James Philip

All Along
The Watchtower

Timeline 10/27/62 – BOOK NINE

Cover concept by James Philip
Graphic Design by Beastleigh Web Design

———

The Timeline 10/27/62 Series

Main Series

Book 1: Operation Anadyr
Book 2: Love is Strange
Book 3: The Pillars of Hercules
Book 4: Red Dawn
Book 5: The Burning Time
Book 6: Tales of Brave Ulysses
Book 7: A Line in the Sand
Book 8: The Mountains of the Moon
Book 9: All Along the Watchtower
Book 10: Crow on the Cradle
Book 11: 1966 & All That

A Standalone Timeline 10/27/62 Novel

Football in the Ruins – The World Cup of 1966

USA Series

Book 1: Aftermath
Book 2: California Dreaming
Book 3: The Great Society
Book 4: Ask Not of Your Country
Book 5: The American Dream

Australia Series

Book 1: Cricket on the Beach
Book 2: Operation Manna

———

Check out the Timeline 10/27/62 website at
www.thetimelinesaga.com

I hope and pray that in the days, weeks and years to come that Americans will remember this day as the dawn of a new age. An age in which no American's character will ever again be judged on account of the colour of his or her skin, religion or origin. This event was planned as a celebration of everything that we share in common in this great land; but we meet on a day when the future of Mankind hangs again in the balance.

This morning President Kennedy collapsed at the Philadelphia White House. His doctors tell me that he suffered a seizure of some kind. At this time the President is fighting for his life in hospital and it is too early to know if he will make a full recovery.

Earlier today I consulted with Chief Justice Earl Warren and Congressional Leaders, informing them that until such time as the President is able to resume his duties the heavy burden of the Presidency of our nation must fall upon my shoulders.

In the coming hours and days you will hear many rumours, half-truths and lies broadcast in good faith by the nation's newsmen. Franklin Delano Roosevelt once talked about having 'nothing to fear but fear itself'. Never was that more true than now.

I have told the Russians and the British that America does not want war. The United States has not used nuclear weapons in the Middle East, nor will it use nuclear weapons against any foe unless the North American continent is attacked by such weapons.

At the time US naval forces in the Persian Gulf came under attack the Governments of the United States and the Union of Soviet Socialist Republics were on the verge of signing an unconditional non-aggression pact. Under this pact both parties undertook to take the steps necessary to end hostilities in the Persian Gulf and to respect each other's legitimate commercial and strategic vital interests in the region.

Peace remains the only policy of the American Government...

Lyndon Baines Johnson
City Hall, Philadelphia
Saturday 4th July 1964

Chapter 1

Forty-eight-year-old Captain Ben Brown Pickett stood on the listing deck of his ship with his cap pushed back at a jaunty angle, wearing a stern, paternal 'everything is under control' expression. However, behind the calm mask of command his stomach knotted and he felt like he was abandoning his ship, his men, and absolutely everything that was sacred to him.

But he was the ranking surviving senior officer of Carrier Division Seven and there was no way he could actually 'command' the fleet from the USS Albany. The old converted World War Two cruiser had taken three bomb hits, she was down by the head and listing five degrees to port, her radars – even those that were not riddled with splinter damage - were off line, and her missile systems were inoperable even in local control.

Pickett had thought his ship was doomed when those bombs hit her. The cruiser had reared and bucked as if three express trains had crashed into her and choking black smoke had been drawn into every compartment; in the confusion he had only become aware later that two RAF fighters had strafed Albany with thirty-millimetre cannons. After those bomb hits the Albany had been out of the battle; from that point on everybody had been too busy fighting the fires...

He had over seventy dead onboard, as many as one hundred and fifty men wounded, half of them badly. Albany's sick bay was wrecked, her surgeon was among the missing and there was precious little anybody could do for the burned and broken men lying in passageways or under awnings on deck, except pump the last of the morphine into their veins.

Water churned under the cruisers stern, one screw turning just fast enough to hold position in the lee of the British oiler Wave Master. The master of the other ship had stationed her between the fluky Gulf winds and light swells to protect the Albany; and Picket appreciated the gesture, mariner to mariner, knowing that if his ship suddenly gave up the fight there would at least be one seaworthy ship close at hand to pick up her survivors...

A native of Pocahontas, Arkansas, Pickett had graduated from Annapolis in the class of 1938, and had been on the cruiser St Louis (CL-14) at Pearl Harbour on 7th December 1941. He had felt sick to his guts then, too. On the St Louis, and later the heavy cruiser USS Vincennes he had been involved in a series of savage actions in the Marshall and Gilbert Islands, the bombardment of Japanese occupied Attu Island in the Aleutians, and two terrifying night actions in the Central Solomons, in the latter of which, the Battle of Savo Island, the Vincennes had been sunk. He had been awarded the Legion of Merit for his part in the first of those battles, and a star in lieu of a second for the later ones; and somewhere along the line he had acquired the nickname 'Blazing' Ben Pickett.

All that had been in another war; one which had made a kind of sense at the time; twenty-two years later he still did not know why two days ago Rear Admiral William Bringle, the commander of Carrier Division Seven had ordered the attack on the Anglo-New Zealand Centaur Battle Group.

What was a guy supposed to do when the RAF mounted a goddammed Kamikaze attack on the fleet behind the cover of two Hiroshima-sized nukes?

After the loss of the Vincennes in 1942, Pickett had returned stateside. It was around then he had started working to earn a degree in electrical engineering at the Massachusetts Institute of Technology. After the war he had graduated from the US Armed Forces Staff College and the National War College, gone on to command the Porter class destroyer USS Winslow (DD-359), and then the new Gearing class destroyer USS Gyatt (DD-712). In a career which had progressed smoothly, almost elegantly both on shore and at sea, he was subsequently appointed the executive officer of the USS Northampton (CLC-1) – a 1945-war hull completed as the most sophisticated and advanced command and control floating 'platform' in the World – and thereafter, by dint of his wealth of technical qualifications and his experience on the Northampton, given command of the US Navy's first true guided missile cruiser, the Albany.

Pickett had joined the Albany during her four-year conversion from an Oregon City class big gun heavy cruiser to her current positively futuristic incarnation over two years ago. At the time of the October War, he had been readying the ship for her re-commissioning on 3rd November 1962 at Boston. The near miss on the city which had obliterated Quincy on the night of the war had delayed Albany's sea trials for three months, and ought to have been an object lesson to the Navy; forewarning that an attack, exactly like the one the British had executed against Carrier Division Seven had the potential to temporarily blind even the most powerful naval force to an air attack at the critical moment.

It was a miracle that the Albany was still afloat.

In her former big gun cruiser configuration, she would probably have capsized. In her conversion practically everything above the main deck had been stripped away, replaced with what looked like huge, top-heavy boxes and towers topped with air search and targeting radars. However, despite appearances, her new superstructure was lightly built, unarmoured in any way; and whereas in her previous incarnation in addition to her three-triple main battery gun turrets, each robustly built and plated, she had carried six secondary twin five-inch turrets and a veritable forest of forty and twenty-millimetre anti-aircraft guns. This meant that – despite appearances - the ship's post-conversion centre of gravity was actually slightly lower now than it had been in 1958.

The best part of three thousand tons of guns, turrets and armour plate had been stripped out of her as well as her former, war-built superstructure; and replaced with relatively lightweight, sophisticated modern weaponry.

In place of her nine 8-inch guns she now carried a pair of five-inch 38-caliber rifles, two Mark 12 RIM-8 (long-range) Bendix Talos missile launchers, two Mark 11 RIM-24 (medium-range) General Dynamics Tartar launchers, a single Mark 16 RUR-5 ASROC anti-submarine rocket launcher, and two triple torpedo tube mounts...

All of which had done *Blazing* Ben Pickett, his ship and Carrier Division Seven precious little good!

The Captain of the Albany was torn between clenched teeth, angry admiration for his enemies and a roiling rage that the idiots in charge had allowed things to come to this pass!

Of course, nothing made him feel so bad as the realisation that he had no choice but to ship his 'flag' to another vessel. Right now, the Albany was fit for nothing but the scrap heap. She was in such a bad way that if she attempted to switch her generating power to powering up her weapons – realistically, a waste of time because none of her guidance systems were on line – her pumps would stop and she would sink within minutes.

True, she had sufficient steam in two of her four Babcock and Wilcox boilers to drive one of her General Electric geared turbines hard enough to maintain steerage way on her port inner shaft but everything down below was a mess. Although Albany's fires were out; problematically, some of the near misses had caused almost as much underwater damage as the bombs which had struck her decks and superstructure. Everything in the fire rooms and engine rooms was shaken to Hell, mounts were cracked or fractured, pipe work was constantly failing and hull plates were sprung in half-a-dozen places.

The foul stench of bunker oil hung in the air around the stricken cruiser as she wallowed a mile or so north of the shattered bow section of the USS Kitty Hawk.

Even from this far away the great letters **63** on her forward flight deck were clearly discernible to the naked eye. Pickett had watched with horror and disbelief as the final huge explosion had broken the flagship's back. Bow and stern had lifted at impossible angles, the after part of the leviathan drifting away from the bow, the latter going down faster and at an acute angle more swiftly than had seemed possible at the time. The stern had stayed afloat some minutes after the broken stump of the bow section, perhaps three hundred or more feet long had impaled itself on the sandy bottom of the Persian Gulf. And then the stern too, with countless men scrambling, scrabbling for their lives on the doomed carcass of what had been, only minutes before, the biggest warship in the World, had levelled itself, dipping a little deeper in the water, and as if in slow motion, capsized. The upturned wreck, red-leaded and probably over five hundred feet long had rested on the surface like a monumental sea monster, until, with a hissing, rumbling boiling of the sea around her she had finally gone down...

It had been over an hour later while the surviving ships licked their wounds and tended their dead and dying that the commanding officer of the undamaged attack transport USS Paul Revere (APA-248) came over the TBS – the rudimentary unscrambled World War II vintage 'Talk Between Ships' VHF backup system that was now the only means of communication available to the whole fleet – and respectfully suggested that Pickett was the senior surviving officer now.

Captain Richard G. Colbert of the USS Boston (CAG-1) was an Annapolis class of 1937 man and had therefore, been senior to Pickett. Colbert was known to be destined for higher command, in effect operating as deputy fleet commander and Rear Admiral Bringle's closest confidante after Kitty Hawk's, and Bringle's Flag Captain, Horace Epes. Epes had also had seniority on Pickett, which had made for a pragmatic command line in most, if not all foreseeable eventualities. For example, when Kitty Hawk and Boston had paid that goodwill, 'flying the flag' visit to Bombay; Pickett had assumed command of the rest of Carrier Division Seven in Bringle, Epes and Colbert's absence.

The first order Pickett had issued was to disperse the fleet. Albany, the Paul Revere, and the lightly damaged, still fully operational Dewey would stay on station in the immediate area of the recent battle to carry on with search and rescue missions. At that time Albany was in a sinking condition, and several miles to the west the whole amidships section of the William V. Pratt was burning like a Roman candle, her crew in the process of abandoning ship. In the flame-kindled darkness of the night oil still burned downwind of the wreck of the Kitty Hawk in a ghastly, mile-long slick and the water was awash with the flotsam, jetsam and human misery of the aftermath of what was probably going to be remembered as the worst day in the history of the US Navy. There had been no way of knowing if there would be a second attack; so, Pickett had dispersed his surviving ships twenty to thirty miles out from the fulcrum point of the wreck of the flagship, mandating a radar watch on the northern Gulf while he decided what the Hell to do next.

The USS Hull (DD-945), which had been absent during both battles of the previous days, was at that time expected to re-join the fleet overnight after putting into Tarouf Bay. She had supposedly made port to investigate a turbine defect but actually her mission had been to spy on the port facilities and to conduct ELINT - electronic intelligence gathering activity - close inshore to the British base at Dammam. In any event, she was a gunship destroyer with no surface-to-air missile capability; she could stand off the wreck of the Kitty Hawk with the Albany and the Dewey, the latter still had missile-shooting capacity and a more or less intact communications suite.

Meanwhile the Charles F. Adams class guided missile destroyers Towers (DDG-9) and Lawrence (DDG-4), both undamaged, would be paired off with the gunship Forrest Sherman class destroyers – sisters of the Hull - John Paul Jones (DD-931) and Du Pont (DD-941) to act as fleet early warning radar pickets. A third gunship destroyer, the USS Decatur (DD-936), also a sister of the John Paul Jones and the Du Pont, had been detached to perform radar picket duties fifty miles south of the wreck of the Kitty Hawk.

Splinter and concussion damage from a near miss had killed several crew men and injured others and knocked out the Decatur's main battery fire control station. Likewise, both the John Paul Jones and the Du Pont had suffered minor splinter damage from near misses and strafing during the air attack, otherwise all five 'dispersed' vessels were fully operational.

Ben Pickett took a last look around, shook his Exec's hand, saluted the flag flying proudly at the stern of the ship and moved to the rail for the perilous climb down into the USS Hull's whaler waiting below in the oil-fouled water.

The bile rose in his throat.

In less than a minute he was watching his fire-scorched, smashed ship slowly receding in the near distance as the boat carrying him to his temporary flagship pitched across the one to two-foot swells.

The Albany looked like what she was; a floating wreck.

Until the October War Ben Pickett had been the most apolitical of officers; untypically, among his peers he had not rushed to blame President Kennedy for the Cuban Missiles debacle. However, he was fully aware that had he not been a member of the relatively small 'command group' of officers capable of taking the new generation of advanced 'missile ships' to sea - and actually employing them properly - his unwillingness to engage in the politicking of the last twenty months would probably have seen him dumped on the beach at the height of the 'Peace Dividend' cutbacks.

That whole exercise had been a farce.

No, ten times worse than that!

An unmitigated disaster and the consequences of that unforgivable *farce* had just played out for *all* the World to see here in the Persian Gulf!

The people back in Philadelphia had the deaths of God only knew how many US Navy men on their hands.

And now he was asking himself: *"How the fuck did we get to where we are now?"*

Chapter 2

Nathan Zabriski (formerly Captain Nathan Zabriski, navigator and bombardier of the 5136th and later the 100th Bombardment Group B-52 *The Big Cigar*) and Doctor Caroline Konstantis (until a few days ago *Colonel* Caroline Konstantis of the US Air Force Corps of Psychiatric Medicine attached to the Personal Staff of the Chairman of the Joint Chiefs, General Curtis LeMay), had heard what the Vice President had had to say earlier that evening outside City Hall, the temporary home of Congress in Philadelphia, and decided that in the circumstances the only rational thing to do was to go to bed and to fuck each other stupid.

Everybody had honestly believed that the World had gone mad twenty months ago and that *not even* the clowns who governed the United States could get it *that* wrong again; not this soon after they had so comprehensively 'screwed the pooch' and blown up half the northern hemisphere of planet Earth.

Clearly, *everybody* had been wrong!

It was blindingly obvious that the idiots in Philadelphia, wherever the new Kremlin was in what was left of the Soviet Union and in Oxford, the seat of the post-October War British Government in England; were using Nevil Shute's '*On The Beach*' as their geopolitical *playbook* and the likeliest outcome of their latest machinations was going to be a second, almost certainly even more dreadful nuclear war.

The fact of the matter was that neither of the unlikely lovers particularly wanted to live in the World that emerged from that...*outcome*.

On the night of the October War Nathan Zabriski had hit the switch that had dropped 3.8 megaton Mark 39 free fall bombs on Gorky, the fifth most populous city in the Soviet Union, and on neighbouring Dzerzhinsk. Whilst he had been cognisant of the fact that Gorky, formerly Nizhny Novgorod in Tsarist times, with a population of around a million people, was a key regional centre of government, a major transportation hub and a lynchpin of the Russian military-economic complex, and that Dzerzhinsk was the place where the Soviet empire had manufactured many of its vilest chemical weapons since the early 1940s, he lived – always – with the knowledge that he had *personally* murdered over a million men, women and children that night.

No sane man could live with a thing like that and not be *different* the next day, *and* every other day of his life. And then last December fate had decreed that he should be a member of one of the Strategic Air Command crews illegally ordered, by traitors in the Pentagon, to bomb *British* bases in the Mediterranean. It made no odds that he and his brothers in arms – most of whom had died that day over the Maltese Archipelago, gunned down like sitting ducks by RAF Hawker Hunter interceptors – had been told that British V-Bombers had already 'nuked' several East Coast American cities.

On that December day last year, *The Big Cigar* had dropped large 'bunker busting' munitions and a single experimental thermobaric – fuel-air 'blast' device – on the Headquarters of the British Mediterranean Fleet. Two of the big bombs had fallen short, exploding spectacularly but relatively harmlessly in the waters of Marsamxett Anchorage but to this day he did not know how many people he had killed and maimed on Malta. All he knew for sure was that the single thermobaric weapon had 'hit the nail on the head' and killed *everybody* within one hundred yards of its point of impact just inside the walls of the Royal Naval citadel on Manoel Island north of the ancient walled city of Valletta...

Caroline Konstantis had been in Joliet on the night of the October War; she would have died in her apartment in Chicago had she not been visiting friends. Her career, her old life had gone up in smoke as had those of countless millions of other Americans.

It had taken her thirty years to put herself in the frame to be the next Dean of Psychiatry at the School of Medicine at the University of Chicago. At the time her commission as a Lieutenant-Colonel in the US Air Force Reserve had become something of a distraction from her 'real' career.

Perversely, the last eighteen months had been the most marvellous, fulfilling time of her entire professional life. That was over now but that was okay, she had always suspected she was on a mission with a deadline.

Curtis LeMay had had her, and probably others with her particular skill sets, cleaning up – suppressing also, albeit in ways not knowingly detrimental to her patients – the psychological damage, much of it of the deep-seated catastrophic variety, sustained by many of the men who had won World War III in a night back in late October 1962.

LeMay had sacked her last week.

Or at least she thought he had sacked her; the legendary bomber commander was an immeasurably more complicated man than people credited and she would have loved – given her eye teeth, in fact – to have had the opportunity to psychologically profile him.

The Big Cigar (she liked that nickname better than '*Old Iron Pants*'), had summoned her to Phoenix, promoted her to full Colonel, retired and honourably discharged her from the Air Force with a fat, thirty-year pension at the stroke of an imperious pen.

LeMay must have known the shit was about to hit the fan and it spoke volumes of the man behind the myth that, he had gone to such great lengths to ensure the 'little people' around him were out of the line of fire when his enemies came looking for him.

God in heaven, she would have *loved* to have decompressed and profiled the force of nature that was Curtis Emerson LeMay...

But that was never going to happen.

Not even if the World contrived, against the odds, *not* to blow itself up again. She had been on an exhilarating 'professional' roller coaster ride the last eighteen months; and now she was on a 'personal' and 'emotional' helter skelter that was no less harum-scarum.

What was that old Chinese saying?

Riding on the back of a Tiger is fine, getting off is when your problems really start...

Something like that!

It was a sultry summer night and the man and the woman lay on top of the sheets, turned on their sides studying each other in the gloom.

The street lights on Hearst Avenue were still on – that was probably a good sign, the war had not started yet – and their loom filtered through the heavy drapes on the front room windows, casting long, impenetrable shadows.

"You know that the physics of *On The Beach* are all baloney, don't you?" Nathan murmured. "We don't use Cobalt in our bombs so the whole world isn't about to..."

Caroline put a finger to his lips.

Then she rolled onto her back and stared at the ceiling.

"At least back in October sixty-two we knew who we were fighting against, sweetheart," she sighed, knowing why he wanted to talk and yet understanding talking was not going to do either of them a lot of good tonight.

Sweetheart...

Yes, that would do just fine. She had been oddly – weirdly, come to think about it – preoccupied with dumb things like *'what was an older woman supposed to call her much younger lover?'*

Suddenly, that really was not very important.

He was twenty-seven, she was fifty-one.

Get over it, woman!

Nathan was several months her son's junior.

Her son, Simon, was a schmuck; he took after his father, whom she ought to have divorced long before she did. Her ex-husband – a history professor ten years her senior - was in Niagara with one of his colleague's wives the night of the war. Sometimes she wondered if they had been coupling at the moment they were vaporized by the Buffalo bomb.

Simon was a junior houseman at Shore Memorial in Atlantic City, most likely in the firing line if the British wanted to start something...

She stopped herself pursuing that line of thought.

The science, spotty as it was, that she had seen on the subject, postulated that while a second 'major nuclear exchange' would inevitably increase background levels of ionising radiation to levels perhaps scores, or in a worst-case scenario, to hundreds of times pre-Hiroshima levels; globally it might *only* double or treble post October War levels. It was known that people working on the Manhattan Project, and workers at Los Alamos, Hanford and several other experimental atomic power plants had all been exposed, inadvertently in the main, to exactly those elevated levels of radiation since 1945. While what epidemiological data that was publicly available already confirmed a statistically significant correlation with a higher than 'population norm' rate of cancers in this group, fears of a 'sample-wide' massively accelerated 'die off', say, in middle age, had not yet been identified by either the pre-war, or the emerging post-October War evidence.

All of which was frigidly cold comfort on a night like this.

Nathan might be right about the improbability of an '*On The Beach*' style *end of life on Earth* scenario if there was a renewed global atomic war; but all other bets would be off.

The most pernicious fission products contributing to the already significantly elevated background radiation levels; Strontium-90, Iodine-131 and 133, each had half-lives measured in tens of years.

Mankind was already twenty months into a terrifying millennia-long physiological experiment in living with what previously had been regarded as *very* high *short-term* dosages of ionising radiation, exposure to which would have permanently disqualified *any* worker in the nuclear industry from *ever* working with radioactive substances again.

The fallout from the October War had blighted the face of the Earth for generations, and anything that made the situation worse was an...*abomination!*

Caroline rolled back into Nathan's arms.

The lovers re-arranged themselves, intertwining arms, legs, pressing close, closer together. His lips nuzzled her left ear lobe, she shivered with pleasure, and gently raked his back with the fingertips of her right hand.

"I love you, Caro," he breathed.

She half-moaned, half-giggled, her mouth seeking his.

He wanted to marry her.

Sweet boy!

She would marry him if they were still alive in a day or two from now.

But right now, she just wanted him inside her.

"I love you too, baby," she whispered as he slid deep inside her.

Chapter 3

23:53 Hours (EST)
Saturday 4th July 1964
The White House, Philadelphia, Pennsylvania

'A day of infamy...'

No, that did not even begin to describe the day Lyndon Baines Johnson and the American people had just lived through. Nor did it remotely encapsulate the hideous dimensions of the bottomless pitch-black yawning abyss upon whose jagged edge the United States now stood; swaying unsteadily like a punch-drunk fighter with the referee counting down the seconds to...

To what?

To the end of the World?

The great clock high above the ceremonial entranceway onto South Broad Street clicked around another minute.

Lyndon Johnson had requisitioned the monumental former headquarters of the Girard Corn Exchange Trust from its bankrupt owners to be the Philadelphia 'White House' back in February. Its proximity to the relocated House of Representatives apart, the building recommended itself for its interim role as the 'Philadelphia White House' while the rebuilding went on in Washington DC, in many ways; it was truly grand, very obviously 'presidential', it was built like a medieval fortress and had a huge vault – a likely bomb shelter in this troubled age – and a surfeit of rooms within it, and its adjoining thirty-one storey office block to accommodate not just the Presidential Staff but the new Philadelphia offices of *both* the State and the Treasury Departments.

Several alternative sites had been proposed but LBJ had stopped looking the moment he had stepped into the cavernous, cathedral-like Girard Corn Exchange Trust building, an opulent rotunda designed by the architect Frank Furness in 1908 as a reproduction of the Pantheon in Rome. Furness had constructed the exterior structural fabric of the great edifice with nine thousand tons of Georgia marble; and the interior with Carerra marble quarried in Italy. A relief of Stephen Girard, the bank's founder was carved above the colonnaded entrance, and the oculus of the rotunda's one-hundred-foot diameter dome was one hundred and forty feet above where Johnson, his harassed staffers, the chaotic inauguration party and God only knew how many TV, radio and newspaper people jostled and elbowed for the best position on the marbled floor of the old bank.

The desks of the clerks and tellers were long gone.

The old vault beneath Johnson's feet now accommodated a state of the art situation room, thick cemented steel blast doors and an 'atmospheric control plant' ensured that the underground rooms of the old bank and the adjoining skyscraper were bomb proof and survivable, possibly indefinitely.

Johnson and his wife had discussed leaving their daughters behind in Texas when they came back to Philadelphia. The way things were looking he did not think the girls would be any safer back at the LBJ Ranch in Stonewall; and at least this way Lady Bird and his daughters Lynda and Luci were with him...

What was a man without his family?

The crowd had parted as Johnson and his entourage emerged from the bowels of the building. LBJ had had enough of being closeted in that fucking 'situation room'. The one thing JFK had got right on the night of the October War was that he had refused to run away and hide; the man had stayed above ground every single minute. Whatever history eventually said about Jack Kennedy nobody could ever take that away from him.

DEFCON1

Codename: '*Cocked Pistol*'.

Situation: '*nuclear war is imminent*'.

Defence Status: '*maximum readiness*'.

The White House Staff had gathered beneath the towering rotunda, junior rankers leaned on the rails of the first-floor balcony, the marbled floor around Johnson was packed with senior civil servants, many from the adjoining Department of Justice building, mingling with Administration insiders and forlorn Kennedy retainers and the stoic press of tired-eyed men in uniform. There were Philadelphia Police Department cops, Secret Servicemen and M-16 assault-rifle armed Marines guarding every door; outside on the surrounding streets M-60 Patton main battle tanks and M113 armoured personnel carriers blocked the streets and enforced a 'shoot first ask questions later' cordon sanitaire around the White House.

There was the taint of confusion and...*panic* in the air and the temporary capital of the Union was aflame with rumours, filled to overflowing with visitors with nowhere to go and despite Lyndon Johnson's best efforts thus far nobody had put a stop to the accelerating descent into chaos.

Everything had gone wrong all at once; well, within a thirty-six-hour window of abject indecision and executive paralysis in *this* building and Lyndon Johnson knew that he was running out of options.

He still had no idea why the US Navy had started a war with Britain, Australia and New Zealand, and by proxy with all their allies in the Persian Gulf.

He still had no idea why the US Sixth Fleet had allowed itself to be 'interned' by the British at Malta.

He still had no idea why the Israelis had allowed several of the RAF V-Bombers flying out of Cyprus to overfly – unchallenged - the southern Negev Desert en route to attack Carrier Division Seven.

Frankly, he still hardly believed the British had actually *sunk* the Kitty Hawk...

And as for the reports coming out of South Korea, well, one of the reasons Johnson would never have personally sanctioned sending half of the Seventh Fleet to the Persian Gulf in the first place; was to avoid sending the wrong signals to the maniacs in North Korea...

That said, there were always warnings and rumours about troop movements and 'concentrations' across the two-and-a-half mile-wide DMZ – demilitarized zone – separating North and South Korea some thirty or so miles north of Seoul, the capital of the South. The CIA and David Shoup, the Commandant of the Marine Corps had cried wolf over Korea half-a-dozen times since the October War; if the North was going to do more than play 'war games' it would have done it this time last year when the III Marine Expeditionary Force was withdrawn from Pusan, reducing the US presence in the peninsula to less than thirty thousand men for the first time. Since then, further troop withdrawals meant the Marines had left only a skeleton operations and maintenance staff in situ so that III MEF could be reactivated relatively swiftly – ninety to one hundred and twenty days – in an emergency, and large dumps of equipment and war stores had been left behind to facilitate exactly that kind of supposedly 'rapid re-deployment' of men to the region. At the time the Administration had been warned – very specifically, in the most unambiguous of terms – that the 'Peace Dividend' cutbacks were going to bite so deeply into the US Air Force's 'air-lift capability' and the Navy's fleet of fast transports, that only a 'slower' *rapid deployment* of a force the size of III MEF might be practical in the event of a crisis.

As the situation in the Middle East had worsened all available resources had first been positioned, and plans developed to send an Expeditionary Force (coincidentally, of approximately the size of that withdrawn from South Korea) to the Persian Gulf, before the situation in the Midwest had prompted President Kennedy to do a volte face and release those forces for 'homeland defence'. In the event the Administration had countered the military's 'concerns' about future North Korean aggression by falling back on the assumption that not even the leadership of the People's Democratic Republic of Korea – PDRK – would be dumb enough to risk provoking an annihilating nuclear retaliation...

Curtis LeMay was worried about Korea; that was his job.

Right now, Lyndon Johnson had matters much closer at home to worry about.

For example, how for the love of God had the Philadelphia PD and fifty or sixty heavily armed Pennsylvania National Guardsmen, allowed a bunch of crazies – no more than a couple of dozen of them - and a several hundred strong lynch mob to overrun the British Embassy in Wister Park; all this at the very time Doctor King was leading his March on Philadelphia up Broad Street towards City Hall, the pro tem home of the US House of Representatives...

It was way beyond this old dog's comprehension!

Yesterday...

He corrected himself, no, *still today*, just. There was a minute or so to go to midnight.

Yesterday...had been supposed to be the day America allowed itself to start to put the last great iniquity of its history behind it. Martin Luther King was destined to lead his faithful to the steps of City Hall, the home of the US Congress, and together with the President (JFK) usher in and endorse a new era in American race relations.

So much for the plans of mice and men!

As LBJ waited for the abbreviated inauguration ceremony to commence, John Fitzgerald Kennedy, the 35th President of the United States, was fighting for his life at Thomas Jefferson Memorial Hospital just four or five blocks away. In his absence Johnson and King had attempted to play their parts at City Hall, read their lines and shaken each other's hand but it had been a sideshow; events six thousand miles away in the Persian Gulf, and painfully closer to home in the Midwest and in Philadelphia itself had turned the great rebirth of the nation into a...*debacle.*

Johnson had invited Martin Luther King to the White House, but the handsome black man and his small coterie were lost in the chaotic press of bodies beneath the rotunda as pressmen jostled, bad-temperedly to get the best position and flash bulbs exploded. The floor was a tangle of TV and radio cables and by the time LBJ had stepped up to the lectern to face Chief Justice Earl Warren the two old friends and political sparring partners were very nearly swamped, anonymous in the undignified melee.

"Stand back, goddammit!"

Johnson was one of the few men who did not flinch.

If there was one man in the White House that night whose sheer physical presence and bull horn-like bark could restore order it was General Curtis LeMay. The veteran bomber commander who had become Chairman of the Joint Chiefs of Staff Committee *during* the Battle of Washington last December, had had enough.

"MARINES!" *Old Iron Pants* bellowed. "Clear these people away from the dais. Arrest anybody who makes trouble!"

Le May stepped up beside Johnson.

"This is a fucking turkey shoot, sir," he growled apologetically, rather in the fashion of a bear whose sudden arrival has just sent day trippers fleeing in terror from a forest picnic area. A lot of what had gone wrong in the last forty-eight to seventy-two hours had happened on *his watch*, so he felt *responsible*; but *everybody* knew that practically everything that had gone wrong had gone wrong because *nobody* had been listening to *his* advice since the Soviet invasion of Iran and Iraq in early April.

"Yeah," the tall, craggy fifty-five-year-old Texan whom his stricken President had exiled from Camelot in recent weeks – with obviously catastrophic consequences – grunted sourly. "Just remember we're going to need some of those 'turkeys'," he added, nodding at the mortally offended newspaper and TV men, and a smattering of women, being driven back from the lectern, "come Thanksgiving, General."

LeMay chuckled and threw a glance at the Vice-President.

Everybody was as jumpy as a cat on a proverbial hot tin roof;

everybody was terrified of making a decision, any decision. That was what happened when people did not know who was in control. If somebody did not get a grip soon – very soon – *somebody* was going to have to do something about it and Johnson understood as well as the Chairman of the Joint Chiefs that if *he* did not fully assume the position of Commander-in-Chief then Lemay would. The airman would have no alternative; the country was sliding – rushing - towards anarchy.

"We've got to get to Thanksgiving first, sir," LeMay observed grimly.

"We will," Johnson rasped. Given that LeMay had advised him earlier that evening that he had three options, and 'not a lot in between', his observation was chilling.

Option one: hit the Soviets hard NOW.

Option two: hit the British hard NOW.

Option three: hit the Soviets and the British hard NOW.

LBJ had asked the Chairman of the Joint Chiefs of Staff if he had any other ideas.

'Those are your *military* options, sir,' *The Big Cigar* had informed him deadpan.

A few hours ago, Johnson had told the American people that '*Peace remains the only policy of the American Government*'.

Johnson tried not to scowl at LeMay.

"With God's grace, we will get through to Thanksgiving, General," he declared, privately thinking that the fourth Thursday in November was an awfully long way away from where he stood today on the marble floor beneath of the rotunda of the old Girard Corn Exchange Trust Bank.

A four to five-yard-deep semi-circle was opening before Earl Warren, Lyndon Johnson and Curtis LeMay. Stone-faced Marines were pushing the butts of their M-16s into the chests of protesting journalists and photographers, while Secret Servicemen snarled a stream of low threatening words of *advice* to hold back the crowd.

The ceremony ought to have started several minutes ago.

Johnson's wife, Lady Bird, and his daughters, twenty-year-old Lynda, and Luci, whose seventeenth birthday had been just two days ago, struggled to hold their positions behind the lectern party. This ought to have been the proudest, not one of – if not the – saddest day of the Vice-President's life.

He had had to shout in the face of the head of his Secret Service detachment to get it across to the man that whatever happened, *nothing* mattered more than the safety of his wife and daughters.

It was a crazy, mixed up world when one father had to explain a thing like that to another husband and father. Shit, the man was only doing his duty; he knew that. Maybe, in the morning he would make amends, some way, or more likely Lady Bird would take the man by the arm and do what she always did when her husband overstepped the mark; make everything okay again.

Heck, perhaps he ought to get her to talk to that mad woman

Thatcher in England. *That* woman was not taking any of the calls he had tried to put through to Oxford in the last couple of hours!

Curtis LeMay had assured him that the fighting in Illinois and Wisconsin had had 'no impact on SAC'; Strategic Air Command's bomber and missile bases in Omaha, Nebraska and the Dakotas and that those key strategic assets were 'all secure', and 'a long way away from the trouble over by the Great Lakes'.

The B-52 wings and other 'tactical assets' allocated to suppressing the rebellion in Wisconsin and northern Illinois had not, nor would they be, re-tasked unless 'operationally necessary'.

The war in the Midwest continued unabated, whatever else was happening in the World.

Johnson looked to the big clock.

Some days it felt like the whole country was coming apart at the seams; except he understood that it was not. Not yet, anyway.

California, Oregon and Washington State might have proclaimed their 'West Coast Confederation', the troubles in the Deep South were getting worse every day, there was the uprising in the Midwest, the ongoing problems in the bombed cities but the Union remained rock solid, for now at least.

Overseas, well, that was a whole other crock of shit. If the Kennedy boys had screwed up at home it was as nothing to the FUBAR – to borrow one of Curtis LeMay's favourite acronyms – that they had overseen beyond the country's borders.

Fucked Up Beyond All Repair just about summed up the condition of the Republic's international relations.

A state of war, albeit officially as yet undeclared existed between the United States and its oldest ally, the United Kingdom, not to mention miscellaneous of its 'Commonwealth' allies. Canada, normally the best of neighbours had gone – at the highest levels of inter-governmental communication - worryingly 'quiet' in the last twenty-four hours. If Canada 'went bad on the US' or refused to co-operate fully in NORAD – the North American Aerospace Defense Command – then the longest land border between any two countries on Earth, the US-Canadian, suddenly became the most exposed 'flank' on the planet. It hardly bore thinking about...

The US *might* be at war with the Soviet Union; there was no way of telling and somewhere along the line JFK had offered the Russians an open-ended armistice of some kind; the crowning glory of the present FUBAR!

The price of peace with the Soviet Union apparently, had been war with the British. Nobody in the White House or at State had asked, not for a single moment, how the British would react. Presumably, they – the President, Bill Fulbright and likely, Robert McNamara at Defence – had assumed the British would meekly accept it all as a fait accompli.

LBJ simply did not have the vocabulary to describe his true feelings about that kind of thinking. 'Asinine', 'complacent', 'half-witted', 'infantile', just plain 'dumb' did not get close!

After the Japanese had bombed Pearl Harbour the country had smelled the coffee, awakened and the US Navy had kicked the butt of the Japanese all the way back to their home islands. What the fuck did JFK think was going to happen if the US Navy carried out – possibly inadvertently, if that was possible - a sneak attack on the British in the Persian Gulf?

Okay, maybe nobody could have foreseen the 'arrest' of the Sixth Fleet at Malta; or predicted that the British were remotely capable of sinking half of Carrier Division Seven and the biggest carrier in the World...

But *somebody* ought to have figured out that there would be...*consequences*. When you stabbed your buddy in the back, sooner or later you had to know that you were going to feel the pain, too!

The craziness boggled his mind.

Shit, British V-Bombers could already be making bombing runs on US cities!

The minute hand of the big clock above the Broad Street entrance to the White House moved; another minute closer to midnight.

"Let's get on with this Earl," LBJ said to Chief Justice Earl Warren. Until that moment he had hardly noticed the dapper, grey-eyed young man at Warren's shoulder who had delved into his attaché case and passed a slim Manila file to his boss.

Dan Brenckmann, Johnson recollected. He was the son of the Ambassador in England, married to Claude Betancourt's oldest girl, Gretchen.

Now...she was something...

Claude Betancourt had been Joe Kennedy's go to litigator in the thirties, and the man JFK had called in to 'clean house' after the old bootlegger had succumbed to a stroke and 'War' influenza last year. Up until forty-eight hours ago Claude Betancourt had been quietly stitching together a challenge to the primacy of the Kennedy dynasty – a bloodless coup - ahead of the upcoming Democrat National Convention, scheduled to take place in around seven weeks' time at Boardwalk Hall in Atlantic City.

All those plans were history.

What happened if JFK did not make it; would Bobby step up to the plate?

Bobby would be as big a disaster for the Party as his brother; tainted forever by the October War and his part in the post-war failures of the Administration...

But that was a headache for another day.

Johnson eyed the young man at Earl Warren's shoulder. He had heard that Claude *and* Earl Warren each thought equally highly of the Brenckmann kid, he ought to ask around, find out more. Maybe, he was a guy he wanted to keep close.

That however, would definitely have to wait for another day.

Earl Warren taped the biggest of the half-a-dozen microphones tied and screwed to the lectern in front of him.

"In my capacity as Chief Justice of the United States it falls to me to officiate at the swearing in of the President before he enters upon the Execution of his Office. The Majority and Minority Leaders of the House of Representatives and I; having satisfied ourselves that President Kennedy, is presently and for the foreseeable future, incapable of discharging the duties of his office, and has *de jure,* stepped down – we all pray temporarily – from that high office, we are here tonight to witness the swearing in of the Vice President, Lyndon Baines Johnson, as President."

Earl Warren and Johnson faced each other.

"Please place your right hand on the Bible, sir," the Chief Justice requested sternly.

With a momentarily hesitation, the tall Texan complied.

"Please say after me," Warren demanded, his voice raised over the diminishing hubbub on the floor of the White House. "I, Lyndon Baines Johnson do solemnly swear..."

"*I Lyndon Baines Johnson do solemnly swear.*"

"That I will faithfully execute the Office of the President of the United States."

Johnson swallowed, dry-mouthed.

"*That I will faithfully execute the Office of the President of the United States.*"

"And will to the best of my ability, preserve, protect and defend the Constitution of the United States."

"*And will to the best of my ability, preserve, protect and defend the Constitution of the United States,*" the new President said with a tear forming in his eyes. "So, help me, God!"

And after a breathless interval.

"*God bless America!*"

Chapter 4

07:01 Hours (Local) – 00:01 in Philadelphia
Sunday 5th July 1964
HMS Eagle, Port Said, Egypt

Forty-seven-year-old Captain Francis Jellicoe Maltravers stood rock steady beside the binnacle on the bridge of the Royal Navy's only remaining operational fleet carrier. His hands were clasped behind his back and his clean-shaven face – he had got married in February and his wife had robust and decidedly trenchant views on 'piratical beards' – was suffused with that particular grace that only a lifelong mariner can understand. No matter what the circumstances the moments before casting off were uniquely special, revelatory.

Frank Maltravers had commanded HMS Ark Royal, Eagle's sister ship during Operation Manna the previous winter, staying with that gallant old warhorse until she had broken down so badly that she had finally had to go into dry dock. He had been offered a posting on shore but Jennifer – the new Mrs Maltravers - had been marvellously understanding when he had accepted the First Sea Lord's unexpected invitation to 'work up' the Eagle after her four-year, stop-start, war-interrupted modernisation.

Or at least, he hoped Jennifer had meant it when she said she 'understood'. He had loved and lost her twenty years ago; like an idiot he had gone off to the Pacific onboard HMS Formidable to fight the Japanese without first getting down on one knee and doing the sensible thing. She was the sort of girl who would have waited for him, however long it took had he plighted his troth. Instead, he had gone East, had a whale of time and got back eighteen months later to discover that, interpreting his absence of a proposal of matrimony as an unambiguous sign of indifference, she had married a chum of her brother's back on leave from Germany, and was already six months pregnant.

All of which was ancient history.

She had written to him last December, welcoming home 'the conquering hero' and things had developed from there. Jennifer's first husband, just out of the Army, had been in London on business, staying overnight at his club – The Army and Navy in Pall Mall – the night of the October War, her children, a boy and two girls in their latter teens, had been with her in Shropshire, and survived.

Frank Maltravers's stepson, Michael was now at the Britannia Royal Naval College at Dartmouth, the girls, aged fifteen and seventeen were safely ensconced at a well thought of school reserved for the 'daughters of officers' in rural Shropshire, a mile or so from the new family home in Much Wenlock. Maltravers occasionally had a pang of guilt about the privileges bestowed on senior officers in the armed services and their families; but not very often. The system had been introduced last year to single out and to favour those whom the state considered 'essential' to its survival. It had been instigated for good reason. In these straightened times what other inducements could poor old Great Britain realistically offer its defenders?

The country was on its uppers, fighting for its survival.

The reality of post-October War life was that workers at home got fed in return for their labour, and anybody who refused to play the game was left to fend for themselves. The post-World War II settlement – the welfare state that had underpinned Attlee's Labour Government, and subsequently the administrations of Churchill, Eden and Macmillan - had sought to do away with that sort of bare-faced institutionalised iniquity; but the October War had plunged the country back into some kind of twisted Victorian-Edwardian time warp.

Things were so smashed up and basically, wrecked in England that the only thing he could do about it – about anything, in fact – was to do his duty and thereby, do his best to keep Queen, country and his newly acquired family safe. It did not matter to him if Jennifer might well have been partly motivated in seeking him out to bring herself – and her children – under the protective umbrella of the 'Armed Forces Dependency' regulations; he had been absolutely delighted to accommodate her. He got to belatedly marry the love of his life, and she the guarantee of a roof over her head and a better future for her children, outcomes to be greatly desired by both parties to the contract. They lived in an age in which the possible and the pragmatic were kings, and in which dreams and dreamers fell, hungry and scorned by the way.

Nevertheless, what with one thing and another he had very nearly bitten the then First Sea Lord's – Sir David Luce's – hand off when he had asked him if he was 'up to taking on the Eagle?'

A voice to his right broke him out of his reverie.

"Scorpion has weighed anchor, sir."

"Very good. You may proceed to sea, Mr Fairbrace," the Captain of the Eagle informed his Navigator.

Lieutenant-Commander Cecil Jolyon 'Johnny' Fairbrace, late of Her Majesty's Royal Australian Navy, had 'hitched a ride' to England onboard the Ark Royal, one of many Australian Navy men who had embraced the renewed unity of the Royal Navies of both the old and the new countries during the course of Operation Manna. Men like him had ensured that famine and pestilence – or more correctly, the worst extremities of both curses – had been banished from what was left of England's fair and pleasant land for the majority of the population last winter. His reward had been a 'joint commission' in both navies and on Maltravers's personal recommendation, a posting to the most important operational ship in the Royal Navy.

Eagle's crew was an increasingly 'Commonwealth' community; with as many as four hundred of her two thousand five-hundred-man complement hailing from places as disparate as Australia, New Zealand, Canada, South Africa, and Rhodesia. The ship's roster also included two men from Port Stanley, the capital of the now Argentine-occupied Falkland Islands, men from Tristan da Cunha, Singapore, Fiji and Hong Kong, and even several *Americans*.

It was a funny old World.

Frank Maltravers tried not to dwell on how many of his Commonwealth *brothers* had died alongside their British crewmates onboard the Centaur and the other ships which had gone down in the Persian Gulf in the last seventy-two hours.

A naval aviator in his younger days he had flown a Hawker Sea Fury FB11 off the Centaur during her first commission, the swansong of his flying career...

Even as his thoughts wandered, at another level he was focused with marksman-like precision on what was going on around him on the bridge, eyes circling the compass binnacle, engine telegraphs, wind gauge and the lights on the Divisional Ready Board.

Vice Admiral Sir Nigel Grenville, Commander-in-Chief of the Mediterranean Fleet had flown his flag on Eagle during the passage from Valletta to Alexandria but returned by air with his personal staff to Malta twelve hours ago, handing command of the squadron to Maltravers.

At Alexandria, Egyptian Navy men had swarmed all over the Eagle; Nasser himself had been due to come onboard in Port Said later that day before 'events' intervened. To paraphrase the thoughts of the late, sadly missed and much lamented, Sir Julian Christopher, there was nothing quite so expressive of the projection of national power, and of the muscular value of one nation's 'friendship' with another, as a '*bloody great big grey warship*'.

Eight years after the Suez debacle President Nasser's ceremonial welcome aboard the biggest ship in the Royal Navy, would have sent an unmistakable message to the whole Middle East, quite apart from having been viewed by the regime in Cairo as the old imperial overlords ritually abasing themselves at the feet of the putative master of the Arab World.

The C-in-C had not been looking forward to that part of the 'goodwill' visit, and, neither, truth be told, had Frank Maltravers. These were indeed strange times.

The anchorage was broad and deep enough even for a ship the size of the Eagle to manoeuvre safely, with relatively generous margins for error; but Johnny Fairbrace was taking no liberties. Lengthening the stern chains to let the wind – hardly more than a light breeze work on the great slab side of the carrier – he was continually calculating angles. A big 'canal tug' stood ready, churning muddy water at a respectful distance, as if admiring the ship handling mastery of a real, professional navy.

The Navigator called orders.

Acknowledgments flowed back.

Everything was very quiet, business-like and today, a little grim even though there was no way that the news of what had happened in the Gulf could yet have circulated throughout the whole ship.

Frank Maltravers would broadcast to the crew as soon as the ship was clear of the harbour.

On a ship the size of the Eagle the distant, very distant clanking of the anchor chains and growling of the capstan motors was transmitted, rather than heard through the steel fabric of the carrier.

Maltravers eyed the second of Eagle's escorts, the Battle class fast air direction destroyer HMS Oudenarde, a sister of the never to be forgotten Talavera of Battle of Malta fame, gliding past the harbour boom.

He was old-fashioned enough to view the radical nature of Oudenarde's conversion with less than ecstatic eyes. Of her original late 1940s build only her hull, engines, funnel, forward superstructure and main armament remained. Abaft her bridge a giant lattice foremast had sprouted – the footings of which straddled the forty-foot breadth of the ship – topped with a four-ton Type 965 AKE-2 double bedstead radar aerial. An additional Type 293Q array was mounted on a platform beneath the huge bedsteads. The Type 965 aerial was the ship's long-range 'eyes', the Type 293Q was the most recent derivation of a Second World War-vintage gunnery control 'range and height-finder'. All the destroyer's former torpedo tubes and light AA armament had been discarded aft of the funnel where a big, blocky deckhouse containing generators and radar rooms had been inelegantly welded to the main deck. Between this new superstructure and the old aft deckhouse, a new lattice mainmast carried a Type 277Q height finder dish and several ESM - Electronic Warfare Support Measures - and Direction Finding (DF) aerials. Near the stern the existing after deckhouse had been extended and strengthened to mount a quadruple GWS 21 Sea Cat surface-to-air-missile (SAM) system. On what remained of the cramped quarterdeck that the ship retained – everybody assumed as a design oversight – was the ship's original Squid Anti-Submarine (A/S) mortar.

The Scorpion – a smaller hull by several hundred tons – had had a scaled down version of the same modernisation rebuild, the primary difference being that she only mounted a single two-ton Type 965 AKE-2 aloft. The Weapon class ships, of which Scorpion was a member, were famously mechanically 'tender' and nobody liked to manoeuvre too close to one of them at speed on account of their cranky, under-powered reversing turbines.

Notwithstanding, the captain of the Eagle was content that he was in company with two proven ships with tested and reliable crews. He had fretted while the carrier's *little friends' bunkers* were topped off, now the race was on.

HMS Blackpool, the Eagle's third escorting warship lay a cable to port of the flagship, anchored fore and aft, a wispy plume of grey-white smoke rising from her single stack. The Whitby class anti-submarine frigate had a problem with her starboard turbine's reduction gear. Blackpool would be staying behind in Port Said with the Royal Fleet Auxiliary oiler Appleleaf.

Port Said to the Grand Harbour, Valletta was over a thousand statute miles, some nine hundred and thirty nautical miles.

Therefore, the Big E, the most powerful ship in the Royal Navy was over thirty hours hell-for-leather steaming from the one place in the Mediterranean she needed to be...now!

As soon as the carrier cleared the boom he would work her up to twenty-eight, twenty-nine or thirty knots if she could sustain it, make her course three-zero-zero degrees to find sea room before pointing her stem at the Maltese Archipelago and driving due west until basically, something broke.

Unfortunately, this latter was not an unlikely consequence of driving the 'Big E' too hard for too long.

An uninformed observer might have reasonably expected a twelve-year-old ship like the Eagle, which had just spent the last four years in dockyard hands being, in essence, 'rebuilt' would have returned to sea 'as good if not better than new'. However, this ignored the fact that the great ship had not emerged fresh from her chrysalis on her commissioning day in October 1951; having been first envisaged in the late 1930s – as a bigger more robust, thirty-six-thousand-ton version of the twenty-three-thousand-ton Implacable class fleet carriers ordered in 1938 while Neville Chamberlain was still Prime Minister. Eagle's keel had actually been laid at the Harland and Wolf shipyard – Yard number 1220 – in Belfast as long ago as October 1942. Launched in 1946 she had been years in the building, the name ship of the four planned carriers of the Audacious class. Like her sister Ark Royal, formerly named Irresistible, Eagle had only acquired her current name at her launch, the ship intended to carry that name having been scrapped at the end of the Second World War when just twenty-three percent completed, and the fourth ship of the class, HMS Africa, having been cancelled on the stocks. So, the Eagle was no spring chicken with just eight years water under her keel. Deep down in her bowels she was a twenty-year-old war time-build – built to corner-cutting wartime standards – and her long sojourn in dry dock had not been so much to rejuvenate her, as to simply keep her old bones going a while longer.

Notwithstanding, Portsmouth Dockyard had given her an angled – at 8.5 degrees – armoured flight deck with two new steam catapults, increasing her width across the flight deck by over thirty feet and adding several thousand tons to her displacement, making her sit nearly four feet deeper in the water; leaving her main machinery largely untouched. The Dockyard's brief had been to 'do what had to be done, no more'.

Four of the carrier's original twin 4.5-inch turrets had been retained aft; and the plan to mount as many as six Seacat GWS 21 surface-to-air missile launchers abandoned. In the end six twin 40-millimetre Bofors mounts had been recovered from a forgotten ordnance store and welded to the sponsons prepared for the now, non-existent Seacat systems.

Oh, whatever become of the plans of mice and men...

It was all academic, anyway.

Eagle had emerged from her 'long refit' capable, in theory of operating an air wing of up to forty-five modern – but not supersonic - aircraft. The real 'problem' was not that Eagle was not a brand new, state of the art fighting machine, it was that she was the *only* fleet carrier left in the locker, and that it had *only* been by scraping up every serviceable aircraft from the Ark Royal, and by collecting the Hermes's 'orphaned aircraft' on route to Malta at Gibraltar, and by requisitioning several 'unserviceable' airframes and practically all the spares at RAF Luqa, that her air group of thirty-two machines had been begged, borrowed and stolen 'into being'.

The Navy's and the country's 'cupboards' were bare.

No matter, one fought wars with the ships and the aircraft one had to hand not the ones one wished one had, and Captain Francis Jellicoe Maltravers was inordinately proud of his command. With her bunkers topped off she surged out to sea tipping the scales somewhere in excess of fifty-three thousand tons and despite her vintage and the incompleteness of her recent refit, she was by any standard a 'mighty' machine of war. And right now, with the USS Enterprise in dock back in Norfolk, Virginia, the USS Independence locked up in the Grand Harbour at Valletta and the Kitty Hawk – Centaur's murderess – lying on the bottom of the Persian Gulf, until such time as the US Navy got one of its other, mothballed super carriers back to sea, HMS Eagle was the match for any carrier afloat.

"Revolutions for twenty-seven knots, if you please," Maltravers demanded as Scorpion and Oudenarde took station on either beam of the flagship in the brilliant morning sunshine. The sea was aquamarine blue, millpond calm for as far as the naked eye could discern.

The engine room telegraphs clanged, the ship began to tremble as far, far below his feet the carrier's four two hundred feet long shafts began to spin her great propellers faster, and faster under her stern.

"I will address the crew, now."

Chapter 5

05:07 Hours (GMT) – 00:07 Hours in Philadelphia
Sunday 5th July 1964
Drakelow Tunnels, Worcestershire, England

The Secretary of State's RAF Westland Wessex helicopter swooped down onto the dusty pad - that was still under construction - a hundred yards to the west of the main entrance to the underground complex. The first pale gleaming of the coming dawn had already turned the star-studded inky blackness of the eastern sky to grey although the long shadow cast by the great sandstone hill in the west still lay across the roughly laid concrete landing pan.

Fifty-two-year-old Alison Monro had eschewed the heavily armed bodyguard detachments so favoured by many of her ministerial colleagues. Even the pair of ever-present Special Branch officers seemed to her *excessive*, barely tolerable; recent events had provided ample evidence that no number of Marines or Secret Servicemen or fighting ships or aircraft were any guarantee of 'safety' in this craven new post-apocalyptic epoch.

A British Prime Minister – Edward Heath – had been murdered by one of President Kennedy's secretaries in the Oval Office of the White House, the Queen and her family could easily have been killed at Balmoral, and Her Majesty and the Prime Minister, Margaret Thatcher, might have perished in the blink of an eye at Brize Norton, victims of Irish - and possibly, rogue American - inspired terroristic plots. Goodness, three months ago the Commander-in-Chief of all British and Commonwealth Forces in the Mediterranean had died defending his headquarters from Red Army paratroopers...

No, what with one thing and another the Secretary of State for Supply – and by default, overseer of the Energy and Transportation ministries, and therefore an irreplaceable linchpin of the Unity Administration of the United Kingdom – was of the opinion that too many of her colleagues worried far too much about their, and their families 'security', and rather too little about that of the people they were actually supposed to be serving!

Moreover, she had said as much in Cabinet, and in a couple of inadvertent moments of exasperation, to the journalists who were forever snooping around her offices. That was her own fault – they understood that she was not a politician and therefore, occasionally she was careless with her words - but the damage was done and she had never been a woman to worry about 'what might have been'.

She had been in the process of removing her designated 'war station' from RAF Chilmark in the Chilterns to the Drakelow Tunnels, a location that she personally, judged to be much better suited to the requirements of her ministry in an emergency, in the weeks before the current crisis blew up. Problematically, the military wanted everybody in a single 'emergency governmental shelter'; which was just plain stupid and besides, if the worst happened she had no intention of allowing the generals and air marshals – few of whom seemed to know anything about anything other than drill, guns and aeroplanes – meddling with the smooth running of her bailiwick!

Fortunately, the Prime Minister was of a like mind, and had initialled her draft relocation plans over a month ago enabling her to hasten the planning for the move to the underground complex designated Regional Seat of Government - RSG 9 - in the latest WEAP (the very appropriately abbreviated, she thought, 'War Emergency Administration Plan').

In the event it had been more than somewhat vexing to be whisked off to Wiltshire the moment the news from the Gulf began to trickle into Oxford. The Army, she had learned, was still working with the *previous* WEAP, not having caught up with the fact a new version had been partially activated over a fortnight ago! Thus, she and her officials had wasted the best part of a day unravelling the mess – the veritable dog's breakfast, in fact - that the Army, specifically 'Home Command', had made of implementing the latest WEAP '*Ministerial Movement Schedule*'.

However, these days one tried to look on the bright side.

Nobody had actually attacked the British Isles, *yet*; and it paid to be thankful for small mercies.

About the only thing which had worked properly was that she had been supplied, as per the latest WEAP, with a set of combat fatigues which actually fitted her, although she had insisted on keeping her own, well-worn and re-heeled, very comfortable – civilian – shoes. If there was to be another global thermonuclear war she was damned if she was going to survive it with blistered heels and toes!

If the only thing one had to take one's mind off the firestorms and the fallout was the discomfiture caused to one by one's corns and bunions, the World would have really gone the Hell in a handbag!

Alison Munro stood for a moment in the doorway of the helicopter.

It was dawn on a summer's day.

She sighed.

But...the hour is getting late...

Stepping down from the Westland Wessex as the big rotors spooled to a standstill above her head she adjusted the strap of her handbag in the crook of her left arm and shook hands with the middle-aged staff officer at the head of the small welcoming committee.

It was three weeks since the Secretary of State had last inspected the extensive works she had authorised to bring RSG 9 into the second half of the twentieth century. Up until three months ago the complex had been half-boarded and blocked off. At the time of her visit the tunnels had been a chaos of cables and noise, the atmosphere heavy with dust, the stink of the diesel exhausts of the dozens of generators, and coolly humid despite the operation of all the giant extraction fans.

"Is the control room operational, Colonel Wilson?" She asked the

Garrison Commandant of RSG 9 as the reception party walked towards the main logistics entrance to the complex.

Above the thick steel blast doors, the ground, sparsely forested rose in a natural sandstone dome several square miles in area. Nothing these days was invulnerable to a direct hit by the largest hydrogen bombs but the three-and-a-half miles of tunnels deep under the Drakelow Hills four miles north of Kidderminster, was a tough nut to crack and frankly, nobody believed the Soviets had the wherewithal to drop a really big bomb anywhere in particular in England.

Of course, the Americans could probably land one of their bombs on a sixpence...

"Yes, Minister," the soldier, a man in his fifties with a Guards Officer's erect, stiff bearing confirmed tersely. "We have established secure ground line and back up radio communications with Oxford, Chilmark and several overseas commands."

"What about Abadan?"

"No, not with Abadan, Minister. Nor with any of our surviving ships in the Persian Gulf. Communications with Cyprus are also a little bit," the Commandant of the RSG 9 Garrison shrugged apologetically, "variable at present."

RSG 9 was supposed to be operating as a fall-back command and communications station, ready to take over the national and international co-ordination of military and civil defence activities if Oxford or the Chilmark facility 'went off air'.

According to a 1961 civil defence review there ought to have been a dozen other RSGs by now; however, the price tag attached to the necessary works had always been viewed as prohibitive by the then Macmillan government. Work had commenced at Chilmark and at Drakelow, but progress at the latter had been snail-like before the October War. Most of the other stop-gap RSGs, set up on relatively miserly budgets – in comparison to the vast treasure that was being thrown at the V-Bomber force – had been located in big cities, obvious Soviet targets in the event of war. For example, four such 'centres of emergency administration' had been located in London, and predictably, all four had been obliterated on the night of the October War. Other RSGs in Birmingham, on Merseyside, near Leeds and Edinburgh had taken the strain until Edward Heath's United Kingdom Interim Emergency Administration had coalesced around the Chilmark bunker and set up shop in nearby Cheltenham. Other, RSG organisations had since been created across the country; but none was so well placed or potentially, as secure as the Drakelow Tunnels facility located in the heart of England within twenty miles of the country's largest surviving intact city, Birmingham.

Outside the main entrance Alison Monro stopped and turned to look back on the world she was about to leave behind. A world that she might never see again as it was now, with the dawn of a bright summer morning suddenly illuminating a quintessentially 'English' vista. To the west the land fell gently to a rambling brook through trees in full leaf, beyond there was a patchwork of fields, several cottages, farmsteads and the sky was oddly...silent. Not customarily a woman given to idle wanderlust she could not help but be struck by the poignancy of the moment.

Everything around her could be vaporised, or incinerated, or both at the same time in a nanosecond if there was a new atomic war. And then what would become of England...

Another woman might have lingered longer on this nightmare premonition, yet in a way her life had uniquely prepared and tempered her for exactly this moment.

Orphaned at the age of thirteen shortly after her parents had transported her and her two siblings to South Africa she had returned to England to be educated at St Paul's Girls' School, and graduated from St Hilda's College, Oxford with a degree in philosophy, politics and economics. She had been pregnant when her husband, an RAF test pilot had been killed in a flying accident during the 1939 war. Notwithstanding, she had gone to work at the Ministry of Aircraft Production, initially as a humble typist, later becoming the personal assistant of the legendary Sir Robert Watson-Watt, the inventor of radar. During the 1945 war she had worked such long hours with the great man that within the Ministry she was rumoured to be his mistress; precisely the sort of gossip that a woman of her mettle was never going to dignify with a comment, let alone a denial.

After the war Alison Munro had passed the Direct Entry Principal Civil Servant interview in a year in which only fifty candidates were actually selected, and entered the Ministry of Civil Aviation, then in the process of 'managing' the United Kingdom's 600 plus – many wartime-built – airfields. By the 1950s she had become a leading figure in the international negotiations for European and ultimately, world-wide air traffic regulation and rights.

Operating in a male-dominated environment in which inflated, overly fragile egos confronted her at every turn she was famous for one particular clash. Condescendingly asked by a former Italian Fascist Air Force general, a conceited, bumptious man called Abbriata: 'What rank did you hold in the war, Mrs Munro?' She had retorted: 'General, I held no rank but I was on the right side!'

Even the Americans had been in awe – and possibly, often in despair – at the way she ruthlessly fought for the rights for BOAC (British Overseas Airline Corporation), BEA (British European Airways) and other home-based airlines to fly to practically every corner of the World. By the end of her stint at the Ministry of Civil Aviation, the cigar-smoking, combative and tireless force of nature that was Alison Munro had risen to be Permanent Under-Secretary for International Relations in Whitehall and that, it seemed, was destined to be the high-water mark of her Civil Service career.

In the years before the October War the nincompoops who ran the Home Civil Service – many but by no means all of whom had been 'retired' during the night of the October War – had seen fit to transfer Alison Munro to the Railways Department of the Ministry of Transport, presumably hoping that they would never see or hear of her again.

Ironically, it was at that department where a little over a year ago she had come to the then Minister of Supply's – Margaret Thatcher's - attention on account of the fact that she was one of, perhaps, the only senior official in the Ministry of Transport who actually seemed to be doing something constructive to ensure that the national railway system was restored to some kind of good working order.

The rest was, as they say, history.

The latest War Emergency Administration Plan contained a revised 'precedence list'; mandating that if Margaret Thatcher and five senior members of the government were killed or incapacitated Alison Monro would become the acting Prime Minister of whatever remained of the United Kingdom.

The Secretary of State for Supply was not entirely sure she knew how she felt about that. Moreover, she was aware that the re-drafted 'precedence list' had put a host of male noses seriously out of joint.

Precedence in the event of the death or incapacity of the Prime Minister to be as follows: No. 1, the Right Honourable L.J. Callaghan, MP; No. 2, the Right Honourable George Edward Peter Thorneycroft, MP; No.3, the Right Honourable A.M.S. Neave, MP, No. 4, the Right Honourable W.S.I. Whitelaw, MP; No. 5, the Right Honourable R.H. Jenkins, MP.

And then *her...*

She had no idea why the Foreign Secretary was not in front of her - he was number seven on the list - or why the three names below his did not precede hers. However, the Prime Minister had seemingly 'agreed' the list with Jim Callaghan, and she was assured that Blenheim Palace had been consulted and concurred with the order of the list of 'precedence'.

In a way it made perfect sense if the upper 'political' echelon was wiped out to turn to the 'technocrats' in the Cabinet; although whether with most of the UAUK in effect, *gone*, the surviving military 'rump' would see it that way was of course, an entirely different kettle of fish.

Presently, she was far too busy to worry about it.

Inside the long, wide curving entrance tunnel – curved to deflect the blast of a near miss – the atmosphere reeked of fresh paint, lubrication oils of several varieties, and there was a hint of dampness, generator fumes, and an underlying musty reek of long blocked drains.

Sten gun hefting soldiers guarded the doors into and out of the currently 'open' air locks beyond the steel blast doors. If there was a fallout alarm everybody entering the complex would be required to strip naked and shower before admittance and the air locks purged to keep radiation out of RSG 9.

Anybody considered to have suffered a terminal radioactive dose would be refused entry. Anybody whose name did not appear on an approved list would be refused admission. In fact, if there was a war, hardly anybody would be allowed into the bunker. It was not so much being cruel to be kind; but as being cruel to survive.

The party's feet rang dully on the concrete floor.

Originally designated the 'Drakelow Underground Dispersal Factory' as part of the huge program to construct 'shadow factories' impervious to German bombing in the 1939-45 war, the complex had been designed by Sir Alexander Gibb and Partners. Built between June 1941 and 1942, the Rover Car Company – then making components for Bristol Beaufighters and other aircraft – had begun to fully utilise the site in the spring of 1943.

The complex was so vast that even though it was now divided into storage, dormitory, office, washing and toilet areas, with a communications complex attached to a partially-equipped BBC studio, many of the tunnels were still empty.

This was a thought that chaffed Secretary of State more than somewhat. After the October War one might, reasonably, have expected the people responsible for civil defence to have got their act together!

If her department had not stepped in the Drakelow Bunker would have been unusable in this current emergency. As it was there had only been time to half-activate it, and to provision it for a maximum six-week occupancy by approximately a thousand people.

"Is the Prime Minister still in Oxford?" Alison Monro demanded as she was escorted into her office, located adjacent to the 'operations centre' some two hundred feet below the rolling Worcestershire countryside.

"Yes, Minister. She has announced that whatever happens she will remain in that city."

The Secretary of State nodded and took her seat behind her desk, which was as yet uncluttered; exactly the way she planned to keep it.

The Deputy Prime Minister, the Leader of the Labour Party, James Callaghan was safely ensconced in the bowels of the Chilmark bunker. She was here. Personally, she hated the idea that at least two of the men ahead of her on the 'precedence list' were – basically – seeing this thing out 'above ground' but nobody had consulted her and in the final analysis, she was a Civil Servant and whether she liked it or not, obliged to follow her orders.

There was a suggestion that William Whitelaw, the Defence Secretary – in this day and age he really ought to be using the old, prematurely discarded title of 'War Minister' - fourth in line of succession might be peripatetic in this crisis, presenting a 'moving target'. More likely, he also would stay close to the Prime Minister.

Peter Thorneycroft, the last of the surviving pre-cataclysm Tory grandees still in government and as Chancellor of the Exchequer, very much the quiet man of the UAUK in recent months and second in line of 'precedence', had apparently, categorically refused – on principle - to 'hide away in a hole in the ground'.

A lot of people felt that way; if there was a new war then who on earth would want to go on living in the ruins?

Alison Monro liked Peter Thorneycroft. He was a man who might have vied for the Premiership or stirred up constant trouble for

Margaret Thatcher. Instead, he had fallen into line behind her much to the wrath of many of his old friends in the splintered ranks of the pre-war Conservative Party.

"Tell the BBC people that their studio needs to be up and running as soon as possible," she demanded. "If they start making difficulties withdraw their rations until they are ready to go on air."

If she could not broadcast to the outside world there was no point in her being at RSG 9.

"That will be all for the moment."

Alone in her sandstone cell deep beneath the hills overlooking the valley of the River Stour to the east, Alison Monro shut her eyes and fought to collect her wits.

She wondered where her son was now...

Chapter 6

Lieutenant-Commander Walter Brenckmann junior had discharged himself from the overcrowded auxiliary sick bay of the four thousand ton guided missile destroyer, when he discovered that the passageways and decks outside it were filled with men much more badly injured than himself. He had a busted left forearm (probably), his head felt like he had run into a wall at a sprint, and he hurt all over but he could just about stand on his own two feet, and he was getting in the way. So, he had swung his legs over the side of his cot, asked if somebody would loan him a jacket and limped up to the Dewey's bridge to report to the ship's captain.

Commander William Vandeput II, a dapper forty-year-old New Englander, had eyed Walter thoughtfully before passing a weary hand through his thinning fair hair. The two men had met a couple of times on the Kitty Hawk but not spoken, other than in passing.

A nurse had given Walter a shot for the pain in his arm – morphine he assumed – soon after he was pulled out of the sea. Thereafter, the hours waiting for the Dewey's Surgeon and his exhausted sick bay attendants to splint his arm and check him over, had passed in a merciful blur in which he had completely lost all sense of the passage of time. Thinking about it he guessed he had lost perhaps half a day, possibly much longer while he was doped up. The lingering effects of the opiates still cloyed at the edges of his consciousness even though he had refused further medication after the agony in his arm had quietened. He needed his head to be as clear as possible, so as to *not* forget anything important.

He was one of the few men alive who actually knew what had *really* happened two days ago – was it that long ago? – when Carrier Division Seven had, without warning, suddenly attacked the much weaker 'friendly' Centaur Battle Group.

He had been in the Kitty Hawk's CIC – Combat Information Centre – throughout. And later he had witnessed the death of the great carrier...

As fate would have it he doubted anybody still alive had had a better ringside seat to the calamitous 'second' battle...*yesterday.*

Or was it the day before now?

The missed hours, the drugs, the time he was in the water in the night blurred; he had to focus every ounce of his befuddled strength to re-construct a meaningful timeline.

The British had attacked Carrier Division Seven at around dusk, sunset in the Persian Gulf on Friday.

That was on the 3rd of July.

Now it was after eight o'clock (local) on what, the 5th July?

So, when was yesterday?

The 4th of July?

Slow down, slow down...

That meant that the British attack was two days ago; so that meant this must be about thirty-five, no thirty-six or seven hours later?

Yes, that made more sense!

Search and rescue evolutions had been ongoing ever since; although in the last few hours only bodies were being plucked from the sea. The majority of the survivors onboard the Dewey were off the Kitty Hawk, only a handful were off the Boston. The way the cruiser had gone up it was a miracle anybody had got off the cruiser alive...

The Dewey was idling in the water, launches, life rafts and debris periodically bumping against, down and along her sleek five hundred and twelve feet long hull; the sound of pumps reverberating around the ship, was unnaturally loud above the subdued rushing of the ship's fire room blowers. Even in the confines of the bridge the atmosphere reeked of the bunker oil that still artificially calmed the sea all around.

Vandeput viewed the splint on Walter's left forearm, noted the blood weeping from between the stitches on his brow and bandaged hairline.

"I got a report you'd discharged yourself from the sick bay without permission, Commander," he grimaced wearily. Nobody on the bridge had slept, other than catnapping for three days.

Walter would have shrugged apologetically but it would have hurt too much.

"I'm fine, sir."

"You don't look it."

Nobody had yet asked Walter Brenckmann what he – Carrier Division Seven's Anti-Submarine Officer – had been doing on a Sikorsky SH-3 Sea King bound for the USS Paul Revere (APA-248) at the time of the air attack on the fleet; and it was highly probable that the small circle of senior officers onboard the Kitty Hawk who had known exactly why he had been banished from the flagship were now dead.

However, to Walter that was incidental; when he had joined the Navy, he had raised his right hand and pledged his allegiance, honour, *everything* that mattered to him to the service of his country and nothing which had happened in the last few hours had changed the way he regarded *his* duty, or the spirit in which he had taken and in the years since, honoured that oath.

'I, Walter David Brenckmann, do solemnly swear that I will support and defend the Constitution of the United States against all enemies, foreign and domestic; that I will bear true faith and allegiance to the same; that I take this obligation freely, without any mental reservation or purpose of evasion; and that I will well and faithfully discharge the duties of the office upon which I am about to enter. So, help me God.'

A little over twenty months ago he had been the Torpedo Officer and Assistant Missile Officer of the George Washington class Polaris submarine Theodore Roosevelt (SSBN-600).

That night the order to flush the boat's birds had been received and authenticated and he had done his duty with, if not a clear conscience, then in the sure and certain knowledge that he was doing *his* duty by *his* President, the constitution of the United States of America, the Navy, and *everything* he knew and loved 'back home'. He had bad dreams about that night which were not going to go away any time soon, if ever. But, he had not felt in any way as 'dirty' about flushing those birds – and killing all those Russian citizens – as he had felt witnessing the cold-blooded murder of over two thousand *allied*, and *friendly* fellow mariners of the Australian, British and New Zealand (ABNZ) Centaur Battle Group.

No part of that 'cowardly sneak attack' by Carrier Division Seven on a hugely weaker and unsuspecting quarry had been consistent with *anything* he had sworn to uphold when he joined the US Navy.

"Sir," Walter told the captain of the Dewey, attempting and inevitably, failing to come to attention because his battered body simply would not, could not play ball. "I respectfully request to be placed in custody pending forthcoming trial."

Vandeput had frowned in obvious confusion.

The younger man who had stumbled, self-evidently still concussed and no doubt drugged up to the eyeballs, onto his bridge seemed to him more than a little delirious.

Walter ploughed on regardless.

"At the time of the attack on the fleet I and several other men from the flagship were in transit to the Paul Revere. There to be confined pending court martial proceedings at a time and place of the Navy's choosing."

The rest of the bridge watch was listening in now.

Vandeput, who had been about to focus his attention on a mug of coffee when the younger officer had made his appearance, threw a mildly vexed look into the faces of the nearest men. This was amply sufficient to ensure everybody kept their minds on the job in hand.

"Okay," he decided. Ignoring Walter for a moment he called; "OOD, you have the deck. I will be in my sea cabin."

The days when a captain's 'bridge bunk' was literally just that, a bench in a cubby hole somewhere in the upper works of a ship were long gone. Vandeput's 'sea cabin' was immediately adjacent to the chart room; it was a small, tidy stateroom large enough to accommodate conferences with several officers.

Vandeput shut the bulkhead door at his back.

"What's this about, Commander?" He demanded, not sure if he needed to be angry, or sympathetic.

Walter hesitated. He had the uncanny sensation that there was somebody inside his skull swinging a hammer at his temples and he badly wanted to lie down and to go to sleep. His discomfort was hardly lessened by the knowledge he was wishing away what remained of his career. Given the circumstances this latter ought not to have mattered as much as it did but he had never claimed to be any kind of a saint.

"I was in the Kitty Hawk's CIC when we fired on the Centaur and her escorts *without provocation or warning*, sir," he said guiltily. He had just been a witness, powerless to halt the madness and yet he still felt culpable, somehow responsible for *all* those deaths.

"No, that's not right," Vandeput protested. softly. "Those guys switched on their attack radars and started out on torpedo runs..."

"No!" Walter retorted grimly. He knew that either the Dewey or her sister ship, the William V. Pratt (DLG-13) had fired the first shots of the unequal battle, downing two of the British light carrier Centaur's fighters.

The ABNZ squadron ships had been steaming in a normal escort pattern twenty miles away approximately *parallel* to Carrier Division Seven, at the time the Dewey and, or the William V. Pratt had flushed their Terrier surface-to-air missile rails. Both ships had been working up to flank speed and heading directly *towards* HMS Centaur.

"No, that's not right," Vandeput repeated, less happily this time. "Dewey was slaved to the flagship's air defence board. I got the signal to manoeuvre between the fleet and the Brits. My CIC reported 'incoming'..."

Walter tried his best to straighten again.

"There were no 'incoming', sir," he reported. "In fact, the *Brits* did not turn on their targeting radars or take any evasive, or aggressive action until some minutes into the engagement. That would have been *after* they had already taken casualties. Thinking about it, I honestly don't think they believed what was happening at first. I guess they thought it was all some kind of dreadful mistake and that sooner or later we'd figure it out and stop shooting at them. Centaur's combat air patrol was operating on the *coastal side* of the ABNZ flotilla, and that was the direction the Brits were looking when we shot them in the back. By the time they realised they weren't fighting a surprise Red Air Force attack, or such like, we'd already shot down several of their aircraft and our big gun ships had closed the range with the nearest escorting ship, the New Zealand frigate Otago."

Vandeput had gone pale.

"Let me get this right. You're saying it was all some kind of awful mistake?"

"No, sir, I don't think it was a mistake. Kitty Hawk had over twenty birds in the air and more on the catapults at the time the 'action' commenced, and the Boston had already manoeuvred so as to open her 'A' arcs on the Centaur and her escorts."

The captain of the USS Dewey was connecting up the dots. Walter had painted him a picture and no man was handed the command of one of the Navy's newest and most formidable warships, unless he was one of the best and the brightest of the available candidates.

Vandeput took a deep breath, collected his wits; he back-tracked as he tried to get a handle on what he was being told.

"Okay, you say you were in transit to the Paul Revere?" The Dewey's commanding asked; he was suddenly hard-eyed as he reassessed the situation. His was one of the few fully battle worthy major units in the fleet and for all he knew the Soviets might seek, at any time, to take advantage of the vulnerability of the surviving elements of Carrier Division Seven as the search and rescue operations continued.

"I requested to be relieved of my duties," Walter explained. "Admiral Bringle wanted me off his flagship. I and about a dozen other men were onboard an SH-3 when the first nuke lit off. When I came around my life jacket had automatically inflated and I was in the water with a ringside seat. I almost got run down by the Boston before she was hit..."

Commander William Vandeput sucked his teeth.

"Jeez," he murmured. "I'm not going arrest you, Commander," he decided. "We're using the brig as a first aid centre and I sure as hell don't have men to spare to guard you. Anyhow, you look like shit. You need to get your head down. All this will have to be sorted out when we next touch shore."

Chapter 7

The stocky man standing impassively at the back of the crowded ground floor lounge of the historic house style hotel - popular with visitors to the city because of its proximity to Independence Hall and the old, revolutionary city of eighteenth century Philadelphia - had noted the clock move on to a minute before midnight as the thirty-sixth President of the United States completed the swearing of his oath of office with the customary flourish: 'So help me God!'

His two principals, Republican Presidential pretenders; the billionaire Governor of New York State Nelson Aldrich Rockefeller, and former Vice President Richard Milhous Nixon, the most ambitious and possibly one of the most ruthless men he had ever met were locked in conversation. Neither of the men, two of the three remaining contenders for the Republican Presidential ticket on 3rd November, had witnessed the hastily organised televised swearing in of Lyndon Johnson with more than half and eye or ear because right now it seemed to them a certainty that *whoever* was on the Grand Old Party's ticket in November would be the *next* President.

This was a thing given inordinate frisson by the fact that the third contender for the ticket, fifty-five-year-old Arizonan Senator Barry Goldwater was starting to look like a spent force. Rockefeller, Nixon and Goldwater had shared the spoils in last month's California primary and ever since, Goldwater had, in gratuitously pandering to the prejudices and insecurities of the libertarian, conservative right of the Party, irretrievably alienated two thirds of the rest of the GOP's traditional caucus.

Goldwater was elsewhere in Philadelphia angrily denouncing the 'traitors in the White House'; if he had wanted to nail down the lid on the lead-lined coffin of his hopes for the nomination – and bury it in that special crypt where all political careers go to die - he could not have done a better, certainly not a more comprehensive job of it, than he had in the last few hours.

All this the stocky man standing a little apart at the back of the lounge saw, and thought, and contemplated with the same perspicacious eye with which he analysed both international and domestic affairs. He was no politician, nor even a technocrat, but the man with the banker's appearance, the almost Roman nose with the cool, steady eyes of gunslinger saw and understood that he was witnessing another turning point in American history; a turning point that was perhaps, even more profound than that represented by the global catastrophe of the October War.

While it was maddening to have to follow what was going on via ABC, or by random snatched bites of information lurking amongst the largely uninformed hyperbole on public radio, or having to rely on the distorted morsels journalists traded for his – and his candidates' – time, he was relatively confident that he had formed a sound general, working, appreciation of the extraordinary, fascinating slow motion global car wreck which had unfolded, step by bloody and avoidable step over the last three days.

Of course, the roots of the disaster actually lay in the abysmally poor judgements and flawed decisions taken weeks and months ago, probably starting as far back as in the hours immediately after the October War when the Washington elite had still been half-traumatised, thankful just to still be alive. President Kennedy and his closest advisors had emerged from the valley of the shadow of death men inwardly broken, twisted and morally corroded, it was hardly surprising that subsequently they had made a series of – in retrospect - very bad mistakes.

JFK and his lieutenants were men of a former, pre-apocalypse age with far too much blood on their hands to rebuild either the US or the devastated post-war World order, even had they known what they were doing.

Posterity would rightly conclude that the fact that the Cuban Missiles Crisis had ended in a nuclear war underlined a fundamental truth; the Kennedy Administration had not known what it was doing in October 1962. While it was legitimate to ask if the Administration was distracted by the Sino-Indian War, its focus blurred by the incendiary racial tensions in Mississippi and elsewhere in the Deep South, and therefore caught off guard by the sudden discovery of 'the missiles' on Cuba, it changed nothing. Foreign affairs are complicated and Presidents and Secretaries of State have to keep any number of balls in the air at any one time; Jack Kennedy and Dean Rusk dropped the most important ball they were juggling and hundreds of millions of people died.

All of which was crying over spilt – and very scorched – milk and achieved precisely nothing and to Henry Kissinger's astute, and pragmatic mind it did not really matter who replaced the men who were currently in and around the White House, because none of the viable – that is, electable - candidates for the Presidency in November could possibly do a worse job.

Well, setting apart George Wallace, an ignorant and bigoted man would probably be hard pressed to find California on the map, let alone Cairo or Sverdlovsk, that was...

But Rockefeller, Nixon, or even Goldwater *could not possibly* do a worse job than JFK, and assuming he did not blow up the World in the next few hours, Lyndon Johnson was going to be the lamest of lame duck Presidents in the next four months (strictly speaking the next six months because the new President would not be inaugurated until late January, 1965).

From what Kissinger had heard Johnson was hardly likely to stand, anyway. There had been talk of Senator Hubert Humphrey being Kennedy's running mate, Eugene McCarthy, the poet politician from Minnesota was pushing hard and there was no telling how JFK's convention surrogates would actually vote, and that was before one even asked if LBJ would want to stand in the first place knowing that George Wallace – a racist demagogue - was going to fatally torpedo the Southern Democrat caucus that any Democrat had to carry if he was to get elected come 3rd November.

It was for this reason that the forty-one-year-old Director of the Harvard Defense Studies Program had concluded that even if the Democrats pulled a rabbit – the biggest most electable presidential rabbit of all time – out of the hat at their forthcoming Atlantic City Convention, that either Nelson Rockefeller or Richard Nixon was going to be the next President of the United States.

Unfortunately, this made his personal situation...*problematic*

Everybody assumed he was Nelson Rockefeller's man, his National Security Advisor in waiting, and had been for some years. However, in the last fortnight Henry Kissinger had realised – reluctantly, because he liked and respected Rockefeller and much of what he stood for, essentially, 'reason' within the GOP - that if, as seemed likely, the nomination came down to a no holds barred arm wrestle, then Rockefeller simply did not have the guile or the killer instinct to 'put away' Nixon.

Kissinger's quandary was heightened because he also understood that neither man was likely to catch the imagination of the Republican 'base' in the country, and that whoever became the next President was unlikely to have any kind of substantive, let alone 'moral' popular mandate from the people.

Rockefeller was an American aristocrat, the descendent of the man who created Standard Oil, he was fabulously rich and an unrivalled doyen of the arts with a purse as deep and generous as a modern day Andrew Carnegie, but politically he was a 'conservative democrat' who sat far to the left of the GOP, with little in common with the millions of people he needed to vote for him if he was ever to become President.

In contrast to the erudite, charming, patrician Rockefeller, Nixon liked to present himself as a Republican hawk, a man not unsympathetic to the 'rollback' to some non-existent utopian past – ever more unrealistic - preferences of the right of the Party. He had been the loyal Vice President of Dwight Eisenhower, the man who was, after George Washington, Robert E. Lee and Ulysses S. Grant, the greatest American soldier in history, a living legend. Ike's Administration had peacefully resisted Marxist aggrandisement and expansion wherever it had threatened for eight years; whereas JFK had not made it to his second anniversary in office before blowing up the World. Everybody knew that and Nixon shamelessly played on his long association with Eisenhower morning, day and night; the past was kinder than the present and he was a man of *that* past.

Rockefeller just 'looked' so much better than Nixon.

The Governor of New York was tall, handsome, telegenic and radiated 'presence' in a crowd; Nixon was serious, staid, less than spontaneous, a man whose temperament would always exhibit the reticence of his Quaker upbringing and who was pathologically incapable of entirely masking his resentment that he had never been given the credit he was due for being Ike's loyal lieutenant all those years...

Kissinger realised he was wool-gathering.

There had been talk among Nixon's entourage, less so from Rockefeller's, that the executive actions LBJ had taken in the hours between the President falling ill and Johnson's swearing in had been 'unconstitutional' and would, down the line be grounds for future impeachment proceedings.

That was the trouble with Nixon's people, they were attack dogs first and staffers second. That was going to be a big problem if they ever got into the White House. People had put up with the Kennedys treating Washington DC as their family playground; but the lies and the incompetence which had characterised the period after the October War had eroded a great deal of the historic aura around the Presidency. In the future the man in the Oval Office was going to be under the microscope every minute of every day and if he crossed the line, by a single inch, all the TV, radio and newspaper men who had played along just to keep in with the Kennedy boys, were going to be on his case like wolves upon the fold.

Kissinger did not think either Rockefeller or Nixon had worked that out yet. LBJ had not – self-evidently – because he had only been in the hot seat a day and he had already left a trail of litigation-worthy missteps in his wake. The veil of secrecy around Jack Kennedy's long-standing health and his present prognosis at the Thomas Jefferson Memorial was already fuelling rumours of a bloodless coup d'état.

That is Hell of a way to begin your Presidency, Mr Johnson!

Kissinger guessed that JFK's various illnesses – several of which in a more rational political system which actually implemented the checks and balances it so proudly claimed were the bedrock of the Constitution - ought to have disqualified him from holding *any* senior role in government, let alone one that gave him absolute command of the US's nuclear arsenal. Even if he lived, the fundamental 'unconstitutionality' of JFK's tenure in the White House was always going to bring him down.

As to what was behind his sudden collapse; that was already a monumental cause celebre. Rumours were rife: JFK was finished, either Dr Feelgood, or some other whisky doctor, had shot him so full of uppers, downers, opiates and God only knew what other quackery that his body had just given up on him. Either that or Addison's disease, which he had hidden from the nation, had finally caught up with him. Nixon's people said the President had had a couple of doses of the clap while he had been in the White House, which probably had not helped...

God bless America...

It was after midnight already.

The air reeked of the intoxication of fear...and generational opportunities. The politicians and their acolytes gathering around the

TV sensed that their moment was nigh.

The civil war in the Midwest and the disasters half the World away in the Mediterranean and the Persian Gulf, the latter having at a stroke emasculated US naval hegemony over the distant Western Pacific, hardly registered in the heady atmosphere; the party was in full swing...

"Have you decided whose side you're on yet, Dr Kissinger?"

The Director of the Harvard Defense Studies Program blinked out of his sombre reverie.

H.R. 'Bob' Haldeman stood beside him watching Richard Nixon and Nelson Rockefeller leaning close, nodding to the TV on the other side of the lounge closest to the small set in the corner.

Haldeman had been Nixon's point man – the senior staffer who always went ahead of and broke the ground ahead of his arrival – during the 1956 and 1960 general elections, and later managed his abortive campaign to become Governor of California. He was an out and out straight arrow raised as a Christian Scientist, an erect, commanding figure with his trade mark 'flat top' crew cut who was on an extended leave of absence from the J. Walter Thompson advertising agency. Wherever he went John Ehrlichman, Haldeman's friend from his UCLA days was never far away.

Nelson Rockefeller had a host of well-paid flunkies around him all the time; whereas Nixon had a small, hard core of true believers who would, if it came to it, go to the wall for him.

"I am on the side of my adopted country, Bob," Henry Kissinger observed flatly.

Haldeman backed off for a moment, recognising the other man had just fired a warning shot across his bows.

His companion had been born Heinz Alfred Kissinger in Furth, Bavaria to a family of German Jews, his family had fled Nazi persecution and arrived, via London, in New York in September 1938. He had not actually become an American citizen until after he was drafted into the Army in 1943.

"Yeah," Haldeman grunted. "What would you be telling LBJ if you were *his* National Security Advisor right now, Henry?"

Kissinger ruminated for several seconds.

Rockefeller's people assumed *he* was their creature; that he was *their* prince's liegeman. Nixon's people took nothing for granted and that made it a lot easier to speak to them and to know that Nixon was getting the message. Rockefeller thought he had been playing the great game all his privileged life; whereas, after so many years sitting like a faithful puppy at Eisenhower's imperial left-hand Nixon yearned to play it for 'real'.

"Sooner or later," Henry Kissinger said, deep in reflection, his voice ringing with low baritones, rumbling with certainty, "hopefully sooner, the President will accept that he must fight an all-out war *or* come to a humiliating accommodation, the terms of which will be – in the fullness of time - repugnant to the vast majority of Americans. He will be damned whichever choice he makes. These are the worst of times, Bob."

He sighed, nodded to himself as if he was thinking out aloud.

"Sometime in the next week," he continued, "the Corps of Engineers will begin demolishing bridges across the Mississippi above Clinton, Iowa because that is the only way to *temporarily* halt the spread of the Wisconsin-Illinois rebellion. It would be well to remember that the Governors of the West Coast Confederation States stamped out nascent insurgencies like that in Chicago despite of, not in league with the Federal Government. The Administration delayed and then prevented similar action being taken in the Midwest; thus, creating a disaster which, I believe, will have a much more damaging and certainly, a longer term deleterious impact on the Union than the so-called Cuban Missiles War."

Bob Haldeman knew Henry Kissinger well enough to know better than to ever expect a 'yes' or a 'no' answer to anything, either in general or particular. He waited patiently for the shorter man to reply to his original question. Henry Kissinger was the cleverest man in every one of the rooms Haldeman had ever been in with him; so, he cut the guy plenty of slack.

"The President is probably being advised," the Director of the Harvard Defense Studies Program speculated, "that in the Middle East, or the Mediterranean, or in respect of the 'European situation', principally, that the evident hostility of the British is the most important problem. *It is not.* The instability the loss of Carrier Division Seven will foment in the countries of the Western Pacific Rim; Japan, China, Korea, the Philippines, Vietnam, Malaya and throughout Indonesia, is a far greater existential threat to American global interests in the medium-term. However, everything pales in comparison to the situation in the Midwest, which might only be a prelude to other internal conflicts breaking out across the South."

Haldeman raised an eyebrow.

"So, you'd tell Johnson to bomb the Hell out of the British and concentrate on putting down the Great Lakes insurgency?"

Henry Kissinger gave the man who was, to all intents, Richard Nixon's chief of staff, a withering look. He knew that Haldeman was testing him, goading him; with Nixon's people one was either 'in' or 'out' and there was nothing in between. They had given him licence thus far, now they needed to know if they could rely upon him in the future.

"As to what Lyndon Johnson will, or can do today, or in the hours to come is a matter of conjecture. I do not have the information necessary to form a concrete view of what will be required to begin to remedy the current *situation.*"

Chapter 8

Lady Patricia Harding-Grayson was beginning to think she was the last sane person in the asylum. In her former, pre-October war life she had been a fading socialite, a more than moderately well-known authoress of superior, if not always best-selling detective stories, and the estranged and then divorced wife of a brilliant man. She had enjoyed occasional dalliances, more often than not with much younger admirers, and relished the freedom to travel widely and the society of her numerous friends. Summers on the Riviera, autumns in New England, shopping forays to New York and Paris, the stimulation of the London post-Second War literary set but actually, in hindsight, her life had become increasingly footloose, directionless in those years and she had become no more than an aging – albeit gracefully, thanks to the bone structure and robust constitution she had inherited from her dearly departed parents – observer watching the world slowly drift past.

The cataclysm of October 1962 had changed all that.

She had re-married the only man she had ever loved and at the end of last year found herself propelled, unwittingly – as the wife of the British Foreign Secretary - into the very heart of the most tumultuous events in her country's history. She had been riding the insane rollercoaster ever since. Unfortunately, right now it looked as if the ride might end very, very messily at literally any moment, and practically all the people who had any chance of applying the brake were either incommunicado, or frankly, temporarily a little deranged.

None of this would have mattered half as much if Margaret Thatcher was more, well...*her old self.* The trouble was that ever since the news of what the military men were calling the 'First Battle of the Persian Gulf' had burst like a hand grenade in the midst of the Prime Minister's private office overlooking the marvellously picturesque Old Quad of Hertford College, trying to reason with her younger friend was...*impossible.* Much like Queen Boadicea of the Iceni had been beyond reason when the Romans stole her kingdom, publicly flogged her to within an inch of her life and raped her teenage daughters; Margaret felt *violated* and she was to all intents, utterly deaf to reason.

Boadicea had led her tribal horde on an orgy of killing, looting and burning to avenge herself of the heinous wrong done to her, her daughters and her people, seeking to brutally purge her lands of the evil overlords. Two millennia later history was being repeated; unfortunately, everybody seemed to have forgotten that in the end the Romans utterly crushed Boadicea's rebellion and went on to rule over *Provincia Britannia* for another three hundred and fifty years.

Reports from the Middle East were still trickling in to Hertford College about the 'Battle of Kharg Island'. The Navy preferred 'the

Second Battle of the Persian Gulf' but the RAF felt that 'title' in some way diminished their roles in the sinking of the USS Kitty Hawk and several of her larger consorts. It was Pat's impression that even the RAF was a little put aback, shocked by the success of the airborne assault on the US fleet. Meanwhile, in the Mediterranean the fact that the US Sixth Fleet at Malta appeared to have meekly surrendered to Air Marshal Sir Daniel French's much weaker forces without a shot being fired was, well...nothing short of astounding.

The problem was that like the mostly mythical Boadicea of popular history these successes had, far from satiating the Prime Minister's lust for retribution merely whetted her appetite for more of the same.

The United Kingdom was at war – mercifully as yet undeclared – with the United States; and only the lack of any extant aggressive plan of action in such an extraordinarily improbable event had put a hold on the immediate prosecution of hostilities.

Pat Harding-Grayson had been in the room when Margaret Thatcher had angrily berated Field Marshall Sir Richard Hull, the Chief of the Defence Staff when the poor man had explained – very patiently, with positively heroic gentlemanly correctness under the severest of provocations - that no 'offensive war plans existed' covering the 'contingency of waging an aggressive war against the United States'.

When pressed he had conceded, ruefully, that around the time of the Operation Manna convoys last year plans had been formulated in the event the US Navy interdicted those convoys in any way; but that was then and this was now.

The old soldier had withstood the Prime Minister's fury with paternal forbearance and great dignity.

'Prime Minister,' he had sighed eventually, seizing his moment when at last Margaret Thatcher paused for breath. "The greater part of our submarine fleet is occupied prosecuting the war in the South Atlantic against the Argentine. Our naval assets in the Mediterranean are outnumbered and significantly out-gunned by the Sixth Fleet, whose continuing quiescence is the *only* guarantor of our tenuous presence in that region. The naval situation in the Mediterranean is further complicated by the fact that our most valuable asset, HMS Eagle is currently paying 'goodwill visits to Alexandria and Port Said the best part of a thousand miles from Malta. The Eagle will have departed Port Said by now but even at maximum speed she cannot be in range to launch her aircraft to support the Malta garrison for at least twenty-four hours, and the earliest she could actually be off the Grand Harbour breakwater at Valletta is approximately thirty-six hours from now.'

The Prime Minister had wanted to bite back at him.

Sir Richard had smiled sadly. 'Our forces at Gibraltar and on Cyprus are relatively week. Our air forces in the Eastern Mediterranean and in the Persian Gulf theatre are capable of only very limited offensive operations. There are less than twenty operational V-

Bombers available for operations at airfields in England, and three,' he paused, 'just *three* based in the Mediterranean theatre of operations.'

Margaret Thatcher had been pacing the room like a caged lioness.

'As for the defence of the British Isles,' Field Marshal Hull had continued, 'while the RAF possesses several squadrons of fast jets, including two equipped with the new Lightning supersonic fighter, both based in Scotland, and several cities are protected by batteries of Bloodhound surface-to-air missiles, realistically, we are ill-equipped to repel a sustained aerial assault. And, of course, we can have no defence whatsoever against missile attack. As to civil defence, well,' the old soldier, a veteran brigade and divisional commander from Hitler's War had spread his hands, 'we are better organised than we were in October 1962 but frankly the Army at home is over-stretched just keeping the peace now...'

'So, what is your recommendation, Sir Richard?' The Prime had asked, sarcastically. 'That we should meekly sit on our hands awaiting the next betrayal?'

The soldier had stiffened. However, when he responded his tone had been measured and his attitude respectful when at last he replied.

'British and Commonwealth ground forces are still engaged in the Abadan sector and south of Basra. All the indications are that the Red Army has been pushed back from Umm Qasr and thwarted opposite Basra. Albeit at a heavy cost. It is now clear that the Australian, British and New Zealand Persian Gulf Squadron under Rear Admiral Davey's flag has been destroyed. Other than a frigate recently arrived in the Indian Ocean and a handful of minesweepers we have no meaningful naval presence in the area at this time, other than the former aircraft carriers Triumph, and HMAS Sydney, neither of which possesses significant offensive capabilities. The First Sea Lord reports that subsequent to the 'second' battle in the vicinity of Kharg Island our surviving small ships and auxiliaries are assisting in ongoing search and rescue operations...'

British and Commonwealth casualties at sea and on land in the Persian Gulf ran into many thousands, and at least eight major Royal Navy, Australian and New Zealand warships had been sunk. US Navy losses must be as bad, possibly much worse and the fighting on land in southern Iraq and Iran was continuing unabated.

Upon hearing of the storming of the British Embassy in Philadelphia by a mob of armed men and a huge crowd of 'protestors' Margaret Thatcher had refused to speak to the American Ambassador, a man both she and Pat Harding-Grayson considered to be honourable and decent, and moreover, a personal friend. Not content with banishing her enemy's solitary honest broker, the Prime Minister had peremptorily ordered that 'all measures be taken to prevent the US Embassy communicating militarily sensitive information to Philadelphia!'

It was this which had led Pat's husband, Tom to 'have words' with the Prime Minister. Needless to say, Margaret Thatcher had given her Foreign Secretary short shrift and he had stormed out of the room cursing.

Now the stupid man was talking about 'resignation'.

'Don't be so bloody stupid, Tom!' Pat had cried in despair.

Her husband had disappeared for about an hour and returned to Hertford College with the reek of alcohol on his breath. His wife had grabbed him by the arm and dragged him into an ante chamber on the ground floor; before he could get anywhere near the Prime Minister. She had wanted to slap him, hard.

Husband and wife glared at each other.

"If you hadn't gone off in such a sulk you'd know that Margaret has already back-tracked on cutting the US Embassy off from the rest of the world. She knows as well as anybody else that we need to be talking to the Americans, she just can't bring herself to do it herself right now."

The bright morning sunshine was threatening to slide over the nearby rooftops and to bath them in brilliant post dawn light and warmth. For the moment they stood in the gloom, both sorely tried by two sleepless nights and the relentless tide of dreadful news.

His wife's intelligence on the 'communications front' had not come as news to the Foreign Secretary. He knew that the only way to stop the US Embassy talking to Philadelphia would have been to bomb it; and not even the Prime Minister was ready to do that quite yet.

"Willie's with Margaret at the moment," his wife told him. "He took Peter Carington in for moral support. The First Sea Lord is waiting to go in. Hopefully, when Margaret's had a little more time to think about what a mess we're in she'll be a little more reasonable..."

Sir Thomas Harding-Grayson shook his head.

He doubted if Defence Secretary William Whitelaw, or Minister for the Navy, Lord Carrington, another charming and very able man, was going to get a great deal of sense out of the Prime Minister.

Margaret Thatcher was a woman scorned and the fact of the matter was that she had a perfect right to be inconsolably incandescent about what had happened in the last few days. What was the point of trying to talk to 'friends' who had just murdered thousands of one's people in a sneak attack at the very moment British and Commonwealth forces were embroiled in a backs to the wall last gasp battle – which any rational US Administration ought to have fought shoulder to shoulder with the Commonwealth - against a vastly superior enemy force on the ground in Iraq and Iran?

Instead, the Kennedy Administration had, for reasons best known to itself because he could not begin to fathom it, decided to give the Soviets a free hand in Iraq; in exactly the same way Harry Truman had *not* given the Russians, or the Chinese a free hand in Korea ten years ago.

Perhaps, Margaret was right. How exactly did one conduct 'talks' with people who had just stabbed one in the back, *again*?

"I tried to get in to the US Embassy to talk to Walter Brenckmann," he confessed. "I'm the bloody Foreign Secretary and the bloody Yanks wouldn't let me in!"

There had been an angry crowd gathering in the streets around the American diplomatic compound even as dawn broke. From the look on the faces of the US Marines outside the Embassy they would not hesitate to shoot if anybody was so unwise as to breach the combined Police and Army cordon.

"So what? Drinking helps?" Pat snapped acidly.

Her husband threw up his hands in mute surrender, turned and went to the window. He stared morosely out through the ancient leaded panes.

"No, it doesn't help," he confessed. "It never did."

Pat relented. Their marriage had never been any kind of homage to domestic contentment, nor anything remotely conventional. Tom had had *his* work, his career, his dreams and she had had *her* life, and now and then, *her* very discreetly conducted affairs. They had lived their separate lives; that had never been a problem. They were friends, intimate confidantes from the beginning, even – in retrospect - when they had become martially estranged, now they were even closer. There had been a time when they were sexually interested, fascinated one by the other; years ago now but that had never been the glue that bound their lifelong tryst. They were each other's moral strength, vindication, emotional and intellectual safe harbours in a world gone mad.

"I got the bottle out," he said. "Threw the bloody thing on the floor. I ought to change my jacket. The filthy stuff must have splashed all over me."

"Your breath smells."

"I had a snifter before I got angry," the man retorted mildly.

Pat touched her husband's elbow. "This isn't your fault, darling."

"Isn't it?" Tom Harding-Grayson snorted.

Husband and wife gazed at the ivy-festooned walls across the other side of the Old Quad, immersed in their thoughts.

There was a light knock at the door.

"Ah, I heard you'd re-appeared," Sir Henry Tomlinson, the unflappable, grey-haired Head of the Home Civil Service and Secretary to the Cabinet, observed as he came in and gently pressed the door shut at his back. He nodded to Patricia Harding-Grayson, smiling wanly. "I see Pat stopped you making a damned fool of yourself again, Tom."

"Somebody jolly well ought to make a 'damned fool' of himself before we all get blown to blazes, old man!" The Foreign Secretary declared. "Be that as it may be," he went on calmly, 'had it occurred to you that *the lady* might – inadvertently admittedly – be resolutely pursuing the one strategy likely, in the short-term at least, to stop the US Air Force bombing old England 'back to the Stone Age'?"

No, that had not occurred to either his oldest living friend or to his wife.

"Look," Tom Harding-Grayson groaned, "we're reasonable people, we honestly believe, despite the evidence to the contrary, that there must be some kind of way out of *here*, this unmitigated hole we have got ourselves into. Maybe we are wrong, maybe there is no way out?"

The Cabinet Secretary viewed the Foreign Secretary ruminatively. For the first time since Margaret Thatcher had half-inherited, half-stumbled into the premiership, the governance of the United Kingdom had about it a whiff of 'headless chicken' disarray; it was *his* job to ensure that something was done about that. Getting upset was not going to help. Likewise, empathising with the openly expressed existential angst of Her Majesty's senior ministers was, self-evidently, going to achieve precisely nothing.

He met Tom Harding-Grayson's stare.

"Do you not think that we are where we are because of the inherent incoherence of American post-Cuban Missiles War geopolitical policy, Tom?"

The Foreign Secretary thought that went without saying.

He nodded.

"Good," Sir Henry Tomlinson acknowledged. "At least we agree on that."

"Yes, but..."

The Head of the Home Civil Service was inscrutable as he shook his head.

"You were the fellow who successfully manufactured circumstances propitious for a coup in Egypt, which prevented Nasser queering the pitch in the Arabian Peninsula while we were engaged in the Gulf," Sir Henry Tomlinson suggested to his oldest friend, "while adroitly convincing the Israelis that if they put a foot wrong – say by an armed incursion into Sinai, or some other 'initiative' to Colonel Nasser's detriment – they would be fighting us, too?"

The Foreign Secretary nodded.

"And," his friend continued softly, "you were the chap who untied the Saudis from the American camp so successfully that the Kingdom will feel obliged to stick with us through thick and thin, if only for honour's sake, for years to come? We won't talk now about how much drawing the Australian, New Zealand, and to a lesser extent the South African and Rhodesian governments into *our* camp will assist us in the years to come. Nor will we dwell upon how the reinvigoration of Anglo-Portuguese relations has neutralised Spanish territorial ambitions and safeguarded Gibraltar."

The greying eminence grise at the very heart of the UAUK allowed himself a tight-lipped, somewhat crooked smile.

"To sum up: you have played an appallingly weak hand as well as you possibly could, Tom. None of us knew the Soviet Union was only 'playing dead', or that the United States – parts of which, incidentally, appear to be openly at war with others – would renege so spectacularly on so many of its international commitments, or be so terrified of a second nuclear exchange with the Russians that it was willing to go to any, frankly outrageous lengths, to avoid it. You are, my old friend, the most rational man I have ever met in my whole life. So, I ask you; how on earth were you supposed to fathom the true dimensions of the insanity and the mendacity of our enemies, let alone that of our so-called *friends*?"

Tom Harding-Grayson shifted on his feet in his discomfiture.

"That's jolly decent of you to say, Henry..."

The other man deflected this with practiced charm.

"We shall agree to differ," he suggested. "Returning to my central thesis," he added, "I'm not going to let you go anywhere near Margaret right now."

"But I..."

"You'll try to talk what *you* think is 'sense' into the Prime Minister's head, Tom. The Chief of the Defence Staff tried that, and I'm sure the Secretary of State for Defence and Lord Carrington are trying just as hard, even as we speak. The truth of the matter is that apart from sending our entire V-Bomber force – what's left of it – on a one-way suicide mission to New York, Boston and Philadelphia there's really not a lot we can do to prosecute an aggressive war against the 'lost colonies'. Even assuming, that is, that it is a remotely sensible thing to do, which, of course, it isn't. All we can do is batten down the hatches, call back our submarine fleet from the South Atlantic, try not to provoke the Sixth Fleet to set fire to the Mediterranean, and hope against hope that the Soviets are as afraid of Strategic Air Command as we are, and desist in ground operations in Iraq and Iran. That is all we can hope for or do at present. That, and hope that there are no more *surprises!*"

Tom Harding-Grayson's analysis of the situation was a little more nuanced; otherwise, it was not dissimilar to that his old friend had so eloquently just expounded.

He said nothing.

"However," Sir Henry Tomlinson remarked, a ghost of a saturnine smile touching his pale lips, "I very much doubt if the current Administration in Philadelphia is in any way as 'clear-eyed' about the realities of the current situation. Whether she meant to or not, the Prime Minister's – somewhat visceral - response to events in the Persian Gulf has done a great deal to ensure that it may well be hours, or days before the fog of war lifts in the corridors of the White House. In my opinion this is all to the good in so far as it gives us some small hope that we will not necessarily be swatted out of existence sometime later today. The important thing is not that Margaret sees 'sense', but that acting President Johnson and his advisors stay their hand until things become less...*opaque.*"

Patricia Harding-Grayson blinked.

Over the years she had become tiresomely fluent in decoding Civil Service double speak. Sometimes she wanted to scream. Honestly and truly, there were occasions when Henry and her husband could be talking in demotic Greek!

She frowned at Sir Henry Tomlinson.

"If I understand you correctly," she checked, "what you are saying is that all we can do is wait to see what happens, Henry?"

"Just so, dear lady," the Cabinet Secretary agreed resignedly.

Chapter 9

Forty-two-year-old Captain Troy Simms was a tall, flaxen-haired man with an uncharacteristically overlarge, well-muscled frame for a submariner. He was a native of New London, Connecticut whose great grandfather had captained a whale ship under sail. Both his grandfather and father had been Navy men through and through, and he had been brought up with the salt sea running in his veins. Command of the USS Sam Houston had been and remained the crowning pinnacle an accomplished career launched back at Annapolis – in a wholly different, lost world - in 1939.

Troy Simms had been ashore on the night of the October War in command of the boat's Blue crew onboard the submarine tender USS Proteus (AS-19), at Holy Loch, Scotland. His Blue crew had finished its shakedown off Cape Canaveral and had brought the boat to Scotland, where, only days before the war he had handed the boat over to his Gold crew counterpart. If everything had gone to plan he would have flown back to Charleston at the beginning of November 1962, spent a week's R and R in Connecticut visiting his parents and re-acquainting himself with his fast-expanding horde of nephews and nieces – he was the only unmarried child among the five Simms siblings – and reported to Groton to participate as a 'visiting skipper' in the scheduled fourth quarter Nuclear Boat Command Course as an instructor/adjudicator. The first Blue crew deterrent patrol had been pencilled in to start on Christmas Day, 1962. Of course, all those plans had gone to Hell after the October War.

His small cabin half-a-dozen steps from the Control Room was filled with the low, muted thrumming hum of the boat, every sound partially deadened. Actually, it was so quiet that it took a man a long time to actually realise the background noise was there at all.

There was a firm knock at his door.

"Come!"

The Chief of the Boat, Master Chief Petty Officer Ronald Rickson stepped into the cabin and straightened respectfully. Simms and the 'Bosun' were the only two men onboard the SSBN who had seen service in the Second War; Simms in the Atlantic on DDEs – destroyer escorts – escorting convoys, Rickson on the 'pig boats' that, had not Paul Tibbett's Enola Gay intervened, would surely have starved Japan out of the war sometime in mid-1946. The younger men on the Sam Houston were, rightly, in awe of the Bosun; he had been on the USS Wahoo when her skipper fired his last fish 'down the throat' of a charging Japanese destroyer. The Wahoo's skipper – Kentuckian Dudley Walker 'Mush' Morton, a Submarine Service legend - had coolly remained at periscope depth, with his periscope up to bait the trap for the oncoming enemy warship.

Now that was style...

That spring the Navy had abandoned the 'two-crew' Polaris boat system, the SSBN's Gold and Blue crews had been whittled down to a single complement and SSBN command deemed to be 'Captain only' duty. Simms, pleasantly surprised to be gifted his fourth ring several years earlier than anticipated, had pushed his luck and made damned sure he got the 'best men' from both crews. Right at the top of his 'best men' list had been Ron Rickson.

"I'll be addressing the boat in a few minutes, Chief," Troy Simms explained matter-of-factly. "As soon as you hear my voice on the horn I want men posted outside the radio room and this cabin, and an armed man to escort the Missile Officer at all times when he is on duty."

The older man – he was fifty-one and but for the October War might have been on the beach by now – absorbed this without so much as batting a grizzled eyebrow.

"Aye, sir."

"That will be all, Chief."

Troy Simms had spent most of the middle watch on one of his extended informal 'tours' of the boat. The Exec scoured the boat daily, inspecting, harassing, checking that everything was clean, in order and that their people were clear-eyed, and on top of their game; that was the Exec's job. *His* job was to command and sitting in a high castle bawling orders had never been his style. So, every now and then he 'walked the boat'. He had nine officers and one hundred men under his command; each man had a family, scar tissue, hopes and fears, weaknesses and strengths the half of which never appeared anywhere in his Service Jacket. The Navy had given him four stripes and one of its deadliest weapons; it was up to him to *earn* and to *retain* the respect of *his* crew.

Inevitably, there had been minor frictions in merging men from the Gold and Blue crews; each crew had regarded itself as the 'real' crew of the Sam Houston, and the men who had been on the boat on that October night in the Barents Sea when she had flushed her birds were apart, indefinably not – quite – as other men were in the submarine service. Personally, Troy Simms would have liked longer to meld the crew into a closer fraternity but what one wanted and what one got in this brave new post-apocalypse World was rarely ever one and the same thing.

One week to shake down off Chesapeake Bay, then six days at Charleston offloading and re-loading missiles before provisioning ship for a ninety-day patrol was all he got.

After the October War the Sam Houston had re-loaded a fresh battery of Model A-2 UGM-27 Polaris Missiles with W-47 600-kiloton warheads. At Charleston nine of these reloads had been replaced with upgraded Model A-3 missiles fitted with the new W-58 'cluster' warhead comprising three separate 200-kiloton devices.

The A-3 could hit targets up to 2,500 miles away with a mean circular error probability (CEP) – in layman's language, an average accuracy – of about eleven hundred yards. An A-1 or A-2 Polaris missile, if it went off, which was a problem with the W-47, lacked the range of the A-3 and had a theoretical CEP of between one-and-a-half to two miles. That sounded okay until one realised that unless the boat flushing those birds knew exactly – within feet and inches – where it was on planet Earth CEP meant precisely nothing.

The Sam Houston's SINS (Ship's Inertial Navigation System) operated by dead reckoning, which was accurate to within hundreds of yards even after a long voyage. However, for targeting purposes that was not always good enough. For this reason, it had always been planned to back it up with a satellite-based system called TRANSIT. The problem was that TRANSIT had not yet been launched into space, or rather, attempts to launch it and to get it operational had thus far, failed. Therefore, even the advanced guidance system of the brand-new A-3 missiles might completely miss a target like a major city, especially at extreme ranges beyond two thousand miles from the point of launch.

Troy Simms had not worried a great deal about that until a few minutes ago. He had had enough to think about in the last few weeks; not least sneaking furtively into the Mediterranean through the Straits of Gibraltar, and then negotiating the relatively narrow, shallow ninety miles gap between North Africa and Sicily undetected.

Fleet Headquarters at Norfolk Virginia broadcast twelve-hourly position updates on the three SSNs – the USS Thresher (SSN-593), USS Barb (SSN-596) and the USS Skate (SSN-578) – attached to Sixth Fleet in the Mediterranean, enabling the Sam Houston to stay well clear of them; otherwise up until he steamed east of Malta it had been a nerve-jangling ride. It was only in the last few days crossing the abyssal depths of the Ionian Sea into the almost equally bottomless Levantine Basin that the commanding officer of the Sam Houston had allowed himself to breathe, every now and again, an occasional very secret, silent sigh of relief.

The way things were at the moment a chance encounter with a British destroyer or submarine was fraught with disastrous potentialities. Thresher, Barb and Skate were operating – or had been until the last few hours – alongside and in support of the Royal Navy, a pair of them bottling up the sea lanes to east and west of Crete, effectively blockading the Aegean, while the third stalked the Libyan Sea ready to hurtle north if 'a situation developed'.

SIXTH FLEET INTERNED VALLETTA...
FLEET ACTION SOUTH OF KHARG ISLAND 3 JULY...
CV-63 PRESUMED LOST...
ALL SURFACE AND UNDERSEA FORCES...DEFCON2...
SAC STRATEGIC BOMB WINGS TO...DEFCON1...
HOLD AT FAILSAFES AND AWAIT EXECUTIVE CMD...
SUBRON15...SUBRON14...DEFCON1...
1930 HOURS ZULU...READY ALL BIRDS...

Last fall Troy Simms had taken the USS Sam Houston to sea,

opened his patrol orders and discovered the boat was being sent to 'mark' Australia. That had been so dumb and so well, absurd that he had risked his career – and probably jail time – and queried his orders; thereby being instrumental in uncovering a monumental breakdown in the Polaris boat chain of command.

But for the Battle of Washington, the troubles in the South, Soviet adventurism in the Middle East and what sounded horribly like a civil war in the Midwest, the 'chain of command' scandal which had simultaneously hit the Navy and the Air Force last November and December would have been headline, not footnote news, for most of the last seven months.

"Captain on the bridge!"

Troy Simms stepped across to the tactical plot. No contacts. That was good.

Ever since commencing her patrol in the Eastern Mediterranean the boat had been beset with 'ghost' contacts; possibly due to some gremlin in the forward sonar array. The boat had needed time in dry dock, not to be sent straight out on another patrol and it was not beyond the bounds of possibility that the sonar room was periodically reporting internal, rather than external 'soundings'. That said, the regular alarms kept everybody on his toes. He pulled out the big map of the Levantine Sea and spread it across the electronic table. There were over four miles of water beneath the SSBN's keel hereabouts. A little to the west the Pliny Trench dove down over six miles into the pressured blackness of the abysmal deep. To the south west lay the Nile Delta and the Herodotus Basin, this latter four to five miles deep.

He felt a presence at his shoulder.

The Sam Houston's Missile Officer, a crew cut thirty-seven-year-old Pennsylvanian, the grandson of Danish immigrants joined him staring at the map.

"Ever since the Suez Canal was opened in 1869 salt water from the Red Sea," Troy Simms grimaced, "it being nearer the equator and therefore higher, tides being higher at the equator, and such like," he went on as if he did not have a care, "has been pouring into the Mediterranean. The water from the Red Sea is saltier, so the salinity levels in the Eastern Mediterranean have been slowly rising in the last hundred or so years; some scientists reckon it will kill off the sardine fishery in these waters sooner or later."

The other officer cracked a grin.

"I guess that sucks if you're a fisherman around here, sir."

"It sure must," Simms agreed. "The other thing that's supposed to be happening is that tropical species of fish and crustaceans from the Red Sea are slowly migrating into the Mediterranean. It's called the 'Lessepsian migration', after the guy who built the canal, Ferdinand de Lesseps. They think something similar is going to happen on the Great Lakes now the St Lawrence Seaway is open. But they don't have enough information about that yet. The Welland Canal was only deepened in when," he pondered his rhetorical question, "back in 1919? These things can take a long time to have an effect."

Deciding that he had convinced the control room that he was still, in effect, on one of his 'walking-talking' tours of the boat he gathered his wits.

Carefully organising his game face, he stood up from the map, stepped to the command chair and picked up the telephone handset.

"Put me on boat-wide broadcast please," he asked quietly.

He waited until he got the confirmatory wave that the channel was open. There were no bells or gongs, nor any kind of warning tone to alert the crew of the submarine.

"Hear this! Hear this!" Simms intoned. "This is the Captain speaking. This is the Captain. Listen up!"

He gave the off-duty men roused from their cots a few seconds to turn on their ears.

"A few minutes ago, I received a communication from Fleet HQ that the alert level has been raised to DEFCON1. I repeat, this boat is now operating at DEFCON 1."

The horrible quietness around him told him how this news would be greeted in the rest of the boat; like an unexpected punch in the gut from a five-hundred-pound gorilla.

"It is my sad duty to tell you that the United States is now at war." Another pause, unavoidably breathless now. "I have been ordered to prepare all our birds to be flushed at sixty, six-zero minutes notice any time after twelve hundred hours (local), that's five hundred hours (Zulu) in Philadelphia."

Troy Simms met the eyes of the men nearest to him.

"It is not our job to double guess the guys in Philadelphia. If the President orders me to flush our birds; that is exactly what *I* will do. That is exactly what *this* boat will do. That is exactly what *we* will do."

Out of the corner of his eye Troy Simms noted the arrival of the Bosun in the compartment. He and the older man exchanged curt nods.

"I am confident that every man will do his duty. I am confident that every man will stand to his station and that whatever happens in the coming hours we will not let down our country."

One last moment of reflection.

"That is all, Captain out."

Troy Simms turned to the Officer of the Deck.

"The boat will go to Missile Stations," he said quietly.

Chapter 10

00:25 Hours (EST)
The White House, Philadelphia, Pennsylvania

The Kennedys had never moved into the Philadelphia White House. The President had used it for meetings, to impress visitors and now and then to humour the Chiefs of Staff and his National Security Team in the cold, antiseptic splendour of its subterranean bomb-proof Situation Room.

Jackie hardly ever came to Philadelphia; she and the kids spent most of the time at Camp David guarded by the Marine Corps in the Catoctin Mountains forty miles north of DC, or at the Kennedy Family compound at Hyannis Port at Cape Cod.

Lyndon Baines Johnson did not need to be in the Situation Room – separated from *his* people by the former President's men, it was going to take a while before he got used to the idea that he was the top man now – to know that he had just been thrown the shortest hospital pass in history...

Heck, that was so *not* funny!

The thirty-fifth president of the United States was in a coma at Thomas Jefferson Memorial and he was whining about winning the rattle snake in the lucky dip!

Johnson slumped into the chair behind the big desk in the first floor Oval Office of the Philadelphia White House. Here in the former bank building on Broad Street South the room was actually a gently curving rectangular – its outer wall convex, its inner concave - of similar general proportions to that in the still rebuilding actual White House at 1600 Pennsylvania Avenue NW in Washington DC.

"Pull up chairs, gentlemen," the President directed gruffly. Sofas and armchairs had been brought to Broad Street from DC but the tall Texan was not in the mood for a quiet, fireside chat with anybody, let alone the men who had, for whatever reason – the inquests could wait for later, if there was a 'later' – allowed Jack Kennedy to 'drop the thermonuclear football' a second time in less than two years.

The British had used nukes in Iraq against the Soviets and in the Persian Gulf against Carrier Division Seven. He was within his rights to retaliate; except he was not going to do that.

Not yet.

Curtis LeMay had told him SAC and the Navy's Polaris boats could wipe the British Isles off the face of the map. LeMay had also told him that the British probably had enough bombs and bombers to 'hurt' the Continental United States.

The trouble was once you started shooting ICBMs that was it; nobody could predict what happened next. There was no magical tap at his right hand with which he could turn off the fiery thermonuclear flames...

LeMay did not know what the Red Air Force was capable of and had refused to speculate, other than to indicate that 'most of the capability the USSR deployed in Iran and Iraq had been a 'really big surprise to us'.

LBJ had got the message.

Even an all-out first strike – every Minuteman, every B-52 in the air and every single Polaris boat flushing its birds – would not, could not possibly guarantee the safety of the American people.

"We'll cut out the horse shit!" Johnson growled as the others settled in the hard chairs he had ordered to be brought into the Oval Office. He was well on the way to working himself up to share several – middlingly vile and angrily blasphemous - profanities with his guests when a door opened.

His wife Lady Bird and his daughters entered bearing coffee trays. The men who had been settling in their chairs stood respectfully, as did Johnson.

The President's wife had already removed all the ash trays in the room; at the same time his daughters had quietly emptied the drinks cabinet his predecessor's people had always kept well-stocked. The World might be about to catch fire again; LBJ's family was not about to allow him to backslide into his former ways. He had a bad heart back in 1955 and they had been on his case ever since.

Cups and saucers clinked as coffee was poured.

It was some minutes before the ladies departed.

By then the President's ire had cooled several degrees.

Johnson sighed, reflecting that his wife and daughters had timed their entrance to perfection.

He had been about to launch into an ill-judged invective-laden rant and that would have been a really bad way to start his Presidency, however long it was destined to endure. For all he knew Jack Kennedy would regain consciousness in five minutes time and demand to be reinstated. If JFK was physically and mentally capable and he could find a doctor to certify as much that was his right; the Constitution was straight up and down about that shit.

Johnson knew he could not afford to get distracted by things like that. He took a mouthful of coffee, put down his cup, clasped his hands together across his gut and made eye contacts with the men he had no alternative other than to trust with the fate of the nation.

"Where's Westy?" He asked, abruptly.

"I sent him to take control at Wister Park," General Curtis LeMay said, his tone indicating that he had not sought anybody else's council, or permission, to despatch his point man, three-star General William 'Westy' Westmoreland, in the Secretary of Defence's Office to take command of the forces now besieging the British Embassy compound in the city's north eastern suburbs.

Secretary of Defence, Robert McNamara's expression was thoughtful as he removed his rimless glasses and polished the right-hand lens. Westmoreland was his bridge between the military and the political wings of the Pentagon organisation, the man who had managed the tortuous inter-service liaison between the Chiefs of Staff and his office for over a year. He knew LeMay had ordered Westmoreland out of the White House partly because he was the best man to restore order at Wister Park; but mainly he had done it to score a cheap point. He glanced myopically at Lemay, said nothing.

Seated on McNamara's left-hand side Secretary of State J. William Fulbright stirred uneasily. He was the man Jack Kennedy had brought in to steady the ship after the assassination of his predecessor, Dean Rusk, during the Battle of Washington. In retrospect it was now obvious that Fulbright had inadvertently steered the ship of 'state' onto a reef that somebody, somewhere ought to have noticed long before the vessel ran into it at flank speed.

"Nobody in England is talking to us," Fulbright explained, seething. "We're in communication with the British Embassy in Dublin. Their Ambassador, Maclennan, is a good man. He's promised to pass on everything we send him to his people in Oxford."

Johnson held up a hand.

These comedians *did not* get to tell him their stories the way they wanted to tell them. He was beyond that. He, *LBJ*, the guy the Kennedy boys and their retainers in the Administration had undermined and treated like a redneck country hick all these years, was President *now* and *he* had had enough of doing things the 'Kennedy way'.

The first thing he had insisted upon was that business was *not* going to be conducted in the presence of a room full of gawkers, pen-pushers and fucking Kennedy family insiders!

He knew who he needed to be talking to and right now he had those six men in the room: The Chairman of the Joint Chiefs, Curtis Lemay; LeMay's immediate political boss, former President of the Ford Motor Company, Robert McNamara; Bill Fulbright, the man Jack Kennedy ought to have appointed Secretary of State back in 1961 but had not had the guts to do it; US National Security Advisor McGeorge 'Mac' Bundy; Deputy US Attorney General, Bobby Kennedy's wingman at the Department of Justice, Nick Katzenbach; and sixty-six year old Georgian long-time Chairman of the Senate Committee on the Armed Services, the former Governor of Georgia and his long-term mentor and friend, Richard Brevard Russell junior.

Johnson pointed to Bundy.

"You first, Mac. How bad does this get?"

Curtis LeMay frowned; Johnson ignored him.

The Chairman of the Joint Chiefs of Staff Committee wanted to bang on about the dangers of North Korean 'adventurism'. Johnson had already given him licence to transfer the 5136th Bomb Wing from Nebraska to Guam. If the regime in Pyongyang entertained any 'ambitions' to exploit the current situation that ought to be sufficient to warn it off; if twenty more B-52s 'in theatre' did not bring the hotheads to heel he was damned if he knew what would!

Hopefully, in a day or two the transfer of the 5136th to the Pacific could be cancelled; those 'big birds' were still needed in the Midwest...

The news from Wisconsin deeply troubled Johnson's soul in

exactly the way the pessimism of the CIA and the military about Korea did not.

Yes, he knew a lot of the troops on the ground in the Western Pacific were lines of communication men, that the 1st Marines apart there was no Divisional-sized combat unit in the region but that was because there was a Polaris boat permanently patrolling within a thousand nautical miles of Pyongyang and there were already several B-52 bomb squadrons based in the Philippines, the Marianas and Japan, over thirty aircraft all told. Moreover, even after Carrier Division Seven had sailed away the Seventh Fleet was not exactly 'impotent'. The guided missile cruiser USS Chicago (CG-11) and a dozen other major surface units were based at Kobe, and several SSNs – nuclear attack submarines – could be on station off the Korean peninsula within days in an emergency. If Korea 'blew up in his face' he could order LeMay to flatten the goddammed place; whereas quelling the insurgency in Wisconsin and Illinois was susceptible to no equivalent solution.

First rule of government; there is always something else to worry about...

Right now, the President wanted the latest glimpse of the 'big picture' first up; the sort of thing the Central Intelligence Agency and the listening services fed into the system, not the cold raw statistics, or the blunt assessments of LeMay's own intelligence 'assets'. If the British or the Russians pulled the trigger he already knew this would be a wholly military matter. Presently, the crisis was – in some meaningful way - still *political* and the longer it stayed that way the better.

Practically everybody in the Administration suspected that Jack Kennedy had re-appointed McGeorge Bundy US National Security Advisor to take the fall when the Warren Commission on the *Causes and Conduct of the Cuban Missiles War*, eventually reported its findings to the House of Representatives. The other thing *everybody* had decided was that Earl Warren would inevitably conclude that the Administration, perhaps JFK personally, had screwed up on the day of the war. However, *nobody* anticipated, not for a single second, that the Kennedy brothers were going to just sit there and take it on the nose.

Hence, 'Mac' Bundy had been recalled from the sick list, even though the man looked like a cancer patient in the middle of a punishing treatment regimen. Still only forty-five years old a stranger would have taken him for a man in his sixties. His face was deathly pale, now and then his emaciated fingers trembled, and his voice fell away in breathlessness; only the eyes remained clear, windows onto what was still the finest, sharpest mind in *any* room he sat in.

Anybody who did not think Bundy knew, and accepted, his role as the Administration's future sacrificial lamb was a fool. That was why Lyndon Johnson wanted him in this initial, critical conference of his sudden Presidency. Mac would tell him how it was without fear or favour because that was what you got when you put a question to a condemned man.

"Mister President," the US National Security Advisor prefaced. "With respect you might want to call Ted Sorenson back from Thomas Jefferson Memorial. We're going to have to sell the American public a lot of..."

"Crap?" Curtis LeMay muttered sarcastically.

"*Unpalatable* news in the next few hours or however long this thing lasts. We need to be ahead of the TV and radio networks, and the newspapers, obviously..."

Johnson thought about it.

Ted Sorenson and Arthur Schlesinger had probably won the 1960 General Election for Jack Kennedy. Sorenson had been JFK's campaign trail speech-writer and confidante par excellence; Schlesinger the scholarly wordsmith, special assistant and Kennedy 'court historian' extraordinary. Schlesinger had died in the post-October War influenza nearly eighteen months ago and Sorenson's magic was probably damaged goods, but Bundy had a point. If you had to fight a war you did it with the soldiers you had, not the ones you wished you had.

The President picked up the phone.

"I want Sorenson at the White House. If he doesn't want to come, tell the Secret Service to bring him here anyway."

He clunked the handset back onto its cradle.

Bundy nodded.

"Okay," he began reflectively, "what we have is a situation in which nobody is talking to anybody else. It is unclear whether this is deliberate or because lines of communication are," he shrugged, "inoperable at present. The, er, *situation* in Wister Park with the British Embassy compound somewhat complicates matters. The silence of the British might be attributable to their interpretation of that *situation* having been of the Administration's making..."

William Fulbright groaned in exasperation.

"We don't incite crazy people and mobs to storm foreign embassies!"

"Yes, well," Bundy sniffed wearily, "we know that; but that's not the question, is it, Bill?" He focused anew on Johnson. "General LeMay will talk to military matters in detail but to my knowledge British and *Empire* forces have made no aggressive or threatening moves against us in the last twelve hours?" It was phrased rhetorically towards the Chairman of the Joint Chiefs, who nodded curtly.

"What about CIA and NSA?" Johnson inquired. "Aren't they talking to their opposite numbers in England?"

"Not to my knowledge, sir," Bundy replied poker faced. "The British reduced their intelligence presence at the Embassy recently. The woman accredited as MI6's Head of Station," he sighed, "*The Polish Woman*, as Director McCone at CIA calls her, was believed to be in the compound when it was taken over by the, er, insurgents."

"So, we think the British are sitting on their hands?"

Bundy contemplated this briefly.

"They may be. But absence of evidence of aggressive intent is not the same as an absence of aggressive intent."

Lyndon Johnson bit back a curse.

What he did not need was more of the self-same Ivy League fucking sophistry that had got them into this mess in the first place!

"What about the Mediterranean?"

"No further developments. The British Commander-in-Chief is permitting Admiral Clarey to send regular 'updates' to Fleet Command at Norfolk. British troops are now onboard many of our ships at Malta. The British are still demanding our nuclear submarines in the Mediterranean surface and surrender themselves. Admiral Clarey has sent out orders to the four boats..."

"And?" The President demanded.

Even as he spoke he did an inadvertent mental double-take.

Had Bundy just said 'four' boats. No, that had to be wrong; he had seen an 'intelligence summary' listing the Thresher, Barb and Skate?

"None of the boats has acknowledged receipt of the orders at this time, Mister President," Curtis LeMay muttered disgustedly.

"Okay," Johnson decided. "The Mediterranean is not our main problem right now. Unless the Navy screws up again!"

LeMay began to object.

Johnson held up a hand.

A fourth nuclear boat in the Mediterranean?

No, Bundy must have misspoken...

"I'm an old Navy man, I know what I'm talking about," Johnson decided. The men in the room knew his 'Navy time' amounted to political window-dressing; he did not care. "Tell me about the Gulf, Mac?"

"The one thing we know for sure is that the Soviets have not responded, either diplomatically, or on the ground in Iraq to your ultimatum that they should withdraw to the 31st Parallel and to immediately cease all ground and air operations south of that line. We believe fighting is still going on south of and around Basra, and on Iranian territory south of the 31st Parallel north of and around Khorramshahr and Abadan. Moreover," Bundy paused to catch his breath, his voice hoarse, "there is evidence of greatly increased Soviet air activity over eastern Turkey and the southern republics of the central Soviet Union. We can only interpret this activity as an attempt to seek out, and or deter, our B-52s currently holding at failsafe positions beyond Soviet radar coverage, from overflying Soviet territory, Iraq, or Iran and carrying out bombing attacks..."

Johnson glanced at Curtis LeMay.

The veteran bomber commander pursed his lips.

"We told them we were coming, sir," he reminded Johnson, his tone solemnly sanguine. "We'll take casualties if we go for Sverdlovsk or Chelyabinsk. Maybe over the Gulf, too, the big problem is my boys can't keep flying a holding pattern forever. Sooner or later the Soviets will figure out where I'm keeping my tankers."

The President's threat antennae were buzzing.

A fourth nuclear boat...

Tankers? KC-135s?

"What the fuck are you talking about, Curtis?"

The Chairman of the Joint Chiefs frowned.

"We've had four KC-135s at bases in the Negev Desert for over a month, Mister President," he reported. "They were there to support reconnaissance and other over-flight operations in the Middle East theatre..."

Johnson's heart skipped several beats.

Two horrible thoughts flashed across his mind.

The US Air Force had had 'assets in theatre' which, presumably, had sat out the attack on Carrier Division Seven; assets which if identified by the British, the Russians, or even the Egyptians could easily be a new catastrophic flash point...

LBJ turned on Bundy.

"You said there were *four* US Navy submarines in the Mediterranean, Mac?"

The emaciated US National Security Advisor nodded.

"Thresher, Barb, Skate and the Sam Houston, Mister President..."

Lyndon Johnson started as if he had been jabbed in the ribs with a steak knife.

"We've got a goddammed SSBN out there?"

The other man seemed surprised he did not know.

"Yes, sir. In the Eastern Mediterranean. President Kennedy authorised the deployment of the USS Ethan Allen shortly after the Battle of Malta and at the end of her sixty day patrol several days ago, the Sam Houston relieved her..."

Bundy's voice trailed off because Johnson was suddenly looking at him as if he had just handed him an angry five-foot-long Diamond Back Rattle snake.

"What else haven't I been told?" He asked, wanting to reach across the desk to throttle Bundy.

"I don't know, sir," the other man replied poker faced.

There was a deathly silence in the Oval Office.

Johnson took a sip of coffee, struggling to get a handle on his roiling anger. Okay, if that is the way these arseholes want to play it, well, I can do that, too.

"Tell me about the Gulf," he invited, gruffly.

"In the Persian Gulf itself," Bundy continued, "it seems the British broadcast a conditional ceasefire to allow for recovery operations to proceed. Thus far this has been observed by both sides. It is believed that small Royal Navy warships have rescued as many as two to three hundred US personnel in the last twenty-four hours. Other good news; the Saudi government has opened its ports and hospitals to the US Navy. Riyadh airport has also been opened to 'humanitarian' flights." He paused. "I don't think the Saudis, or the Egyptians or the Israelis actually believe what has happened in the last couple of days."

Johnson looked at him from behind hard eyes.

"Yeah, well," he groaned, "I'll tell you for nothing that I'm having a hard time believing it, too, gentlemen!"

The silence was instantly oppressive.

The men in the Oval Office were relieved when the black phone on the President's desk rang softly.

Johnson picked up.

Marvin Watson, White House Chief of Staff and an LBJ friend and collaborator of many years standing, sounded like he was a thousand miles away rather than two doors down the corridor.

"I've just had a heads up that our *visitors* from California have just been picked up by the Secret Service at the airport. They should be here sometime in the next thirty minutes, Mister President."

"Thanks, Marvin."

The others were watching him closely.

"Let me know as soon as they get here."

"Yes, sir."

The President put down the phone, sucked his teeth.

"When we found out what was going down in Wister Park," Johnson explained, knowing he was one, possibly two steps ahead of the others, and a little disappointed by the fact, "I put a call through to Governor Brown in Sacramento. Ninety minutes later the British Consul to the West Coast Confederation was onboard an American Airlines DC-9 headed for Philly."

This drew blank looks for a moment until recognition dawned. The first response to the crisis from the man who had been Washington DC's ultimate deal maker for a decade, literally the ringmaster of the Senate in the second term of the Eisenhower Administration, had been to start looking around for people to *talk to*.

This was not a thing that ought to have come as any kind of surprise to the men in the room. Or at least, it ought not to have come as a surprise on any other day; one man in Philadelphia had been thinking clearly as the tsunami of crises began to break across the beleaguered Administration.

The President savoured this small triumph.

It was only then that Johnson recollected that Marvin Watson had very deliberately used the word 'visitors' rather than *visitor*.

No, maybe that was my imagination...

"That kid Christopher?" Curtis LeMay queried, less than impressed. "What the Hell can he do, Mister President?"

Chapter 11

08:29 Hours (Local) – 00:29 in Philadelphia
USS Dewey (DLG-14) south of Kharg Island

When the sun had risen burning red over the eastern rim of the horizon the bow of the great carrier had emerged out of the patchy mist wreathing the oil-slicked sea. There it reared, eighty or ninety feet in the air, the great painted '**63**' on her forward flight deck glinting darkly in twilight's first dawning that morning half-a-world away from her home port.

Hardly a breath of wind stirred the air and as far as the eye of any man standing at the rail of the USS Dewey could see, the water was littered with the flotsam and jetsam of the giant wreck and her sunken consorts.

Walter Brenckmann stared at the bodies drifting, the wreckage of rafts, and the splintered woodwork in the AVGAS-streaked oily calm. The Forest Sherman class destroyer USS Hull circled close in to the looming, rock-like bow of the Kitty Hawk. Beyond the Hull the British minesweeper HMS Bronington was slowly sweeping the waters downwind from the wreck of the Kitty Hawk. Yesterday the four-hundred-ton vessel armed with only a single 40-millimetre cannon had transferred over a hundred survivors from the sunken William V. Pratt to the Dewey and the transport Paul Revere, before setting off again in search of more men in the water.

The British Royal Fleet Auxiliary oiler Wave Master was still standing alongside the crippled guided missile cruiser Albany. The big tanker was holding station after taking off several of the cruiser's most severely injured men using her undamaged whaler and captain's barge.

There had been no spoken or unspoken truce, no official ceasefire in the desperate hours after the battle. It was just that nobody had any appetite for carrying on the fight. Once the last spasm of violence and retribution subsided, there was no rekindling it. The men on the rail of the Dewey viewed the British ships with hooded, angry eyes but both sides had fought themselves to a pyrrhic standstill and neither side began to understand how things had come to...*this*.

Walter Brenckmann constantly replayed what he had witnessed in his mind's eye. He did not want to relive it; it was simply that his waking consciousness would not let it go.

He had seen an RAF Canberra bomber attack at wave-top height, skip its bombs across the water and fly into the side of the heavy cruiser Boston at five hundred knots; the bombs had gutted the fifteen-thousand-ton ship and the impact of the hurtling twenty-ton fuel-laden aircraft had lit up the six hundred and seventy feet long doomed ship like a Roman candle. The Boston had died within minutes as had most of her thousand-man crew.

A forest of bomb geysers had surrounded the USS Albany, rising high above her towering radar masts, the World War II converted guided missile cruiser had lurched and shouldered through the forest of near misses until at least two bombs, perhaps three, had found her. Livid crimson flashes of fire had splashed across her superstructure and erupted near her bow and after that she had been a listing, burning hulk.

Bobbing in the water, dazed and disorientated, Walter had not seen the William V. Pratt's end. Hit by several bombs she had burned like a distant torch and gone down overnight.

Those events had been almost explicable.

A little over two decades ago another Navy man, Texan-born Ensign George Gay had witnessed something very nearly as surreal as Walter had survived, at the height of the Battle of Midway. Gay, the pilot of an obsolete Douglas TB Devastator torpedo bomber had found himself the lone survivor of the USS Hornet's Torpedo Squadron 8, in the water surrounded by Japanese aircraft carriers, and had watched the tide of the whole Pacific War turn in a few extraordinary minutes. In diving down to massacre the slow, manoeuvrable torpedo bombers the enemy's fighters had left their carriers undefended against the wave of dive bombers that suddenly fell upon them that afternoon in June 1942. George Gay had seen three Japanese aircraft carriers - the *Akagi, Kaga* and *Soryu* - bombed into burning wrecks.

Ensign Gay had found himself on the cover of *Life* Magazine in August 1942 but Walter somehow doubted his own fate was to be similarly feted and garlanded.

The Second War aviator had had to wait over thirty hours before a PBY, a Catalina seaplane, had picked him out of the water; Walter had been more fortunate, fished out after the dimming flashlight on his Mae West attracted one of the Dewey's splinter-damaged, leaking whalers around midnight.

Whatever the Navy did to him the things he had seen would live with him forever. What *he* had witnessed would surely have beggared even George Gay's credulity. Even now his recollections had more in common with a fever dream than anything...*real.*

As the sun had set in the west the ships of Carrier Division Seven had raced, twisted and turned with great bones in their teeth between the falling bombs, or lain dead in the water beneath towering pillars of grey and jet-black churning smoke rising like pillars of Biblical salt above the damned...

Guns had thundered ceaselessly; missile contrails had criss-crossed the darkening skies...

Kitty Hawk was dead in the water...

Walter had watched the old-fashioned turboprop British Fairey Gannet torpedo bombers – at a distance the things looked uncannily like old WWII Grumman TBF Avengers – picking their way through the surrounding escorts to drop their fish at point blank range. One after another water spouts had erupted under the stern of the flagship and afterwards, the giant carrier was drifting like an eighty-thousand-ton barge...

He had seen two RAF fighters barrel in from the dark eastern horizon and strafe the Albany with thirty-millimetre Aden cannons...

More missiles had stabbed up into the heavens above the crippled flagship, their rooster tails of fire and smoke like the fingers of a vengeful lesser god probing the coming night for victims; yet down through this aerial killing – death zone – the bombs of now broken bombers still fell, falling in ever-quickening unstoppable ballistic arcs.

And still the USS Kitty Hawk had lain dead in the water...

Walter had watched the swarm of smaller bombs, specs like motes in the corner of his eye but each one a five hundred or a thousand-pound agent of death begin to fall around the flagship. Tall geysers of water approached the great ship's bow, and then the missiles began to hit the great ship. The yellow-red flashes had walked across her flight deck and the aircraft parked beside and aft of the catapults had begun to burn.

Kitty Hawk might have survived those hits.

Her crew might have put her out her fires, got the leviathan under way again had not the coup de grace already been delivered, high above the doomed ship.

The V-bombers blown apart by the escorting ships' Terrier surface-to-air missiles - and sliced and diced by the barrage of radar predicted gunfire of the surviving ships of the fleet which formed an impassable umbrella of scything cannon and exploding heavy-calibre shells over the carrier - had already been in terminal dives when they were hit. Each aircraft had been carrying six-ton Tallboy, or ten-ton Grand Slam munitions and when the bombers disintegrated their cargoes of death whistled down regardless.

Walter was mesmerized by the descent of the great black dart that could only have been a ten-ton Grand Slam. The bomb appeared be falling vertically; except it was not. When the explosion came it had seemed to envelope the entire forward half of the massive ship; even over a mile away from the detonation of the bomb's four-ton Torpex warhead the shock wave had hit him like an unexpected punch in the guts. He had been dazedly astonished when as the water settled the flagship was still...*there.*

Then he had heard the screaming in the sky.

His disbelieving eyes had glimpsed the silvery arrowhead silhouette...

In the time it took him to realise that what he was looking at was the wreck of an aircraft falling to earth minus is wings and most of its tail plane the stricken V-bomber – a Victor - had burst through the umbrella of anti-aircraft fire.

Large parts of the bomber peeled away and there were at least two small explosions seemingly just behind its nose; perhaps cannon hits...

Walter saw Kitty Hawk clear her stern Terrier rails one last time.

Too late...

The Victor was too close, too fast and no guidance system known to man could 'lock up' a missile falling from the heavens at twice the speed of a rifle bullet.

The bomber had dived vertically into the middle of the Kitty Hawk's flight deck very nearly next to the carrier's island superstructure.

Walter thought – it all happened to quickly for the human eye and brain to *know* the exact sequence of events – that there were two, or possibly three explosions.

The first marked the impact of the bomber just aft of the carrier's bridge; it was as if a two-thousand-pound bomb had gone off on the deck.

A fraction of a second later the entire mid-third of the biggest warship in the World was consumed by a massive double detonation.

The bomber must have still had her bombs onboard...

The ferocity of the detonations was such that as he bobbed in the water over a mile away pieces of the ship had fallen in the sea all around him...

Now the bow of the USS Kitty Hawk jutted out of the waters of the Persian Gulf like an uncharted rock, a great, jagged shard of metal marking the place of death of as many as five thousand American Navy men.

Chapter 12

Dwight Christie blinked in and out of consciousness trying to differentiate between what was dream-nightmare and what was real. He had no idea what the time was or how long he had been propped up in the corner with his right wrist handcuffed to a radiator pipe. The air stank of burning, urine, mustiness and...*faeces*. He would have wrinkled his nose but it felt as if it was broken and he guessed the reason he could not see out of his left eye was because of the crusty, congealed blood on his face and down the left side of his chest.

"You're still alive then?" The woman sitting on the floor a few feet away – chained to the pipe work at the other end of the old iron radiator – asked.

The man struggled to focus his good eye on her.

With only the light coming into the room from the small rectangular window above the door for illumination practically everything, including her face was deep in shadow.

Who was she?

When they first brought him up here; yes, this was upstairs somewhere on the first or second floor, he remembered that now...

There had been a woman on the bed in the corner...

"Do you have a name?" The woman asked.

Christie thought he detected an eastern European, or perhaps, a Russian lilting accent. *No, maybe I imagined that.* His thoughts were scrambled and every time he moved his head he felt sick.

"Christie," he muttered. His lips were fat and slurring, he had bitten his tongue and a couple of his lower teeth felt...loose.

I was on a bus...

There was a crash...

And then what?

Nothing, there was a big void where there ought to have been memories...

"Dwight Christie," he said, spitting what could have been phlegm or blood. He retched thin air for several seconds, afterwards his head was less muzzy and he was a little less nauseas.

He focused on his companion.

She looked like he felt.

Her nose was bloody, her hair matted and plastered over her face. Her blouse was torn practically off her shoulders, and her left wrist was handcuffed exactly the same way his right was to the ancient pipes.

Christie squeezed his good eye shut.

The bastards had had her on the bed.

Three of them; taking it in turns to rape her.

Two holding her down, the third on top of her.

She had bitten and kicked and spat in their faces, clawed at them, put one of the clowns on the floor and stamped on him before the others pulled her off...

"You...okay?" He grunted, ashamed without knowing why.

It was hard to make out her expression in the shadows.

"Men have done worst things to me," she sniffed with a matter of fact indifference that sent a chill down Dwight Christie's spine. "They called *you* a traitor?"

The man almost laughed.

"Yeah, that would be me..."

"Were you unconscious or were you just playing dead before?"

"Out cold, maybe," he speculated, resting his aching head against the wall at his back. "Until a while ago, I guess."

"I didn't get a look at the big guy who raped me the first time," the woman remarked.

Again, the cold, utterly emotionless tone.

"He got two of his people to hold my arms while he fucked me from behind," she went on. "One of them pulled so hard I think my left arm popped in and out of its socket. Then the others came in..."

"I don't remember that..."

"That's okay. I'll know them all the next time I see them."

Christie swallowed dry mouthed.

"Sorry, I don't even know where we are?"

"We're in the second-floor room of one of the Embassy secretaries..."

"The Embassy?" The man checked. This was getting crazier every second.

"Wister Park. The crowd outside stormed the compound at the same time somebody crashed a bus through the main gates. There were men with automatic weapons. There was a lot of smoke and I ran out of ammunition at the wrong time. Either that or the bloody gun jammed. Anyway, somebody hit me and I came around being dragged up the stairs. The whole place was full of people by then. There was a lot of shooting, every room was being ransacked. They brought you in a while later; it was as if they wanted you to see what they were doing to me. Why would they want to do that, Dwight Christie?"

The man's mind was racing.

"Who are you, lady?"

"You don't need to know that."

Dwight Christie thought that was funny, he coughed a painful snort of amusement.

"What do you mean I 'don't need to know that'?" He protested, starting to get very light-headed.

The woman looked at him in the gloom.

Silently, she looked.

"What?" He demanded, unnerved.

"Who are you, Dwight Christie?" She asked. Before the man could reply she followed up: "And what do you know about the people who crashed that bus into the gates?"

"Maybe, you don't need to know that."

Again, silence except now Christie was hearing movement and other sounds in the building, booted feet on distant bare boards, muffled voices on a floor beneath them, machinery noises from outside.

And he was remembering the shouts and screams emanating from rooms adjacent to this one. There were other women in other rooms on this floor of the Embassy...

"Maybe," the woman said unthreateningly, "I'll just wait until you pass out again and strangle you, Dwight Christie."

He had no doubt whatsoever that she would do it.

Even though he had no idea how she would get anywhere near him; he believed she would kill him if he gave her cause. Any cause, any doubt, without a scintilla of hesitation or regret.

"I used to be FBI, a Special Agent out on the West Coast," he said, not recognising his own voice.

"You used to be?"

"Yeah, it's a long story."

"You're not going anywhere any time soon."

"This is true," he admitted. He wanted to laugh, did not know why; assumed it was hysteria brought on by concussion. Every moment he made he became more aware of how beat up he was. His head was cracked, obviously but his chest hurt like Hell every time he breathed and his right arm felt *wrong.* Hopefully, that was on account of it having been chained up for so long, blood not circulating properly or such like. "I went bad a long time ago, lady."

"It happens," she said, half-sympathetically.

"I worked for the Reds. Or at least I thought I was working for the Reds. I may actually have been working for something called Red Dawn..."

"Krasnaya Zarya."

"Krasnaya..."

"It doesn't matter. You worked for the Soviets?"

"Yeah. All that went south after the Battle of Washington. After that I took to hunting monsters..." It was all coming back to him now. "The Feds caught up with me in Texas. After that, I made a deal, which I broke. In a way. I went after a monster called Galen Cheney..."

"I heard some of the insurgents use that name."

"Yeah."

I went looking for Cheney in the forests of New Jersey and the maniac chained me to a seat in an old school bus that...

"I remember being on the ground after the bus crashed," he said, musing out aloud. "I tried to get up and something knocked me down. I don't remember anything else until dreaming, seeing, I suppose, those guys on top of you on the bed."

Inadvertently, he rattled his chain on the pipe above his head, anguished that he had not been able to do anything about what she was going through.

"So, what are you?" He asked, breaking from one circle of thoughts into another. "You a secretary or something?"

Even in the darkness he could tell this amused the woman.

"No."

"Oh, right, then what?"

"You said you hunt monsters, Dwight Christie," she reminded him with a sigh. "Perhaps, I won't strangle you in your sleep after all."

"You think I care, lady?"

"Yes," she decided after a short delay. "I think you probably do." In the quietness they listened to the sounds of the building. Booted footsteps clumped along the corridor nearby, receded.

"Cheney and his crazies attacked the Embassy to kill as many people as possible," Dwight Christie said lowly.

"He discussed this with you?"

"No. Does it look like I'm the kind of guy he *discusses* that sort of thing with, lady!"

"I don't know, it's very dark in here," the woman observed with impatience and scorn in her momentarily *very* Russian vowels. "So how would you know a thing like that?"

"He left his family back in Texas so he could go up to Atlanta to assassinate Dr King. He took his boy, Isaac, and just up and left. Isaac's kind of slow but a dead eye with a long gun. Galen ordered him to break his cherry with a twelve-year-old virgin before he and the kid left home."

"Isaac?"

"Yeah."

"Tall boy, afraid to look one in the eye?"

"Could be..."

"He was in the room *watching* when they started on me."

"That figures..."

Dwight Christie hesitated, realised that keeping secrets was not going to do him any good.

"The Feds busted me when I took Sarah, the kid Isaac raped and beat up on, to a hospital. He got her pregnant and she was too young, damaged," the former Special Agent shrugged, words choking angrily in his throat, "she miscarried and was bleeding out. Heck, the Agency would have caught up with me sooner or later but, later would have been better."

"You must have had a chance to kill Cheney?"

"I didn't plan on getting killed getting even, lady."

"What about now?"

Dwight Christie thought about it and realised he did not know the answer.

"What about you?" He posed, turning the question on its head while he wrestled with his courage.

"If you were a *real* monster hunter you wouldn't ask me that."

The man opened his mouth to press the woman again on who she was, thought better of it. If she had wanted to tell him she would have done so by now and she did not seem to be the sort of girl a guy hit on twice.

And besides, at that moment the door swung open with a crash and the single overhead electric light glared into life temporarily blinding him.

Two men in grubby combat fatigue stomped into the room; a pair of Galen Cheney's boys, neither of whom had exchanged a single word with Christie in his short time at the Atsion Lake camp in the woods of Wharton Forest.

The former Special Agent squinted through the glare to get his first good look at his fellow member of the room's chain gang. Although it was hard to tell because of the blood on her face he guessed she was in her thirties, slender and might have worn her tattered blouse and torn calf-length dress with a model's catwalk elegance; she was *that* type. Definitely, not a secretary! A diplomat's wife, perhaps? No... She had said she had a gun; that made her different, singular and her accent was not 'British'.

So, who was she?

"You going to make trouble?" The older of the two men brandishing handguns at her asked.

There were others out in the corridor.

And Dwight Christie felt his gut twisting.

He knew what was going to happen next was wrong beyond his imagining and so did the woman, and there was absolutely nothing he could do about it.

The room was filling with bodies, each man ignoring the former FBI Special Agent as if he was invisible. The woman's chain clanked. She made no attempt to resist, fight back; there were too many strong hands and arms restraining her, forcing her down on the bed, tearing, lifting her ruined skirt, wrestling her legs apart...

Isaac Cheney was the first to climb on top of her.

As he clumsily violated her he started giggling...

Chapter 13

Forty-six-year-old William 'Willie' Whitelaw, Her Majesty's Secretary of State for Defence in the Unity Administration of the United Kingdom (UAUK), had not been under fire this severe since that time at Caumont in Normandy, when he was in command of a troop of Churchill Tanks. On that occasion, very nearly twenty-two years ago – virtually half his life – he had been under fire from the *Panzerjägerkanone 43*, 88-millimetre rifles of several German *Jagdpanthers* (Hunting Panthers). Right now, the fire from those guns – in whose sights any target up to two miles away was a sitting duck, the equivalent to point blank range – firing a twenty-three pound round with a muzzle velocity of over three thousand feet per second capable of slicing through five inches of armour plate up to a mile distant, would have been infinitely more preferable than the verbal barrage that he, and his friend and colleague, Peter Carington had had to endure in the last few minutes.

Willie Whitelaw, since 1955 the Member of Parliament for Penrith and the Border, was by nature a serene, jovial, affable man, a throwback to a more 'clubbable' age in which all the old-fashioned virtues of politeness and everybody knowing their place were taken for granted. He had not quite attained the status of a genuine Tory grandee by dint of still being some distance short of his fiftieth birthday at the time of the October War, but in a decade or so – if he had had the patience to stick it out - he would almost certainly have become an automatic candidate for *Primus inter pares*, first among equals, in the company of the elder statesmen in the Conservative and Unionist Party of the United Kingdom and Northern Ireland. Because of the war he had got where he was *always* going to get to sooner rather than later, with in fact, uncommon and very discomforting haste.

His friend, Minister for the Navy, Peter – 6th Baron Carington and therefore strictly speaking 'Lord Carington' - had been a rung or two higher up the greasy pole of government by October 1962, and but for his failing health he would have stayed ahead in that race, and might by now, conceivably been prime ministerial material.

Like Whitelaw another old soldier, Carington was sorely tempted to dive for cover as the tirade continued. At one point he had opened his mouth to try to intervene, to utter some feeble excuse or apology, anything which might mollify the lady. In the end he was left to reflect on how little his career to date had actually prepared him for this, the greatest crisis of his life.

William Whitelaw tried to tune out the Prime Minister's existential ranting. Born on the family estate at Monklow in Scotland, his father had been killed in the First World War without ever setting eyes on his infant son, leaving Whitelaw to be brought up by his mother and grandfather. Educated at Winchester College and Trinity, Cambridge – where he earned a blue at golf – he had earned a regular, as opposed to a temporary wartime commission in the Scots Guards, in 1939, serving with the 6th Guards Tank Brigade. Field Marshal Bernard Montgommery had pinned a Military Cross on his chest after that little affray at Caumont; and had it not been for the death of his grandfather, necessitating his return home to manage the family's Lanarkshire estates, he would have stayed in the Army after the war. As it was he had come to politics relatively late...

"Willie!"

The hectoring voice punched a hole in the Secretary of State for Defence's normally impenetrable psychological carapace. He blinked, momentarily alarmed as if he had been caught in the headlamps of a rapidly approaching lorry.

"Willie! I don't think you've been listening to a single word I've been saying for the last five minutes!"

"To the contrary," he retorted stiffly. "You were - if I may be so bold as to venture, somewhat intemperately - berating my department for its inability to provide you with a significant second, or retaliatory nuclear strike option against the continental United States, Prime Minister."

Nothing in William Whitelaw's adult life had schooled him in how to deal with a woman like Margaret Thatcher. It was not that he was uncomfortable in the company of intelligent, persuasive, strong-willed members of the fairer sex. He was none of those things, although if pushed he might admit to occasionally responding with – less than wholly gentlemanly - mild irritation when *any* woman took it upon herself to tell him *his* business. That sort of thing was well, just bad form; a woman's place was in the home, her rightful role that of an obedient wife and as the supportive soul mate to her husband, or whichever other man with whom she shared her life, work, or amusements. That was the way of things; a view by and large heartily shared by the majority of his fellow MPs, old school and college friends and certainly by all the men he employed on his still extant, post-October War, Scottish estates.

While there were times – not so many lately – when he would have been the first to confess, that he was as much under the lady's spell as anybody else; frankly, he had just about had as much as he could take from her!

"Quite," the Prime Minister enunciated coolly.

Still Whitelaw fought to be reasonable, urbane.

"The cupboard is bare, Margaret."

"So, when the bloody Americans come calling with their contemptible demands and threats what do I say to them?"

Margaret Thatcher had been pacing like a Tigress.

She halted.

The men in the room had been ordered to sit down; all the better to take their medicine. Like lambs to the slaughter, they had done as they were told, sat on the hard, rickety chairs in the middle of the Prime Minister's room while she paced, backwards and forwards against the stilettos of sunlight now silhouetting her slim figure in the window.

"Yes, sir! No, sir! Three bags full, sir! Whatever you say, Mister President! How many more of my people would you like to murder this time? Which ship or town or aircraft do you want to attack without warning this time?"

Whitelaw looked to his left. Peter Carington half shrugged in despair. Beyond him the third man in the room – who clearly felt he had come to the wrong meeting – had been as silent as a church mouse once the brief, uncomfortable opening civilities had been exchanged was frowning.

Thirty-five-year-old Nicholas Ridley, the Member of Parliament for Cirencester and Tewksbury and since the untimely death of Iain MacLeod, his predecessor as Minister of Information – the UAUK's chief propagandist – coughed.

His two male Cabinet colleagues looked to him and Margaret Thatcher halted a heartbeat before resuming her pacing. The Minister for Information coughed again, this time adding an impatient shake of his head.

The second son of a viscount and the daughter of the architect Sir Edwin Lutyens, educated at West Down School, Winchester, Eton College and Balliol College, Oxford, Nicholas Ridley's innate inability to tolerate fools was always going to be a problem when eventually, after soldiering and pursuing a career in civil engineering, he entered the political arena. Outside politics he still retained his territorial commission and painted, with great accomplishment much in the style of his famous grandfather. In other words, he had always been and would always be his own man.

"Prime Minister," he ventured, "if I may offer an unsolicited thought on our somewhat unfortunate predicament?"

Margaret Thatcher halted, folded her arms across her breasts and scowled at Ridley.

"By all means, Nick."

Ridley's name had been at the top of a very short list when she had hurriedly had to find a replacement for her friend, and sometime detractor and opponent, Iain MacLeod. She did not know Ridley very well – she suspected he was a hard man to know in the same way she was probably a hard woman to know, so they had had that at least in common – but that had not been a problem. Ridley had reputation for being a 'thinker', a man who questioned accepted wisdom and looked for new ways to do things. There were few enough original minds in Parliament, even fewer 'doers', that was why her own immediate predecessor, Edward Heath had co-opted Tom Harding-Grayson into his Cabinet, she had brought Alison Munro into hers and relied so heavily on the advice of Sir Richard Hull...

She had treated the Chief of the Defence Staff abominably earlier that morning and the minute she finished this session, she would dash off a note of abject apology....

"It seems to me," Nicholas Ridley observed glumly, "that since we have quite obviously already played every card in our hand that we contemplate – if I may employ another card game analogy - the best way in which to 'stick', rather than to 'twist', Prime Minister."

Margaret Thatcher was about to slap him down; hesitated not quite knowing why. People used to tell her not to be so 'literal', not to take everything that was said to her at face value. People said she was humourless; she was anything but, it was just that she 'did not get' a lot of the jokes she heard because much of the innuendo and punning that had others 'rolling about in the aisles' flew straight past her. Basically, she spoke plainly because she expected others to speak plainly to her.

"How so, Nick?" She demanded, a little of the wind spilling out of her sails for a moment.

"We have already done everything that it is in our power to do, Prime Minister," the man replied levelly. "Our forces have repulsed – temporarily at least – the Russians in Iraq. We have defeated a superior American naval squadron in the Persian Gulf, albeit at the price of surrendering that battlefield to the surviving US vessels in the area. At Malta we have interned the bulk of the US Sixth Fleet; thereby, seizing a valuable negotiating card. Likewise, it is my understanding that you have left the Administration in Philadelphia in no doubt as to our resolve to battle on, regardless of the cost. Events in the Gulf and elsewhere have also enabled us to claim the high moral ground, both in the Commonwealth and in Arabia. Moreover, we have demonstrably – at great cost - stood by our allies, and they have stood by us. However, realistically, what more can we possibly do?"

The Prime Minister huffed and puffed.

Presently, she corralled her skirt and sat in the hard-back chair next to her desk beneath the window and viewed the most junior of the three men in the room.

"We have put our V-Bombers on standby," she stated tersely. "Orders are being drafted to bring our submarines in the South Atlantic home, the major surface units of the Sixth Fleet are being disarmed..."

"Prime Minister," Ridley retorted, without rancour, "the US Navy has at least three nuclear submarines operating in the Mediterranean. *We* are therefore, somewhat 'bottled up' in Malta whether we like it or not. The Americans – if they get their act together – will soon realise that their Navy and their bombers still call the shots in the Gulf. As for the V-Bombers, how many have we got? Ten? Fifteen? Twenty? The Americans have over a hundred B-52s and a dozen Polaris missile submarines, quite apart from all those missiles in silos in the Midwest. As for the Russians," he shrugged, "they thought they had a cast iron deal with the Americans a day ago! Goodness knows what they will do next. The point is that *we* have to be pragmatic about our *real* options."

Margaret Thatcher's steely blue eyes narrowed.

Nicholas Ridley went on, a little perturbed that he was the one who was having to tell his Prime Minister what ought to have been patently apparent to his senior colleagues.

"If we make *any* further aggressive move against the Americans they might simply swat us aside. Since they are capable of doing this at the flick of a switch, this ought to be foremost in our deliberations."

"Our submarine fleet..."

Ridley cut off the woman.

Raising a hand, he groaned: "We can inconvenience the Americans for a few days before all our submarines are sunk, that is all, Prime Minister. I'm sure the Chief of the Defence Staff belaboured this point to you in your recent interview with him so I will not rehash any of that. Likewise, I think the argument that the Soviets – for all the treasure they have poured into Iran and Iraq – will almost certainly have held back significant military and political assets, must be factored into the, er...*equation*. It seems to me that militarily right now we ought to be doing precisely...*nothing*, Prime Minister."

Doing nothing was a concept that Margaret Thatcher had never entertained in her life or career to date, and yet...

"So, your advice would be to *do nothing*?"

"No, Prime Minister," Ridley reposted tartly. "We ought to be 'doing nothing' as *aggressively* as possible, just so nobody gets the impression we intend to do anything else!"

This was far, far too tautological for Margaret Thatcher.

"So that's what I tell the Queen?"

Willie Whitelaw stirred, ponderously as if from a long slumber.

He had been, and remained, appalled that Her Majesty, His Highness Prince Philip, Prince Charles and Princess Anne were still above ground at Blenheim Palace in nearby Woodstock. However, now that he had had a little more time to get used to the idea, the Royal Family's determination to 'tough it out' with the British people presented both propaganda, and concrete political possibilities.

"Yes, Margaret," the Secretary of State for Defence declared, gently clapping his large hands on his knees. "I think that is exactly what you should say to Her Majesty. Ideally, I would suggest, it might be helpful if Her Majesty subsequently said it herself in front of Nick's Ministry's cameras and sound recordists for broadcast to the Commonwealth, and the rest of the civilised world!"

Chapter 14

As the big limousine glided into central Philadelphia Captain Sir Peter Christopher, VC, gave his wife's hand one last gentle squeeze, took a very deep breath and tried, yet again, to compose himself. For her part his wife – as if oblivious to the presence of the two men sitting opposite the couple in the armoured passenger compartment of the custom-built Presidential Lincoln – applied counter-pressure to his hand and when he glanced to her, his forced smile tight-lipped, she met his gaze for moment and then nuzzled his shoulder with her brow. He planted a kiss in her hair, and suddenly felt – albeit momentarily – a new man capable of facing whatever outrageous slings and arrows of misfortune were thrown at him.

Each great new American city Peter Christopher and his small party had stopped in or passed through filled him with awe; each one, New York, Philadelphia, San Francisco were like kingdoms apart, city states joined together in a Union of literally untold power and potential, each with streets like canyons, with teeming populaces seemingly untouched by the privations of the October War.

He recollected the previous – surreal - occasion he had visited the Philadelphia White House, then as an aide-de-camp to the Prime Minister.

In Xanadu did Kubla Khan, a stately pleasure-dome decree: where Alph, the sacred river, ran, through caverns measureless to man down to a sunless sea...

For all that he regarded himself as the most modern of men – both in his scientific bent and, away from the deck of one of Her Majesty's warships, a man of the most liberal of views; there were times when he conceded that his largely wasted Public School education had, in some ways prepared him better for his new role than anything he had learned at the Britannia Royal Naval College at Dartmouth, or working with Ferranti at the company's research establishment in Crewe Toll in Edinburgh before the war, or in his time onboard HMS Talavera.

Dear old Samuel Taylor Coleridge might not have been thinking about Philadelphia or any of the other mighty city states of the New World, but nothing quite captured the mood of visitors abroad in this great and fascinating land like the words of the old, long dead opium eater.

And 'mid this tumult Kubla heard from far ancestral voices prophesying war! The shadow of the dome of pleasure floated midway on the waves...

In some ways a man like Coleridge would have been more at home, attuned to these times than many 'so-called modern' men; the World had gone mad, and now perhaps the time had come for poets to attempt to explain the unexplainable.

In the towering palaces of the cities on the North American plain one turned every corner half-expecting courtesans, Princes keeping the view from their lofty castle keeps all along the watchtowers, and bare foot servants, too, jokers and thieves, the philosopher kings of the topsy-turvy World in which they all lived these days...

Peter Christopher caught himself in his reverie.

He felt his face heat, hoped his cheeks had not coloured too deeply; he quirked a self-deprecatory grimace to his wife.

Marija was smiling at him as if she *knew* where, briefly, his thoughts had gone to hide from reality. Although they had not actually met, face to face until five months ago – five months and a day, actually - yet she knew him better than he knew himself.

In the front seats, looking backward as the Lincoln rolled imperiously down the empty street in the middle of a cavalcade of Army jeeps and Philadelphia PD cruisers with their blue lights spinning in the night, Chief Petty Officer Jack Griffin – late of Her Majesty's Ship Talavera – never stopped scanning the street, gauging the distance to the escorting vehicles, his right hand ready to twitch towards the Model 1911 Colt forty-five nestling in the shoulder holster under his left arm pit.

Not so long ago a motor cycle assassin wearing a 'stolen' - according to the Philadelphia PD, not the most reliable of authorities on any particular subject - uniform had attacked the car containing his two 'Maltese ladies' as it drove away from a service at *this* city's Roman Catholic cathedral. If he had not taken out the assassin, by the uncomplicated expedient of throwing himself under the wheels of the attacker's Harley, the 'two wives' he had sworn to protect with his life might easily have been killed.

The crew cut Secret Serviceman sitting next to him was probably very good at his job but he did not have *his* 'history' with the people he was guarding; Jack Griffin *did* and that was why he had had not thought twice about throwing himself out of a moving car onto a busy street to dismount a grenade-throwing assassin on a Harley Davidson the last time he was in Philadelphia.

It had been his thirtieth birthday two days ago and the two Maltese wives – the two princesses in his care – had baked him a cake in honour of the occasion. Nobody had ever done that before but then until the last couple of years he had been, to put it charitably, something of a lost cause. Lost to himself, the Navy, and to his irrevocably estranged family whom to a man and a woman had been consumed in the cataclysm, mostly in the hole in the ground that was all that was left of the Kentish town of Chatham and its once great naval base on the River Medway in Kent.

As his eyes quartered his surrounding they made passing contact with Peter Christopher's.

Jack Griffin's Captain – he would never be anything other than his 'Captain', that was just the way things were – was a little more than two years his junior, albeit broken from a different, and superficially more privileged pattern. Peter Christopher was the son of the hero of

Operation Manna, a real honest to God legend in his own lifetime in the Royal Navy. Yet still only aged twenty-seven the son had already outdone the father; the 'fighting admiral' who had died defending his headquarters at Mdina against Soviet paratroopers and Spetsnaz killers the day the son had eclipsed his long shadow.

Jack Griffin had had a small part in that; he and Lady Marija's little brother, Joe, had fired the torpedoes that sank the two biggest battleships in the Soviet fleet bombarding Malta...

"Two minutes," the man beside Jack Griffin growled under his breath.

The American had a boxer's face, a nose which was as broken as Jack Griffin's, but wore no beard to conceal his square, nicked and chipped lantern jaw. The man had had a hard life; that much was for sure. His name was Jake Karlsen, he was thirty-eight and he had come back from the Korean War with a collection of Purple Hearts. He did not talk much about that, or anything else. He was a strong, silent type and had been with 'the English party', as the Californian press called the Consular delegation to the West Coast Federation, ever since it departed from Philadelphia a month ago.

"Two minutes," Jack Griffin echoed, his hand inadvertently moving inside his jacket to check the positioning of his Colt.

In a few weeks, a month or two at most, he would be fully recovered from the scrapes, bone deep bruises, strains and miscellaneous cracked and broken extremities he had incurred 'falling' out of the car carrying the two wives; Lady Marija and her 'sister', Rosa Hannay, the wife of the Captain's deputy, Alan Hannay. Commander Hannay had been the last man standing on the Talavera's aft deckhouse when the ship began to sink. One of the gentlest, most modest men Jack Griffin had ever met in his whole life, Hannay was probably the only man alive who had engaged a First World War-era dreadnought battlecruiser at point blank range with an anti-aircraft cannon!

What with one thing and another Jack was very nearly as devoted to the Hannay's, husband and wife, as he was to the man and woman currently holding hands in the back seat of the bullet-proof Presidential limousine.

Looking back, he still did not begin to understand what had happened when the Talavera's fresh-faced, apparently bookish beanpole new Electronic Warfare Office (EWO) had summoned him to a meeting on the stern of the destroyer one late summer evening nearly two years ago.

Jack had had the ship's EWO down as just another upper-class toff slumming it in the Navy until something better came along. Son of an Admiral! Probably still wet behind the ears!

'Mr Montgommery," the then humble *Lieutenant* Christopher, had begun, invoking the name of the Talavera's Executive officer, had explained, man to man; none of the normal bull as the two men stood looking out across the dockyard basin at the lights of Chatham town as the dusk settled, "tells me that you have it in you to be a first-rate warrant officer, Griffin."

Lieutenant-Commander Hugo Montgommery was one of the better executive officers Jack had served under, well respected if not universally liked by most of the men who served under him. Montgommery had been killed in the Battle of Cape Finisterre, reduced to a fine mist of gore as he lay badly wounded on the aft deckhouse auxiliary steering position by the cannon fire of an *American* A-4 Skyhawk as the ship lay dead in the water, disabled by two bomb hits...

Jack Griffin shrugged off that memory, allowed his mind to walk back to the quietest, most uncompromising 'talking to' he had ever experienced, either in or out of the Navy. Coming from any other man it would have been water off a duck's back but afterwards he had known, known with utter certainty, that if he ever crossed Peter Christopher again that Mr and Mrs Griffin's troublesome son and the Royal Navy were finished with each other. It was not until then that he had realised what he was about to lose.

When the A-4s had swooped in to strafe Talavera that awful day last December he had rugby tackled Peter Christopher to the deck as cannon shells demolished the Talavera's Combat-Information-Centre (CIC), probably saving both their lives. A few days later the destroyer's commanding officer, Captain Penberthy, had sent him ashore in Portugal with Peter Christopher, and basically, he had regarded himself as his, and later the two Maltese wives', guardian angel ever since.

It had been, as their American friends might say, 'one heck of a ride' the last few months.

Jack Griffin had followed Peter Christopher up onto the bridge of the Talavera the night Captain Penberthy was wounded off Lampedusa; and hardly believed his eyes when he – by then the second-in-command of the destroyer - had coolly conned the ship *inshore* of the crippled HMS *Leopard* drawing the fire of and engaging *all* of the enemy shore batteries while the other ship was taken under tow. Hardly surprisingly, his father, the fighting admiral – by then C-in-C in Malta - had left his son in charge of Talavera after that!

They had hardly pumped the old destroyer dry and patched all her holes from the Battle of Lampedusa before Talavera and Scorpion had gone under the stern of the USS Enterprise to fight the raging fires her own crew could not reach while bombed up aircraft blew up on the big ship's deck...

The Captain had not flinched when a burning F-4 Phantom toppled out of the flames and the smoke high above the destroyer's bridge. Jack Griffin had shut his eyes and waited as the wing of the twenty-ton jet had scythed down like a huge cutlass. A random eddy had pushed Talvera's bow to port, the wing tip had scoured a gouge half-way down the hull to the waterline and they had got on with fighting the fires...

Belatedly, the hard-bitten warrant officer realised Lady Marija's gaze had fixed upon him. The 'Christopher Party' had departed

Philadelphia last month before he was released from hospital and he had only caught up with it at Huntsville, where it had 'stopped over' for ten days as guests of the National Aeronautics and Space Administration (NASA) while plans were finalised for its arrival and ongoing security in California. The 'wives' had thrown a barbecue in *his* honour and greeted him with huge hugs and kisses as if he was a prodigal returned!

Somewhere along the line the people sitting in the back seat of the Lincoln, and the Hannays, had become more than just his superior officers and their wives, they had become *friends*, and...*family*.

Off Cape Finisterre, off Lampedusa, on that day when Talavera nosed under the burning stern of the USS Enterprise, and later when the old destroyer took on the entire Russian Navy off Malta, he and Peter Christopher and Alan Hannay could easily have died. But they had survived and whenever he was anywhere near the Captain or Lady Marija, or the Hannays – whatever else was going catastrophically wrong in the World – he knew, he just knew, that everything was going to turn out okay. It was irrational, stupid really but that was how he felt whenever he was around *these* people.

"This time, Jack," Marija said, mischief twinkling in her almond eyes. "There's no need to jump out of the car before it comes to a stop, Jack."

Jack Griffin tried to be stern.

He snorted an involuntary guffaw.

Peter Christopher winked at him, smiled wryly. The World was going to hell in a hand basket and he had not the slightest inkling why exactly the man in the White House – had President Kennedy miraculously risen from his sick bed or was it Lyndon Johnson at the helm? – had demanded *his* presence. *He* was the most junior post captain on the Navy List, *he* was no diplomat; *he* and his friends had been sent to America to do a flimflam job, to court TV, radio and newspaper men, to have their photographs taken and to say nice things about all things American. For all *he* knew World War IV had broken out and had already been fought and won by the same aircraft and missiles that had won the US the October War in a single night.

Twelve hours ago, he and the others had been settling into the hillside chalets allocated to his party above Sausalito across the bay from San Francisco. Two days of exploratory talks with Governor Brown's people had been, well, at best 'inconclusive' and at worst, 'pointless'. The Governor did not know why the 'Christopher Party' had come West, or what to do with his guests now they had arrived in his 'back yard'.

The White House's request that *he* return to Philadelphia had been couched in terms which implied that it was made 'in consultation' with Lord Franks, the Ambassador. Things were obviously a little chaotic in Philadelphia and cables from the Embassy confirming 'this business' would no doubt, catch up with him eventually. So, Peter had called his small staff together, broken the news that his presence was required 'back in Pennsylvania' and Marija had begun to pack overnight bags.

'I am coming, too,' she had declared.

He would have argued but what would that have achieved?

Yes, his wife was the best part of four months pregnant; she was a nervous flier, understandably so after her first fraught flight from Malta to England in April, and a long continental flight would be trying for her, but...it had taken him half a lifetime to meet her face to face, to hold her in his arms, and really and truly, it would have broken his heart to leave her behind in California on a day when the World was apparently, once again, going stark, raving mad.

Jake Karlsen, the Secret Serviceman raised an eyebrow.

Griffin was way too close to *these* people.

He liked to think that he would have done what the bearded warrant officer had done that day outside the cathedral; did not know if he would have, you never did until it actually happened. But being *close* to people complicated things; it might slow you down at a critical moment, distract you when you ought to be looking twice at something that did not quite seem right at the edge of your peripheral vision.

He seriously doubted he would ever understand the Brits. He had been told that they were obsessed by class and went around like they had rods up their arses. However, his five weeks with the 'Christopher Party' had unsettled most and over-turned many of his preconceptions; and he was nowhere near reconciled with that yet. Something rebelled against the notion that *these* people were just – what they seemed to be - regular guys and gals. The man sitting across from him was a gold-plated hero, and an aristocrat to boot!

And Lady Marija...

Jeez, you could put her at a table between Elizabeth Taylor and Debbie Reynolds and she would have the two of them shaking hands and making nice over Eddie Fisher! Heck, Liz and Debbie would be so pissed off the photographers only wanted to take pictures of the little Maltese princess that they would probably end up in a no holds barred cat fight!

Shit!

Now who's getting distracted!

Peter Christopher sighed, patted his wife's hand and grinned ruefully at Jack Griffin.

The car was slowing and the escorting Philadelphia PD cruisers were peeling off to form a crawling, impenetrable wall of steel around the Presidential Lincoln.

"Just between the four of us," the fair-haired, boyish man whose face had adorned the front pages of the World's newspapers, magazines, TV and Pathé news reel films ever since the Battle of Malta confessed ruefully, "I think I was a lot less nervous conning Talavera down the muzzles of the Yavuz's eleven-inch naval rifles than I am now!"

Chapter 15

The complex was buried deep beneath the bedrock of the eastern foothills of the Ural Mountains.

The increasing yield of thermonuclear devices and ever more disturbing intelligence from sources in the West about the pinpoint accuracy of the latest American inter-continental ballistic missiles, had raised warning flags about the 'invulnerability' of the underground facilities outside Chelyabinsk long before the Cuban Missiles War, or more recently the RAF had wrought such havoc with old-fashioned, but very big, conventional iron bombs. The Politburo's response had been to authorise the construction of half-a-dozen new, genuinely 'bomb proof' facilities in the spring of 1960.

None of the six sites had actually been operational in October 1962 – although one, outside Moscow had been handed over to a Red Army engineering brigade to install an air filtration system ahead of its planned commissioning in January 1963 – and subsequently, the shortage of labour and resources of every imaginable kind, had made it impracticable to resume work on the undamaged, forty percent completed complex in the Soviet Far East on Sakhalin Island near Krasnogorsk, or the less well progressed site at Tomsk in Siberia. The Moscow bunker, as had those partially built at Kiev in the Ukraine, and the complex ten kilometres from the naval base at Murmansk in the Russian far north-west, were located in areas so badly damaged as to be considered 'dead zones' and had been left to rot.

The late Marshal of the Soviet Union Vasily Chuikov had had the job of sending survey teams into those 'dead zones' on his list of 'things to do'; but never got around to it. Operation Nakazyvat – the invasion of Iraq via northern Iran - had sucked up every available spare man, tank, bullet, gallon of fuel, tactical and transport aircraft, ship and surviving engineer in the whole USSR!

Or at least that was what the backsliders and revisionists in the Politburo were probably muttering behind their hands, fifty-seven-year-old Leonid Ilyich Brezhnev assumed as he paused for a moment after the armoured door of the BMK-80 armoured personnel carrier which had transported him from the airfield, five kilometres distant to the entrance of the Project Sevastopol Complex, clanked noisily and swung open.

Forty-year-old Colonel Viktor Vasilyevich Konayev stepped forward and saluted crisply. Konayev had been a project engineer in the Engineering Brigade of the Red Army before the Cuban Missiles War. He had spent most of his career building bunkers, frontier and port fortifications...and bomb proof dachas for the more than usually paranoid members of the Politburo. It was this latter work which had first brought him to the attention of Alexander Shelepin, earned him an – at first – honorific rank of Major of the Construction Corps in the KGB, and after several years, two further promotions. The war of October 1962, had seen him appointed Chief Engineer of Project Sevastopol.

Konayev's combined Red Army and KGB hour guard snapped upright, rifles and Ak-47s clicking metallically to the 'present'. The Red Army troopers and his green-uniformed KGB men – strictly speaking border control troopers rather than soldiers – stood in two ranks, each viewing the other like the members of two mutually antagonistic alien species. The sour-faced General Secretary of the Central Committee of the Communist Party of the Soviet Union walked past Konayev's salute without bothering to glance sidelong.

Not that anybody had ever accused Leonid Brezhnev of flaunting the 'common touch'. Like many of the old Bolsheviks who had led the Motherland into the unmitigated disaster of the Cuban Missiles War Brezhnev had the arrogance and the manners of a Tsar. However, he was no Stalin, no 'man of steel', he lacked the imagination or the powerbase within the Party, and while people were sometimes afraid of him, he was hardly a man born to spontaneously inspire bladder or bowel evacuating terror in those around him.

In the end *Project Sevastopol* had been the obvious candidate for prioritisation. Not least because it was the complex most likely to remain out of sight, hidden from the Soviet Union's enemies longest and when finished, to be the hardest nut to crack.

The nearest town, Krasnoufimsk lay on the Ufa, a tributary of the Kama River approximately two hundred kilometres west of Sverdlovsk, and nearly two hundred kilometres south-south-east of Perm, the two closest major centres of population. Founded in 1736 as 'Krasnoufimskaya', a fortress built as a buttress against raiding tribes in a still wilderness region of the Russian Empire, it had not been recognised as a town in its own right until 1781. At that time and for around a century-and-a-half thereafter the Cossacks had been its primary ethnic grouping, a thing Stalin's purges had ended between the First and Second World Wars. The town had been so isolated that the railways had not come to it until late 1916.

Before 1941 Krasnoufimsk had been a farming town, with little industry other than that sufficient to maintain and produce, in small numbers, tractors and a small number of essential agricultural manufactures.

After 1941 whole factories, research and training bureaus from western Russian had been moved into the forests around Krasnoufimsk; among others the prestigious Kharkov Institute of Mechanics and Machine-Building, and the All-Union Institute of Plant Cultivation had arrived in the foothills of the Urals. Many of the transplanted institutions and factories had moved away after the Great Patriotic War, but their footprint on the land remained and the upgraded war-time rail and road links to the town had, during the 1950s, threatened to transform the still remote settlement into a relatively comfortable, prosperous enclave in the wilderness.

Nevertheless, it remained the sort of place that was unlikely to attract the attention of the motherland's enemies. The town had no obvious military connections or significance and it was literally kilometres – hundreds of them – from anywhere strategically significant. It probably did not even appear on the maps of US and RAF navigators!

It was the perfect place to construct a command centre from which to wage, or to sit out, a nuclear war.

Viktor Konayev held his salute, contemptuously eyeing the perfunctory rituals lavished upon the arrival of the new Tsar of the post-war Politburo. With Kosygin and Chuikov gone, murdered by the British, his own chief, Alexander Shelepin had become number two man in *Brezhnev's* Politburo, and probably to his surprise, Admiral Gorshkov had found himself the third most important man in the USSR. But that was just a quirk of Party politics; the consequence of the Red Army having no obvious 'consensus' candidate ready to step into Vasily Chuikov's boots. The soldiers had had to back Gorshkov or face having to live with a third 'civilian' apparatchik on the ruling Troika.

Stepping into the afternoon sunshine of what had been a balmy sunny day that belied the mounting crises wracking the globe, the General Secretary of the Central Committee of the Communist Party of the Soviet Union, had been confronted by a man who had entertained hopes of being promoted into the Politburo, or even appointed to the ruling Troika as Minister of Defence when Vasily Chuikov had been killed in the British raid on the Kursk Bunker at Chelyabinsk.

Not that sixty-four-year-old Chief Marshal of Aviation Konstantin Andreevich Vershinin's expression betrayed his disappointment as he had marched forward, and stiffly come to attention and saluted Brezhnev. The grizzled old veteran of the Revolution, the Civil War, and the fight against the Nazis had lived too long in the dangerous, rarefied upper echelons of the Soviet state to allow his feelings – any feelings at all, in fact – to percolate to the surface where they might advertise the true workings of his mind outside of his own, close-knit loyal inner circle.

Brezhnev acknowledged the older man's salute with a curt nod before the two men shook hands and exchanged the obligatory kisses of welcome, a charade all old-timers performed for whoever was watching just to perpetuate the myth that the leadership remained united. It was of course, anything but united and both men knew as much.

"Rudimentary communications have been restored with Baghdad and Basra, Comrade Chairman," Vershinin reported gruffly. For all that he lacked Vasily Chuikov's cherubically gnarled threatening solidity, he was a man hewn from the same Russian mettle. "We have *secure* land line and radio voice links back to Sverdlovsk. The Air Defence Centre in the capital will be fully operation within the next twelve hours. If there is a 'problem' we can take over sooner."

Brezhnev already knew this.

Following the abject failure of the Red Air Force to defend the motherland in October 1962, practically everybody had expected Vershanin, its commander since January 1957, to fall on his sword or to be ritually purged. Left to his own devices Brezhnev would probably have let the re-constituted post-war Politburo have its way and by now, Vershanin would have died anonymously in some distant Siberian labour camp. However, Brezhnev's now dead companions in the original leadership Troika, Alexei Kosygin and Vasily Chuikov, although recognising the need to make 'a few' – well, in the end several thousand, exemplary examples – had both lobbied for Vershanin to be kept in post, and it had proven to be a sound decision.

Old Bolsheviks like Vershanin tended to be non-political, less inclined to join the camps of ambitious younger men competing to fill the vacant ranks within a Party hierarchy decimated in the war, and by illness since. Older men from the Great Patriotic War generation who had lived under Stalin's regime also tended to be more 'reliable', and as a group they tended to spend a lot more of their time actually attending to their duties than fomenting plots and coups.

Brezhnev and the Commander of the Red Air Force walked heavy-footed towards the open blast doors at the entrance to the five-metre-high semi-circular tunnel that drove hundreds of metres into the wooded hillside above them. From the air the surrounding terrain would look like impenetrable forest right up to the foothills of the Ural Mountains.

"Comrade Alexander Nikolayevich's aircraft was delayed by technical difficulties," the Red Air Force man reported as they trudged out of the daylight into the glaring illumination of the buried complex.

Brezhnev snorted. "He's probably still trying to shake off those idiots from Pyongyang!" He growled, having wearied of the ever more strident entreaties of 'Supreme Leader' Kim Il-Sung's entreaties. The bloody man had almost started a nuclear war back in the early 1950s! Now he wanted the Soviet Union's backing to do it again!

Brezhnev did not envy Alexander Shelepin's job of keeping the representatives of the Democratic People's Republic of Korea – the DPRK – at arm's length. The trouble with people like Kim Il-sung and his ultra-obedient apparatchiks was that if he, or they, got so much as a sniff of encouragement from anybody in Sverdlovsk, they might easily take it as their cue to send their always ready tanks into the DMZ and open up yet another front in the war with the West.

Leonid Brezhnev had no intention of going to war with the USA over a Far Eastern peninsula singular only for a million shitty paddy fields!

Besides, South Korea was a mess; the North had come out of the October War sitting pretty. Undamaged in the war, with its giant northern neighbour, China, still paralysed by the destruction of most of its industry and torn by post-Maoist factionalism and countless local civil wars, the regime in Pyongyang presided over a growing economy looking across the DMZ at a corrupt, failing state.

If Kim Il-sung waited long enough the South would collapse

anyway; but for now, it remained – in American eyes, at least – a vital strategic bulwark in the defence of the Japanese Archipelago and South East Asia. Axiomatically, if Kim Il-sung invaded the South the US would be forced to retaliate.

Shelepin was just the man to put the delegation from Pyongyang straight on the realities of global realpolitik. If the idiots made a fuss he would probably disappear the lot of them! Good riddance, to Brezhnev's way of thinking!

Brezhnev felt the cool air from the ventilation fans on his face, smelled the unmistakable tang of new equipment, wiring and the merest suggestion of generator fumes. The worst teething troubles with any new underground facility were always those associated with the air filtration and circulation plants.

The air stank of stale tobacco smoke, even this near to the surface. The party began to pass rooms filled with men and women in uniform too busy to notice the commotion outside their own claustrophobic, murderously high-pressured little bubbles of frenetic activity. Two month's commissioning work was being accomplished in hours; everybody knew the Americans or even the British might strike at the motherland without warning.

Brezhnev was as wary of Alexander Nikolayevich Shelepin as any man. A lot of his old friend Vasily Chuikov's surviving people were as preoccupied with the revenge the Head of the KGB and his clique would take on them, as Brezhnev was. Shelepin had begun plotting against him the day after the smoke and dust of the Cuban Missiles War began to settle; and he was under no illusion that his scheming would have gone into overdrive with his recent elevation to the Troika.

All this Konstantin Vershanin took for granted; as he took it for granted that an old Bolshevik like Leonid Ilyich Brezhnev was doing everything he could to stay one step ahead of the malevolent young pretender foisted upon him by a panicked Politburo.

People allowed themselves to be distracted by Brezhnev's leaden footed, clumsy gait and social awkwardness, foolishly misinterpreting his long silences in meetings for slowness of mind and thought.

In the Soviet Union a leader needed to cultivate a persona every bit as much as any Western so-called democrat. To many people Brezhnev personified the dignified Russian bear; a dumb, brutish man who relied upon others, like the late Alexei Kosygin to pull his strings. However, those who knew Brezhnev quickly discovered that beneath the stolid carapace was a brain the equal of any of his Politburo contemporaries allied to an iron will.

"Yes," the General Secretary of the Communist Party of the Soviet Union grunted. "There are matters that you and I and Admiral Gorshkov need to discuss before Comrade Alexander Nikolayevich arrives."

Vershanin said nothing for several seconds. Gorshkov, like Vershanin a long-time Deputy Defence Minister and the Commander-in-Chief of the Red Navy, had leap-frogged him into the Troika as Vasily Chuikov's replacement and immediately found himself catapulted into the – apparently disastrous, although it was almost impossible to know exactly what had happened in southern Iraq, Iran and the Persian Gulf in the last few days - final denouement of Operation Nakazyvat. Vershanin and Gorshkov had been opposed to the whole 'Mesopotamian' adventure but Vasily Chuikov and Hamazasp Babadzhanian's Red Army 'faction' had ridden roughshod over the objections of the 'junior' services.

Operation Nakazyvat was madness, it had always been madness. Seizing the oilfields of Kurdish Iraq made a kind of sense, likewise giving the Anglo-US surrogates in Tehran a bloody nose before they started developing their own territorial ambitions in the Caucasus. That part of Operation Nakazyvat had chimed with everybody; but as for grabbing a warm water port in the Persian Gulf and attempting to gobble up the British fortress at Abadan before first securing the Iranian flank of the two – the *only* two operational tank armies likely to be at the disposal of the motherland for the foreseeable future – well, that smacked of a compulsive gambler's last throw of the dice...

"Gorshkov is still in Iraq," Vershinin informed Brezhnev. He was tempted to add 'clearing up the shit *you* created' but instead he went on respectfully: "I was warned that several other Politburo members would be arriving here later today?"

"Yes. The whole crew, I should imagine," Brezhnev snorted. The War Plan required at least two of the three members of the Troika to be together to make 'global decisions' regarding the prosecution of hostilities and, or the management of 'All-Union' civil defence protocols. Other Politburo members had specific Party, political and military responsibilities which required them to be as close as possible to other national or regional centres of command and control. However, right now most of the Politburo's august members – with one or two notable exceptions – were much more preoccupied with finding the safest possible holes in the ground for themselves, their families and their retainers.

In a day or two the Sevastopol bunker complex would be full of wailing children, mistresses and conniving middle-ranking Party apparatchiks wasting space and eating their way through the food stores that were supposed to last – the people who actually needed to be in the bunker – up to a year.

"But I think we can rely on Comrade Alexander Nikolayevich's people to evict inessential personnel from the facility," Brezhnev growled.

Vershinin chuckled, in that moment reminded his dead friend, Vasily Chuikov.

Brezhnev grinned, shook his head.

It was a good thing Alexei Kosygin had stopped him purging the Air Force man; in these troubled times the dwindling number of old Bolsheviks, like him and Vershinin, had never needed to stand together more resolutely.

Chapter 16

08:15 Hours (Local) – 01:15 in Philadelphia
HMS Eagle, 32 nautical miles NNW of Port Said

The Captain of HMS Eagle eyed the latest message 'flimsy' he had been handed with a ghost of smile on his lips.

"And so, the game is afoot!" He said to himself, very privately. Beneath his feet the fifty-thousand-ton carrier was thundering through a three to four feet cross swell, her deck thrumming softly as she shouldered through the water at over twenty-eight knots. The engine room had promised him another knot, perhaps two; but for the while the leviathan would hold this speed. Eagle was a ship laid down twenty-two years ago with machinery already older that some of the sailors manning her; a smidgeon of caution was not unreasonable this early in the race to the west.

Eagle, Scorpion and Oudenarde had operated a radio blackout since clearing Port Said over an hour ago and would continue in that mode until they got to Malta or, as was more likely, the *enemy* made contact.

Frank Maltravers passed the flimsy to the Officer of the Watch, Lieutenant-Commander Johnny Fairbrace.

"Flash this to our little friends, if you please."

This was like the good old days; radio silence in case the Germans or the Italians or the Japanese were listening in, the constant clacking and flashing of Aldis signal lamps between ships and new flags continually chasing up and down halyards.

Fleet Headquarters in Malta had signalled that at least one of the US Navy's three-boat Mediterranean SSN squadron was believed to be moving to 'cover the approaches to the eastern harbours of the archipelago'.

Fair enough, if he was the skipper of one of the American nuclear-powered hunter killers he too would have ignored the 'surface and surrender' demand. If he was in charge of the US Navy he would have ordered all three back to Malta, and probably, declared a blockade.

Or to just start shooting...

If he had been the captain of the USS Independence and somebody had come onboard and suggested he surrender his command; he would have had the blighter escorted straight off the ship. Had the 'request' arrived when he was feeling a tad liverish he would probably have had the bearer of the missive thrown overboard!

As for meekly surrendering one's whole fleet; well, that beggared belief unless the Yanks had been caught completely unawares. This latter he found somewhat implausible, it spoke of good men being asleep at the wheel and having met Vice Admiral Bernard Clarey, the Commander of Sixth Fleet he was inclined to reject the 'sleeping at the wheel' or 'caught with one's pants down' explanation for the US Navy's 'surrender' at Malta.

Actually, it was all very odd.

The news from Malta ought to have galvanised the Kitty Hawk Battle Group in the Persian Gulf. For that matter Carrier Division Seven ought to have been capable – more than capable - of fighting off a much heavier and more sustained aerial assault than that which had – at a stroke – destroyed the US Navy's peace dividend-stunted capacity to 'project power' in the Indian and the Western Pacific Oceans. It was as if the Americans had lost their belief in themselves; nothing else began to explain how two massively superior – numerically and technologically – US fleets had been either defeated in battle or imprisoned in the last two days.

Wars are won and lost in the minds of men...

What was it Andrew Cunningham, C-in-C Mediterranean Fleet had said during the evacuation of Crete in 1941? At that time the Luftwaffe had complete command of the air, and politicians and army generals were telling him that the twenty thousand British and Dominion troops left on the island would have to be abandoned. The cost in ships of mounting an evacuation *they said* would be far too high; it simply was not worth the candle.

Cunningham had taken this suggestion as a heinous calumny on the proud escutcheon of the Royal Navy. At Aboukir Bay Nelson had taken his ships *inshore* of the moored French Fleet and scuppered Napoleon's ambitions in Egypt, at Trafalgar he had split his line to get to grips with a more numerous and more heavily-gunned Franco-Spanish fleet, the Nelsonian tradition was alive and well and as a famous American had declared at the height of the Civil War: 'Dam the torpedoes!'

Knowing that his ships would be severely handled, and many sunk evacuating the Army from Crete Cunningham had said '*the Navy must not let the Army down*'. And that was that, the dictum was unambiguous, the statement of a truth universally known to the men who had fought in that war, and this latter, altogether crueller conflict.

'*It takes the Navy three years to build a ship. It will take three hundred years to build a tradition. The evacuation will continue...*'

Back in 1941 the Royal Navy lost three cruisers and six destroyers in rescuing over sixteen thousand men from Crete. Many of the ships involved in the evacuation had shot themselves 'dry' fending off wave upon wave of air attacks.

Frank Maltravers recollected a friend – who had been serving on a destroyer at the time - telling him that his captain had ordered the small Royal Marine detachment onboard his ship to throw open the arms locker, and to issue small arms to 'men who didn't have anything better to do' so that they could go up on deck and blaze away at the Stukas and Junkers 88s dive-bombing his otherwise defenceless vessel with Lee Enfield rifles and Webley service revolvers.

Now there was a tradition to die for...

"I have the latest on that weather that's coming up from the south, sir."

Another 'flimsy' was pressed into Frank Maltravers's hands.

There was a nasty, squally summer storm developing between the squadron and its destination, things would get rough for the two escorting destroyers in the next few hours. Mediterranean storms, particularly in the summer months although relatively rare, could be vicious affairs. Often lasting only a day or two they swept out of the wastes of Cyrenaica like great dust devils. Over the sea they became huge squalls, twenty or thirty-mile-wide electrical storms with lashing rain and briefly, steep and unpredictable waves that could buffet even a leviathan the size of the Eagle.

Especially, if she was in a hurry!

The carrier's Captain might have worried more about the notion of a potentially hostile – very hostile, likely vengeful – US Navy nuclear submarine steaming to intercept him if there had been anything he could have done about it. Hopefully, Fleet HQ was going to send out a couple of the old Amphions - 'A' class diesel-electric submarines - to drive the American interloper deep, or despatch aircraft from Luqa to drop sonar buoys in the waters around the Maltese Archipelago.

His job was to get *his* air group within range of Malta to support the garrison. If he could do that then Eagle, for all her deficiencies remained the biggest beast in this sea and she packed a formidable punch. The Admiralty might have scaled back the original 1959 plan to 'stretch' her hull and to install brand new modern geared steam turbines – creating an only slightly smaller version of the big US super-carriers – but Eagle had nevertheless, emerged from dockyard hands with a panoply of improvements.

Her 'island' bridge superstructure had been completely reconstructed, and a modern 3D Type 984 radar installed to serve a command and control system capable of tracking up to a hundred separate targets. She had a new one hundred and fifty feet long bow catapult, and two hundred feet long one in her waist enabling simultaneous launches off both the bow and the angled amidships flight decks. She had the latest mirror deck landing system, a ship-wide electrical set up which was 'as good as new' with nearly twice its pre-refit output, and powerful standby generators in the event of battle damage. Already as heavily armoured as any carrier in the world – with four-inch belt armour at the waterline and over her machinery spaces, and one to two inches more on the walls and floor of her great hangar deck, her flight deck, built as a rigid 'strength deck' was effectively a two-and-a-half-inch slab of cemented plate.

The 'Big E' was a tough 'old beast'!

And now that her air group was as 'worked up' as it was ever going to be, Eagle was a tough old beast with deadly fangs.

The 'Air Readiness Board' currently showed eight out of her ten De Havilland Sea Vixen interceptors 'READY'; all three of her Supermarine Scimitar fighters 'READY'; four of her five Westland Wyvern turboprop attack aircraft 'READY'; six of her eight rugged modern Blackburn Buccaneer jet bombers 'READY'; her three Fairey Gannets – operable in airborne early warning, anti-submarine, or torpedo bomber roles 'READY', and two of her three Westland Wessex helicopters 'READY'.

Maltravers walked out onto the port side flying bridge to observe the ongoing activity on the Eagle's vast flight deck. A Wessex was parked clear of the bow catapult, two Scimitar fighters were on deck on QRA – Quick Reaction Alert – and aft of the bridge Sea Vixens and Buccaneers lined the starboard side of the ship. Two thirds of the carrier's aircraft were down below in the cavernous armoured hangar. Unlike her bigger American 'cousins' – like the Independence or the sunken Kitty Hawk – Eagle only had two elevators, both on the centre-line of the ship, a design layout that harked back to her World War Two genesis, and this limited her capability to 'load' the flight deck with the substantial part of her air group and to safely conduct flying operations at the same time.

The Navigation Officer joined him.

He nodded to the north-west where HMS Oudenarde was forging ahead of Eagle and her close escort, the Scorpion.

"Oudenarde is painting a single high-altitude target at fifty thousand feet, circling forty-six miles out, sir."

"Ha," his Captain snorted.

The 'target' was most likely a US Air Force, or CIA – it mattered not one jot which – Martin B-57 or Lockheed U-2 spy plane. Probably, it was the same one which had periodically stalked Eagle and her consorts all the way to Limassol, Haifa and Port Said in the last week.

He was tempted to launch one or both of the QRA Scimitars. This despite knowing that none of his aircraft had the fleetness of foot or the operational ceiling to get within missile, let alone gun or eyeballing range of the spy in the sky.

Frank Maltravers might have asked himself where exactly the American aircraft had come from but then a man did not have to be any kind of military genius to work that out. After paying a short, somewhat frosty 'goodwill' visit to Haifa he had detached Scorpion and Oudenarde to 'scout' and to skirt the twelve-mile international limit 'as close as possible' all the way down the coast of Israel, Gaza and the Sinai coast. The two destroyers' radars and listening equipment had probed deep into the deserts while Eagle's Gannets had cruised – with Egyptian permission – south over Sinai all along the Israeli border down to the Red Sea, listening, gathering ELINT, priceless electronic intelligence.

The spy in the sky, and presumably other US Air Force airborne war-fighting, support and intelligence assets were based in the deserts of southern Israel, far from prying eyes. Those kind of 'assets' could not easily be transplanted overnight, therefore they had to have been 'in place' for weeks, or months watching and not inconceivably, meddling in the events of the region while in the United States, President Kennedy, and or, his associates had pretended to be a fourth blind monkey.

Before the October War Frank Maltravers would have felt, to say the least, a little queasy about entertaining Egyptian military and electronic intelligence officers onboard his ships at Port Said. However, strange times made for strange bedfellows and for better or worse, his country and that of Colonel Nasser, were allies in this topsy-turvy post-cataclysm world.

Discussions with the Egyptians had turned to mounting a low-level penetration of Israeli air space over the Negev Desert to investigate 'interesting hotspots' south of the settlement of Dimona. It was the sort of thing Frank Maltravers's Buccaneer jockeys were itching to have a go at; but unfortunately, it was also the sort of thing which needed explicit prior authorisation from Oxford. He had no idea if an official proposal had been forwarded back to England before the First Battle of the Persian Gulf. Afterwards the Chiefs of Staff would have been far too busy organising the 'Second' Battle to worry about a piffling little 'ELINT jaunt' over Sinai. Now it was academic, Eagle had pressing business elsewhere in the Mediterranean…

"Launch the QRA fighters to chase that bastard away," Frank Maltravers ordered abruptly.

He realised he had been brooding.

That would never do!

Knowing there was not a proverbial snowflake's chance in Hades of the two sub-sonic Scimitars getting within twenty or thirty miles of the interloper before it turned away, made the decision easy. It turned a do or die gesture into a useful training exercise for the two pilots involved and the carrier's still, inevitably, rusty deck crew.

He grinned piratically, rather missing his old beard to stroke; a thing he had tended to do in moments of stress in past years.

"We can't have these bastards thinking they can push us around!" He declaimed cheerfully. "That would never do!"

Chapter 17

09:15 Hours (Local) – 01:15 Hours in Philadelphia
Abadan Island, Iran

Major Julian Calder of the 22nd Special Air Services Regiment of the British Army stood on the south bank of the Karun River studying a scene of – very nearly – unimaginable carnage.

Out on the muddy brown Shatt-al-Arab smoke still rose from the grounded, burned out wrecks of the cruiser HMS Tiger, and the Australian destroyer Anzac.

To the south roiling black pillars of smoke rising out of burning oil tanks mercifully veiled the cratered battlefield which until a few weeks ago had been the biggest oil refinery complex on the planet. Here and there the muzzles of the long rifles of the handful of surviving British and Australian Centurions flashed defiance in the smoky gloom. Hundreds, thousands, God only knew how many men had died in the battles south of the Karun River and on those wrecked ships out in the mainstream below the sandy islands of the Om-al-Rasas; but the execution south of the Karun and out in the Shatt-al-Arab south of Basra had been as nothing compared with ongoing killing match still in progress on the northern bank, and in, around and across the deserts north of the devastated town of Khorramshahr.

The Tiger and the Anzac had broken the Red Army's advance, emerging out of the fog of war to pour an avalanche of naval gunfire into the packed armour waiting to cross to the south. Eventually, the weight of Soviet firepower – mainly the 115-millimetre rifles - of the surviving T-62 main battle tanks had subdued the two warships but not before Tiger's six-inch guns hurling fifteen to twenty rounds per barrel per minute, and Anzac's four point five-inch twin turrets shooting almost as fast had destroyed the fighting power of the last available tank corps of the 2nd Siberian Mechanised Army. In a battle fought at ranges of less than half-a-mile with the big guns of both sides shooting over open sights the slow moving or stationery, closely packed Soviet tanks and armoured personnel carriers had been helpless. In the end the survivors had turned and run, in a rout, leaving the much smaller armoured spearhead which had already crossed onto the southern bank of the Karun unsupported as it rumbled into Lieutenant General Michael Carver's carefully prepared killing grounds north of long abandoned RAF Abadan.

The Soviets had since put infantrymen and Spetsnaz troopers across the Karun, and no doubt, they had done their share of killing in the last few hours but the battle had been over the moment the Tiger and the Anzac steamed slowly out of the drifting dust and smoke.

The cannonade north of Khorramshahr rose and fell, its epicentre moving slowly towards the Shatt-al-Arab in the north-west opposite Basra. The Red Army units desperately attempting to escape the Hell of the north bank of the Karun River and the constant shelling of Khorramshahr had suddenly discovered fresh, dug in, unengaged Iranian and British armour on its right flank.

The slaughter had proceeded apace.

Farther north the Centurions, M-48s and M-60s of the 2nd Brigade of Major General Hasan al-Mamaleki's 3rd Imperial Iranian Armoured Division had crashed into the infantry and logistics traffic jam idling along in the wake of the massed Soviet armoured attack. Needless to say, the Iranian armour had sliced through the Red Army's unsuspecting rear echelon like a hot knife through butter just south of the Iraq-Iran border and placed itself squarely across 2nd Mechanised Army's former line of advance; and of course, blocked its line of retreat.

Now it seemed that the 1st Brigade, with all of al-Mamaleki's up-gunned Mark II Centurions and three squadrons of M-60 Patton main battle tanks was driving what was left of the Soviet armour back onto the Shatt-al-Arab while 2nd Brigade's artillery pinned the enemy in the north.

Calder looked around him.

If he had had something to eat in the last few hours he would have been sick. The stench alone was enough to make a strong man blanch. When guns the size of those on the ships in the river and in the turrets of the scores of knocked out tanks in the sand around him and across the Karun River exchanged fire at any range, let alone virtually at arm's length the consequences for mere flesh and bone were uniformly predictable and...*catastrophic.* T-62s still burned fiercely in the near distance, their crews strewn around them like lumps of charcoal, or frozen in their contorted death agonies

Iranian infantrymen had moved through the wreckage shooting into the back of smashed vehicles, putting bullets in the heads of broken, barely living men spread-eagled or lying in the sand between the burning tanks and shattered big-wheeled BTR-60 and 80 armoured personnel carriers.

Calder had tried to stop the murder.

Given up...

There was nobody to administer medical care to the wounded; and in many ways a bullet in the head was a kindness. And besides, the Russians had come to this land to steal its riches and to lord it over its people. Tehran had been destroyed by a nuclear weapon on the first day of the invasion. One way or another Hasan al-Mamaleki's men had every right to exact their revenge. This was their country; they made up the rules.

He heard the jeep grind to a halt nearby.

Half-turned as a ragged figure staggered to his feet from behind the wheel and waved.

"Bloody Hell!" The newcomer observed, trudging through the sand to stand by Calder's left shoulder. "It's a bit of a mess, what!"

"I wondered what had happened to you, Frank," Calder grimaced, glancing to the man who had been his mentor – and briefly, something of a hero to him – when he had first joined 'the Regiment' the best part of a decade ago.

Colonel Francis St John Waters, VC, was one of the founding fathers of 22nd SAS Regiment, one of David Stirling's 'originals'; the five officers and sixty other ranks of 'L' Detachment, Special Air Service Brigade formed in July 1941 to deceive the Axis powers into thinking there was a 'special' paratrooper unit operating in North Africa, which had set about 'proving' its existence by mounting a series of dramatic – reckless, near suicidal – commando raid at 'long-range' behind the lines of the Afrika Korps in the Western Deserts of Libya. The men of what became known – incorrectly - at the time as the 'Long-Range Desert Group' were legends within the Regiment and no man more than Frank Waters. Even if he had not gone on to become a regimental 'star' in Borneo, among other places, he was a one off. He was also a cad, a serial philanderer and very, very dangerous to be around. That was not to say he was not also charming, brave as a lion, patriotic to the point of obsession; characteristics which in recent years had endeared him so much to the top brass that no matter how many of his people got killed, his career had prospered right up to the day – or rather the evening – he had seduced the wrong senior officer's wife and worse, the news had got abroad!

Frank Waters had found himself exiled a couple of years before the October War, footloose in postings to embassies in parts of the World that ought to have communicated to him that his career was over. Not Frank Waters, he had stuck it out and eventually found himself despatched to Iran on a 'training and liaison' mission; where, in April he had had an opportunity to have 'an inordinate amount of fun tweaking the Russian bear's tail!'

Now the man was an even bigger hero!

Of course, the Army always won in the end; that was why its newest, or rather, most recently 'rediscovered hero' had been retired and shortly thereafter, transferred into the pastoral care of the British Broadcasting Corporation.

Not that you could possibly keep a man like Frank Waters down for long. Before anybody knew it, he had wangled a job 'reporting' on the war in the Middle East and just like a bad penny, turned up at Abadan. If he had not – wisely by his standards - gone straight to the C-in-C's wagon and successfully made his peace with Michael Carver he would probably have been on the first aircraft back home.

"What have you done with your BBC friends?" Julian Carver inquired wearily.

"I left one chap with a bit of savvy at HQ. He knows which end of a gun the bullet comes out of and there are still a lot of Russians creeping around in the dunes down there. I detailed the other chaps off as stretcher bearers. Pleasant enough fellows but they were cramping a fellow's style, what!"

Calder viewed the older man thoughtfully.

He had a bloody bandana around his head, his battledress smock was ripped and spotted with – presumably, somebody else's gore – and his left hand was encased in a dirty makeshift dressing which went most of the way up his arm.

Julian Calder raised an eyebrow.

Frank Waters chuckled. "I got buried by a near miss and then some bloody sniper clipped me just above the wrist. I got the medicos to stitch me up. Be good as new in a day or two."

An increasingly toothy grin began to dominate Frank Waters's grubby, unshaven face as he surveyed the utter devastation littering the whole of the north bank of the Karun River all the way back to the southern outskirts of ruined Khorramshahr.

"We thought you were on the other side of the bally river?" Frank Waters remarked.

"The engineers the C-in-C sent up here to recce the options for putting a new pontoon bridge across the Karun gave me a ride back over on one of their boats. I used their radio to update General Carver on the state of play in 3rd Armoured Div's sector just before you got here."

The older man mulled this.

Presently, he looked east across the Shatt-al-Arab, eying the wrecks of the Tiger and the Anzac.

"The Navy doesn't do things by half," he remarked cheerfully. "What is the news from the north, by the way?"

Julian Calder hesitated.

"Michael Carver gave me leave to wander about on condition I report back to him at regular intervals," Frank Waters explained.

"You're supposed to work for the BBC!"

"Yes, but the only thing I bother about with that is the 'British' in the title, old man."

Calder told Frank Waters what he knew, or rather, what he now suspected was going on beyond the town on the north bank of the Karun River. He concluded by mentioning that the Iranians were taking no prisoners.

"Probably for the best," the older man declared sanguinely. "You and I both know that if we let the bastards go they'll only be back again in a few weeks, or months or years."

"Does anybody know what's going on across the other side of the Shatt-al-Arab over towards Umm Qasr?" Julian Calder inquired, unsurprised by his former mentor's callousness.

"We think the RAF hurt the Reds' forward units around Umm Qasr more badly than anybody realised at the time. The Aussies and the Saudis may have enveloped a couple of laagered armoured regiments and cut the road north to Basra."

The younger man absorbed this without comment.

"We also think," Frank Waters went on, "there may be some kind of popular uprising going on in Basra. But it could just be the Russians mistaking Basra for Budapest."

Calder found himself staring again at the scorched, shell-torn flanks of HMS Tiger.

"No more news about what happened in the Gulf?"

Frank Waters shook his head.

"Sorry, no idea, old chap. All we know for sure is that we've got no air cover. None at all and apart from a couple of minesweepers in the Shatt-al-Arab and some Navy cargo ships in the Gulf nobody is broadcasting or acknowledging our calls anymore."

"No air cover?"

"The Yanks have gone off air, too."

They had all seen the flashes in the sky far to the south.

Who had nuked whom?

"God," Calder groaned, "isn't it a mess?"

This prompted a snort of amusement from his companion.

"Goodness, I know you were always a bit of a misery guts, Calder," he exclaimed jovially, "but you really must try to look on the bright side of things, what!"

The younger man turned to face Frank Waters.

He eyed the older man bleakly.

"The bright side?"

"Dammit," the SAS legend beamed broadly, "we're standing here – more or less in one piece – and the bloody Russians are in full retreat. What the Devil do you mean asking me about the bloody 'bright side'? We're jolly well winning, don't you know!"

Chapter 18

"Why how great it is to meet you," Lady Bird Johnson cooed as if she was welcoming guests to an 'at home' down at the LBJ Ranch in Stonewall, Texas. "*Both* of you!"

Marija did not know if one was supposed to curtsy to the acting-First Lady. On those occasions when she had been introduced to Jackie Kennedy at Camp David things had been relatively informal, and she had settled upon bobbing a small nod of the head in respect. It was a good compromise; unless Peter held her arm she was likely to fall over attempting to do a 'proper' curtsy. When she had met the Queen at Blenheim Palace in April she had indeed, very nearly fallen over but that had been as much through nerves as the enduring legacy that her childhood injuries still had on her sense of balance...

Beside Marija her husband stood tall and straight, bowed his head momentarily and carefully shook Lady Bird Johnson's small tanned hand.

For some reason Peter Christopher kept remembering – or thinking he was remembering – lines from Kubla Khan.

There was no sign of the President or any other senior member of the Administration; although a lot of people seemed to be running around the Philadelphia White House brandishing pieces of paper and generally looking flustered. Lady Bird Johnson was flanked by her daughters and an ever-changing sub-cast of other women, secretaries or the wives of officials, he knew not which.

A damsel with a dulcimer in a vision once I saw: it was an Abyssinian maid, and on her dulcimer, she played...while all the women came and went...

No, that last bit was wrong.

Try to remember you are an officer in Her Majesty's Royal Navy; forget metaphysics, concentrate on the matter in hand, man!

"May I introduce my wife, Ma'am," he said easily, very much as if to the manner born in a way that still surprised and somehow, made Marija very proud.

Actually, everything he did made her very proud, obviously, but since they had come to America she had discovered that her new husband, the man she had loved for over half her still young life, was a natural diplomat. He just 'got on' with people, with everybody without ever really seeming to have to...*act*.

"We were only expecting Sir Peter, Lady Marija," the older woman explained, gushing in that particularly welcoming way that Marija suspected was one of the hall marks of the old American South. Rather '*Gone With the Wind*', a very long book both she and her sister, Rosa, had religiously read from cover to cover in an attempt, possibly an overly ambitious attempt, to better understand the culture and the history of the states through which they had recently travelled.

Marija smiled seraphically at the President's wife and made brief eye contacts with the tall young women who flanked her; the two daughters whom she had heard Lyndon Johnson worked so hard, and wisely, to protect and shield from the political hurly burly and any whiff of public scrutiny.

"I will lose Peter again to the Royal Navy too soon," she explained, philosophically. "Sooner or later, they will give him a big grey warship to sail away in. Until then I will be at his side."

This pronouncement somewhat flummoxed Lady Bird Johnson.

Marija quirked a twinkling-eyed grimace.

"Besides, every time I let him out of my sight he can't stop himself doing something insanely dangerous. Like that business with your big aircraft carrier, the Enterprise. And as for sinking those Russian battleships just off the coast of Sliema," she shrugged, "what can I say? His father tells him to steam away as fast as he can and what does he do? He hears the sound of guns and turns around!"

The President's wife honestly did not know what to say or do; behind her, her daughters, Lynda and Luci were trying very hard not to smirk.

Peter Christopher decided the only thing to do was to stare at the ceiling for a few seconds. His wife had a way of just 'taking over' and there was really not a lot he could do about it until she gave him his cue to step in.

Marija unconsciously passed her left hand over her abdomen.

"Things are very bad," she said, very soberly. "I think we must all do what we can before we make a world in which none of us would wish to raise our babies."

Lady Bird Johnson accepted this and introduced her daughters to her guests. "The President has asked me to escort you to our private rooms. He is in conference with his closest advisors at present. I'm sure he won't be long." A look to Marija, whose tiredness was palpable. "In your condition you should be sitting down, my dear," she decided.

Jack Griffin and Secret Service man Jake Karlsen had peeled off to stand at a respectful distance from their charges. Now they followed the President's wife and daughter, and Peter and Marija up to the first floor as the party slowly ascended the grandiose staircase of the former bank. Everybody climbed the steps painfully slowly; which always irked Marija. She was perfectly capable of keeping up with them and if she missed her step Peter would catch her; she had discovered he was really good at that and it made things so much easier. Eventually, the doors closed at their backs and the Christophers were ushered to a tastefully patterned chaise longue in a big room furnished by somebody who had no idea which chair, table or lamp stand belonged to which era, or style.

"Jackie hardly ever came here," Lady Bird Johnson explained, as if reading her guests' minds. "How was your flight?"

"I am not a very good flier," Marija confessed. "I am not sure if that was because the first time – the only other time I've flown - our aeroplane was very nearly shot down."

Again, while both the Johnson daughters perfectly understood that Marija was trying to lighten the atmosphere; their mother missed the joke, possibly because unlike her girls she was aware that the aircraft which been shot down coming in to land at Cheltenham on the day in question had been shot down by a an experimental *American* air-to-air missile which had been misappropriated from a US Army arsenal by either Irish Republican American sympathisers in the US Army, or according to Philadelphia tittle-tattle, the CIA....

"What can I offer you to drink?" The President's wife went on, hopefully. "You must be hungry?"

"Might I have a very weak cup of tea please?" Marija suggested. "No milk?"

Peter Christopher had no idea how his wife could be so calm. His stomach was so knotted with anxiety he felt physically sick. Marija was supposed to be the one with morning sickness, not him! He was tempted to ask for a stiff drink. A very stiff drink!

"A coffee, please," he murmured, forcing a rictus smile.

The Johnson daughters instantly flew into action.

"Forgive me," the man continued. "We've had no news since we left San Francisco. Has the situation at the Wister Park Embassy been sorted out? Have there been any other *untoward world* developments, Ma'am?"

Lady Bird Johnson visibly flinched. "I, well," she wrung her hands on her lap. "It is probably better if I leave it to the President to, er..."

Marija read volumes into this unhappy obfuscation and thought for a moment that she was going to faint. President Kennedy was ill, there had been two great battles in the Persian Gulf, supposedly between the US and the Royal Navies, atomic bombs had been used in Iraq, there had been an attack on the Embassy in Wister Park...

What had happened to the Ambassador and their friends; had anybody been hurt?

What else had happened while they were in the air?

"Might I inquire why Lord Franks is not at the White House at this time, Ma'am?" This Marija heard her husband asking in a quiet, half-choked voice.

She had been a little surprised when there was nobody from the Embassy at the airport to greet them off the plane. She had hoped Rachel Piotrowska or Mary Drinkwater, the Ambassador's wife's Personal Secretary might be waiting in the arrivals hall and had looked forward to renewing acquaintance with Lady Franks, Barbara, who had been like a protective mother hen to both her and her sister Rosa during their time at the Embassy. Barbara would want to know all about their travels...

The President's wife avoided Peter Christopher's eye.

"Please. What has happened to our friends?" Marija asked, suddenly terrified.

Chapter 19

It would be Lieutenant General Viktor Georgiyevich Kulikov's forty-third birthday tomorrow; not that he was in a particularly celebratory mood.

"That fucking idiot Babadzhanian left the leading echelons of 3rd Caucasus Tank Army hanging in thin air down below Basra," he roared in pain and disgust, "and handed all my fucking armour over to those two fucking clowns Puchkov and Kurochnik!"

Admiral of the Fleet and freshly appointed Troika member, Defence Minister of the Soviet Union Sergey Georgiyevich Gorshkov was not normally a man overly inclined to listen to whining Red Army generals. Unfortunately, as he rested his tired, aching limbs in the big chair behind the former Provincial Governor of Basra's huge, polished desk, he knew that on this occasion the aggrieved general pacing like an enraged Snow Leopard, actually had a genuine grievance.

Up until two or three days ago Army Group South had been – on paper at least – the most formidable ground force on the planet. Admittedly, many of its men and an uncomfortably high proportion of its best tanks were in need of – respectively - rest and urgent maintenance, and its two constituent Armies, 3rd Caucasian Tank and 2nd Siberian Mechanised, had been operating at the end of horribly long and exposed lines of communication for over three months, but all in all, Marshal of the Soviet Union Hamazasp Khachaturi Babadzhanian, its hugely experienced and outstandingly able commander, had done a remarkable job carrying Operation Nakazyvat very nearly to a stunningly successful conclusion.

But two or three days was an awfully long time in modern war; suddenly the Red Army's invincible sword arm had been reduced to a bloody stump, by a series of brilliantly co-ordinated enemy counter attacks which had fallen on Army Group South's exhausted right wing and the flank of the supposedly unstoppable thrust down the eastern bank of the Shatt-al-Arab like thunderbolts from the Gods!

Nobody, absolutely nobody had seen the disaster coming.

The enemy had seemed beaten; his situation hopeless.

Yes, there was evidence that Babadzhanian knew about the presence of a 'weak' Iranian armoured force 'somewhere' north of the Karun River; and that the enemy was attempting to build up some kind of 'armoured barricade' along the Kuwaiti border in the south west. But Basra had been taken without a fight, Khorramshahr was there for the taking, indefensible, and Abadan was besieged, at the mercy of Kulikov's as yet barely engaged, largely intact 2nd Siberian Mechanised Army.

"Comrade Hamazasp Khachaturi must have had a brainstorm," Gorshkov agreed quietly, ruminatively stroking his dark moustache as he spoke. He might be a sailor not a soldier but the rules and the realities of war were common to both trades. Babadzhanian might be forgiven for underestimating his enemy once, on one quarter of his front; but *everywhere*, no that spoke to some catastrophic aberration of judgement, madness really...

Major Generals Vladimir Andreyevich Puchkov and Konstantin Yakovlevich Kurochnik, Babadzhanian's favourites, were not just 'hard chargers', they were natural born '*hard chargers*'; or as events had proved, reckless adventurers.

Puchkov was a man of Babadzhanian's own age with a weather-beaten face and a shaven head exhibiting the public scars of that day back in 1943 when a German Tiger tank had knocked out three of the four T-34s under his command at Kursk. His gunner had put a seventy-five-millimetre round through the side of the Nazi behemoth but not before the Tiger's eighty-eight-millimetre canon had put a solid shot into his tank's engine compartment.

Kurochnik had come to Babadzhanian's attention after his brilliant handling of the mission to assassinate the Shah and to decapitate the Iranian state in Tehran, the precursor operation to the launching of Operation Nakazyvat. Since then, he had distinguished himself at Urmia in Iranian Azerbaijan, and in ruthlessly subduing the northern cities of Kirkuk and Mosul. He had more than earned his two rapid promotions from lieutenant-colonel to major-general; but placing an airborne forces man in command of massed armoured formations at such a critical time was...*bizarre.*

And in the circumstances, this was now irrelevant because both men were missing, presumed dead or if they had been very unlucky, captured. The latest reports indicated that while the British and the Australians were taking prisoners, the Iranians were not and any man who allowed himself to be captured by 'the natives' probably considered himself lucky if he got away with just a bullet in the head.

Babadzhanian had been one of Nikita Khrushchev's 'special' generals after he sorted out that little local difficulty in Hungary in 1956 – earning the sobriquet of 'the butcher of Budapest' – and after October 1962 he had been Vasily Chuikov's unchallenged number two in the Red Army. He was undoubtedly a great man; a great man whose reputation would, regrettably, be forever tarnished by the events of the last days of his life.

The only way Gorshkov could explain Babadzhanian's decision to relieve Kulikov – a competent, albeit rather too 'political' general not wholly trusted by many in the hierarchy of the Red Army – of command of his best armoured units was by assuming Babadzhanian must have completely lost his mind or grown so paranoid that he was convinced Kulikov was plotting against him. And as for giving command of the last full-strength tank corps in the Motherland to two 'hard chargers' who had obligingly walked – no, sprinted blindfold – into what now looked like it had been a masterfully conceived and executed bear trap, well, Gorshkov did not know where to begin to start to unravel the psychopathy of that!

In any event, that was an exercise he would leave for future historians to ponder; presently, he had more immediate problems. Every few minutes the rumble of another distant explosion somewhere in the city reverberated throughout the Palace, the crackle of small arms fire was continual, although hardly intense which insofar as it went, was a morsel of good news he was happy to clutch at with both hands.

The Iraqi Army garrison of Basra had melted away before the leading echelon of 3rd Caucasian Tank Army; now it was re-emerging from its holes in the ground inflaming what had all the hallmarks of a popular revolt across the whole city.

The other members of the Troika – Brezhnev and Shelepin – had told him to base himself in Basra so as to be well-placed to 'negotiate with the British and the Americans'. A lesser man would have brooded on the iniquity of his being expected to clean up somebody else's shit; specifically, Comrade Leonid Ilyich's shit.

However, Gorshkov had been cleaning up other people's shit all his life; that was how he had made himself indispensable to Stalin, Khrushchev and Brezhnev.

"So, what do we do now, Comrade Sergey Georgiyevich?" Kulikov asked, finally sufficiently in control of his emotions to resume his chair in front of Gorshkov's desk.

Gorshkov sat forward, steepling his fingers under his chin.

"If we acceded to the American's *request* to withdraw our forces north of latitude 31 degrees," he posed, very much rhetorically, "how and more importantly, where, would we anchor our line?"

"There's nowhere south of Baghdad," Kulikov snapped back without pausing for thought. "Karbala, possibly," he added, dubiously, "in the west on the Euphrates. Perhaps, Numaniyah on the Tigris in the east? But frankly, we might as well go home!"

Gorshkov smoothed his moustache for several seconds.

"No, I don't think we'll do that. The Yankees were so afraid of going to war with us again that they stabbed their natural allies in the back. When we find out more about the reverse the American Navy suffered yesterday," he shrugged, "or the day before," he went on, unwilling to trust a single word that any US President said to his own people over the radio. Moreover, he was sceptical that the powerful fleet the Americans had sent into the Persian Gulf could possibly have been mauled as badly as people back in Sverdlovsk claimed.

That said, the situation developing in Malta with the US Sixth Fleet effectively 'quarantined' by the British suddenly opened a wealth of new opportunities in the Eastern Mediterranean.

It was painfully obvious that the Politburo had been wrong to *ration* the shipments of arms, technical supplies and combat advisors to the anti-western, anti-fascist groups in France and Germany. Authorising 'one off', 'exploratory' actions like the attack on that Royal Navy destroyer by those idiots on Corsica had brought down a predictably crushing retaliation. He had told the fools that such 'adventures' were pointless unless conceived as part of a wider 'game'.

For example, because the Krasnaya Zarya leadership on Corsica had been allowed to launch an 'isolated action', the opportunity to set a 'missile trap' for British bombers over-flying the island or mining the waters off Ajaccio to sink submarines sent to Corsican waters to bottle up the destroyers based in the port, had not been explored, let alone exploited. Consequently, the RAF had bombed the town and the docks to rubble and sunk several irreplaceable modern warships, a British submarine had destroyed both the vessels responsible for carrying out the otherwise, entirely successful interception of HMS Hampshire, and now other British submarines effectively blockaded the sea lanes between Corsica and the coast of Southern France. The whole thing was a fucking disaster!

He forced himself to focus on the current...*disaster*.

Any opportunities missed in the Eastern Mediterranean in the last month paled into insignificance in the light of what had been allowed to happen in Southern Iraq and Iran in recent days.

It would take years to rebuild the striking power of the Red Army...

Gorshkov had ordered that a message be broadcast to the British every five minutes seeking 'armistice negotiations in the Iraq-Iran theatre of operations'. The message made it clear that he spoke for 'the Collective leadership of the USSR'.

This latter was untrue; in fact, whatever he agreed, or failed to agree with the enemy would almost certainly be denounced by the dolts back in the Motherland who were, at this very minute, more interested in finding somewhere to hide than facing up to the consequences of their actions.

"My communication to the British will have been broadcast by now. We shall see if they are in a mood to talk soon enough."

"And if not?" Kulikov inquired grimly.

Gorshkov did not reply.

Operation Nakazyvat had turned into a monumental self-inflicted wound upon the Motherland, the future belonged to the pragmatists, not the diehard Party men. Brezhnev, Kosygin and Chuikov – the 'old Troika' – had carried their lackeys in the Politburo with them on a misbegotten crusade that threatened to plunge the Soviet Union into a second, inevitably final nuclear war.

To avoid that Sergey Georgiyevich Gorshkov would gladly – in fact he had already asked himself if that was what he had already actually done – make a pact with the Devil.

As for Basra, well, like any other ground which had to be surrendered all the enemy would inherit would be scorched earth.

He realised Kulikov was about to jump to his feet and re-commence his pacing.

Gorshkov waved for him to remain seated.

"The war is lost, Comrade Viktor Georgiyevich," he sighed, viewing the other man with dark, unblinking eyes. "Harsh times are coming to us all. Hard decisions need to be made."

Kulikov was impassive; waiting to hear more.

Gorshkov interpreted that as a good sign.

"We are both patriots and good Party men," he went on. "Had I any doubt about your loyalty to the Revolution we would not be having," he shrugged, "this little talk."

It would not have been lost on the Acting Commander of what was left of Army Group South that Gorshkov's bodyguard detachment of twenty heavily armed Red Navy Marines had effectively, taken control of the Headquarters building within minutes of their chief's arrival.

"You mean I'd be dead by now if you didn't think I was the right sort of Red Army general, Comrade?"

Kulikov had posed this more in sadness than irritation.

"Quite," Gorshkov acknowledged, pausing to light a cigarette. He sucked in smoke, exhaled wearily. "Like others I believed Operation Nakazyvat was a catastrophe for *our* cause. Whatever its strategic merits we were too weak to exploit it even in the unlikely event it achieved all its initial objectives. To that end we abandoned the Krasnaya Zarya offensive in Anatolia, the Aegean and the Balkans," his face twisted with distaste, "diverting irreplaceable assets we could ill-afford to squander to crush local rebellions, we pulled out of Crete and Cyprus, and by expending the greater part of the Black Sea Fleet in the Malta Operation, we put all our eggs, as it were, in the Operation Nakazyvat 'basket'."

Viktor Kulikov's bushy eyebrows arched.

Gorshkov had just voiced the most devastating – positively excoriating – condemnation of State and Party policy he had ever heard in his whole life!

"Let me be straight with you, Comrade General," Gorshkov continued, rapidly disappearing behind a pall of cigarette smoke. "The men responsible for the current," he snorted, "*abomination* that we find ourselves in have betrayed the Revolution. Frankly, they have betrayed us all and in so doing demonstrated a fantastic political incompetence and geopolitical ineptitude that proves to me, at least, that it is inconceivable that *whoever* steps into their shoes would not be an improvement."

Oh, shit...

Kulikov did not, of course, say that out aloud but he suspected that, even through the fog of vile tobacco smoke, Minister of Defence and Admiral of the Fleet Sergey Georgiyevich Gorshkov was reading his mind.

Unconsciously, the Red Army man had delved in his pockets for his own cigarette case. He flipped open the battered, tarnished silvery lid of the memento recovered from a knocked out German Panther tank in the Ukraine in 1944, and jammed an un-tipped Turkish cigarette between his numb lips.

Gorshkov had risen from behind his desk. His petrol lighter flared viciously. Stepping back, he half rested against the table, looking down at Kulikov.

"*Whoever*, Comrade?" The soldier inquired.

"Yes," the other man retorted quietly. "Presently, there is too much confusion."

"Far too much..."

"What must be done must be done quickly, without hesitation. Are you with *me*?"

Kulikov took a long, deep drag on his cigarette.

He looked Gorshkov unwavering in the eye.

"Yes," he heard himself say, very hoarsely.

Chapter 20

Sir Thomas Harding-Grayson studied the cup of tea his wife had planted before him on his desk in the Foreign Office Annexe overlooking the darkened southern cloister of the ancient quadrangle.

The Prime Minister was locked in consultation with the military; diplomacy was dead it seemed.

Diplomacy was dead and things were, basically, going to pot. Great and convoluted plans had been laid, widely promulgated and discussed for this sort of *'end of everything situation'*; the only problem was that now that the worst had – or was about to happen – nobody was paying anything more than lip-service to 'what we ought to be doing'. In one way it was wholly explicable; and utterly irrational in another.

The United Kingdom was, *de jure*, at war with the United States and therefore doomed so what was the point going through the motions? Better to die with one's trousers on with one's head held high than to spend the last minutes, or hours of one's miserable existence cowering in a hole in the ground somewhere, or wasting time and energy clearing one's in tray. Half the people who were supposed to be manning the various RSGs – Regional Seats of Government – located in nuclear bunkers of varying robustness across England, Scotland, Wales and Ulster, had either refused to leave their normal posts above ground, or had since the declaration of the emergency re-surfaced in Oxford.

Everybody had thought an attack was imminent after the First Battle of the Persian Gulf. Nobody had had any idea whatsoever what was going to happen after the 'arrest' of the US Sixth Fleet at Malta, or the deployment of Arc Light against the USS Kitty Hawk's battle group.

The grim-faced, beetle-browed man who had dumped his meaty frame in the chair he had dragged, squealing across the bare boards of the old don's room now commandeered for 'the duration' - however long that turned out to be - rumbled impatiently.

"Look, I'm sorry if it's put your nose out of joint my turning up back here," he apologised, without the least conviction. "But Edna and I decided that if the worst came to the worst we'd rather be blown to smithereens here in Oxford than rot in a fetid bunker beneath the Chilterns until the food ran out!"

The Foreign Secretary raised his gaze for a moment.

"Fair enough," he murmured.

The arrival of his younger colleague – people imagined he was one of his protégés but Denis Healey, the Member of Parliament for the still intact constituency of Leeds East was nobody's *protégé*, or for that matter, *fool* – had interrupted his meditations.

He could well imagine his friend's wife, Edna, if not 'putting her foot down' then being a willing accomplice in Denis Healey's return to Oxford. The couple had met at Oxford when she was studying English at St Hugh's College and he was at Balliol, marrying in 1945 as soon as Denis came out of the Army. Edna had been the first girl at her school, Bells Grammar at Coleford in Gloucestershire, to gain a place at Oxford, and from his first acquaintance with the Healey's, the Harding-Graysons had found them to be the most erudite, and fascinating of dinner guests. Edna harboured as yet unrequited literary ambitions, poetic pretensions and had never really been reconciled to the life of a political wife; so, she and the Foreign Secretary's wife had in many ways been closer before the October War than the two husbands.

The Healey's three teenage children were at his home with Denis's brother, Terence and his family, in Alfriston, in East Sussex. There was no room for the families of 'nominated persons' in any of the RSGs; another mistake they were going to have to put right if they were ever in this sad pass again. Demonstrating a British 'stiff upper lip' was one thing, leaving one's kith and kin above ground when the Government of the day wanted you to be underground, was another.

"Pat will be pleased to hear that Edna is back in the city," Tom Harding-Grayson remarked.

"That's all right then!" Denis Healey declared affably. He was a larger than life character who had shouldered his way back into the hierarchy of the mainstream Labour Party in recent weeks after overcoming, for the while at least, the debilitating illnesses which had afflicted him on and off, ever since the October War. If nothing else his reappearance had shaken up, and immeasurably strengthened Jim Callaghan's faction of the Labour Party, and his appointment as the Foreign Secretary's 'Personal Advisor' had put any number of Foreign Office staffers' noses out of joint.

Tom Harding-Grayson sipped his tea.

He had guessed that Healey would be among the first 'early returners' to Oxford. Like his friend he had no appetite to be the 'Foreign Secretary in waiting' for the end of the World in a bunker beneath the Chilterns.

If there was a nuclear war then Jim Callaghan and Alison Munro in their respective bunkers would make the best of a bad deal; or rather, they were welcome to try.

The Foreign Secretary suspected his friend was a little bit 'behind the latest news' so he brought him up to speed at the risk of restating what the other man already knew.

"We sank the Kitty Hawk getting on for thirty-six hours ago," he declared, partially opening and leaving ajar a window into his thoughts. "We'd previously interned the Sixth Fleet. That was just after Margaret gave Jack Kennedy that Churchillian 'we'll fight you on the beaches' talk and threatened to fight Uncle Sam with her own 'eye teeth' if that was what it came to."

Denis Healey viewed his friend thoughtfully, his expression

suddenly very sober.

"And presumably, you're wondering why nothing unpleasant has happened yet?"

"Something like that," the older man confessed. "If the Vice President was a less capable man than Lyndon Johnson I'd suspect the onset of a temporary paralysis at the top in Philadelphia, but," he shrugged, "I don't know. One can so easily read the wrong thing into the Americans' apparent inertia."

"What if they aren't in any state to *act*, Tom?"

The Foreign Secretary contemplated this in silence.

He said nothing.

"We gave them a fearful knock in the Gulf," Denis Healey went on. "We've got their Mediterranean Fleet bottled up at Malta..."

Tom Harding-Grayson stirred.

"And they've still got the air force that won the October War in a single night, Denis," he reminded his friend. "And scores of Minutemen and Polaris missiles pointed at us right now. As for the naval balance of power; they still massively out gun us in the Persian Gulf, and if things turn nasty at Malta they must know that the Sixth Fleet would prevail. We don't even have the option of waging submarine warfare in the Atlantic; all our newest submarines are thousands of miles away bottling up the Falkland Islands and blockading the mouth of the River Plate. We've got say, twenty serviceable V-bombers, half-a-dozen squadrons of jet fighters to defend the British Isles and what little remains of our Fleet scattered all over the place. For goodness sake, we can't even keep the peace in Northern Ireland!"

Denis Healey already knew that.

"Changing the subject," he grimaced, "is the PM still dead set on expelling everybody at the American Embassy?"

"No, no, that was just a tantrum..."

There was a light knocking at the door.

"Come!"

The Foreign Secretary's wife stepped into the room.

"Hello, Denis," she smiled. "I thought you'd turn up sooner or later."

"Bad pennies and all that," Healey remarked cheerfully as he jumped to his feet to exchange pecking kisses with the newcomer. "Edna's gone off to reclaim our lodgings," he added, "before some Don comes out of the woodwork to re-establish his tenure!"

Pat Harding-Grayson cut short the pleasantries.

"Walter Brenckmann is in the lobby. He says he's not going anywhere until he's talked to you, Tom."

"How on earth did he get through the cordon?"

The Foreign Secretary's wife frowned.

"He told the Police that the only way they were going to keep him out was to shoot him, I should think..."

Tom Harding-Grayson was already on his feet.

Every diplomat worth his salt understood that in time of war you never stopped talking to your enemies.

The American Ambassador rose to his feet as hurriedly as his aching, sleep-deprived frame permitted as the two Englishmen, pursued by Pat Harding-Grayson virtually tumbled down the steps to the ground floor lobby where a nervous policeman and a hard-eyed Royal Marine hefting a Sten gun were watching over him.

Walter Brenckmann senior had been the US Naval Attaché to the United Kingdom in December; the last time the old transatlantic allies had very nearly come to blows. Looking back that contretemps now seemed like a mere hiccup in international relations, hand bags at forty paces, rather than the overture to World War IV that it had seemed at the time.

Hands were shaken.

"Please leave us," Tom Harding-Grayson ordered the US Ambassador's minders.

"There's more news about what happened at the Embassy in Wister Park," Walter Brenckmann explained, unable to wash the shame from his voice as chairs were drawn up before the big desk in the Foreign Secretary's room, and cups and saucers rattled as Pat Harding-Grayson fussed around the visitor.

Denis Healey arched an eyebrow in an unspoken question.

"I've been in contact with the State Department in Philadelphia," the US Ambassador explained, "via the relay station in Ireland and a US Navy ship stationed in mid-Atlantic. We've got scrambled voice and other systems up and running."

Tom Harding-Grayson nodded mutely. The 'facility' outside Dublin in the Irish Republic was a joint US Air Force – Central Intelligence Agency enterprise whose primary role was to spy on the United Kingdom.

"I believe that Station 'D' has already approached Sir Ian Maclennan," Walter Brenckmann went on, "your ambassador in Dublin, with a view to opening up an alternative channel of communication with the UAUK?"

The Foreign Secretary nodded.

His American friend was going prematurely grey. Normally the most reserved, impeccably groomed, calmest man in any room he was clearly a little rattled.

"This whole thing is getting way too out of hand, Tom," he said miserably.

"I think it's worse than that, old man."

"Oh, God," the American groaned, briefly running his hands through his hair before taking a deep breath, and literally, re-gathering his wits. "President Johnson is likely to come under extreme pressure to order the Sixth Fleet to 'break out'; and to send in the B-52s in the Middle East. All Hell will break loose in the papers and across the networks as American wakes up. Right now, the man and the woman on the street back home has no real idea what is going on, just that whatever it is, it's really bad. In a few hours they are going to discover that thousands of Americans are dead and that the

Sixth Fleet is being held hostage…"

He realised he had allowed himself to be distracted.

"Sorry, I know I'm telling you what you already know. That's not why I wanted, *needed*, you to hear what I came over here to tell you, from *me*, rather than a stranger."

His listeners stiffened.

"I have more information about the attack on the Wister Park compound," the Ambassador continued, his tone grim. "We have reason to believe that agents provocateur in the mob around the Embassy at the time of the assault, by a gang of 'insurgents' claiming allegiance to the 'Council of the Great Lakes' rebels in the Midwest, incited a mass 'break in' at the time of the initial armed 'incursion'. Previously, I was led to believe that the compound had been breached and partially besieged, and that British diplomatic staff were being held hostage. That was untrue. What actually took place was that the staff in the Embassy were, by and large, left to their own devices to defend themselves against the insurgents who drove a bus into the front of the building and then stormed it from the city side. At the same time a mob – several hundred, perhaps several thousand strong stormed the rear of the compound. Philadelphia PD men and troops protecting the perimeter failed to open fire on the crowd…"

Tom Harding-Grayson opened his mouth to speak.

Walter Brenckmann shook his head.

"Subsequently, the mob ransacked the compound. Two outbuildings were set on fire. At around sunset last night several bodies were dumped in the yard in front of the main Embassy building."

The US Ambassador was close to tears.

Tears of shame.

"The bodies are believed to include those of the Ambassador, Lord Franks, his wife Lady Barbara, and the Chargé d'affaires, Sir Patrick Dean…"

Chapter 21

02:40 Hours (EST)
British Embassy, Wister Park, Philadelphia

Dwight Christie had thought she was dead. After the bastards had finished with her – about a dozen of them crowding into the small room, all over her for what seemed like forever – they had walked out, strutting like Peacocks, laughing and joking, patting each other on the back for being such brave warriors, leaving her unconscious, spread-eagled on the narrow single bed. The former FBI Special Agent had rattled the handcuff chain that locked him to the old iron radiator just feet from the foot of the bed, enraged, and sick to his stomach with helpless impotence.

The animals had left the room's single, overhead light on.

His right eye was crusted with dried blood but open, a slit, now. He tried not to stare at the body on the bed, instead he began to study his surroundings. The room was smaller than he had imagined in the darkness, Spartan. The sort of accommodation a low-ranking visitor from back home might be allocated for a short stay. Besides the bed there was a matchwood desk in the far corner and a hard chair for when the occupant needed to attend to his, or her, papers. There were documents on the floor, strewn carelessly, as if everything on and in the desk had been tipped onto the bare boards; a small bottle of black ink which had come to rest by his right foot suggested there might be a fountain pen somewhere under the detritus around the desk...

Once more he rattled his chains.

The woman had made no attempt to resist.

The bastards had pinned her down and then one after another they had climbed on top of her. She was a piece of meat, they had been like pigs at a trough, grunting, cursing, goading each other on and she had just lain there, limp, inert as they held her legs apart and formed a queue, playing with themselves...

Christie had not recognised any of the bastards apart from Isaac Cheney...

Two or three of them were just kids, college age jocks. They were all white, Galen Cheney's kind of people. Deadbeats, no-hopers, guys who *never* got it that the reason they were *never* going to 'make it big' in the world was that they were too ignorant, too inflexible, too prejudiced or just too stupid; representatives of the white underclass, the people who felt they never got a fair shot, and were convinced that somewhere in the Constitution it said that the rest of America owed *them* a living. He had been investigating, and arresting arseholes like these guys all his adult life. Hating, demeaning, resenting women came with the territory. In their heads these morons were players, important men who needed somebody physically weaker, under their power to lord it over to feel like they were 'real' men. So, when the crazies took over and somebody said it was okay to prey on women and blacks, or anybody weaker than them, that was just fine with scumbags like these guys.

There must have been other women in the Embassy...

He thought he had dreamed of hearing screams and pleas for mercy in the next-door room...

Again, he rattled his chains.

Where else in Philadelphia had the insurgents struck?

Where else were these lowlifes killing, raping and looting?

And how the fuck had they managed to seize the British goddam Embassy?

She had just stared at her attackers until the bastards were so unnerved they pulled her skirt over her face. That was how they had left her, naked from the waist down with her blouse and her frock over her head. Her stockings were down around her calves, she was unmoving, cruelly exposed. But then that was the object of the exercise, to dehumanise, to humiliate, to destroy that which the lowlifes feared and loathed the most. It was not enough to win; one's enemies could not be allowed any...*dignity.*

Christie dragged his eyes away from the woman's pale nakedness. There were red welts on her legs and abdomen, the shadows mercifully veiled the damage her tormentors must have wrought between her thighs. One of the animals had tried to choke her; that had almost started a fight because there had still been a queue back out to the corridor at the time and the others were worried they were going to miss out on their 'piece of the action'.

He shut his eyes.

Galen Cheney had only kept him alive so he could see *this*, and probably much worse to come before he put a bullet in his neck. He reckoned he could hardly feel any worse than he did already; but Cheney would not worry about a little thing like that. Dwight Christie did not need to be told that his whole life was a bad joke, or that he had got practically *everything* wrong.

He had betrayed his country, murdered fellow FBI men, run for a while with Galen Cheney's insanity before attempting, and failing to take the monster down. All along he had honestly believed he was doing the right thing, except in retrospect the reason he was chained to a radiator witnessing the gang rape of a helpless woman was that for the last twenty years he had been making ever more disastrously bad life decisions.

He had been nineteen years old at the time of Pearl Harbour, dropped out of college, and walked through the US Army's officer candidate selection board. His brothers had gone overseas, he had spent the war stateside, fought his war with the most beleaguered unit in the whole Army; the small band of brothers, the 'damned', charged with policing the procurement process that fuelled the US war effort and poured treasure – quite literally beyond the dreams of avarice - into the coffers of a handful of American robber baron industrialists.

Christie had never been any kind of all American boy traduced by some kind of national 'dream'. That baloney had only ever seemed real in the movies. However, he had not grown up as any kind of socialist or rebel either. It was only when he saw American industry systematically fleecing and gouging the American people, and the way in which so many obscene fortunes had been shamelessly founded upon the still warm bodies of countless dead GIs, that his personal worm had slowly turned.

Even so his internal conversion had been slow, reluctant. He recollected no particular *Damascene moment*, no sudden conversion on a par with St Paul's on the road to Damascus; there was simply the daily drip, drip, drip of unequivocal, unambiguous evidence. Wall Street bankers, steel men, shipbuilders, Ford, General Motors, Chrysler, Boeing, and all the other great contractors, and the ever taller, wider wall of lies...

The Rockefellers and yes, the Kennedys got richer and richer while American GIs died on the beaches of Iwo Jima and Normandy, in the jungles of the Philippines, the mountains of Italy and in the Ardennes forest of Luxembourg and Belgium. While the war profiteers and their political place men – Congress was a willing accomplice throughout, its members amply compensated for their largesse at the time, and in the years since - salted away their millions young American soldiers, sailors and airmen bled to death thousands of miles from home; and the *American system*, worshipping the great god of the market economy, solemnly blessed the thieves and charlatans for whom the war could not go on long enough!

Ask not what your country can do for you!

Yeah, sure...

Christie's kid brother, Vernon, a corporal in the 101st Airborne had died of wounds sustained in Normandy in June 1944. Christie's older brother, Frank, a lieutenant in the Marines, had been killed at Iwo Jima. Frank and Vernon's deaths had destroyed his mother and father; they had both died young in their fifties, broken and inconsolable.

Ask not what you can do for your country!

Ask what you can do for your country!

When the Soviets – the NKVD in those days – had recruited him around Christmas 1946 he had been a soft touch. Just out of uniform, guilt-ridden for having 'hidden' at home while his brothers died on foreign fields for the greater good of the stock price of US conglomerates, he had been drinking himself into a hole ahead of going back to college under the auspices of the GI Bill. He had no longer believed in...*anything.*

His handlers had channelled his rage and given him a new purpose. In 1947 he had applied to join the Federal Bureau of Investigation in California, completed his college education, become a G-man and the rest, as they say, was history...

He blinked.

The woman on the bed was watching him.

She was propped on her right elbow having re-arranged her skirt to conceal again her violated modesty.

Dwight Christie realised that her tormentors had removed her handcuffs – discarding the same on the floor by the bed – probably having been forewarned that previously she had employed the restraints as knuckle-dusters.

The man blinked myopically at her for some moments.

She was oddly composed, detached.

Her eyes flicked warningly at the door as she slowly sat up, easing her legs over the side of the bed with the measured caution of somebody who is expecting to be doubled up by excruciating pain without warning.

She sat there as if waiting for her head to clear.

Or perhaps, hardly believing she was not in more discomfort than she actually was; whichever it was she took several deep breaths and with a grimace, turned to view Dwight Christie.

The man shivered.

He knew then – he just knew – that the killing had only just begun.

She sighed.

"I haven't heard anybody in the corridor for about ten minutes," she said lowly.

Chapter 22

10:34 Hours (Local) – 03:04 Hours in Philadelphia
Leningradsky Prospekt Hotel, Chelyabinsk, Soviet Union

Fifty-nine-year-old Llewellyn E. 'Tommy' Thompson, Jr., who was that most unlikely of Americans; a man who had, if not fallen in love with, then always missed Russia when he was elsewhere, looked out of the window of the bare-walled apartment where his green uniformed KGB minders had corralled him for the last twenty-four hours.

He was trying very hard not to despair.

The man President Kennedy had sent to Russia to broker a non-aggression pact – at any cost – with the Troika, was the son of a Coloradan rancher who had entered the US Diplomatic Service in the late 1920s while working in the Georgetown office of Price-Waterhouse in Washington DC. During the Great Patriotic War – nobody in the Soviet Union troubled to call Hitler's War the 'Second World War' – he had been Second Secretary at the Moscow Embassy and become a fluent Russian speaker. Posted back to Moscow in the late 1950s he and his wife had enjoyed several happy years, becoming friendly with the Khrushchevs, and almost but not quite Russophiles. While other senior members of the diplomatic corps viewed the Soviet Union as a bleak, drab place dominated by tractor plants with Red Army and KGB men standing guard at every corner, Thompson's Russia was a place of yes, bleak functional architecture and rigid social regimentation but also of immense natural beauty populated by a people made hard by their privations; yet as brave as lions and no less human than any American.

He had heard the helicopter's thrumming approach several minutes before it was visible, now he watched as the camouflaged Mil-6 swooped down towards a patch of open ground partially hidden by two grey apartment blocks several hundred metres away between the Leningradsky Prospekt Hotel and the River Miass.

The negotiations had, he thought, been progressing relatively smoothly until about thirty-six hours ago.

Vasili Vasilyevich Kuznetsov, the former First Deputy Foreign Minister of the Union of Soviet Socialist Republics who had replaced Alexei Kosygin, the member of the Troika whose responsibilities had included both the administration of the post-Cuban Missiles War Five-year Plan and Foreign Policy, and they had been making – Thompson believed - real headway.

Understandably, the Soviets wanted everything he was offering, and more, and both sides had sent provisional 'final position' papers back to their principals in Philadelphia and Sverdlovsk.

Thompson had come across Vasili Kuznetsov now and then over the years. The man was an engineer by profession who had been given permission to study in America – between 1931 and 1933 – at Carnegie Mellon University in Pittsburgh. For most of his career in the Soviet Foreign Ministry, sixty-four-year-old Kuznetsov had worked in relative obscurity, a trusted Party apparatchik who had eventually ended up working for that most remarkable man, the late Andrei Andreyevich Gromyko.

President Kennedy's special envoy to the 'new' Soviet Union suspected that had Gromyko survived the Cuban Missiles War the Motherland might not have marched back down the road to a new, never-ending war. But that was his heart talking; his head said that the war faction – even after it had broken the back of Krasnaya Zarya within the Soviet Union – would probably have won out in the end whatever Gromyko had said or done.

Kuznetsov had been accompanied by Major General Sergey Fyodorovich Akhromeyev, in his last meeting with Thompson. Thompson knew nothing of Akhromeyev; which was probably exactly why the Red Army had sent him as its representative to that particular meeting. Thompson's colleagues back home viewed sending a soldier to a 'diplomatic' meeting as a provocation, a deliberate discourtesy but he recognised it as simply the Russian way. It was pure hypocrisy to pretend that the US State Department did not routinely pull similar 'fast ones'.

Thompson went on waiting.

A door opened behind his back; he forced himself not to turn.

"Forgive me, Ambassador," Vasily Kuznetsov apologised gruffly, pausing to catch his breath.

He and Thompson shook hands.

"I was detained receiving the latest situation reports," the Soviet Foreign Minister explained. "Things are," he sucked his teeth, "not good. Comrade Alexander Nikolayevich will be here shortly. That was his helicopter that landed just now. He will have the latest intelligence."

Forty-five-year-old Alexander Nikolayevich Shelepin, the head of the *Komitet Gosudarstvennoy Bezopasnosti* – the Committee for State Security (KGB) – entered the second-floor apartment with two bodyguards. The newly appointed Troika member had never been a man to take chances and he was not about to turn over a fresh leaf now.

He and Thompson shook hands with perfunctory courtesy.

Strong men often blanched when confronted by Shelepin.

With Kosygin dead the cold-eyed, ruthless KGB man was the last of Stalin's men in the Politburo. Even before the Cuban Missiles War there had been no more dangerous or secretive operator in the Union of Soviet Socialist Republics than Comrade Alexander Nikolayevich Shelepin.

Before the October War dark rumours roiled around Shelepin like an impenetrable cloak wherein evil resided. Inevitably, not every rumour was true, or could in fact be true, but if not all the mud stuck then some of the blood could never be wiped away. He was one of those men whose mere presence in a room seemed to chill the air.

Thompson looked Shelepin in the eye.

The younger man met his gaze, held it a second or so and glanced to Kuznetsov.

"My people have taken over the communications centre, Comrade Vasili Vasilyevich," he announced levelly before turning his full attention back to the US Emissary.

This was Shelepin's game now.

Thompson had not needed this to be signposted but Shelepin was not the sort of man who left anybody in doubt as to when they were trespassing on *his* turf.

It was said the Khrushchev had installed Shelepin at the Lubyanka, the headquarters of the NKVD, the predecessor of the KGB back in the 1950s, because only a man with his particular 'gifts' was capable of 'cleaning out the stables'. Other whispers claimed that Shelepin had been the man who 'cleaned out the stables' when German and Polish exiles in the West and the American government started asking awkward questions about the twenty thousand Poles murdered in the Katyn Forest, a crime committed in April and May 1940, over a year *before* Hitler invaded and conquered *that* part of Russia in the Second World War.

"If there is war between our countries Chelyabinsk will not be safe, Ambassador," Shelepin explained in Russian, knowing Thompson had no need of an interpreter. "Time is short and we have much to discuss."

The American could not disagree with that.

"There have been certain," Shelepin hesitated, "bizarre developments in the Persian Gulf and elsewhere," he half-choked on his next admission, "and the Red Army has experienced certain...*setbacks*, in the final phase of its operations to invest the southern regions of Iraq and Iran."

Setbacks?

To Thompson's highly attuned diplomat's antenna, that word coming from the lips of the Head of the KGB, sounded a lot like '*disasters*' to him.

"Setbacks?" He inquired, his tone that of a man intent on making polite, inconsequential conversation.

"Yes. *Setbacks* exacerbated by the failure of your government to fulfil its solemn undertakings to the Union of Soviet Socialist Republics."

Thompson froze inside.

What is going on?

"You have me at a disadvantage, sir," he objected. "I have been under house arrest for the last two days with no access to news of events outside Chelyabinsk."

The Russian did not need to be reminded of this, nevertheless, it irritated him and for a moment he allowed his anger to add a razor-sharp edge to his voice.

"President Kennedy undertook to deploy his bombers to compel the British to lay down their weapons..."

"No," Thompson interjected, not prepared to be browbeaten. "*We* undertook to separate the opposing forces *if*, and only *if*, that was operationally viable, and was likely to be conducive to promoting a meaningful ceasefire on the ground."

Strategic Air Command 'assets' and the formidable naval air wing of the USS Kitty Hawk ought to have been more than sufficient to cow even the British into accepting the inevitable.

What could possibly have gone wrong?

Alexander Shelepin might have been reading his mind.

"Lyndon Johnson has declared himself President," he explained acidly, "anti-Soviet elements in your capital may have mounted a coup. There are reports of fighting and civil disturbances on the streets of Philadelphia. Possibly, this is a thing orchestrated by that witch Thatcher in England. Who knows? It does not matter. The United States has reneged on the undertakings you made to us. Now your General LeMay is perhaps making plans to try again to bomb the Motherland 'back to the Stone Age'?"

Chapter 23

The Oval Room briefing had continued with participants coming and going and new, frightening and sickening reports being delivered by tight-lipped, troubled aids until shortly after three in the morning, the President had called a temporary halt to proceedings.

"Everybody in this room needs to get up to date with their own people. We will reconvene in this place at four-thirty. Uncle Dick and I have to talk to our English guests."

The room cleared quickly, and soon Lyndon Johnson was alone with the man who had been his mentor and friend most of his Senate career.

Sixty-six-year-old Richard Brevard Russell Jr was at once flattered, a little surprised, and somewhat disconcerted that his friend, and now President with whom in recent times he had been a little estranged politically although never personally, had invited him straight into the inner circle of the Administration and started treating him as if he was a fondly, and much revered Vice Presidential calming figure in the White House.

Very few men understood LBJ the way he did; it went unspoken that Russell was standing next to the President in this hour of utmost national calamity not because Johnson had been overcome by some sentimental quirk, but because LBJ needed him. The two men had been drifting apart on issues like Civil Rights but Johnson – after over three years, mostly on the fringes of the Kennedy Administration – badly needed some kind of powerbase within, if not the national polity, then at least the Democratic Party, and bringing a founder and leader of the Conservative Coalition in the House into his first 'kitchen cabinet' was a wise opening gambit of the kind that might actually make it possible for him to continue to govern beyond the immediate crisis.

Johnson, a much taller man than Russell watched the others depart.

He turned to his old friend, his lived-in face craggier and wearier than it had any right to be for a man whose fifty-sixth birthday was not due for the best part of another eight weeks.

"Heck," he muttered, shaking his head. "We've got the fucking Russians on the line all the time; and the British won't pick up the goddamned phone!"

Johnson had taken a call from Canadian Prime Minister Lester 'Mike' Pearson an hour ago.

The other man had congratulated him on becoming President and inquired after the wellbeing of Jack Kennedy; then he had dropped an unexpected bombshell.

The Canadians had been left to their own devices to clean up the mess left by crashed Red Air Force bombers shot down over its territory on the night of the October War. Without the resources or the expertise necessary to survey and clean up the wrecks of at least eight 'nuclear crash sites', huge tracts of the country had been effectively quarantined ever since. Pearson had warned Johnson that if a single Soviet 'atomic bomber' was shot down over Canada, his country would 'pull the switch' on NORAD north of the US-Canadian border.

Curtis LeMay had looked like he was going to blow a gasket when he got the news.

Pearson had also informed Johnson that American aircraft on or suspected to be on 'offensive missions against the British Isles' would be 'liable to be fired upon without prior warning' if they entered Canadian air space.

LeMay had indicated this called for 'positive action'.

'We seem to be already at war with the British,' the President had observed, ignoring the Chairman of the Joint Chiefs of Staff Committee's discomfiture, 'we may be at war with the Soviet Union. I have no intention of going to war with this country's next-door neighbour. Do I make myself clear?'

LeMay's spluttering acknowledgement had been somewhat less than unambiguous.

Right now, there were a dozen foreign Ambassadors knocking on Secretary of State, Bill Fulbright's door. Some, like those of Australia, New Zealand, and South Africa would want to know why US ships and aircraft were killing its citizens. Others would be demanding protection from the re-born aggressive Imperialist Anglo-Saxon freebooters, and the Argentine Ambassador had been sitting on the Secretary of State's doorstep for the last seventy-two hours demanding guarantees that the British would not nuke Buenos Aires!

Lyndon Johnson knew that he had to put all that 'background noise' aside for the moment; the main thing was keeping Americans safe. If he had to go to war to do that, he would but only after he had tried, if not everything else, but as many other things as possible in whatever time was left to him.

Russell sucked his teeth.

The older man was a doyen of the Southern Democrat caucus, a former Governor of Georgia who had sat in the Senate for over thirty years. An arch segregationist he had stood as a staunch New Dealer in the bad old days of the Depression, and never deviated from the view that Government had a duty to intervene when markets failed. In that peculiar Southern tradition, he was in favour of the segregation of the races by dint of colour, and axiomatically, upheld white supremacy; without ever condoning or joining in the 'race baiting' – which he positively loathed - of so many of his Conservative Coalition fellows.

Russell had run for the Democrat Presidential Nomination in 1948 and 1952 but his real stalking ground was the Senate where his lawyer's training and masterful command of the legislative process had made him one of the most formidable members of the House. In his role as Chairman of the Senate Armed Service Committee he had bitterly and very publicly fallen out with the Kennedy Administration over the 'Peace Dividend' cuts which had, as he had predicted 'crippled and denuded our national defences and astonished and appalled our friends and enemies alike'.

Although he was proud of his part filibustering the 1957 Civil Rights Act, Russell was still greatly respected for his earlier chairmanship of the Senate hearings into the sacking of that deeply flawed national icon General Douglas MacArthur. His conduct of that inquiry in the dog days of Harry Truman's ill-starred second term had successfully defused the most explosive elements of a huge political firestorm; and served as an object lesson in setting the rules of engagement for an appropriate relationship between the military and civilian authorities in a democracy. It spoke eloquently to his stature and reputation in the House that his appointment to the Warren Commission on the *Causes and the Conduct of the Cuban Missiles War* – effectively as Earl Warren's deputy - had gone through on a unanimous nod in an otherwise bitterly divided Senate.

Johnson and Russell's friendship dated back to LBJ's arrival in the Senate where, having been advised that 'all senators are *equal*' but that 'Russell was the most *equal*', he had swiftly allied himself to Russell. Nobody doubted that it had been Russell's support that had facilitated Johnson becoming, first Senate Minority Leader in 1953, and then two years later Senate Majority Leader.

"I don't like what I'm hearing coming out of Korea," Russell said sombrely.

Lyndon Johnson shrugged.

'Clashes', mostly isolated cross-border shelling had been reported at the eastern end of the DMZ. Now there were reports of the same kind of thing around Cheorwon on the southern side of the border some fifty miles from the South Korean capital, Seoul. Inevitably, at times like this a US President was reminded that the outskirts of Seoul were only around thirty miles south of the DMZ.

"Just the goddammed so-called People's Army flexing its muscles," LBJ retorted distractedly. "Those boys know what will happen to them if they go too far."

Russell had suffered minor injuries during the Battle of Washington and recently spent spells in hospital with the emphysema-like symptoms of the 'war influenza' which periodically swept New England. A normally well fleshed man he had lost a lot of weight in recent months; a thing Lady Bird Johnson had teased him over, demanding that he dine more regularly with her and LBJ whenever they were 'in town'.

On the subject of Korea, the older man was nowhere near as sanguine as his one-time protégé. Nor, he suspected, was Johnson's Secretary of State. Bill Fulbright had been looking over his shoulder at the Far East ever since the US Seventh Fleet was split in half and the 'war winning' Kitty Hawk part of it was sent to the Persian Gulf.

However, concluding that for the moment LBJ had no intention of focussing on Korea, he changed the subject.

"The papers will be hitting the streets in New York and Boston in two, three hours," Russell remarked glumly. "This will be all over the radio networks by now; it's just that nobody's listening at this time of day. You're going to have to go in front of the cameras..."

"Maybe," Lyndon Johnson conceded. "Maybe, this is not one of those things anybody can get out ahead of? Maybe, that's not the way to go? The American people will never forgive us, well the Administration, for this, whatever we do. Maybe, all we can do is try to stop the bleeding?"

Russell made no attempt to reply immediately.

His one-time protégé was prone to violent mood swings, mostly of the melodramatic, for effect, variety. It was part and parcel of the package that was the whirlwind of political scheming, arm-twisting and persuasion that was Lyndon Baines Johnson. Throughout the second half of the 1950s if something needed to be done LBJ was the man to do it; once he made up his mind he was like a dog with a bone in his teeth. It was the manic side of his personality which had likely induced the heart attack which had left him prematurely aged, and possibly lost him the 1960 Presidential Nomination to the rich kids from Massachusetts (and their daddy's bottomless Chicago war chest).

The one thing Russell knew for a certainty was that if Johnson had been in the hot seat in October 1962 they would all be living in a very different world today!

"Stopping the bleeding would be a good start, wouldn't it?" Johnson asked.

"That would be a good start, Lyndon." Russell grunted a deprecatory laugh. "I suppose I have to call you Mr President now? I sure as Hell ain't going to call you 'sir'!"

Johnson chuckled involuntarily.

Summoning 'Uncle Dick' to the Philadelphia White House had been smartest thing he had done for years.

Forgetting, for a moment, the ignominy of the United States' most powerful concentration of naval power – the Sixth Fleet – being held hostage in a foreign port, what had happened less than two days ago in the Persian Gulf was easily the worst day in the history of the US Navy. The bare – very provisional - statistics were a crushing indictment of the bankruptcy of US post-October War strategy.

Carrier Division Seven had lost three ships and suffered six thousand casualties. Three ships confirmed lost: USS Kitty Hawk [CV-63] - crew approximately 5,600 souls of whom 737 were survivors thus far including 174 seriously injured/wounded; USS Boston [CAG-1] – crew 1,150 souls of whom 24 were survivors including 6 seriously injured/wounded; USS William V. Pratt [DLG-13] – crew 360 souls of whom 207 were survivors including 28 seriously injured/wounded. Other fleet casualties on ships which survived the Second Battle of Kharg Island: USS Albany [CG-10] – 78 dead or missing presumed killed in action and 103 injured/wounded; USS Dewey [DLG-14] – 2 killed in action and 12 injured/wounded; USS Decatur [DD-936] – 4 killed in action and 3 injured/wounded.

It was known that men had also been injured on other ships; when warships manoeuvred at high speed and the air was full of bullets, people got hurt. That was war. However, four major surface units of Carrier Division Seven – the guided missile destroyers Towers (DDG-9) and Lawrence (DDG-4), and the older gunship destroyers John Paul Jones (DD-931) and Du Pont (DD-941) - had escaped either with minor damage which had left their fighting systems unimpaired, or unscathed.

It was the worst day in the history of the US Navy; over six thousand men were dead or missing, over three hundred of the survivors seriously injured or wounded, with the largest surviving ship – the Albany – battling to stay afloat. The whole of the Kitty Hawk's air group was gone, bar half-a-dozen aircraft which had managed to land safely in Kuwait and Saudi Arabia.

The casualties in the Persian Gulf and the 'arrest' of most of the Sixth Fleet at Malta had at a stroke, gutted the Navy. It did not matter that Strategic Air Command was intact, albeit at a fraction of the strength of its pre-October War strength, or that the US currently had eight Polaris boats, and as many as eleven hunter killer nuclear powered submarines on patrol beneath the surface of the oceans of the northern hemisphere; submarines could not take or hold ground.

The President of the United States was the most powerful and the most cursed man on Earth. Deploying SAC's bombers or missiles, or the Navy's submarine-launched ICBMs meant Armageddon and only a madman would pull the trigger...

"We need to start talking to the British," Lyndon Johnson decided abruptly. He turned on his heel. "Let's do this!"

Chapter 24

He heard voices as if they were whispers at the end of a very long tunnel. Syllables, words, sounds that made no particular sense, jumbled in his mind; it was a dream in which everything was painted in different shades of red. He had a fragmentary memory of the world around him disintegrating and of falling, impossibly fast, and then hitting something incredibly hard. Later he had briefly come to coughing fouled sea water, or at least, that was what he thought he remembered. It was hard to trust things that came in and out of focus in his head like the impossibly scrambled Technicolor visions of a fever delirium. For example, he imagined he had been carried – no matter how he attempted to thrash his limbs nothing happened – into a place that reeked of pungent antiseptics, bleach and he was suddenly very cold, he could not breathe...

"Somebody get hold of his arms," a coolly collected, very tired voice demanded. "Do we know anything about him?"

Do we know anything about him?

Panic coursed through his veins.

For a moment he had no idea who he was.

He tried to open his eyes, everything was a pale crimson blur and his face was a sea of pain.

"They thought he was dead so they laid him out on the stern, sir," somebody said.

A woman's voice...

He heard this and inwardly, deep down within his broken body and shocked psyche, he actually...*chuckled.* But the people around him were not to know that.

Lazarus rising...

"How did that happen?"

"It's a mess back there," the target of this question apologised; a man this time, his tone gruffly respectful. "Anyways, somebody saw him move, well twitch; that's why we brought him straight to the front of the queue, sir."

"Okay, okay," the man who was obviously in charge relented. "Tell your men they did the right thing, Chief," he added. "We'll take it from here."

He felt himself lifted, firmly but gently and laid down again on something a lot softer and yielding than whatever he had been lying on until then.

"Eye movement, sir."

Yes, definitely a woman's voice.

"I see it. Get a saline line into him while we get to work."

His arm was grasped, there was a stabbing finger of fire in his left hand, momentarily. Mentally, he flinched but his limbs were limp like a doll's.

"What do we think happened to this man, sir?"

The woman's voice again.

American?

Perhaps, she was the one who was carefully stroking, soothing his burning face. No, not stroking, cleaning...

"I haven't seen too many cases," the man standing over him speculated.

He could imagine the other man's brow knitting in concentration as he considered his reply.

"But I'd say this man survived a high-speed ejection. No dog tags or anything indicating this man's blood type?"

"No, sir. I'm on that now."

More pricks in *his* arm.

He had become like a witness, listening, feeling, experiencing his helplessness from somewhere inside of himself; yet detached from and oddly, disinterested in what was happening to him.

"The deck crew must have cut off what was left of his flight suit when they were trying to revive him," the woman suggested, unconvinced. "I've read about high speed ejection trauma..."

"The literature is thin because below five thousand feet most of them result in the death of the pilot," the man retorted, a little distractedly. "Apart from the normal compression injuries to the spine caused by the explosive exit from the aircraft the body is immediately subjected to very high g-forces and a – normally – catastrophic pressure differential. That's why hardly anybody survives a supersonic or near supersonic ejection. Basically, at those speeds ejecting from an aircraft is like being fired out of a gun into the supersonic airstream."

That did not sound good...

"I'd say this man still had his helmet on when he ejected."

"Why do you say that, sir?"

"From the look of him the *pressure shock* instantaneously engorged and ruptured all the blood vessels in his face, and eyes," he paused, "we'll check that in a minute, the event may have caused significant cranial trauma. If he hadn't still had his flying helmet on, his head would probably have exploded."

That sounded really bad...

The swishing overhead fans wafted air over *his* naked torso as several pairs of hands worked on him. A soft pillow was positioned under his head while the swabbing and probing continued unabated.

"Can you hear us, buddy?" A soft, lilting Southern drawl asked, virtually in *his* left ear.

He tried to speak, could not open his mouth. His face was not working, frozen, numb.

Try to move something, man!

"His fingers moved!"

"Yeah, I saw that," confirmed the man who seemed to be in command.

He was aware of a face close to his.

"You're going to be okay," a woman cooed. "You're safe now."

"I think his jaw's bust," another voice reported.

A mask had been eased over *his* face.

Oxygen...

His head cleared; his chest hurt a little less.

And then *he* remembered who *he* was; except that was impossible.

He had specifically ordered *The Angry Widow's* ground crew to de-activate – or remove, he could not recollect which – the explosive charges from his and his co-pilot's seats six hours before take-off...

Chapter 25

Captain Frank Maltravers waved for his senior officers to take seats where they could in his stateroom deep beneath the bridge. The latest updates from the Persian Gulf, Mediterranean Fleet HQ in Malta and a personal signal from the First Sea Lord had come in as the two Scimitars returned from chasing away his small flotilla's unwanted high-altitude voyeur.

From the spy plane's fleetness of foot; the evidence that it had screamed away to the north in level flight rather than climbing to still more rarefied heights, it seemed as if it had been a Martin B57, most likely the 'E' *big wing* variant of the English Electric Canberra twin-engine jet bomber. A U-2 could soar to seventy thousand feet but there was no way it could show a clean pair of heels to two interceptors capable of breaking the sound barrier in a shallow dive.

Eagle had subsequently launched two Sea Vixens to loiter astern of the squadron as it forged west at twenty-nine knots. Ideally, one of the carrier's Fairey Gannets would also have been in the air at all times, its onboard radar scanning far beyond the horizon but all three aircraft had countless time-expired components and Maltravers had decreed that they would be 'saved for when we need them most'. In this instance, that was going to be to scout ahead 'over the horizon' as the squadron approached Malta.

The Captain of the Eagle was not one of those men who invariably kept his cards close to his chest. Several of his most experienced officers had been with him on the Ark Royal throughout the homeward phase of Operation Manna; they had been through a lot together and basically, he preferred for everybody to 'be in the know' as much as was possible unless there were over-riding operational and security considerations. Today, there were no such considerations. They were up against it and they were all in it together, a band of brothers.

"I'll keep this as short and as sweet as possible, gentlemen," he prefaced as two stewards brought round trays bearing mugs of tea. "I don't know what the situation will be when we get within flying-off range of Malta. However, it is quite likely we will be steaming straight into a war zone; and that is what we must be prepared for."

This opinion was greeted with nods so apparently sanguine that a third party witnessing the gathering without knowing any of the personalities involved, or the collective shared experience of the group in the last twenty months, might have been horrified.

Maltravers had asked his secretary, a middle-aged lieutenant with whom he had served in the Pacific in 1945, recalled from the reserve shortly before he took command of Eagle, to circulate the sheaf of message 'flimsies' which had come through since the squadron departed Port Said.

Nevertheless, he briefly summarised the picture they painted.

"It seems as if Tiger and the ships that steamed up the Shatt-al-Arab to support General Carver's land forces have been lost or disabled in the river with heavy loss of life. That means we have no major surface units left in the Persian Gulf. Apparently, HMAS Voyager, which had a fouled port shaft and reduction gear problems sufficient to put her in dry dock at Aden, is to be sent back to the Gulf soonest, but otherwise, apart from the Sydney and the Triumph," two old deactivated aircraft carriers operating as a fast transport and a heavy repair ship respectively, "all we've got in theatre are a few minesweepers and patrol craft. What success our forces have had on land in Iraq and Iran may, therefore, be temporary. Thanks to the Yanks everything we have achieved in the region may now be for nothing."

Frank Maltravers was not the man to worry about a little thing like that. He sniffed, paused to whet his whistle with a sip of scalding hot, moderately vile black tea.

"There is nothing we can do about that!"

He moved on.

"Likewise, we don't have an anti-submarine escort with us and I can't afford to have our Gannets throwing away all our precious sonar buoys in the water on the way to Valletta. We'll let HQ in Malta worry about 'the submarine menace'."

His guffaw was echoed around the windowless stateroom.

Basically, if the US Navy wanted to carry on with the war that was fine by him; every man in this room had known somebody, or many men who were now most likely dead in the two battles in the Persian Gulf. Nobody was mincing their words. What had happened to the Centaur and her escorts was not war, it was plain simple *murder* and right-thinking men could not let that stand. There was a price to pay for that sort of thing; sinking the Kitty Hawk and a couple of her accomplices was a good start; but if the US Navy believed that was an end of the matter, it had another thing coming to it!

For example, now that he had had a little time to think about it there was actually quite a lot the C-in-C in Malta could do about the US Navy's freelancing SSNs in the Eastern Mediterranean. He could organise a picket line of diesel-electric submarines around the Maltese Archipelago, put listening buoys in the water and mount continuous airborne patrols from RAF Luqa. If things came to it he could start taking hostages...

No, that was just...un-British.

Nobody in Malta was going to go down that road...

"My intention is to steam as hard as Eagle will steam," Maltravers asserted, putting his last, subversive thought aside, "and to sit twenty miles off the Grand Harbour breakwater."

He let this sink in.

"We will give the authorities on Malta any or all support required. If necessary I will order our aircraft to sink every US Navy ship in sight. If necessary," he hesitated for the merest fraction of a second, "we will deploy *Arc Light*."

Before departing Malta ten days ago Eagle had taken onboard three 'special munitions' ferried to her slung in nets beneath her Westland Wessex's from the bomb dump at RAF Luqa. Physics technical officers had assembled the weapons – four hundred kiloton Green Grass all-British bombs - after the ship had cleared Valletta. Two of Eagle's No. 892 Naval Air Squadron Sea Vixens were currently unavailable for operations because they were being modified to carry these weapons. Similar conversions had already been completed on two of No. 805 Squadron's Buccaneers.

"On a more mundane note," Eagle's commanding officer went on, "with the bulk of the Mediterranean Fleet somewhat preoccupied watching over the *prizes* at Valletta, one or two subs apart and a couple of ships in transit, *we* are all that is flying the Royal Navy's flag in the Med. If, as we surmised after the Battle of Malta three months ago the Russians held back surface units and submarines for opportunistic commerce raiding and other nefarious purposes, this is probably when they will make their move. Obviously, once we're on station off Malta we can do something about policing the seas around those parts but even so, our outposts on Pantelleria, Linosa, Lampedusa and various other islets are going to be on their own until normal service resumes."

Behind his mask of jovial sangfroid Frank Maltravers wanted to spit. All the blood and treasure which had been expended regaining the freedom of navigation from one end of the Mediterranean to the other looked like being wasted. Enemies in Spain, South France, Corsica, Sardinia, mainland Italy, in the Aegean and Turkey would surely catch the taint of blood in the water; whatever happened in the next hours and days, the Royal Navy would inevitably be weakened still further and be even less capable of holding the line...

The bloody Yanks...

The report from Malta spoke of all the 'bigger prizes' being 'marked' by a submarine, frigate or destroyer, with torpedo tubes primed; of batteries of anti-aircraft guns trained on American ships in the Grand Harbour, and the crews of the seized ships mustered on deck in plain sight.

It was a nightmare, a powder keg which might be ignited by a single misstep, a single small mistake or miscalculation.

Perhaps, the Big E's arrival off the Grand Harbour breakwater might concentrate minds.

Either that or it would start World War IV...

Chapter 26

11:15 Hours (Local) – 03:15 in Philadelphia
Field Headquarters, 4th Armoured Regiment, Abadan Island

Lieutenant-General Michael Power Carver had sent out a search party for a translator soon after the Red Army in Basra had started broadcasting. Normally, he would have had several Russian-speakers on his staff but 'mopping' up the Soviet forces which had got across the Karun River before the counter-attack north-east of Khorramshahr, had been a bloody and costly, all hands to the pump sort of business. His HQ at RAF Abadan had nearly been over run at one stage, and even now sporadic bursts of gunfire in the distance told of desperate, ongoing actions as the last pockets of enemy resistance were snuffed out.

"4th Armoured," Carver informed the two somewhat dusty and ragged new arrivals in the command tent, "have a couple of communications wagons in good working order; hence my transfer up here from the airfield. We think the Russians may want to talk about an armistice or ceasefire but we've ignored their blandishments thus far. Tell me what's going on north of the Karun River?"

Frank Waters had dumped himself in a canvass chair before he fell over. One of the C-in-C's aides pressed a lukewarm mug of something muddy that stank of brandy into his trembling hands. He drank deep and felt the healing 'medicine' scorch his insides.

Major Julian Calder presented a rather more soldierly figure although he was filthy from the desert and his camouflage fatigues were splashed with blood. He and Frank Waters had transported a couple of badly wounded gunners back to the nearest field dressing station on their return to report to Carver. One of them had thrashed about a bit, poor chap, and they had had to restrain him for his own good.

The SAS man glanced at Frank Waters, who waved for him to carry on while he regained his strength and stepped over to the torn map stretched across a trestle table. Despite the pall of smoke hanging over the battlefield the burning summer sun had turned the tent – more an awning stretched between two trucks – into an airless oven.

Calder was a tall, patrician man – a less scholarly, younger version of the C-in-C - with clear blue eyes and a manner that strangers often misinterpreted as haughty. Men who got to know him or were fortunate enough to soldier with him for any length of time soon saw past that apparent haughtiness. He delivered his report concisely, without embellishment and waited respectfully for his superior to question him further.

Michael Carver looked to Frank Waters, then to Calder again.

"Do we know what happened to the survivors of the Tiger and the Anzac?"

"They piled onto rafts and a gaggle of boats that came down from Basra around sunrise, and let the current carry them down river, sir," Calder replied. "I have no numbers and the information I have comes from third parties. Shortly thereafter, demolition charges were seen to detonate on board both ships; presumably, destroying equipment that could not be allowed to fall into enemy hands. The survivors on those ships could have had no idea that the Soviet armoured push had been so comprehensively repulsed overnight."

Carver had refrained from commenting when the younger officer had told him that their Iranian allies were 'not taking prisoners'.

Eventually, Frank Waters picked himself out of his chair and joined the other two men at the map table.

"What's the news from the west, sir?"

Carver brightened a fraction, quirked a wan half-smile and jabbed a finger at the small port settlement of Umm Qasr just above the border with the Emirate of Kuwait on the other side of the Faw Peninsula.

Concisely, he explained what he knew.

The Centurions of Major General Thomas Daly's hastily thrown together Anzac – Australian and New Zealand, stiffened with cadres of the 4th Tanks – brigade, supported by several troops of Saudi Arabian M-48s had sliced through the Red Army's ramshackle perimeter east of the port and enveloped the exhausted forward echelons of as many as three Red Army divisions, in the process cutting the road and rail links connecting Umm Qasr to Basra.

Privately, Carver had hoped that this operation would be no more than a diversion; a follow up spoiling attack in the wake of the one-off bombing of the enemy's most southerly positions. He had *hoped* to delay the Soviet's inevitable advance into the oilfields of Kuwait. Instead, Tom Daly's armour had rolled straight over several Red Army formations pulverised by the previous night's bombing and, with minimal casualties, captured hundreds of square miles of territory and thus far, at least ten and perhaps as many as twenty thousand prisoners.

"I should imagine the Soviets still don't know what hit them south of Basra," he concluded drily.

"They certainly don't know what hit them at Khorramshahr, sir!" Julian Calder observed.

Michael Carver was not overly confident about that. By now the men in the tanks and vehicles of every description that were streaming back north along the eastern bank of the Shatt-al-Arab ought to have painted a pretty definitive picture for the benefit of whoever was in command of the Red Army in Basra. Moreover, no matter how many tanks and soldiers he had captured, killed or routed Carver had no illusions about one thing; he was still heavily outnumbered and outgunned. Tom Daly's marvellous Anzacs and his friend Hasan al-Mamaleki's 3rd Imperial Iranian Armoured Division currently held the field but both would be low on fuel and ammunition by now, and each was as over-stretched and vulnerable to a concerted armoured counter attack as the other. Daly's Anzacs and Hasan's Iranians were all he had, there were no reserves, and the logistics locker was empty; already the offensive operations of each force, no matter how outrageously successful they had been, were winding down.

On the Shatt-al-Arab and at sea the ABNZ Persian Gulf Squadron had been wiped out bar a handful of coastal minesweepers; the Americans, whatever their losses in the recent battles still actually commanded the waters of the Persian Gulf and therefore his exposed – positively naked – southern coastal flank.

Everybody had pretty much fought each other to a standstill. That was what happened in war. Every battle, each campaign had its own natural, profoundly bloody rhythm and presently a brief hiatus was settling over the vast theatre of death.

"There's some talk about the Americans wanting the Soviets to withdraw north of the 32nd parallel," he explained, thinking aloud.

Frank Waters grunted his disdain.

"If they agree to that they might as well pack up and go home," he observed disgustedly, recognising it as a sure-fire recipe for even more bloodshed.

"Quite."

"What does Oxford say about that, sir?" Julian Calder inquired.

"I have absolutely no idea," the C-in-C replied, standing tall and sniffing the air. "All the lines on the airfield are down. My people are trying to raise one of our ships in the Gulf, thus far without success."

He did not dwell on this misfortune.

The British Army expected its officers to look to their front, to confront what was there, and to carry on carrying on and that was exactly what he planned to do.

He looked to the battered and bloodied former SAS man.

"In the meantime, I need you to get on the radio and talk to whoever's trying to attract out attention in Basra, Frank."

Chapter 27

Peter and Marija had been 'parked' in an ante room by the President's wife who had been unable, or possibly unwilling, to answer the questions they had fired at her about the fate of their friends at the Wister Park Embassy.

After a few minutes they had been joined by a man in his forties who introduced himself as: 'Walter Jenkins. I'm one of the President's aides.' The newcomer had viewed the young people with what seemed like transparently gentle and very real sympathy. 'This must be as rough for you as it is for us?'

When the President had appeared a few minutes later, 'Walter' had stepped respectfully into the background.

Peter and Marija had not known what to think. Although many family members and a number of Embassy staff deemed inessential had been sent to Canada after the car bombing of the Wister Park compound in June, there had still been between thirty and forty people remaining at the time 'the Christopher Party' had departed on its roundabout route by road and rail to California four weeks ago.

Other junior Embassy staff had transferred to the old United Kingdom UN Delegation building in New York or gone up to Ottawa in the intervening weeks. However, the Ambassador, Lord Franks and his wife, the Chargé d'affaires, Sir Patrick Dean, and about twenty secretaries, attaches and liaison officers had stayed on. As had Rachel Piotrowska's *Intelligence Section*, and the cipher clerks manning the Embassy's communications equipment. There had also been a small detachment of 'security staff' under the command of a Captain of the Blues and Royals.

Peter Christopher had met Lyndon Johnson several times, but always when he was playing the 'quiet man' supporting role to the President; or rather, the former apparently indisposed incumbent, John Fitzgerald Kennedy.

He had never been introduced to the older, shorter, stockier man who entered the room at the President's shoulder, whom he knew to be Senator Richard Russell, Chairman of the Senate Committee on the Armed Services.

Peter Christopher looked to his wife.

Marija had dried up her tears for the moment, in many ways she was stronger than him; they had both lost too many people. She had lost her brother, Samuel, and her friend and mentor Margot Seiffert, murdered during the battle of Malta; he had lost his father in that fight, and best friend in Christendom. Miles Weiss, to his wounds shortly afterwards, and so very, very many of his brave Talaveras...

Now more of their friends were most likely dead or injured at the Wister Park compound, betrayed yet again by Uncle Sam!

"Sorry to keep you kids waiting," the President began, exuding a fatherly stern bonhomie that cut very little ice with Marija and none at all with her husband. "A lot's been going on."

Marija made a grab for Peter's left hand. She had *never* seen her husband so livid, literally trembling, shaking with rage, as he had been when Lady Bird Johnson had haltingly broken the news about 'the attack' on the Embassy. He was not just angry, he was *insulted*. It was as if the news had touched a raw, unhealed nerve. It was as if somebody had spat on the on the grave of his father or besmirched the sacred memory of his dead Talaveras.

Peter shook the President's proffered hand, did not react at all as the President covered his right hand with his own in a brief two-handed grip. The two men locked eyes.

The craggy Texan was, by a fraction, the taller of the two men. Renowned for staring down opponents and cowing men by towering over them until they succumbed to his sheer force of personality, he wasted none of the famous 'LBJ treatment' on the young naval officer standing before him.

He released Peter's hand and introduced Russell.

Marija shook hands, wordlessly.

The President made eye contact again with Peter Christopher and flicked a glance at his wife. He opened his mouth to speak.

"With respect, sir," Peter said abruptly, as urbanely as any mortal man could speaking through very nearly clenched teeth, "neither I, nor my wife, are 'kids', and I would be obliged if you would at least observe the common courtesies of diplomacy and address us with the respect we are due, and have more than earned in the last months at the cost of the blood of more of our friends than you, over here in your undamaged cities filled with well-fed citizens, can *ever* imagine. Sir!"

Senator Russell stiffened with offence.

Lyndon Johnson carried on eyeing the younger man with inscrutable eyes.

Neither American spoke.

"You may address me," Peter went on, aware that his wife was squeezing his left hand, digging her nails into his palm in a vain attempt to stop him ruining...*everything*. "As *Sir Peter*, or as *Captain Christopher*. You will kindly address my wife as *Lady Marija*." He had forgotten to breathe, finally he gasped: "Or our business today, is concluded, sir!"

This bounced off the lined visage of the President. He raised an eyebrow. He sighed. Picking a fight with a man was easy; picking the right time to pick that fight...well, that was another thing.

"Is it true you disobeyed a direct order from you father to pick a fight with those big Soviet ships back in April?" Johnson asked, with a genuine curiosity in a tone which suggested he had taken no lasting offence to what had just been said to him.

"No, sir," Peter replied, flatly. "I was ammunitioning ship in the Grand Harbour opposite Valletta at the time. My father ordered me to cut Talavera's lines and to get out to sea."

The two men eyed each other, neither knowing whose move it was next.

Marija coughed, forced a smile.

"Everybody thinks I'm the stubborn one," she declared, a little coyly. "But I'm not. Peter's father ordered him to take his ship out to sea." She shrugged, apologetically. "Which was where the big ships were. I did not know Peter's father as well as I would have liked to have got to know him, he was a remarkable man, I think. I believe he knew exactly what Peter would do that day whatever he ordered him to do. We are not 'kids', Mr Johnson. Nor are we fools; please do not treat us as children."

Lyndon Johnson's whole career had been an exercise in 'doing what a man needs to do to get the job done' and this little standoff – which he ought to have seen coming and avoided – was an object lesson in how his country had blundered into so many crises in the last couple of years. The one thing you never did was let your pride or your dignity get in the way of 'getting the job done'.

"I stand corrected, Lady Marija," he grinned.

The atmosphere warmed by a degree or so. The two American old-stagers detected the subtle change; understood immediately that if they were to deal – in any meaningful way – with the angry young Englishman before them they were going to have to bring his almond–eyed princess along with them on the journey.

Both men caught themselves wondering, idly, if she, Lady Marija, had made sure that she was here precisely because she had worked that out for herself. No, that was ridiculous, she looked so...down home and well, goddammit...*cute.*

Peter Christopher ignored the President and his oldest political ally for a moment to focus on his wife. She in her turn, relaxed the hurtful pressure of her finger nails on the palm of his left hand, satisfied that he had regained control of his emotions. Only just but that was sufficient for the moment.

She sniffled, wanting to cry again.

"Our friends would want us to help these gentlemen," she said simply. "If we can. That is our duty, husband."

Peter heard this, took it to heart over the following seconds.

"Yes," he muttered hoarsely. Oblivious to the widening eyes of the two powerful men watching he nodded to himself and bowed his head to plant a kiss in his wife's hair. Right then there was probably nothing in the World capable of calming his soul so effectively, so profoundly as the scent of Marija's hair. He took a deep breath, gently disengaged his hand from hers and turned to face President Johnson and Senator Russell.

He met Lyndon Johnson's stare.

"You have us at a disadvantage, sir," he stated with quiet purpose. "If it is your intention to stop the blood-letting, before *we* can be of assistance *we* need to know what is going on."

Chapter 28

A Berkeley PD cruiser had rolled past the house twice in the last hour spinning its blue lights. It was unnaturally quiet other than the background, barely audible whispering and clicking of Cicadas and other insects in the darkness of the sultry night.

CITIZENS ARE ADVISED THAT A SUNSET TO SUNRISE CURFEW HAS BEEN DECLARED STATE-WIDE BY THE GOVERNOR...

Sweltering in the stifling humidity which had worsened throughout the evening Nathan Zabriski had opened all the windows hoping a fluky breeze off the mountains or rolling down from Strawberry Canyon would eventually alleviate the worst of the evening heat.

People said that these 'pressure cooker' nights had been common last summer across the Bay Area. There was speculation that back in October 1962 the smoke from the burning cities and the huge forest fires that must have raged in the Soviet Union, China and Europe, might have in some way 'blocked' the Sun's rays so significantly to have changed the Earth's winds, and therefore weather patterns randomly causing 'freak' unseasonal icing and warming conditions across the globe. Some said there had been a 'nuclear' winter across Europe in the months after the October War; although strangely, the winter gone by had been relatively mild in North America in comparison with those Nathan remembered in the 1950s.

The truth was nobody knew if the weather was 'wrong', or why the Bay Area was being afflicted with 'pressure cooker' nights like this that suddenly developed, unpredicted and steamily reminiscent of the most enervating of tropical nights; more like Manila or Guam than anything people who had lived their whole lives in the Bay Area – renowned for its mists and temperate summers – had always taken for granted.

IF THE FALLOUT ALARM SOUNDS ALL DOORS AND WINDOWS SHOULD BE SHUT AND CITIZENS MUST RETREAT TO THE SAFE AREA OF THEIR DWELLINGS...

"Yeah, sure," Nathan groaned.

Caroline Konstantis sat opposite him at the rickety kitchen table. Although she was wearing a thin white slip and nothing else, perspiration constantly formed on her brow.

The man was in his skivvies, dripping with sweat.

In retrospect they ought not to have got even more hot and bothered having sex but they had awakened in the warm darkness feeling horny and things had...just happened. Now they were red-faced feeling like the blood in their veins was several degrees too hot.

The tap water tasted a little metallic. All the houses in this part of town had been thrown up in wartime, and the contractors had not worried overly about the quality of the materials employed to construct the water supply to the area, or the plumbing in the buildings along this stretch of Hearst Avenue. Although the man and the woman had re-hydrated somewhat the heat seemed ever more oppressive.

The radio buzzed in the corner; the announcer's words periodically mashed to gibberish by the static that invariably accompanied the atmospheric conditions responsible for these extreme nocturnal heat waves.

Nathan had eventually tuned into KMPX, the FM station with the most powerful signal in the Bay Area. The station normally put out country and middle of the road numbers. KMPX's studios were in downtown San Francisco, its broadcasting beacon high on the Marin Headland above Sausalito.

KMPX was still playing its standard output, interrupted at regular intervals by a drawling California State National Guard spokesman issuing punchy bulletins and stern exhortations to observe the 'civil defence measures' ordered by the Governor.

Anybody who disregarded the curfew was liable to be shot.

Looters would be shot...

A new announcer came over the airwaves.

"...the Office of the Governor of California has authorised the following update to be broadcast," the stentorian tones of what sounded like a middle-aged man who had not had enough sleep in the last forty-eight hours warned his listeners. *"First, news from the Persian Gulf and the Mediterranean Sea."*

Caroline momentarily forgot the hair plastered over her face, worried a little less about what a sight for sore eyes she must present to the young man sitting across the table from her. She had never been any kind of seductress, no movie star lookalike, plain. Years ago, she had had a sparkiness that occasionally interested a man; nothing very obvious. Right now, she was feeling her age, sweaty, bedraggled and listening to the radio knowing that she probably looked very careworn.

"On the direction of the Governor of California acting as the Chairman of the Confederation of West Coast States I am able to report the following account of events in the Mediterranean and the Middle East. This report has been embargoed by the Administration in the Philadelphia but the Council of the Governors of the West Coast believe that their citizens have a right to know why the nation is again at war..."

Nathan reached out for the woman's hand.

"Two days ago, units of the USS Kitty Hawk battle group – Carrier Division Seven of the US Seventh Fleet – operating in the northern Persian Gulf engaged and sank the British aircraft carrier HMS Centaur, and the frigates HMS Palliser and HMS Hardy, and the New Zealand frigate HMNZS Otago. British and Commonwealth sources state unequivocally that aircraft flying off the Kitty Hawk and her escorting vessels attacked the much weaker British and New Zealand Squadron without warning. These sources add that the Centaur, a ship approximately one quarter to one third of the size of the Kitty Hawk

which had not been modernised since World War II, presented no significant threat to the Kitty Hawk or her escorts."

Caroline realised her lower jaw was hanging slack.

Nathan was no less pole-axed.

"That's," he mouthed.

"Insane," she suggested, her voice faraway.

"In response to this attack on its naval forces in the Persian Gulf the British authorities retaliated by 'arresting' all ships, aircraft and men of the US Sixth Fleet based at Malta. At that time the British demanded the surrender of US Navy surface ships and submarines at sea in the Mediterranean Sea and instituted a blockade of the Straits of Gibraltar. One ship, the USS Berkeley tested the blockade and was permitted to steam into the Atlantic unmolested. However, the British have subsequently made it clear that the Berkeley was permitted to depart because of quote 'special circumstances'. Specifically, the Berkeley was the ship that came to the aid of HMS Talavera as she sank after the Battle of Malta in early April. Although the Commander of Sixth Fleet, Admiral Clarey, has thus far complied with British demands the situation at Malta remains tense. All major US warships are currently under the guns or threatened by the torpedo tubes of British ships."

The tone of the announcer warned that the best – or perhaps, the unthinkable worst – was yet to come. Having served the *hors d'oeuvre* in a staid monotone, splinters of emotion – confusion and disbelief mostly – signalled the conclusion of the appetizer and the clearing of the table so that the main business of the report could be served.

"Approximately around sunset – Persian Gulf time – on the 3rd of July, Carrier Division Seven was attacked by RAF V-Bombers, Canberra medium bombers, and a quote 'swarm' of jet fighters and fighter-bombers, and propeller-driven torpedo bombers. Immediately prior to this attack the British detonated two, Hiroshima-sized atomic bombs some ten to fifteen miles distant from the Kitty Hawk. The main attack on Carrier Division Seven was carried out in the confusion following these massive explosions, taking advantage of the damage they would have caused to the electronic equipment and systems onboard the US Navy ships."

Nathan thought his head was going to implode.

The Brits had done it!

They had pulled a move straight out of a pre-war war game 'book' and run with it; the Navy must have seen that one coming...

"The USS Kitty Hawk, having apparently been damaged by a single torpedo strike in the action the previous day was targeted by and brought to a dead stop in the water by enemy torpedo bombers. The flagship of Carrier Division Seven was seen to be struck by several large bombs and sank after a British V-Bomber crashed into her flight deck amidships causing a massive internal explosion which broke her back..."

No, the Navy had not seen it coming...

"It is my sad duty to report that the heavy cruiser USS Boston, and the guided missile frigate USS William V. Pratt are also reported as lost.

The missile cruiser USS Albany is damaged but afloat and at this time we believe that search and rescue operations are still ongoing in the Persian Gulf. Preliminary, and of necessity, very provisional casualty estimates are that as many as six thousand US Navy personnel may have died in the attack on Carrier Division Seven."

The solemn voice paused.

Presumably to spit his disgust and to kick something around the studio, Nathan speculated.

He looked to the suddenly pale, frightened woman across the table whose hand he was clasping as if he was a drowning man about to slip beneath the waves for a third time.

The US Navy had gone into somebody else's waters, picked a one-sided fight with *the wrong* people and then been caught with its thumb up its arse when the British hit back not just in one sea but two.

The Sixth Fleet was in jail and Carrier Division Severn no longer existed.

"This is beyond insane," the woman muttered, swallowing hard in her angst.

"Meanwhile, on land in southern Iraq and around the British fortress of Abadan Island, Defence Department and CIA sources indicate that the Soviet invasion forces have suffered major reverses at the hands of the British, Australian, Iranian and Saudi Arabian defenders. The Red Army has been driven back from the northern Kuwaiti border and the port city of Umm Qasr; and attacks on the Abadan garrison have also been beaten back. Soviet tank losses are said to be 'very heavy'. However, there are unconfirmed reports that all five ships of the Australian, British and New Zealand Persian Gulf Squadron which operated in the Shatt-al-Arab waterway south of Basra during the battles of the last forty-eight hours have been sunk or put out of action..."

Nathan's mind was racing.

The Brits and their allies had crippled the entire US Navy and driven off two Soviet tank armies half-a-world away from their home bases; while *his* government had done everything in its power to undermine the struggles and the sacrifice of the rest of the *Free World* to hold back the tide of Marxist-Leninist aggression!

What the fuck was going on?

"It's like a bad dream," Caroline observed, punch drunk now.

"It is believed that President Johnson has been in conference with his senior advisors since he was sworn in just before midnight, Philadelphia time."

"In conference!" The woman groaned scornfully.

"A spokesman for the Kennedy family told ABC that shortly before he was taken ill President Kennedy had had an acrimonious transatlantic conversation with British Premier Margaret Thatcher whose tone was described as being provocative, intransigent and threatening. The standoff between Army and Marine Corps units and the insurgents inside the British Embassy compound in Wister Park continues. We know no more because the Army and the Philadelphia

PD have declared a complete news blackout until the siege is over."

The concluding sentences of the announcement were something of an anti-climax.

"The Australian, New Zealand and South African governments have broken off diplomatic relations with the United States and announced the unilateral seizure of all US shipping in their home ports. The Canadian government has issued a statement condemning US aggression but stopped short, of breaking off diplomatic relations at this time. However, in the event of an outbreak of hostilities involving the territory of the British Isles, Canadian Premier Lester Pearson has issued the following communiqué. 'US Aircraft and missiles overflying Canadian sovereign territory targeting the British Isles will be regarded as an act of war against Canada. In the event of any hostile action against or effecting the civilian population of the British Isles all military co-operation with the United States will be terminated and the Canadian-US border will be indefinitely closed to US citizens, produce and manufactures.' That is all. I will hand you back to..."

The air – at a frequency of 106.9 megahertz – was handed over to Hank Williams. The strains of *I'm So Lonesome I Could Cry*, by any standard a bizarre thing to play at a time like this, trickled from the speaker.

Outside the amplified Berkeley PD warning seeped into the kitchen.

CITIZENS ARE ADVISED THAT A SUNSET TO SUNRISE CURFEW HAS BEEN DECLARED STATE-WIDE BY THE GOVERNOR...

Chapter 29

Fifty-year-old Major General Thomas Daly gratefully drained the canteen of brackish water offered to him by the nearest of the grinning, grime-streaked tankers standing around the troop of Mark I Centurions blocking the Basra-Umm Qasr Road.

"Right, somebody give me a bunk up," Daly commanded and willing hands propelled him onto the stingingly hot chassis of the nearest armoured beast.

The paint at the business end of the monster's 84-millimetre rifle had flaked off, the bare metal was blackened, and there was a foot-long gouge in the cupola plating of the top of the turret where a Soviet projectile had glanced off into thin air. In a moment Daly was standing on the turret looking north east into the suburbs of Zubayr. He was handed a pair of binoculars, and unhurriedly studied the ground between where he had halted his Anzac spearhead and the town barring the road north east to Basra.

There were scattered fires burning, and smoke mingling with the scorching mid-day heat haze. He had ordered his artillery to drop a 'shell or two' onto the road into the town 'every five minutes'; just to keep the enemy's head down.

He lowered his glasses, grinned down at the dusty faces looking up at him. Beyond them the ground was littered with the abandoned weaponry of Soviet infantrymen whom, already fleeing in retreat, had meekly surrendered to his Anzacs virtually without a whimper once they realised they were surrounded. Faced with the option of fleeing into the marshes and braving the tender mercies of the Marsh Arabs, or trying to escape, waterless, into the western deserts in daytime temperatures of one hundred and twenty to one hundred and thirty degrees Fahrenheit, already hungry, and terrified of renewed bombing, the Russians had thrown down their arms and marched back down the road towards Umm Qasr in their hundreds, and then their thousands escorted by a handful of allied infantrymen.

What Michael Carver had described to Tom Daley as a desperate, last gasp spoiling attack had turned into the sort of adventure that would be written into staff college manuals for the next hundred years under the heading *'classic armoured envelopments of an emplaced superior enemy force'*; and nobody, absolutely nobody, was more astonished about the incredible victory his men had achieved than Tom Daly.

For all that in the last couple of days he had pulled off a masterpiece of armoured manoeuvre that Erwin Rommel would have been proud of, he was an unlikely tank commander.

Daly had not sought out, nor anticipated his posting to the Gulf. In fact, he had honestly believed his fighting days were over after

Korea. A native of Ballarat in Victoria and student of the Duntroon Royal Military College in the Australian Capital Territories, prior to being commissioned into the Light Horse Regiment, back in the thirties he had served in the British Army – literally winning his spurs - on the North West Frontier in India. His career in Hitler's war had been crowded and varied; after a spell as Brigade Major of the 18th Brigade at Tobruk he had moved on to the staff school at Haifa in Palestine, preparatory to transferring to the Far East to join the 5th Division in New Guinea as Senior Staff Officer. He had finished World War II commanding the 2/10th Battalion in the invasion of Balikpapan in Borneo, winning a Distinguished Service Order in the process.

Post-war Daly had attended the Joint Services Staff College in the United Kingdom, where he had met and married his wife, Heather, before returning to Australia. Professionally, up until now he had regarded the time he had spent in Korea in 1952-53 as the crowning heights of his career; during the course of which he had been given command of the 28th Commonwealth Brigade, the first Australian to command a combined Australian-British infantry formation in that conflict.

All that 'excitement' had seemed an awfully long time ago and an unbroken succession of relatively tame, sedentary staff jobs in the intervening decade had hardly been ideal preparation to lead his under-strength Anzac, Saudi and British armoured brigade – hardly a couple of regiments strong – against the spearhead formations of what was probably the finest tank army on the planet.

He knew had been lucky.

Bloody lucky!

His part of Operation Lightfoot was supposed to be limited to punching a hole in the 3rd Caucasian Tank Army's front west of Umm Qasr – hopefully isolating the advanced echelons of the exhausted and depleted 10th Guards Tank Division on his left. The plan had been to take and hold a desert line northwest of Umm Qasr threatening the enemy's communications with Basra, and to invite the Red Army to drive onto his artillery and hull-down armour, thereupon basically, to wait and see what happened next.

His primary objective had been a modest one, simply to delay the preparations for Soviet offensive operations against Kuwait; yet to his surprise – actually, astonishment - the enemy had melted away before his armour, and after he had picked his jaw off the floor, he had decided to push on up the Basra Road. Right now, it was all he could do to stop himself investing Zubayr and moving up to the outskirts of the city of Basra beyond it.

Daly was sorely tempted to push on right now.

The trouble was he had no real feel for what lay in front of him. Had the Russians decided to make a stand at Zubayr or had they just kept on running all the way back to Basra?

Hopefully, the SAS raiding and reconnaissance parties roving ahead of his spearhead would give him an answer to that, sooner or later. In the meantime, he had no option but to call a halt while ammunition was brought forward and fuel bowsers caught up with his leading Centurions. Most of the tanks around him hardly had enough fuel to keep their engines idling and their fans turning over to keep their cabins 'liveable'. Besides which, his boys needed a rest after over forty-eight hours of continuous, hard-charging operations.

Of course, in his place Erwin Rommel would have driven straight into Zubayr. But Thomas Daly was not Rommel, and besides, the Desert Fox had the whole Afrika Korps behind him; all he had were a couple of exhausted, under-strength tank regiments. He had given the Saudis - with their P-48s - the job of guarding his western flank and rounding up stragglers around Umm Qasr and left the trail-blazing in the direction of Basra to his Anzac and British tankers, the latter, few in number but mostly veterans. The men around him were mainly Victorians and Queenslanders, part-timers in comparison with the long-service professionals of the 4th Royal Tank Regiment sprinkled throughout Daly's combined brigade.

In the East the apparently uninhabited, uninhabitable wastes of the Faw Peninsula - the domain of the Marsh Arabs - represented a theoretical 'open flank' to his northward advance. In reality, at this time of year large areas of the peninsula were still flooded from the spring spate of the Shatt-al-Arab, marshy, impassable for his or the enemy's armour. Not even the Iraqi Army had ever really tried to subdue the Marsh Arabs, let alone attempted to maintain a presence below Basra. Nevertheless, his soldierly instincts hated the 'idea' of leaving an open flank and after the exhilarating momentum of the last couple of days, that 'open flank' was suddenly making him both nervous, and very cautious.

If Zubayr was completely undefended he would move forward, otherwise he would dig in here. He had too few tanks and men to get embroiled in a stand-up fight with a significant enemy blocking force, and he could not afford to risk his spearhead blundering onto prepared defences.

The Red Army could lose any number of battles and still exist as a fighting entity in Iraq; if he lost a single, solitary skirmish that was that, game over.

"Right, lads," he declared with the confidence and élan that only a successful general can carry off. "This is where we hold for the moment. Get these 'big boys', he waved around at the parked tanks, "hull down and await replenishment. We'll give the infantry a chance to catch up before we push the bloody Russians all the way back to Baghdad!"

Jumping down he marched directly to the command Centurion.

"General Carver and the Iranians have got the Russians on the run north of Khorramshahr," reported a dusty subaltern boasting a cap with a Royal Armoured Corps badge.

The younger man sounded baffled by the news.

"HQ is saying that Abadan is secure and the enemy is in full retreat opposite Basra, sir."

Tom Daly muttered a private: "Bloody Hell!"

Briefly, he contemplated the startling ramifications of what he had just heard.

Michael Carver was by repute, the cleverest man in the British Army, but even so...

If he had just done an Alam Halfa or better still – unbelievably – an Al Alamein on the Red Army's 2nd Siberian Mechanised Army, that was...

Goodness, he honestly and truly did not have the first idea what that meant!

It was too...*incredible.*

"Try to get me in voice contact with HQ," he ordered calmly, as if he had expected nothing other than a complete rout of the enemy on all fronts from the outset.

Chapter 30

12:15 Hours (Local) – 04:15 Hours in Philadelphia
USS Dewey (DLG-14) South of Kharg Island

Commander William Vandeput had observed the much smaller British minesweeper, HMS Bronington, approach and with a grinding against every available fender thrown over the side of both vessels, bump against the port flank of his ship to begin to transfer several seriously injured men to the Dewey.

The British ship's single forward 40-millimetre cannon mount was trained fore and aft, covered by a tarpaulin. Men lay on makeshift stretchers around the gun and on the four-hundred-ton coastal minesweeper's stern. A slim officer, who looked like a kid straight out of college from Vandeput's elevated vantage point on the bridge wing, jumped onto the destroyer's deck, saluted the first man he encountered and then the US flag flying from the jackstay at the stern.

You could not fault the Brits for their manners...

Vandeput went back onto the bridge and headed down the ladder to intercept his visitor.

"Lieutenant Cyril Mitchell, sir. Her Majesty's Ship Bronington," the younger man reported.

The Commanding Officer of the Dewey had to choke off the bile rising in his throat before he could utter a terse acknowledgement. He returned the kid's – he could not have been more than twenty or twenty-one – salute and after a moment's hesitation, stuck out his right hand.

Mitchell shook it cautiously.

When he had brought Bronington south from her hiding place in a horribly shallow creek, thirty miles to the east of Kharg Island he had half-expected to be blown out of the water without so much as a 'by your leave'. Notwithstanding that he had been ordered to 'retire' from the scene by the Captain of the Wave Master two days ago, he still felt sick with guilt for running for cover after the Centaur was attacked. Sitting out the second battle had been positively shameful. It just was not the Navy way. It went against everything he believed in, a betrayal of the recent exploits of the fleet off Cape Trafalgar, Santander, Cadiz, Lampedusa, Cyprus and Malta. Granted, the Bronington only had a single relatively small cannon and her wooden hull – wooden so as to not set off magnetic mines – made her catastrophically vulnerable in any kind of surface action, but dash it, running away went so completely against the grain as to be...*disgraceful.*

At dawn yesterday morning he had crept out to sea and cut into the American's TBS – Talk Between Ships – frequency and offered his ship's services in 'search and rescue' operations.

It was the second time in the last twenty-four hours that Cyril Mitchell had brought Bronington alongside the Dewey.

He eyed the men on deck.

"As soon as we've transferred the injured across to you I was thinking of searching downwind, sir," he reported. "Fellows in the water could have drifted twenty or thirty miles east, or perhaps, east-south-east since the, er, battle."

Vandeput hesitated.

The kid did not need to ask his permission; heck, they were enemies and their countries were, for all he knew, formally at war with each other. On the other hand, although the British might have long-range aircraft back in Dammam or Riyadh they were not about to risk flying anywhere within fifty miles of what was left of Carrier Division Seven, and without serviceable helicopters all the work had to be done by the surviving ships.

The American cleared his throat.

A few minutes ago, he had received a signal from the Hull – Captain Ben Pickett's flagship – that the unofficial 'truce' had broadened several more degrees.

"We just got word from Tarouf Bay that the HMAS Sydney and HMS Triumph and a couple of tugs are heading our way. The Australian carrier is bringing three helicopters."

Mitchell absorbed this.

The Sydney still looked like a carrier but these days she was a fast transport incapable of operating fixed wing aircraft, and the Triumph a heavy repair ship with her old flight deck cluttered with cranes and workshops. Both ships could operate a handful of helicopters at a pinch but neither had been an aircraft carrier for many years. That said they were big ships, presumably hastily loaded with medical supplies and every medic who could be cajoled or persuaded to come along for the trip.

"The Sydney will fly off her choppers and their ground crews and proceed on to Abadan," Vandeput went on. "She has been granted free passage through this area. HMS Triumph will stand to in this vicinity to offer assistance as required. Neither ship will reach us before this time tomorrow at the earliest."

Cyril Mitchell breathed a heartfelt sigh of relief.

Somebody in authority had picked up the phone and *talked* to the Americans!

Vandeput's weariness now dogged his voice.

"It was my sad duty to report to the captain of HMS Triumph – the senior British Officer afloat - the number of survivors from the Centaur battle group safe onboard US vessels." He swallowed; throat dry. "The count now stands at 59 persons."

There had been over two thousand men on the sunken light carrier and her escorts. Traversing the waters downwind from the 'first' battle thirty-six hours later Bronington was only recovering bodies.

Cyril Mitchell's schoolboyish face hardened.

"Yes, well, we'll finish our business here and then proceed east to search for men who may have been swept further into the Gulf, sir."

"Very good. I will broadcast your intention to the fleet."

Cyril Mitchell hesitated.

"Another Royal Navy ship, HMS Tariton, will be clearing the bar to the Shatt-al-Arab within the hour, sir," he explained. "She is carrying a small number of survivors from Admiral Davey's squadron; many of whom require urgent medical attention..."

Vandeput nodded brusquely.

"I will alert the fleet."

"Thank you, sir."

The two men had suddenly turned stiffly formal.

"Lieutenant," Vandeput said as they tensed before parting. "I wouldn't have chosen things to be this way. Your conduct and that of your ship has been exemplary in this..."

The words might have failed him but Mitchell got the message.

He nodded.

"Thank you, sir. I wish you safe steaming."

Vandeput watched the young British officer step back onto his own ship and jog up the ladder to his bridge house, belatedly becoming aware he was not alone on the upper deck platform below the bridge.

A burly surgeon's mate stood to attention.

It seemed that Vandeput's presence was respectfully requested in the main sick bay.

He walked aft down crowded passageways, past men repairing splinter damage, wounded men on stretchers, and exhausted men dozing at their stations.

Vandeput did his best to project stern, fatherly confidence as he moved past his men and the survivors crowded below decks. The Farragut class frigate could be a claustrophobic home for its normal complement of twenty-three officers and three hundred and thirty-seven other ranks; with well over two hundred rescued survivors onboard – many seriously injured – she was positively *crowded* or just plain *busy*, depending upon whether a man elected to put the best possible spin on the situation.

In any event her commanding officer was under no illusion that fighting his ship with so many *passengers* onboard would be anything other than a fraught affair beset with probably intractable difficulties.

Chapter 31

11:55 Hours (Local) – 04:25 Hours in Philadelphia
Leningradsky Prospekt Hotel, Chelyabinsk, Soviet Union

"It is very simple, Ambassador," Alexander Nikolayevich Shelepin growled as the two men exited the front lobby of the slab-sided Intourist hotel and walked out into the burning mid-day sun. *"You* have a great deal more to lose than *we* do."

Although President Kennedy's Special Emissary to the Troika – the collective leadership of the new Union of Soviet Socialist Republics – Llewelyn 'Tommy' Thompson did not know this for a fact, he suspected that in a rational World his principals back in Philadelphia would understand as much. Unfortunately, 'rationality' was in very short supply at the moment.

The two men settled into the lumpy, frayed seats in the back of the ancient Red Army staff car. The vehicle ground forward, rolling and pitching like a ship in a rough sea as it navigated the pot-holed road.

"So you say, Comrade Minister," Thompson agreed noncommittally. It went without saying that he found Alexander Shelepin, the head of the KGB and – notwithstanding that members of the Troika each had an equal voice, Leonid Ilyich Brezhnev's deputy – *intimidating.* It was said that when Shelepin entered a room the temperature dropped two degrees, and a chill began to settle in a man's bones. "You will appreciate that my understanding of the present state of the USSR is imperfect. I would need to be better informed to make a sound judgement on your contention."

Thompson had been astonished when he discovered that men he considered to be cautious old Bolsheviks – Brezhnev, Alexei Kosygin and Vasily Chuikov – had *impetuously,* gambled everything on confronting British and American post-October War resolve in the Mediterranean and the Middle East.

It spoke volumes that Admiral of the Fleet Sergey Georgiyevich Gorshkov – now promoted to Defence Minister and the junior member of the reconstituted Troika – had apparently sacrificed practically every major naval asset at his command, including several captured Turkish ships, in a dazzlingly audacious operation to seize Malta at the beginning of April. Whether his intention had actually been to seize the most strategically important archipelago in the Mediterranean, or simply to draw the West's attention away from the Middle East at the very moment two Soviet tank armies burst into Northern Iran, was somewhat moot at this remove. The gamble had very nearly over-turned the strategic and diplomatic applecart of the whole Mediterranean World, and by the time the Soviet Union's shocked, positively reeling enemies had awakened to the fact that at least a quarter of a million Red Army soldiers were on the move, much of Tehran had been turned into an irradiated dust bowl and Western hegemony over the great oilfields of Kurdistan, Iran and Arabia was threatened as never before.

That was three months ago and the failure of the Kennedy Administration to react – at all, other than leaving the Sixth Fleet in the Mediterranean – had, not unsurprisingly, convinced the Soviets that America had lost its will to fight. Sending the USS Kitty Hawk to the Persian Gulf – criminally weakening the US Naval presence in the Western Pacific at a time when the North Korean regime was muttering defiance, and the situation in South Vietnam was rapidly deteriorating as Ho Chi Minh's prompted insurgency increasingly undermined the corrupt regime in Saigon - as an afterthought on an ill-defined 'deterrent' mission, had merely muddied the waters...

The 'peace dividend' *process* had already left South Korea horribly vulnerable; and the Kennedy Administration's strategy to keep Hanoi's hands off South Vietnam had been barely coherent long before Marshal Babadzhanian's tanks had crashed into Iran and Iraq. Neither of these things would have in any way have escaped the attention of the Soviets; nevertheless, the outrageous opportunism of the former Troika – and presumably a majority of Politburo members – had caused Thompson to question practically everything he had thought he had known about the Soviet Union.

Now Shelepin claimed that the Kitty Hawk had been sunk by the British. Moreover, according to him the Red Army had unilaterally called a halt to offensive operations and declared the 30th parallel – that is, the line of latitude at that degree from the Kuwaiti border in the west to the eastern boundary of Abadan Island – as the de facto 'Peace Line' in Iraq. In other words, the Soviets were behaving as if they had conquered Iraq and vanquished the British. Notwithstanding that it was unclear if either of those 'claims' – to anybody - Shelepin seemed to be under the impression the Soviet Union had won the war...bar the shouting.

'We chose *not* to destroy the surviving feeble British and Australian forces at Abadan and in Kuwait,' the head of the KGB had explained emolliently, rather like a python hissing with relish before it enveloped and crushed the life out of its prey. 'Moreover, we are prepared to permit American forces to *escort* the surviving Imperialist lackeys back to their outposts in Oman and Aden.'

Thompson had not risen to the bait.

Okay, so the British still hold Abadan...

Where else have they contrived to throw a monkey wrench into the works of the invincible Red Army colossus?

'Of course, if necessary we will invoke the clause in our agreement with your Government demanding,' Shelepin had continued, malevolence flickering behind his eyes, 'that your Strategic Air Command enforces the *Peace Line* in the event that the British make trouble.'

It was at this point that the American had politely reminded his host that what had – thus far – actually been signed, was only a 'draft memorandum of understanding', in effect, 'a working document covering those areas which both parties had agreed to discuss in detail in a spirit of mutual co-operation in the interest of global *stability*.'

Shelepin had brooded.

It was then that he had reported, a little more fully, the outcome of the recent sea battles in the Persian Gulf.

'Your Navy sank the British aircraft carrier Centaur; the British bombed the Kitty Hawk and several other American ships. The Red Air Force destroyed all the warships the British sent up the Shatt-al-Arab.'

Tommy Thompson had just stared at the Russian.

Shelepin had smiled coldly. He was a man who liked his revenge served in cold blood; he enjoyed watching his enemies writhe in agony. Physical agony was better; however, in lieu he would content himself with existential angst, providing that is, it was so acute it was as corrosive to the victim as actual bodily pain.

'Your magnificent,' he sneered, 'Sixth Fleet meekly allowed itself to be *arrested* by the British at Malta. As we speak the crews of your ships are being marched off into open-air prison cages all over the Maltese Archipelago.'

Shelepin had been in no hurry to conclude his business. He was like a cat toying with a bird with a broken wing.

'So,' he had concluded, 'with your vaunted Navy defeated and humiliated for all the World to see, and with the Red Army supreme in Iraq,' he gloated, 'it was to be expected that the war criminal Kennedy would be deposed in a coup by Johnson and his *Southern* friends.'

Thompson had stared out of the grubby windows as the drab city blocks still standing after the recent RAF bombing – like great concrete broken teeth – in the damaged central districts of Chelyabinsk, slid past as Alexander Shelepin's armoured cortège headed towards the east and the bridges across the River Miass.

It took a concerted effort of will to break out of the circle of his premonitions.

"I have told you what has happened," Shelepin said, dully. "You came to us with offers of peace, tempting us with the promise of future 'summits' to determine the changed spheres of influence of your country and the Motherland. Now your *new* President, the *usurper* Johnson has broadcast threats," he shook his head, "as if the Soviet Union is just another Yankee client."

The American emissary did not bother to contradict the Russian. Even if he believed the half of what the man had told him about the war in the Gulf or the situation in the Central Mediterranean, let alone the suggestion that President Kennedy had been toppled in some kind of coup – which he did not believe for a single minute – it was obvious that something had gone badly wrong at home, and practically everywhere else...

What had gone wrong or why was incidental at present; what mattered was that he understood Shelepin's *angle*. And more importantly, whether the Head of the KGB was playing his own game or that of the Troika, both at once, or pitting one against the other?

Shelepin sighed.

"If you make war on us again we shall set free Red Dawn to do its worst!"

Thompson had received a deeply disturbing FBI briefing about 'Krasnaya Zarya' before coming to Russia.

Whereas Red Dawn was embedded, to varying degrees in all the less damaged countries of Western Europe, in the United States it had always been an arm of the NKVD, and more recently, at the heart of KGB attempts to spy on and to subvert the American body politic and the military-industrial complex. It was likely that Red Dawn agents were involved in the uprising in the Midwest, having already been implicated in the smaller scale insurgencies in Washington State and elsewhere in North America.

Krasnaya Zarya tended to be stronger, better organised and immensely more virulent the nearer it existed to the pre-October War borders of the USSR; and it was for this reason that it had, in effect, run wild in Turkey, swarmed onto Cyprus, throughout the Aegean, conquering Crete and eventually spilled over into Greece and the Balkans. Right up until the moment Red Dawn had begun to behave as a state within a state, flagrantly disregarding the authority of the Troika it had worked hand in glove with surviving Soviet forces. It was only when it had threatened to 'run amok' within the Soviet Union that the Troika had brought it to heel with stunning ruthlessness.

It was believed that the purge was 'ongoing' even now, four months after the Red Air Force 'nuked' Bucharest. The Romanian capital had, it seemed, been the 'hub' of Krasnaya Zarya activities in the Eastern Mediterranean and the Balkans, and the main staging post for airborne infiltration into Western Europe.

Notwithstanding the purges Krasnaya Zarya had not gone away, it still existed; for example, as an army of occupation across the Anatolian littoral of Turkey, and in parts of Rumania, Bulgaria and northern Greece. Presently, it was a much more obedient beast, tethered by the throat to the will of the Troika. Not so much a state within a state, but as the adjunct, or auxiliary of the Soviet state and significantly, for old Russia hands like Thompson, under the iron control of the Communist Party and therefore a balance to the previously all-powerful Red Army faction.

Thompson had had plenty of time to ponder the logic of the situation.

Krasnaya Zarya was now Alexander Shelepin's own personal half-tame monster. His man, Yuri Andropov had already been installed in Baghdad as Commissar General of Northern Iraq; and within weeks tens of thousands of Red Army troops would be relieved of their wasteful garrison and policing duties by fresh Krasnaya Zarya units, freeing up troops to renew the offensive in the south. Iraq, with its huge oilfields and ports granting access to the rest of the World via the Persian Gulf, might soon be Shelepin's personal fiefdom, his power base. It was only a matter of time before he turned again on neighbouring Iran and the oil-rich despotic tribes of Arabia...

"Where are you taking me?" Thompson inquired, knowing his analysis was flawed. Something else, something bigger and even more dangerous was going on...

"Somewhere safe," the most sinister man in the Soviet Union replied wearily, momentarily his thoughts a long way away.

Chapter 32

09:30 Hours (GMT) – 04:30 in Philadelphia
Blenheim Palace, Woodstock, Oxfordshire, England

Her Majesty Elizabeth the Second, by the Grace of God of the United Kingdom of Great Britain and Northern Ireland, and of Her Other Realms and Territories Queen, Head of the Commonwealth, Defender of the Faith slowly rose to her feet as her guests followed her Private Secretary, Sir Michael Adeane into the audience chamber of what actually remained, the family seat of the Dukes of Marlborough.

Strictly speaking the Royal Family was not so much 'in residence' at Blenheim Palace – actually a monumental eighteenth-century country house rather than a 'palace' – as *borrowing it* from John Albert William Spencer-Churchill, 10th Duke of Marlborough. These niceties mattered because it was the fine 'detail' of history which taught one so much about how transiently individual lives fitted into the great sweep of the destiny of nations. Or so the thirty-eight-year-old mother of two upon whom a substantial part of the weight of ensuring the survival of the United Kingdom presently seemed to be bearing down reflected after yet another dreadful, sleepless night.

The fine detail of history...

For example, the magnificent building in which she and her immediate surviving family and closest courtiers now lived, had been neglected so sorely in the nineteenth century that it was virtually falling down less than a century ago. Had it not been for the 9th Duke's foresight in taking, for his first wife, Consuelo, an heiress to the Vanderbilt fortune, the Marlborough's would have abandoned the 'palace' years ago; and then where would the Royal Family have found suitable lodgings so near to Oxford?

But that was to miss the point.

The point was that she was standing in an historic, superbly appointed and maintained *British* palace designed by the legendary architect John Vanbrugh, *only* because of the treasure which Consuelo Vanderbilt had returned to the old country from the New World. There was a profound lesson, an unambiguous signal from the past somewhere in that!

Winston Churchill had been born in this massive house, family mausoleum and national monument. Ironically, the court and parliamentary intrigues, and the controversy and the bitter infighting around the building of Blenheim Palace had tarnished the reputation and driven into exile John Churchill, 1st Duke of Marlborough, and his Duchess, Sara. The hero of the War of the Spanish Succession, the victor of Blenheim, Ramillies, Oudenarde and Malplaquet had never found sanctuary or peace at Woodstock, and nor it seemed, would she: *Elizabeth II, Dei Gratia Britanniarum Regnorumque Suorum Ceterorum Regina, Consortionis Populorum Princeps, Fidei Defensor...*

The Queen found herself silently speaking the words in Latin, determined to maintain her air of polite, graceful detachment when every molecule of her being wanted to cry out in despair.

Her Consort, Prince Philip, the Duke of Edinburgh lurched unsteadily to his feet at her right shoulder. He had insisted on 'dressing to the nines' that morning and his ceremonial sword clanked. She too had dressed as regally as her aging Norman Hartnell and Harvey Amis trousseau allowed. Not that she particularly missed the hundreds of dresses, shoes and accessories blitzed and scorched in Buckingham Palace in London, up at Balmoral in Scotland, or at Sandringham in East Anglia.

Sandringham...

This latter royal retreat in Norfolk had escaped direct injury in the October War only to be taken over by the homeless, itinerant and starving in that terrible first post-apocalypse winter. The RAF had eventually got around to surveying the estate, finding mostly ruins. The big house and all the estate cottages had been ransacked and put to the torch some time last year.

In any event...

Today she was wearing a sober dark blue dress, the hem of which danced around her calves and covered practically every inch of flesh between her lower legs and her chin. She had decided to wear pearls; one did not want to look overly dour even on a day as grim as this one!

Margaret Thatcher was accompanied by a man in his thirties whom the Queen struggled to place.

"The Prime Minister, The Right Honourable Mrs Margaret Thatcher; and the Secretary of State for Information, The Honourable Nicolas Ridley, MP."

'Of course,' the monarch said to herself, hugely relieved to be able to place the man in the worn, shiny morning suit lagging a little behind *Her* Prime Minister's left hand.

Ridley was a grandson of Sir Edwin Lutyens!

There used to be several of Lutyens works in the Royal collections...

Ridley's father had died earlier in the year, his title passing to the older brother, Matthew, who was now 4th Viscount Ridley. She recollected encountering the older Ridley brother some years ago when he was aide-de-camp to Sir Evelyn Baring, the then Governor of Kenya. Matthew Ridley was a zoologist, she remembered; legend had it that he had once spent three or four months alone on an uninhabited island in the Seychelles bird-watching, a feat of endurance which had attracted quite a lot of attention at the time!

The Queen motioned for tea to be served as she and her guests moved slowly, haltingly to the pre-laid table beneath ornate, golden chandeliers close to tall, gilded windows overlooking the idyllic parklands which surrounded the palace. Her own injuries – sustained in the atrocity at Brize Norton in April – were well on the way to fully mending; her husband's life threatening wounds suffered in the regicidal attack on Balmoral in December, would take longer to heal, if in fact they ever did but he was nothing if not stoic as he limped gamely across the treacherous, polished floor towards the respite of one of the padded high backed Queen Anne chairs salvaged from Windsor Castle.

Presently, tea cups clinked in priceless bone china saucers.

"It is my view, and that of my senior colleagues in government, your Majesty," Margaret Thatcher prefaced, "that our forces should adopt a defensive global posture until further notice. It is our 'collective' opinion that our policy should be to hold the line, and if possible do nothing to further inflame passions either in Philadelphia or in the Middle East. Consistent with this approach *your* government will make no public comment or protest about the disgraceful attack on our Embassy in Philadelphia at this time, will declare a unilateral ceasefire in the Persian Gulf, and," it was readily apparent that the words were choking her, "a similar temporary cessation of military action in the South Atlantic. Steps will also be taken to reduce unnecessary tensions on Malta consistent with maintaining the internment of the US Navy ships currently in port. In the meantime, HMS Eagle is proceeding to Valletta at her best speed to support the forces on the archipelago. Further, I have drafted a note to Ambassador Brenckmann to this effect detailing our altered military 'posture', and Sir Thomas Harding-Grayson and his wife will shortly pay a courtesy visit to the United States Embassy in an attempt to reinstate 'normal' transatlantic channels of communications."

There was a pregnant silence.

"What of the V-Bombers?" Prince Philip inquired, as if the question was of only passing interest.

"On the advice of the Chief of the Defence Staff no plans have been made to attack North America, sir. However, all available aircraft in the British Isles, Malta and Cyprus have been 'bombed up' and in the event of a Soviet attack on the British Isles will be tasked to attack targets inside the former Soviet Union, including the cities of Sverdlovsk and Chelyabinsk and associated regional suspected command bunkers. A small number of other RAF and Royal Fleet Air Arm aircraft, mainly in the Mediterranean theatre have been, or are being, similarly prepared for operations against Soviet objectives in that Sea and in the Middle East."

The Queen ruminated a moment.

"How many V-Bombers do we actually have left, Prime Minister?"

"Fourteen ready for operations, Ma'am."

The first time she had come face to face with her sovereign Margaret Thatcher had been a bag of nerves and had needed to be coached as to the correct mode of address: *first 'Your Majesty' and subsequently 'Ma'am,' pronounced with a short 'a,' as in 'jam'.*

"In the United Kingdom, the Mediterranean and onboard HMS Eagle," she went on, "we possess between fifteen and twenty aircraft capable of delivering nuclear weapons, although," she apologised, "we have less than a dozen such bombs available for deployment by these aircraft at this time."

The larger part of the country's nuclear munitions stockpile had been used up in the October War and no real effort had been made to re-start bomb production in the time since. Aldermaston and other related facilities remained in effect, mothballed under heavy guard mainly on account of the fissile materials on site. Although over thirty warheads had been returned to the United Kingdom from the bunker at RAF Akrotiri on Cyprus by HMS Hampshire, many had subsequently been dismantled and their 'active' components re-stored at 92 Maintenance Unit, Faldingworth Nuclear Bomb Store (Permanent Ammunition Depot), in Lincolnshire. While theoretically, these munitions could be speedily re-assembled and issued to RAF units, in practice no attempt had been made to 'recover' additional 'bombs' for 'operational exigencies' in the current emergency. The RAF had run out of the skilled technicians needed to effect a fresh mobilisation of 'nuclear ordnance', the Army did not have the men to escort and safely deliver assembled bombs to distant stations; and frankly, even after the successful 'Arc Light' missions over Iraq and in the Persian Gulf, nobody in Government had any appetite for further 'atomic adventures' other than in the event of a full scale attack on the home islands.

Enough was enough...

"What do we know of President Kennedy's health?" The Queen asked quietly.

"Very little, Ma'am."

"Odd that, his being taken ill so suddenly?"

"Yes," the Duke of Edinburgh added, sniffing thoughtfully. "Coming as it did right after the news about the Centaur and your, er," he half-smiled conspiratorially at Margaret Thatcher, "little talk with the blighter?"

The Prime Minister blushed and studied her tea cup.

On the occasion in question, she had spoken before she had allowed herself time to consider her words. In international affairs, *if* there was ever another such time she would hold her peace; but she had been so...*angry.* Jack Kennedy had lied to her time and again, gone back on everything he had promised at the Hyannis Port Summit only a month ago. Then there had been the cowardly attack on HMS Centaur...

Jack Kennedy's Administration had lost – if it had ever had one – its moral compass.

For all she knew the men in the Philadelphia White House and the Sverdlovsk, or Chelyabinsk Kremlin were at this very minute plotting some new perfidious attack.

"I asked Mr Ridley to attend this morning," Margaret Thatcher said, focusing her faculties on matters over which she had some semblance of control, "to crave your indulgence, Ma'am."

The Queen registered her Prime Minister's change of tone and was quietly reassured by the decisive edge in her voice suggesting she had firmly seized again the wheel of the ship of state. That wheel had been spinning out of control for most of the last forty-eight hours, now the monarch could sense the great vessel steadying on a new course.

"I am at the service of my people," she invited.

I wonder if this has anything to do with the two British Broadcasting Corporation lorries that arrived a few minutes ahead of the Prime Minister's heavily armed convoy?

"If we have to, we shall fight on with every weapon at our disposal, Ma'am," Margaret Thatcher averred levelly, her confidence gathering. "However, that will be as a last resort. Mr Ridley will explain how you and other members of the Royal Family may wish to be involved. Suffice to say that having largely exhausted our fighting resources in the exercise of a strategy of 'WAR WAR'; rationally, we must now try to pursue the tactics of 'JAW JAW'."

The Queen arched a curious eyebrow, remained silent.

Nicholas Ridley cleared his throat.

"While we have little faith that an appeal to reason will work with the United States Administration," he explained diffidently, "and even less in respect of the Russian regime, it may be that a more fruitful audience might be the ordinary people of the World, Ma'am?"

"Ah," the Queen murmured, glancing sidelong at her husband who was nodding sagely. "I see. Presumably, you have scripted something appropriate?"

Margaret Thatcher interjected: "We are still working on that, Ma'am. The outcome of the Foreign Secretary's meeting with the American Ambassador may have a bearing on the text."

"How exactly will my, er, message, be broadcast to the, er, world?"

"The BBC, the Chief of the Defence Staff and others are working on that as we speak, Ma'am," Nicholas Ridley assured her. "Tom Harding-Grayson is also seeking Ambassador Brenckmann's good offices – the Oxford Embassy has communication links with a large CIA facility at Dublin, it may be possible to utilise that," he pursed his lips into a thin, pale line, "but we're still investigating the possibilities. The thing is we are hoping to record *your* broadcast in the next few hours."

The Queen did not have to think about it.

"Well, we should get on with it then!"

Chapter 33

12:50 Hours (Local) – 05:50 Hours in Philadelphia
USS Sam Houston (SSBN-609), Levantine Sea

Captain Troy Simms had returned to his cabin to shave and freshen up ten minutes ago. In the last hour the boat had come up to one hundred and fifty feet and trailed her aerial astern; just in case there was something waiting for her in the ether.

The first burst transmission from New England, relayed circuitously via a ship stationed in the mid-North Atlantic and a ground station in Spain had been garbled, the next two transmits had parity checked and were going through the normal decryption protocols. If both 'good' *receipts* 'matched' the signal would be treated as 'authentic'. And then, hopefully, the commanding officer of the USS Sam Houston would know what the heck he and his eight-thousand-ton submarine were doing in the Eastern Mediterranean.

"Captain on the bridge!" Greeted his return to the control room. He stepped over to the plot.

As of zero-two-twenty hours the USS Thresher (SSN-593) had been in the Ionian Sea heading south west like a bat out of Hell; if she had held her course, at flank speed she would be in position to blockade the approaches to Valletta sometime around now. The USS Barb (SSN-596), the Thresher's sister boat was patrolling west of Gavdos, the biggest island in a small archipelago twenty miles south of the Cretan mainland. The third US Navy SSN - the Skate (SSN-578) - in the Mediterranean was guarding the eastern approaches to the Aegean north-east of Crete, watching the channels between it and the islands of Kasos, Karpathos and Saria, and the northern sea lane between Saria and Rhodes, the largest island in the Dodecanese. Like the Barb, Skate's patrol orders required her to keep at least fifteen miles of sea room between her and the nearest landfall.

The Sam Houston had slunk another twenty miles south over the last few hours, running silent. Actually, there was no way an eight thousand ton, extraordinarily complicated machine like the Sam Houston could run 'silently', so 'very quietly' had to do. This said she was currently moving slowly three hundred feet beneath the surface of an unnaturally empty ocean above an abyssal depth that might have been bottomless for all the difference it made to the men onboard.

Twenty-four hours ago, a fifteen-hour old report had placed the British fleet carrier HMS Eagle, two or three escort ships, and an oiler at Port Said. They were in the Delta on some kind of goodwill visit presumably to show Colonel Nasser that the folks back in England were still rooting for him after the failed coup a month ago. That had been a bad business by all accounts, apparently the whole government district of Cairo was in ruins and the round ups and executions were still going on.

Not your problem, Troy!

Given what had happened in the Persian Gulf and at Malta it was not unreasonable to expect that the Eagle and her little friends would hunker down in port until the smoke cleared. Or at least, that's what he would have done if he was the British C-in-C knowing that there were three angry US Navy SSNs patrolling the Mediterranean somewhere between him and the relative safety of the Valletta breakwater.

He stared at the plot, mesmerised by the table.

"Coffee, sir," murmured a man behind his shoulder.

The commander of the USS Sam Houston nodded his thanks and settled in his chair near the periscope stand. He carried on 'working the plot' in his head.

Port Said was 224 nautical miles approximately due south east from the Sam Houston's current position. Eagle and her escorts could cover those miles in seven or eight hours, assuming her fast air detection destroyers, HMS Scorpion and HMS Oudenarde had topped off their bunkers before weighing anchor. The other warship in company with the big British carrier was the Whitby class anti-submarine frigate HMS Blackpool, less heavily armed than the two destroyers but only a little less fleet of foot. Eagle was believed to be the Royal Navy's only operational fleet carrier – the Ark Royal was in dock at Portsmouth, the Victorious a half-wrecked hulk at Malta, and the smaller HMS Hermes was effectively decommissioned at Gibraltar.

The Eagle was it, so far as the Royal Navy was concerned and if there had been any way to get her to the Persian Gulf, Carrier Division Seven might have found itself with a real fight on its hands when it went up against the Centaur Battle Group in the first 'Battle of Kharg Island' two, *no* three days ago.

Troy Simms did not think for a second that the British would lock away their biggest, best war-fighting asset in the Mediterranean in Port Said. If recent history was anything to go by the Eagle would head for Malta at flank speed with – metaphorically – all guns blazing...

Simms still did not know what to make of the terse reports concerning the two 'battles' in the Persian Gulf. Frankly, he was still in a state of not so mild shock. Carrier Division Seven had destroyed a British carrier group; and the RAF had sunk the Kitty Hawk, a cruiser and a modern guided missile destroyer a day later...

Thankfully, it was not his job to ask: "What the fuck is going on?"

However, he sure as heck hoped somebody in Fleet Headquarters back in Norfolk, or at the new Navy Department building in Camden was asking: "*What the fuck is going on?*"

He sipped his coffee.

Periodically, his eye circled the compartment. He checked the SINS position board, listened to snatches of whispered conversation, tuned into the muted soft humming of machinery under his feet transmitted through the deck plating. The lights on the torpedo board showed all four torpedo tubes loaded and 'ready'.

To his right the missile panel stubbornly indicated two UGM-27s, both new A-3s, 'down'.

The people at the Lockheed Missiles and Space Company (LMSC) had still been developing the A-3 when he visited the LMSC plant at Moffett Field, Sunnyvale the summer before the October War. That visit was part and parcel of the familiarization protocol all designated Polaris boat skipper candidates went through. There had been a lot of problems – *a lot* – with the first couple of batches of A-1 UGM-27s, guidance issues mostly. The whole program had been beset with problems; even if people tended not to talk about the warhead reliability and 'safing' glitches that *everybody* in the Polaris program found out about sooner or later.

The Navy had been in a screaming, positively ungodly, hurry to get the first two classes of Polaris boats – the George Washingtons and the Ethan Allens (the Sam Houston included) to sea, and Lockheed had been racing against the clock from day one. The result was that the CEP (Circular Error Probability), or targeting accuracy, for an A-1 was one to two miles at best, and its warhead initiation rate (or in laymen's language, how many of the infernal things could confidently be expected to actually detonate) was a long, long way south of one hundred percent.

The updated A-2s were fine now that their teething problems had been resolved; but the A-3s well, they were another thing entirely and once loaded onboard a submarine, hardware maintenance and repair options were severely limited. Basically, if the missile board lit up a major defect or one of any of a score of launch-adverse risk factors then *that* bird was staying in the tube until the Sam Houston got back to Charleston.

Unless of course somebody specifically ordered him to flush his two faulty birds, in which case he would have to shut his eyes, turn the key and hope that neither of them blew up in the tube or that their W-58 warhead's cluster of three two hundred and fifty-seven pound, two hundred kiloton 'devices' initiated anywhere in the vicinity of the boat...

The notion of the equivalent of forty Hiroshima-sized bombs going off two thousand miles away did not exactly give the commanding officer of the USS Sam Houston any kind of warm feeling inside, the idea that they might light up next to his boat was well...

"Captain to the radio shack!"

"What have we got?" Troy Simms demanded as he stuck his head around the radio room door.

Petty Officer Warren Dokes looked up myopically.

"A two-part executive, sir," he intoned neutrally. He passed the decrypted command verification codes to his commanding officer, clipped to a board.

Troy Simms nodded.

The way it worked was that command orders – or 'executives' – were transmitted to vessels at sea by means of abbreviated code names and numbers. Once decrypted these ought to correlate with those listed in the 'war plans' and 'target' books kept in *his* safe in *his* cabin.

He now needed to manually decode the text of the 'executives' in company with one of the boat's Executive Officer, the Missiles Officer, or the Torpedo Officer, and thereafter, thumb through the 'books' in his safe and any relevant additional operational documentation pertaining to restraints upon his action and or, other 'operational considerations'.

For all he knew he might already be holding orders requiring him to rain thermonuclear perdition on the enemy – whomsoever that might be in this ever crazier mixed up World – or to stand down, or to prepare for some other contingency.

Alternatively, at this stage the codes on the pad Warren Dokes had just handed him might simply be a request for an updated 'engineering defects list', or a routine report on reactor performance.

The Chief of the Boat, Master Chief Petty Officer Ronald Rickson was waiting for Simms in the passageway.

"Pass the word for the Exec to attend me in my cabin please, Chief," he grunted.

In his cabin Troy Simms opened his safe and retrieved the folder containing the command codes. The Exec would recover a second set of the codes from a safe located in the Missile Compartment before he reported to the cabin.

Troy Simms stared at the bulkhead a few feet from his face.

Oh shit!

Here we go again!

Chapter 34

It was growing light outside but the heavy drapes on the first-floor windows of the old Girard Corn Exchange Trust Bank excluded the new day.

Captain Sir Peter Christopher and his wife had been shepherded into another reception room when the President and his stern-faced companion, Senator Richard Russell were called away by a harassed aide. Since then, he and Marija had been cooling their heels in a state of angst-ridden turmoil.

The bodies of the Ambassador, Lord Franks, his wife and the Chargé D'affaires and the youthful Blues and Royals officer who had commanded the small Embassy protection detail, had been thrown – practically naked – onto the steps of the Wister Park Embassy.

Peter and Marija had only been at the Embassy a little over a month or so, during which time Peter had spent several days away at Cape Cod during the period of the Hyannis Port Summit between Prime Minister Margaret Thatcher and President Kennedy. Nevertheless, they had made many new friends – the processes of forming friendships greatly accelerated by the siege atmosphere at the Wister Park compound – and been taken under the paternal wings of the Ambassador and his wife.

Lord Franks had treated Peter much like a long, fondly remembered lost nephew; and Lady Barbara had mothered Marija and Rosa Hannay as if they were her own daughters. Although Peter Christopher did not think he could, or ever would be, at ease in the company of Rachel Piotrowska, the mysterious Polish-born 'spook', the two 'Maltese wives' and the unlikely Head of Station of British Intelligence in Philadelphia had been like sisters. Despite everything, Peter and Alan Hannay – his putative 'deputy consul' in the mission to the West Coast but actually, ever since the Battle of Malta, his de facto aide-de-camp – and their wives had 'mucked in' with the Embassy staff and been welcomed into that community with open arms. Many of their new friends would have gone to Canada or to the legation in New York after the bombing of the compound last month; but it was likely that everybody else was dead, murdered by a gang of religious fanatics and misfits, and a mob...

"The President will be with us shortly," explained the solid-looking, stern-faced man who was ushered into the small room without prior warning or introduction.

Peter Christopher shot his cuffs, straightened his jacket and shook Secretary of State William Fulbright's hand. He and the man who, albeit approximately, was Sir Thomas Harding-Grayson's counterpart in the US Administration, had met previously but never really spoken to each other.

He remembered his manners.

"Good morning, Mister Secretary of State. I don't think you've met my wife..."

Marija had risen unsteadily from the chaise longue upon which she had been sitting and trying, with only middling success, not to succumb to the urge to nap. It was customarily at about this time of day that she started being sick; obviously her body clock, confused by travelling between time zones was determined to inflict her daily morning sickness later, rather than earlier today.   No matter, she would enjoy the respite while it lasted.   If nothing else her life experience – its many childhood and adolescent travails and lately, the loss of so many friends – had taught her the wisdom of understanding that most of the time one's cup was half-full, not half-empty.

She smiled and shook the newcomer's hand.

"I wish we were meeting in better times, Lady Marija," the fifty-nine-year-old Missourian-born former Chairman of the Senate Committee on Foreign Relations said wearily. The older man noted that the young woman's husband had moved to his wife's side as she got to her feet as if ready to catch her if she stumbled. "Thank you both," he went on, making stern eye contacts, "for hanging around while we," he shrugged, "get our act together."

There was a knock at the door.

A second man entered the room.

He was younger, perhaps in his forties, plumper than the Secretary of State and Peter and Marija were struck immediately by his...*presence*.

The Secretary of State wasted no time.

"Allow me to introduce Dr Kissinger."

"Sir Peter...Lady Marija..."

The newcomer's grip was firm, his gaze piercing, contemplative.

"Dr Kissinger is the Director of the Harvard Defense Studies Program," Fulbright continued, "and the principal foreign policy advisor to the Governor of New York, the leading Republican Party candidate to run for the Presidency in November, Mr Nelson Rockefeller. The President has appealed for a bi-partisan approach in the current emergency. Dr Kissinger has come to the White House in that spirit."

While her husband shook Henry Kissinger's hand perfunctorily, his impatience horribly close to boiling over despite his marvellous impersonation of a man completely in control of his emotions; Marija held onto the other man's hand long enough to look him directly in the eye.

This man was different from all the other senior US politicians she had met. She could not put her finger on what exactly was different; he just was...*different*.

It was not the foreign – German, she guessed – accentuation when he spoke, America like her own native Malta was a melting pot of peoples and languages. No, it was the gravitas and the *weight* of every syllable that passed his lips.

"In the present crisis my principals," Kissinger explained, "Governor Rockefeller, with the support of former Vice-President Nixon, has asked me to liaise – strictly confidentially and off the record – directly with senior Administration members in the interests of national unity."

Peter Christopher did not really care about 'domestic' US political 'niceties'.

"To what end, sir?" He asked tartly.

Fulbright recoiled somewhat. He opened his mouth to reply, only to be beaten to the punch by Henry Kissinger.

"To prevent further bloodshed, Sir Peter," he declared lowly.

Fulbright reasserted his authority: "We anticipate opening a direct telephone link to the authorities in Oxford, hopefully within the next sixty minutes. It may be that you will be the United Kingdom's senior accredited diplomat in Philadelphia…"

"May be?" The younger man grated between clenched teeth.

"Yes, so it would seem…"

"What do you expect me to do, sir?"

Peter Christopher felt Marija squeeze his right hand, hard. He was so angry, outraged in fact, that it took an immense effort of will not to spontaneously shake off his wife's grip.

"President Johnson has proposed a number of measures to ensure a peaceful resolution to the crisis…"

"Measures? Such as, sir?"

Marija's heart chilled. She had never seen her husband this close to completely losing control. She was afraid that if she released her hold on his hand he might strike one or both of the Americans. She had married a man who was never, ever going to run away from anything or anybody. He was his father's son. The night he had taken command of HMS Talavera he had steered the thin-skinned destroyer into shoal water off Lampedusa to trade fire with guns ashore at point blank range. The day of the Red Dawn nuclear – mercifully failed - attack on the Maltese Archipelago he had practically 'parked' Talavera's bow under the stern of the burning USS Enterprise to fight that ship's raging fires. At the Battle of Malta, he had taken on the whole Russian fleet without so much as a moment's hesitation…

Her husband did not even know how to run away.

She was proud, and terrified.

"Peter," she blurted, her mouth suddenly horribly dry. "Peter…"

The man she had loved half her life had been about to follow up his angry question. He shut his mouth like a fish out of water gulping air and turned to her.

"We will be angry *later*, husband," Marija said, frightened that she was presuming too much. They had both lost so many friends and loved ones, consumed by the madness of the World; in the last few months the war had taken her brother and the woman who had been like a 'second mother' to her, Peter had lost, buried half his brave Talaveras, his father had been murdered…where was it going to end?

"I'm not, I..."

"We live with our pain every day of *our* lives, husband," Marija murmured, her lips quirking into a sad half-smile. "We find our solace in walking with the ghosts of our loved ones, not in fighting *their* battles forever."

Henry Kissinger had been observing the exchange with detached curiosity. There was no doubt as to who exactly was the real diplomat in the room and it was not the tall, handsome young naval hero.

"Captain Christopher," he grunted, the register of his voice so low it ought to have rattled windows. "It is likely that sometime in the next few hours President Johnson will authorise a massive first strike against the United Kingdom," he shrugged, "and possibly against targets in the Soviet Union." Another shrug. "Moreover, it is my analysis is that there is a significant chance that the Russians may attack British and Commonwealth Forces around the globe with nuclear weapons."

Peter Christopher said nothing.

His breaths came in short, seething intakes.

"If there is a Fourth World War the continental United States will, inevitably, suffer further casualties and destruction but given the balance of nuclear forces, it will be as nothing in comparison with that our enemies will sustain."

Secretary of State Fulbright was nodding.

Kissinger looked from Peter to his wife, thoughtfully, as if he was chewing over a fascinating intellectual puzzle.

Fulbright reclaimed centre stage: "Strategic Air Command and the Polaris submarine fleet is at DEFCON ONE and will be in position to carry out the President's orders within hours."

Marija leaned against her husband.

He was trembling with rage.

"I will," Peter Christopher forced out, "do whatever I must do. But first you will do whatever must be done to recover the bodies of our friends from outside the Wister Park Embassy."

"Sir Peter, that won't be possible..."

"Please don't talk to me about what is, or is not possible, Mister Fulbright. If your people don't have the guts to do what must be done give me a bloody gun and I'll do it!"

Marija shut her eyes, the man she loved had drawn his personal line in the sand and wild horses would not, could never, drag him back from that line.

"And," she heard herself saying in those moments before sudden nausea racked her body, "I will be at my husband's side..."

She remembered the two Americans looking at each other as if somebody had just threatened them with a loaded pistol, and then the world went dark and she had the oddest sensation of falling, falling, falling into a bottomless black void, wondering as she fell, her hair streaming in the wind of her fall, if it would hurt when eventually, she landed...

Chapter 35

14:21 Hours (Local) – 06:21 Hours in Philadelphia
Field Headquarters, 4th Armoured Regiment, Abadan Island

Lieutenant-General Michael Carver listened with only half an ear to the cool, collected, vaguely threatening tone of voice of the man whose voice boomed and crackled over the speaker on top of the field W/T set. The air was thick with flies feeding on the bodies in the surrounding dunes; there had been no time to bury the dead and even had time not been the issue, most of the living – many of them walking wounded – were still fully engaged in mopping up operations south of the Karun River. Now and then the foul stench of death, unspeakable corruption mingled with the scorched detritus of war as it wafted into the open-ended camouflage awning that accommodated 4th Armoured's much shot up communications section. Thirty yards away the turret of a hull down Mark II Centurion poked above the sand, its 105-millimetre rifle depressed so as not to flag the position of the headquarters company in the otherwise uniformly blasted and cratered desert.

Presently, the Russian stopped talking – blustering really - and Carver waited patiently for the translation.

Frank Waters scratched his head, declaimed something in Russian – presumably 'OK chum, I'll pass on what you've just said, don't put down the phone' – and looked to the C-in-C of Allied Forces, Middle East.

"The chappie on the other end is almost certainly who he says he is, Admiral Gorshkov," the former SAS man confirmed, grinning toothily from beneath his bandage-swathed brow. "He's holed up in the 'unassailable fortress' of Basra. He wants to declare a 'peace line' at the thirtieth parallel." He frowned. "That runs south of us and Basra, so that's a bit of a nonsense but there's no telling with these chaps. Anyway, the long and the short of it is that if we don't play ball he'll send in the Red Air Force and the rest of his tanks. He was pretty bullish, sir."

Carver had heard that in the man's tone. "I wonder if he actually has any idea what's going on outside Basra?" He asked, entirely rhetorically.

It was only in the last couple of hours that the completeness – putting aside how temporary it might be – of the victory Allied forces had achieved over the over-extended Red Army formations in southern Iraq and Iran had become evident. The surviving members of Michael Carver's staff were still in a state of mildly euphoric shock.

In the west Tom Daly's hastily thrown together combined ANZAC-led mechanised brigade had enveloped elements of at least three Red Army tank divisions and driven, virtually unopposed up the Basra road to the town of Zubayr hard on the heels of a rabble of routed Soviet troops.

On the western bank of the Shatt-al-Arab, Carver's Commonwealth tanks and infantry had drawn a brigade-sized Red Army mechanised battle group into a trap on Abadan Island and destroyed it in detail. North of the Karun River the cruiser HMS Tiger and the destroyer HMAS Anzac had – in significantly less than twenty murderous minutes – smashed another tank division, the second wave of the massive armoured assault on the Abadan garrison. Simultaneously, the 3rd Imperial Iranian Armoured Division had charged out of the deserts beneath the Zagros Mountains and fallen on the flank of the Soviet 2nd Siberian Mechanised Army logistics train above Khorramshahr and comprehensively routed it.

The killing around the Iraq-Iran border opposite Basra was still going on. The Iranian battle cry had been 'no prisoners' and Carver tried not to think about the atrocities which had been and were still going on in the deserts east of the Shatt-al-Arab.

The situation out at sea in the Gulf was less propitious but thus far the surviving US warships had been too busy picking survivors out of the water - and keeping afloat - to trouble his men on the ground. Now there seemed to be some sort of unofficial ceasefire out at sea with the Americans allowing the HMAS Sydney – a de-activated carrier stuffed full of medical supplies, food and fuel, and carrying a handful of helicopters – free passage across the northern Persian Gulf, hopefully, all the way up to Abadan. The Navy had negotiated a pragmatic quid pro quo; the heavy repair ship HMS Triumph and at least one ocean-going tug would rendezvous with what was left of Carrier Division Seven in due course, so as to offer what assistance it could.

RAF Dammam was trying to get a couple of Canberra bombers serviceable; and there were also two or three other grounded jets – a Supermarine Scimitar and two De Havilland Sea Hawks – at fields in Kuwait. The trouble was that ground crews were spread out all over the place and spares were a huge, possibly intractable problem; so, he was not counting on air support any time soon.

Carver was also aware that the Americans had made – rather ill-considered – threats about 'bombing both sides' into a cessation of hostilities. Well, he would worry about that if and when it happened; recent experience had taught him that depending on the Americans was problematic and he had no intention of forming his plans on the basis of anything an American President had *said.*

Frank Waters scratched his chin; he had not felt this unkempt and dirty since he had been in that Red Army prison cell...

Carver came to a decision.

"Fill in the blighter's card for him, Frank," he said. "Paint him a picture. Let's see what he says to that."

The former SAS man picked up the microphone.

He composed his thoughts and in his best Moskva Russian called: "Vy do sikh por tam, tovarishch?"

Are you still there, comrade?

"Da, tovarishch!"

"Good. General Carver has ordered me to advise you as to the state of play in this neck of the woods. From what you have been saying to me you seem to have a very poor, sorry, well, let's say an incomplete appreciation of the tactical situation!"

This prompted a terse, theatrically dismissive response.

"I have a perfect understanding of the tactical situation in this theatre of operations!"

"Have it your own way, sport!" Frank Waters reminded himself to leave out the quips and to avoid straying too far from the demotic. Russian was a pig of a language without over-complicating things. In his school day's his penchant for lapsing into demotic Greek – plain speaking – had always plonked him down at the bottom of his class when, without undue modesty, he was the only genuine natural linguist for miles around! Greek, Russian, whatever, it was all the same; he got bored with just 'straight talking'. However, today was perhaps one of those days when he needed to contain his high spirits. "I'm sorry, Admiral. I apologise if I have not have made myself clear to you."

"There is nothing to 'make clear'. You still hold ground but you are weak, short of supplies and have no air cover. Your fleet has been destroyed..."

"*One* of our fleets *may* have been partially destroyed, Admiral," Frank Waters riposted, "we have lots more ships and sooner or later they'll be blockading the Persian Gulf again."

The man at the other end of the line said something rather along the lines of: "PAH!"

"Look," the weary SAS man went on, "I hate to kick a man when he is down but we've got your chaps on the run. Well, on the Iran side of the river, leastways. Your chaps can't run away fast enough from our tanks. Down south of Basra your chaps have stopped running away because we've captured thousands of them, so many we haven't even tried to count the beggars. I don't know what your intelligence boys are telling you but our tanks are dug in outside of Zubayr waiting for the order to advance into the southern suburbs of Basra where, presumably, the local populace is waiting to rise up and welcome them as liberators."

The ether crackled and hissed.

"Tell the blighter to get out of Basra or we'll kick him out!" Michael Carver said with uncompromising vehemence.

"Hello!" Frank Waters chortled into the handset. "Are you there, Basra?"

There was another static punctuated interregnum.

"Da, tovarishch!"

The battered SAS man glanced at Carver.

"Twenty-four hours; starting now," the C-in-C intoned.

Frank Waters grinned: "I am to inform you that unless you have pulled all your forces out of Basra, this time tomorrow we will throw you out of the city, Admiral."

Chapter 36

The insurgents had stationed a guard at the door to the second-floor room. Half an hour ago a scrawny girl – she could not have been more than fifteen or sixteen had come into the room and under the supervision of a man with a shotgun, slopped a two-pint jug of water on the floor between the bed, where Rachel Piotrowska lay playing dead, and the radiator to which former FBI Special Agent Dwight Christie was chained.

'Galen says nobody ain't to *molest* her,' she had blurted, pointing at the bed where Rachel lay, apparently unconscious, 'no more', she added tremulously as she backed out of the room.

Dwight Christie had registered this in a thick-eared, concussed sort of way.

The girl had left the single naked overhead light bulb on and he blinked into its fierce glare.

The kid had had a real Deep South accent...

Mo...Lest!

He groaned with anguish realising the water was out of his reach and breathed a loud sigh of abject relief when the woman on the bed rolled over and soundlessly swung her legs onto the floor. She must have been as parched dry as the man, possibly even more desperate to slake her arid, burning thirst but she...

She bent over the jug and sniffed at it.

Put a finger in the water, touched it to her cheek. Dipped her finger again, raised it to her left eye. Waited before finally, she dipped her finger again, touched her tongue.

"It smells like somebody pissed in it but that's all," she whispered. She raised the jug to her lips, drank deep, very slowly, lowering the level in it by about a quarter before moving over to the man chained to the pipes.

She held the jug to his face.

He drank like a dying man in the desert, careless of the vile, putrid taste of the water.

She pulled the jug away.

"Slow down or you'll be sick," she hissed. "Then you'll feel even worse than you do now."

Dwight Christie did not think that was remotely possible; he had never felt this bad in his whole life.

"Slowly," she counselled, moving the jug back to his mouth.

She withdrew the jug while there were still a couple of fingers of liquid in the bottom of it.

"Were you awake when the kid came in?"

The woman nodded.

"You heard what she said?"

Another nod.

"The bastards can't afford to have people," the woman said, "leaving their posts to 'mo...lest' the surviving embassy women anymore. That means the authorities have established a secure cordon around the compound and stopped people coming and going at will. The rebels inside the compound aren't going anywhere. It sounds like *your* friend Galen Cheney is starting to get nervous."

The former FBI man did not know how she could be so rational, so detached after what she had been through in the last few hours.

He said nothing.

"The bastards are all manning the barricades," Rachel went on. She had moved very close to the man, even so her whisper was barely audible. "The party's over!"

The way she said it sent a shiver of ice down Dwight Christie's aching spine.

He knew it was ridiculous: he was sitting in a pool of his own blood and piss, knocked and kicked senseless, chained to a fucking radiator, having been forced to watch the repeated, brutal gang rape of the woman beside him, there was a guard outside the door and they both were so desperately thirsty they had just drunk a couple of pints of what might have been piss, and yet...

Something in the woman's voice told him that the *real* unpleasantness was only just about to begin.

She leaned very close to murmur in his left ear.

"*I* am about to collapse on the floor over there next to the bed. *You* are about to scream your head off until whoever is outside that door opens it and comes in here to punch out your lights."

Dwight Christie's mind raced.

"Then what?"

"Nothing," she mouthed. "Nothing. I just want to see what is, or rather, who is on the other side of that door."

This said she rose to her feet with a strangely balletic grace that defied the many deep hurts she must have been feeling and ghosted to the bed. She turned, pirouetting, raising her arms. She gave the man chained to the radiator pipes one last meaningful look.

He nodded mutely.

And watched as with a loud moan the woman dumped – there was no other word like it – herself on the bare boards and lay, her face to the room's single door, insensible, motionless in an approximation of a heap of hardly articulated bones.

"COME IN HERE!"

"THE WOMAN'S COLLAPSED!"

"SHE TRIED TO GET TO THE WATER!"

It was then Christie realised she had knocked over the jug and that the remaining water was already draining through the cracks in the floorboards.

"HELP US YOU FUCKING BASTARDS!"

Nothing happened, so he kept shouting.

His voice got hoarser; his shouts less loud.

He kept shouting.

It was simple; he was ten times more afraid of the woman playing dead on the floor six feet away from him than he was of Galen Cheney, any of his maniac followers, or the religious nuts and crazies who must have stormed the compound when those two old school buses bust through the front gates.

It was irrational, bizarre in fact; but...

There were three of them; one man hefting what looked like a British Sten gun, the teenage girl who had come in with the jug of water and a shotgun-wielding boy with mean eyes, the sort of little turd who just liked hurting people.

The muzzle of the Sten gun pressed Christie's head back against the wall.

"Pick her up and put her on the bed," the man with the Sten gun growled, like he was incredibly pissed off with the others. "Careful, we need *her* alive."

He waited until the woman was spread-eagled on the mattress.

"Go get the medical box from downstairs, Kitty. Bring it back here. RUN!"

The girl sprinted, she literally sprinted out the door.

"Get back in the corridor, Noah," he instructed the boy.

Noah hesitated.

"Nobody goes into the rooms up here without me or Galen giving the OK, remember? Tell Jeb out there, too!"

The former FBI man registered this.

The man giving the orders was Dan, his *friend* from Cheney's Atsion Wood camp in the Wharton Forest. Dan was the ex-Army guy who had wanted to gut him on first acquaintance and had not mellowed in the intervening days. Either the other man had seen him as a threat to his own status within 'the gang', resented the fact he had obviously known Cheney from 'before', or he had seen through Christie on sight; Dan had been on his case ever since he had allowed himself to be captured in the woods.

Dan, Cheney's number two...

Or at least he probably thought he was the evil sonofabitch's main man; Cheney was not the sort of guy who had a 'deputy'. God was always watching over him so what need did he have for somebody to watch his back?

The kid with the shotgun was guarding the door to *this* room; outside in the corridor another man called 'Jeb' was on duty...

The muzzle of the Sten gun drew away. Dwight Christie squinted at the other man. Dan was smiling but not in a good way. There was blood on his camouflage smock, he was grey with exhaustion.

"Why don't you cap me now?" Christie asked, his words slurring. He shook his head, bad mistake. It felt like there was something wrong with his jaw...

"She said anything to you, FBI man?"

"Yeah, like in between rape sessions she's been telling me her life story?" Christie retorted contemptuously. "You shitheads make me want to throw up!"

"The other women couldn't talk fast enough."

Or *scream*, Christie recollected through the haze of bludgeoned memories. He had thought it was a nightmare, it was actually some poor woman, maybe two or three crying, pleading screeching their lungs out in the adjoining rooms.

Dan had slung his Sten gun over his right shoulder and reached under his smock. As he withdrew a six-inch hunting knife – razor-sharp and curved on one side, serrated on the other – Christie glimpsed the belt and the holstered revolver on his right hip.

What was the bastard doing toting what looked like an old-fashioned forty-five?

The blade of the knife caught the light, glinted dully.

Dan crouched over Dwight Christie.

"I told Galen we ought to have gutted you that day we found you hanging around the lake outside the camp in Wharton Forest. I figured he was waiting for a day when the mood took him, what with him being sick at the time. Never thought he'd start getting soft. Not after what we've been through."

The point of the knife pricked Christie's skin just under his left eye.

"You know these Brits didn't even fire into the crowd when all them boys and girls came over the fence out back?"

The former FBI Special Agent tried and failed to squirm away from the red-hot stabbing pain of the knife tip probing the flesh of his eye socket.

"They just let them come on in. They'd have killed us all out front if they'd been real men. You know what they did? They held up their fucking hands and surrendered..."

Christie thought he felt, definitely *felt* because he saw nothing, the presence of somebody behind the madman who was about to gouge out his left eye with a hunting knife.

But 'Dan', whoever the fuck he was, some loser from Galen Cheney's past maybe, was far too busy savouring the divine moment of maiming to *feel* or to *sense* anything else going on in the room.

There was a muffled 'click; a sickening bone-on-bone sort of 'click'.

Dan's eyes widened.

Afterwards, so many things happened so fast that it was not until the bodies were lying on the floor and the blood – so much blood - was spreading, dripping through the cracks in the floorboards that Dwight Christie began to reconstruct events.

He knew exactly what he had seen; he just did not believe it.

Momentarily he was paralysed, then an instant later all he wanted to do was claw his way through the wall behind him and escape before he too was ripped limb from limb by the monster with whom he now shared the blood-spattered charnel house in which he was imprisoned...

Chapter 37

14:09 Hours (Local) – 06:39 Hours in Philadelphia
Sevastopol Bunker Complex, Krasnoufimsk, Soviet Union

"Where the fuck is Shelepin?"

The middle-aged KGB Colonel to whom the Chairman of the Communist Party of the USSR had addressed this question visibly flinched.

"I regret I am unable to answer..."

Leonid Ilyich Brezhnev's beetle brows very nearly collided above his – these days – increasingly bucolic nose. He had arranged matters so that *he* arrived at the Sevastopol Bunker before his fellow Troika member and the head of the KGB; he had *not* planned to arrive and then to have to hang around indefinitely for the arrival of the fucking man!

The remote communications station in the outskirts of the ruins of the city of Perm over two hundred kilometres away on the other side of a mountain range – just in case the Yankees decided not to talk but just to bomb instead – was set up; the time had come to talk, well issue a counter ultimatum to the Americans; but Brezhnev knew that if he acted without the presence, and the acquiescence of the second most powerful man in the Motherland, Alexander Nikolayevich Shelepin, his enemies and the KGB man's allies in the Politburo, might never forgive him.

"Where the fuck is he?"

Colonel Viktor Vasilyevich Konayev, Chief Engineer of Project Sevastopol and the commander of the bunker complex's KGB garrison, had spent most of his life being berated and talked down to like a serf by men like Leonid Brezhnev. He ought to have been used to it by now.

But no, after the Cuban Missiles War putting up with the Party's shit had become in some, indefinable way *unbearable* in ways it had always been water off a duck's back before. It was as if the cataclysm had opened his eyes, raised his horizons beyond the world of engineering design and construction which had been his refuge, and his joy, since boyhood. He had never cared for politics; his marriage was a distraction although he missed his two boys, Konstantin and Nicolai. But for the blundering of men like Leonid Brezhnev his sons would be twelve and ten years old now...

When he spoke again Konayev's voice was even, carefully modulated with just enough skin-deep respect to avoid unnecessarily enraging the Party Chairman further.

"I do not know, Comrade Chairman..."

"Why the fuck did he fly down to Chelyabinsk?"

Konayev's reply was in one sense, painstakingly truthful and in another, criminally disingenuous.

"I do not know, Comrade Chairman..."

The KGB colonel waited resignedly to a verbal punishment beating.

"Oh, fuck off! Get out of my sight!"

Sixty-four-year-old Chief Marshal of Aviation Konstantin Andreevich Vershinin had witnessed the brief exchange. His face was impassive.

He was still digesting the contents of the long transmission concerning the situation on the 'southern front' in Iraq-Iran that had been received from the Commissar General of occupied Iraq, Yuri Andropov. Andropov was Shelepin's creature and like many Politburo members a military 'virgin'. The man had shit his pants in Budapest in 1956 when the mob had started stringing up Hungarian secret policemen on the street outside the Soviet Embassy, panicked and demanded that Khrushchev send in the tanks.

Andropov's communiqué was phrased in typical 'KGB-speak'.

Army Group South has attacked in massive strength on the Iranian side of the Shatt-al-Arab. Fierce fighting is in progress on Abadan Island. A British naval force has been destroyed by bombing and Red Army artillery south of Basra. Basra is being prepared as a staging area for ongoing operations. 3rd Caucasian Tank Army is consolidating its positions at Umm Qasr and along the Kuwaiti border. Enemy bombing raids have caused sufficient damage to delay 'forward operations' into Kuwait for at least ten days...

It sounded too good to be true and therefore, it was complete bullshit. That was why Gorshkov had flown south. If the situation was bad, really bad, the Troika needed one of its own members to make a realistic assessment.

"Comrade Chairman," Vershinin said, moving to shut the door of his office at his back. This was a thing best discussed privately. "We are running out of time. The squadrons of the 7th Guards Air Division must be moved to their forward operating stations," he shrugged, "otherwise we run the risk of our last nuclear capable bomber force being destroyed on the ground in the event of a Yankee first strike."

Leonid Brezhnev slumped into a chair.

He had been briefly cheered by the news that his wife Viktoria, and his son Yuri and his young family had been admitted to the complex, now his mood dipped anew.

What was Shelepin up to?

The only reason to detour to Chelyabinsk was the presence of Ambassador Thompson, President Kennedy's emissary to the Troika. Surely not even Shelepin would hold a man like that hostage?

Vershinin cleared his throat.

Brezhnev scowled.

"Yes, yes," he groaned. "The 7th Guards Air Division. I hadn't forgotten!"

In the immediate aftermath of the Cuban Missiles War the first systematic inventories had established that as many as two thousand military aircraft had survived the American attack. However, it soon became evident that ninety percent of all the aircraft and aeronautical components manufacturing plants in the USSR had been destroyed, badly damaged or were located in completely devastated areas no longer under the control of the government. For this reason, several key decisions had been taken in the spring of 1963 concerning which aircraft and component plants would be rebuilt and where, and more importantly, which aircraft types would be manufactured and retained by the Red Air Force. The five-year plan which had emerged had unified all existing airframe and engine design bureaus into a single 'Soviet Air Defence Development Project'.

The final decision had been to support only one interceptor type; the Mikoyan-Gurevich Mig-21. Surviving Tupolev Tu-95 long-range strategic bombers, and the handful of civilian variants of the type, the Tu-114 were to be kept operational if possible, whereas the more technologically advanced Myasishchev M-4 Molot – two aerial test beds excepted – was to be abandoned. The primary production plants for the Tu-95 and Tu-114 had been destroyed in the war; but one of the three factories producing the Tupolev Tu-16 medium bomber at Omsk was found to be 'salvageable', if not for purposes of aircraft production then for the ongoing manufacture of spares and components, and as an industrial scale facility for the refurbishment of existing airframes.

Thus, one of the two most numerous post-Cuban Missiles War bomber types available to the new USSR was the Tupolev Tu-16. The type had first flown in prototype form in 1952, eventually winning out over the competing Ilyushin Il-46. Eighteen months ago, the Tu-16 had again won out over another, earlier Ilyushin bomber, the Ilyushin Il-28, as the interim fully supported 'future bomber' of the Red Air Force. In practice a lot of the existing Il-28s had been retained, albeit in unmodernised and minimally maintained configurations. Many of the aircraft lost in the Iran-Iraq campaign – Operation Nakazyvat – had been Il-28s, 'deployable' within the 'kill envelopes' of the British missile defences on Abadan Island, because they were regarded as expendable.

The USSR's carefully husbanded force of over a hundred Tu-16s was anything but expendable. Although the Tu-16 was no Russian B-52; lacking the range, sophisticated electronics and payload of the American Stratofortress, it was the most capable remaining numerous bomber in the Red Air Force armoury and for this reason, eighty-five aircraft of this type had been retained under the command of the 7th Guards Air Division.

The Tu-16 was a large swept-wing aircraft powered by two Mikulin AM-3 wing-root mounted turbojets. With a full bomb load – a FAB-9000 'Grand Slam' type conventional bomb or a 'special' nuclear 'cargo' – it had a one-way range of over four thousand kilometres. Originally designed as a high-altitude bomber it could carry an AS-1, fighter-sized, nuclear or high explosive-tipped cruise missile allowing it to 'stand-off' over a hundred kilometres from its target. In all respects other than its operational range – the Red Air Force had lagged far behind western enemies in air-to-air refuelling capabilities – the TU-16 was a formidable strategic bomber but not, an intercontinental strategic bomber in the class of a B-52 or the scarce and very vulnerable Tu-95.

Of the eighty-five Tu-16's allocated to the 7th Guards Air Division, some fifty were serviceable and available for operations at any one time, and for this reason, no Tu-16 had been deployed in or over Iran and Iraq, or over any other territory beyond the borders of the Motherland since the Cuban Missiles War. The Tu-16 force represented the Soviet Union's single remaining *modern* nuclear strike force.

However, it was not the only 'strategic' bomber remaining in the Red Air Force's locker. In the spring of 1963 – after the nightmare they had all be through the previous October – nobody in the Red Air Force was willing to bet everything on a single horse. Pure, undiluted pragmatism had compelled the planners to turn to the past to ensure that whatever happened, the Red Air Force possessed at least one bomber type that it could maintain, and keep flying, practically forever; or at least until crashes, mechanical failures, old age and inevitably very heavy losses in action erased it from the order of battle.

There was nothing modern, or sophisticated about the Tupolev Tu-4, and because so few of them had been deployed in forward positions in the western republics of the Soviet Union at the time of the Cuban Missiles War – because they were obsolete – a large number, over three hundred, had survived mostly undamaged in a mothballed state. Moreover, because so many of the type were already in mothballs or awaiting disposal, future cannibalisation provided a potentially endless source of spare parts; thus, obviating the need to tool up new production facilities.

The Tu-4 was a reverse-engineered Soviet version of the American B-29 Superfortress. When, during 1944, several B-29s had made emergency landings or crashed on Soviet territory Josef Stalin, recognising the opportunity, had had the complete 'interned' aircraft and all the wreckage delivered to the Tupolev Design Bureau and demanded the bomber be cloned 'as soon as possible'. When Stalin ordered a thing like that it happened 'very quickly', and eventually over 900 separate factories and research bureaus were working on the project.

The intact B-29s in Soviet hands had actually been produced at two separate Boeing plants in Wichita, Wyoming, and at Renton in Washington State, the same plant that fifteen years later was building Boeing 707 airliners. Tupolev dismantled one B-29, used one for flight tests and kept another as a 'measuring horse' against which to quality control the whole gigantic reverse engineering project. The biggest headache had been overcoming the problems converting from US imperial to Soviet metric gauges; but after producing over a hundred thousand technical drawings, within two years Tupolev had produced an initial batch of twenty test aircraft. By the time production ceased in 1952 nearly five hundred and fifty Tu-4s had been built.

In the late 1940s the Tu-4 was actually, in some respects a marginally superior aircraft to Boeing's wartime 'rush job'. The Soviet

AHh-73 engine was at least the equal of the somewhat temperamental Wright duplex-cyclone R-3350s of the original captured B-29s, and the Tu-4's remotely operated gun turrets mounted the Nudelman NS-23 cannon as opposed to the B-29's 50-calibre machine guns. This said the Tu-4 had suffered a history of engine, propeller and equipment failures throughout its career and by the late 1950s was being gradually phased out of service; hence the large number of mothballed machines at the time of the Cuban Missiles War.

Notwithstanding, the availability of so many - admittedly old-fashioned – bombers capable of carrying a large conventional bomb load, or a nuclear weapon to targets as far from the Soviet Union as Los Angeles or the American Midwest (on a one-way flight), was hardly a thing the post-October 1962 Red Air Force, or the Politburo could ignore.

Earlier that day the commander of the 7th Guards Air Division had reported to Konstantin Vershinin that one hundred and seventeen Tu-4s were available for 'long-range' missions carrying either 'normal' or 'special' weapons.

If the Americans attacked the Motherland again they and their allies would not just face a few hastily scrambled Tu-95s and M-4s, or whatever missiles could be readied in the minutes before the first Minutemen, Polaris A-1s and A-2s plummeted down upon the Soviet Union as they had in late October 1962; now the 7th Guards Air Division stood ready to retaliate in kind!

Leonid Ilyich Brezhnev wondered if he ought not to have given the 'dispersal' order before he left Sverdlovsk.

Presently, less than half the Tu-4s and Tu-16s were in transit to, or at their forward, war station bases.

"Do it!" The Chairman of the Communist party of the USSR said grimly. "Disperse the 7th Guards Air Division to war stations!"

All operational aircraft would fly to their 'advanced' bases – minimising the distance and flight times to their targets – and until such time as the 'ready' order was rescinded at least fifty percent of the entire force would be airborne at any one time.

The Americans called their DEFCON 1 state of alert 'cocked pistol'; well, Leonid Brezhnev had just 'cocked' his gun.

Once again, the Soviet Union and the United States stood eyeball to eyeball on their respective continents, each holding primed and monstrously indiscriminate thermonuclear duelling cannons to each other's heads.

Chapter 38

In her husband's absence Marija was being kept company by one, or both of President Johnson's daughters, and occasionally also by the First Lady, and at all times by Petty Officer Jack Griffin. Although she was doing her best not to show it she was finding all the attention a little bit...claustrophobic.

She had not slept properly for thirty-six hours, obviously things were very tense and she was worried, really worried about Peter. Oh, and of course, she was four months pregnant with her first baby. She was allowed to faint now and then and besides; Peter had caught her.

So, what was everybody so worried about?

She sipped tepid weak tea, smiled demurely at her hosts and guardians and attempted to make small conversation. She liked the President's daughters. They seemed nice people, very normal and the older of the pair, Lynda was only six or seven years her junior. Luci, who was seventeen, Marija had discovered, was the chattier of the girls. Their mother was a little distracted, which was entirely understandable in the circumstances.

Having unavailingly suggested to Jack Griffin that she was in the 'safest place in America' and that he ought to 'relax', take a break to eat breakfast 'or something', she had gently embarrassed the bearded, rock-like sailor by regaling the Johnson girls with the tale of how he and her 'little' brother Joe, had fired the torpedoes that sank the two Russian 'battleships' in the Battle of Malta.

Her motives in telling the story were not simply to discomfort Jack but to remind her hosts that she, and her husband, far from having any personal 'beef' against the United States or any of its citizens, were as unhappy as everybody else in the White House that things had come to this very, very sad pass.

"My husband warned the Captain of the USS Berkeley not to come alongside Talavera. You see, he believed she was going to capsize, or perhaps blow up. But the USS Berkeley came alongside anyway and because of the bravery and the sacrifice of the men of the United States Navy my husband," a nod towards the red-headed, scarred man standing at the door, "Jack, my brother and many, many other Talaveras are alive today. In my prayers I always remember Midshipman Alois Rendorp, and Seaman Casey O'Leary of the Berkeley who died that day rescuing badly injured Talaveras from the water when the ship's back broke and she sank." This she concluded with a tight-lipped grimace. "We had hoped – Peter and I and my sister Rosa, and her husband Alan Hannay – to visit the parents of Midshipmen Rendorp in Savannah and Seaman Casey's mother in San Diego, but..."

The one good thing which had come out of Marija's 'fainting

moment' was that it seemed to have snapped her husband out of his uncharacteristic 'angriness'. She admitted that she had a stubborn streak – her Mama had often chided her on the subject although *she* was hardly the one to lecture anybody about 'stubbornness' – but once Peter set his mind to it he could be as immovable as a rock. Worse, because he was a man who did not anger easily – hardly at all in fact usually - when he was angry he was doubly hard to mollify.

However, as she had blinked up at the circle of concerned faces around her she had realised that her husband had, temporarily, put aside his righteous anger. At that moment he was much more worried about her than he was about the World lurching toward World War Four...

'I am all right,' she had protested. 'You must do what you can to save us all,' she had declared, albeit shakily. Peter had swept her up in his arms and was in the process of gently laying her on the chaise longue from which she had unwisely risen shortly before. 'Like at Malta...'

She had almost swooned again at that point.

Chapter 39

07:00 Hours (EST)
Situation Room, White House, Philadelphia

"You should know that I am sitting in the middle of the Situation Room in the basement of the White House," Peter Christopher informed Sir Thomas Harding-Grayson down the remarkably clean, unclicky, static-free transatlantic line. A part of him – the electronics aficionado who had been fascinated all his life by every manner of radio and radar widget and new space age gizmo – wondered what technical wizardry the Americans possessed that could so marvellously 'clean up' an inherently 'dirty' hard-wired very long-distance telephone connection. However, for the moment the officer and gentleman part of him focused on the business in hand. "Everything I say is being overheard by at least a dozen persons, sir."

At this Tom Harding-Grayson's scholarly gravitas cracked momentarily.

"Diplomacy was ever such, Sir Peter."

"I shall have to take your word for that, sir."

The Foreign Secretary became serious again.

"The Prime Minister has given me leave to inform you that *de facto*, well, to all intents, actually *de jure* you are now Her Majesty's Ambassador to the United States."

The man who had been a relatively junior Electronic Warfare Officer – a lowly lieutenant – on the night of the October War just twenty months ago allowed himself a moment to adjust to his latest promotion.

"Please pass my compliments to the Prime Minister, sir. She bestows on me an honour that I have done nothing to deserve. I will do my best to justify her confidence in me."

"I will relay your words to her verbatim."

"Thank you, sir." Peter took a deep breath.

First things first; the man at the other end of the line might think he had a sound grasp of the lay of the land but he did not and could not know, the mood of the men in the bunker around him. That mood was grim and frankly, vengeful. He guessed that to most Americans the sinking of the Kitty Hawk and the deaths of several thousand US Navy men in the Persian Gulf had hit home like the first news of the attack on Pearl Harbour in December 1941.

It was obvious to the young naval officer that most of the people around him had already conveniently half-forgotten about the sneak attack on HMS Centaur; to them it was some piffling little misunderstanding. They were much more preoccupied with what was going to happen when the news about the sinking of the Kitty Hawk and the arrest of the Sixth Fleet at Malta reached 'middle America'. All Hell was going to break lose. In such a febrile atmosphere it was not beyond possibility that the rebellion in the Midwest, the troubles in the Deep South, the humiliation in the Mediterranean and the outright disaster to American arms in the Persian Gulf could, and probably would be confabulated into a single incendiary grievance directed at the United Kingdom and its allies, regardless of the Soviet Union's ongoing aggression...

The Situation Room's low ceiling emphasised its former role as a bank vault; it was easy to understand how men confined down in its depths might quickly succumb to 'bunker mentality'.

"President Johnson has communicated several," he hesitated, "*demands* to me, sir."

"What does he want?" The other man inquired urbanely.

"First; the release from *internment* of Sixth Fleet."

"We're writing this down at our end," Tom Harding-Grayson confirmed drily. "Carry on."

"Second; an immediate ceasefire in the Persian Gulf. Ground forces to stop where they are, or were, at zero-zero-zero-one hours Eastern Standard Time."

"Ceasefire, yes, what next?"

"Third; all parties to the conflict in the Persian Gulf are to attend a peace conference at the old UN building in New York within seventy-two hours. President Johnson to chair the same."

"Oh, that's novel!"

"Quite, sir. Fourthly, an immediate cessation of hostilities in the South Atlantic and a commitment in principle for all parties to the 'dispute' over the sovereignty of the Falklands/Malvinas Islands to convene 'talks'. Again, he suggests the old UN building as a possible venue."

"Um..."

"Fifth; all Royal Navy vessels in the North Atlantic to withdraw east of longitude ten degrees west. Further to this our submarine forces in the South Atlantic are to withdraw to Simonstown in South Africa. Any vessel not complying with this ordnance will be liable to attack without warning."

Peter sighed.

"Sixth and last; Her Majesty's Government will abandon plans to initiate a permanent 'West Coast Embassy' in California and recall all staff currently assigned to that mission to Philadelphia."

The Foreign Secretary ruminated briefly.

When he spoke again his tone was very nearly jaunty.

"Do you have a pen and paper to hand, Sir Peter?"

One of Secretary of State Fulbright's senior flunkies placed both – a foolscap lined notepad and a fountain pen, a Parker, by the new British Ambassador's right elbow.

"Yes, sir." Peter acknowledged, shifting the phone from his left to his right ear and moving the pen and pad to his left side.

"Good. If you would be so good as to take this down. Word for word, please."

"Fire away, sir."

The Foreign Secretary spoke slowly, pausing to enable the younger man to keep up with him.

"Her Majesty's Government thanks the US Administration for clarifying its stance on several of the matters of dispute between our two countries. *Full stop. New paragraph.*"

Peter wrote neatly, in his own time.

"All of which it will take under urgent and serious consideration. *Full stop.* Having heard the US Administration's demands, we note the omission of a reference to the unprovoked attack on HMS Centaur and her consorts of the second instance, *comma,* and to US diplomatic overtures to the Soviet Union designed to undermine the legitimate interests of British, Commonwealth and Arab nations in the wider Middle East. *Full stop. New paragraph.*"

There was a delay while Peter caught up.

"Carry on, sir," he invited.

"Reference President Johnson's 'six points'," Tom Harding-Grayson, his tone now indicating that he had given up punctuating and paragraphing the note Peter was writing.

"Point one. Internment of the Sixth Fleet. HMG may at some point in the future elect to initiate negotiations on this subject based on establishing a quid pro quo for the Royal Navy, Royal Australian Navy and Royal New Zealand Navy vessels lost as a result of the *sneak* attack of second instance."

Peter queried if he had heard the word 'sneak' correctly.

He had!

Around him his hosts looked at each other unhappily as they shifted impatiently on their feet or drummed their fingers on the top of the Situation Room table.

"Point two: matters pertaining to a ceasefire on the ground in southern Iran-Iraq are ongoing between C-in-C Middle East and his opposite number in Basra."

Peter imagined he heard papers shuffling at the other end of the line.

"Oh, yes... Point three: we agree in principle to calling a *general peace conference.* Our preference would be for it to be held on neutral ground. Ottawa suggests itself. Given the assassination of Lord Franks and his staff it will be impossible to lay the necessary ground work for such a conference in seventy-two hours."

Peter's eyes widened a little at the Foreign Secretary's insouciance. He kept on writing.

"Point four; there will be no withdrawal of our submarines to Simonstown. It is not for the US Administration to mandate the naval dispositions of an independent, sovereign power. Point five; the same clause applies," Tom Harding-Grayson guffawed lowly, as if he was shaking his head with disbelief. "As for point six; HMG reserves the right to propose and dispose of its diplomatic missions at its pleasure."

The Foreign Secretary allowed a short interregnum to settle.

"Would you be so good as to read that back to me, Sir Peter?"

The younger man did as he was bade.

"Thank you," The Foreign Secretary acknowledged. "Diplomacy, like politics, is the art of the possible, Peter. The *carelessness* of our hosts in Philadelphia has denied you and I the opportunity to converse confidentially, therefore we must make the best of things and deal with our 'friends' in America via megaphone. Customarily, my instructions to you in your new role would be a private matter between us, the Prime Minister and in extremity, Her Majesty." He paused, letting his audience form their own opinions. "For your information the communications 'channel' over which we are speaking has been facilitated via the Central Intelligence Agency."

"Presumably by that station of theirs in Ireland, sir," the younger man remarked. "The clarity of the channel would be something to do with the equipment onboard whatever ship must be relaying the signal from somewhere in mid-Atlantic," Peter's voice trailed away. He was allowing his parochial, technical fascinations to run wild, and that would never do. "So, the people in Philadelphia are in regular contact with Captain Brenckmann at the Embassy in Oxford?"

"Quite so."

Peter's sigh of relief would have deafened the Foreign Secretary had he not briefly removed the handset from his face.

"What are my instructions, sir?"

"You are to do what can be done."

Independent command; what more could any naval officer ask?

"Very good, sir." He looked up. "I believe Secretary of State Fulbright wishes to speak to you."

It was not lost on him that half the room was suddenly empty.

Chapter 40

07:05 Hours (EST)
British Embassy, Wister Park, Philadelphia

Dwight Christie and the scarecrow teenage girl called Kitty had dragged the bodies of the three men down the corridor and rolled them onto the circular staircase, partially blocking it.

The girl had returned just after the killings.

She had stood frozen in the bedroom doorway in a trance, staring wide-eyed, catatonically at the carnage.

Christie had no idea why she had not simply run away when she came across the body on the landing; she must have stepped over it to get to the door...

Rachel, the blade of Dan's gory hunting knife glinting dully in her hand had pinned the newcomer to the wall with a single look.

'Stand where you are! Don't scream!'

The woman had not had to say *'move and I'll kill you'* because the kid had worked that out for herself by then; and ever since she had been as meek and compliant as a puppy dog.

The corridor floor was bloody underfoot, slippery. A human body contains seven or eight pints of blood and it seemed at least a couple of gallons of it was now slopping around on the bare boards or seeping through the gaps to drip down into the rafters below.

The former FBI man was still piecing it all together...

Trying to get things in chronological order was...*difficult.*

He had been too busy trying to squirm away from the tip of the hunting knife digging into his face – it had opened him up down to the cheek bone below his left eye – and it had been several seconds before he realised it was no longer grating against the bone.

There had been a shadow behind the crouching tormentor.

Dan, yes, Dan...

Galen Cheney's sidekick...

A shadow and a sudden, very quiet non-mechanical, sickening 'click'...

Dan was squatting over him, his head jerked back...

Or was that before the 'click'?

Dan's eyes had started to widen with surprise.

A thud.

And another...

The knife – the one that had been in Dan's hand, the one with the razor-sharp edge on one side and a viciously serrated blade on the other – had flashed and then there was blood, pumping, splattering across Christie's feet.

The bedroom door had opened.

The kid with the narrow eyes, the kid Christie had marked down as one of those people who got his kicks hurting people, had stumbled into the room raising the barrel of his shotgun. Some kind of nineteenth century fouling piece...

The shadow had risen from the twitching, flailing body of the man who had been about to carve out Dwight Christie's left eye – just for the heck of it – and the blade of the knife had glinted wetly.

Held like a dagger it had proscribed a short, unbelievably fast arc and then the kid was staggering towards the bed. The shotgun clattered on the floor, his hands pawing uselessly at his throat.

'*I just want to see what's the other side of that door.*'

That was what she had said.

'*I just want to see what's the other side of that door.*'

Another noise, out in the corridor.

The door slammed almost, but not quite against its frame.

It hit something hard with a sound like a beat-up flatbed truck with a drunk at the wheel totalling a trash can on the sidewalk.

She had unhurriedly opened the door and stepped out into the corridor.

Christie had seen what she had done to the man she slammed the door on a couple of minutes or so later, when she had pushed him and Kitty out onto the landing to start dumping the bodies down the stairs. What looked like a bayonet off an old-fashioned US Army carbine was pinning the third man's lifeless cadaver to the floor boards through the wreckage of his right eye socket.

'Get that out. Wipe it before you give it back to me!'

Christie had done what he was told to do.

She had busted him out of the handcuffs tying him to the radiator with a hair clip in literally two seconds flat...

A goddam hairclip!

Dan had left a satchel containing three spare magazines for his stolen Sten gun, two US Army issue pineapple-type hand grenades and two canteens full of brackish but clean water propped against the wall of the corridor just outside the bedroom door.

'*Idiots!*'

This the woman had observed contemptuously, shouldering the Sten gun and carrying the satchel with her as she looked into the three rooms farther down the landing. There was a dead girl in one bedroom, a woman in her twenties and another in her thirties in two others, both beaten up, and chained as she had been whom she immediately released.

One of the women had called *her* Rachel; both had looked at her as if she was their guardian angel.

Christie, the girl Kitty, and as soon as *Rachel* had freed her, the older of the two surviving women had begun to pile furniture from the bedrooms across the corridor half-way down, about twenty feet from the top of the stairs; beds, mattresses, chairs, tables.

Christie was given the shotgun and the ten cartridges they discovered in the dead boy's pockets. The man Rachel had executed in the corridor had had a Browning pistol, eight slugs in the magazine, but no spare rounds on his body. Dan's antique Colt revolver was given to the older of the other women, who seemed remarkably untraumatised by her ordeal, Christie thought...

Her name was Mary.

The younger woman rescued from the room next to the one in which he and *Rachel* had been held trembled and sobbed uncontrollably in a corner.

Christie had expected more of Cheney's zealots, or a gang of the animals who had stormed the compound to tramp up the stairs at any second.

"Where are these guys?"

"Your friend Dan told them he was coming up here to have his 'turn'," Rachel retorted sarcastically. "His sort doesn't like to be interrupted."

She must have detected his incredulity, quite an achievement beneath the blood and grime encrusting his battered features. She had washed the blood off her face and hands, the worst of it, and made an effort to restore her modesty, re-arranging her torn frock and blouse and pulling on the only partially blood-ruined khaki-dun shirt of the man whose head she had pinned to the floor with a hunting knife.

Her left eye was blotchy and swelling, half-closed and her throat was red, from the choke hold of one of her rapists clearly, brutally apparent. Her voice was a little hoarse; it tended to be for a few days after some madman tried to strangle you...

"These people are ignorant, undisciplined imbeciles led by a handful of lunatic religious fanatics, Special Agent Christie," her lip curled in scorn. "The sort of people who marry their own sisters and think the government is run by the Devil because it won't let them have sex with their children. That's why somebody has to kill them." She sniffed, pushed the tangled matt of hair off her bruised brow. "All of them!"

Christie had been flicking looks at the fire escape door at the end of the corridor.

"Forget it. Right now, if you open that door and it will be the last thing you ever do. The people outside think we're all dead." She thought about it. "Or if we're not that it would probably be a lot better for everybody if we were. They don't want survivors walking about talking to journalists, or going on radio or TV blaming the US government for not respecting the sanctity of diplomatic missions to the land of the free, do they?"

It was Mary, a plump brunette with a fat lip, cradling Dan's old Colt in the folds of her filthy skirt who asked the obvious question.

"How *do* we get out of here, Rachel?"

Dwight Christie picked up his ears; realising that the two women – of an age – were probably more than just coincidental work colleagues, possibly even friends.

Rachel's attention was distracted by movement beyond the other woman's right shoulder.

She held up a hand and threw a nakedly intimidating look at the girl Kitty, who instinctively shrank away.

"Do you want to live?"

"The terrified teenager nodded jerkily.

"Go to the top of the stairs. If anybody shows their face scream at the top of your voice and run back here behind the barricade."

Again, the kid nodded; her face the colour of ash.

"Go!"

Kitty hurdled the low barrier of bedsteads, chairs and mattresses like a startled Gazelle, skidded on the blood on the bare boards and teetered to a halt at the head of the stairs, got down flat on her belly and peeked over the edge to the first-floor landing below.

Rachel returned her full attention to Mary and the former FBI man. She ignored the other, younger woman half-sitting, half-curled in a near foetal position, whimpering softly with unseeing eyes some feet away.

Instead of answering Mary's question her stare settled on Christie.

"One of the reasons 'your friends'," she prefaced with the casual cruelty of a cat lazily clawing an unsuspecting companion, just to make sure she had its undivided attention, "haven't interrupted us again in the last twenty of so minutes is that the layout of the building," she corrected herself, "or rather, collection of buildings making up the 'complex' makes it very hard to secure. This wing – the north wing – unlike its southern sister which is otherwise identical, is only linked to the rest of the Embassy by a single door on the ground floor."

She pointed at where Kitty was lying, sneaking periodic frightened looks through the banister rails at the end of the hallway.

"The main offices are all situated in the largest of the three wings, the 'West' or 'central' wing. The southern wing accommodates the Ambassador's rooms and the suites of senior Embassy officials. Space was at such a premium – this is an old boarding school, after all, not designed for the needs of a foreign embassy - that until the bombing of the compound last month some twenty to thirty staff had to lodge at local hotels, or in the houses of ex-patriots or friends in Philadelphia. The Embassy Protection Detail occupied much of the two floors below us. The basement of this wing houses a boiler room, a storeroom and a small armoury." She hefted the small satchel Dan had left in the corridor. "Clearly, our former captors discovered *that* particular little Aladdin's cave."

Rachel eyed Dwight Christie.

"In any event, this floor of the North Wing of the Embassy complex was designated for accommodation for secretarial and military support personnel. Three rooms on the floor below were for the use of visiting low-ranking staff or guests. *This* floor was specifically reserved for members of the Ambassador and the Charge D'affaires's private offices, and Lady Barbara's personal assistant." She inclined her head towards Mary. "Mary was, in effect, the 'floor mother' to the other women, in addition to her duties as the Ambassador's Diary Secretary."

The other woman had seemed to be on the verge of breaking

down. She squeezed her eyes shut, breathed deep and got a grip of herself.

"I first came to work at the Embassy during Oliver and Barbara's first stint in DC," Mary sniffled defiantly. "I worked as a legal secretary for many years in Washington after 1952 but when Lord Franks was re-appointed Ambassador I wrote to Lady Barbara and she invited me, literally by return of post, to work at the Embassy here in Philadelphia."

Dwight Christie tried to form a reassuring smile on his bloody face; and failed dismally.

"Sorry to meet you this way, Mary," he murmured.

To his astonishment the woman breathed an amused sigh.

"Rachel hasn't introduced us, Mr Christie," she whispered. "I'm Mary Drinkwater." This she confessed with a distinct Maryland-Virginia twang.

"Mister Christie is a disgraced FBI agent who was caught working for the Russians," Rachel snarled like a Leopardess rising to protect her cubs from a marauding Hyena.

"I was 'captured' by Galen's Cheney's maniacs when I was working on a sting with the FBI," the man protested, feeling oddly guilty to be lying, particularly to Mary Drinkwater.

"I've heard them talking about somebody called Galen," the woman observed. "They're all scared stiff of him..."

Rachel frowned impatiently.

"We can all get to know each other better later," she hissed irritably.

Dwight Christie, having rediscovered a little of his moral fibre, drawing no little comfort from the knowledge that at least one of the women in his immediate vicinity was looking at him as if he was a human being.

"You know who I am, who are you, Lady?" He put to Rachel.

Mary Drinkwater was silent.

Rachel ignored the question.

"This wing's telephone exchange is separate from that of the rest of the complex and was therefore unused," she explained. "So far as I know it was never dismantled or disconnected, although several of the more technically-minded of the Royal Marines attached to the Protection Detail may have modified it for their own purposes. If I can get to it I may be able to talk to the people outside the compound."

She let that sink in.

"Since nobody came upstairs in the minutes we were noisily dragging bodies and furniture around it is likely that there may not be any 'intruders' permanently posted in this wing of the complex other than the two men, and," she nodded at Kitty, peering through the banisters at the top of the stairs down to the ground floor well of the building where it connected to the larger, West Wing, "*her*. Kitty," she snapped, "what was your job?"

"I carried messages, ma'am," the kid blurted.

Rachel nodded.

That made sense; the scum infesting the Embassy had not worked out how to operate the telephones.

Why does that not surprise me?

"There is a good reason very few of the intruders are permanently based in this wing," Rachel explained, thinking aloud. "The south and central, main wings are interconnected at every floor and in terms of services; plumbing, electricity and telephones effectively 'one building'. Whereas, personnel sent into this wing are, in effect, lost to the defenders in an entirely separate block and unable to support, or to be supported by the main force currently in control of the complex. Presumably, this was one of Mister Cheney's considerations in locating *we* 'comfort women' here, rather than in the south and central wings where he needed his people focused on 'manning the barricades' rather than on 'looting and rapine'."

Rachel did not dwell on this.

She glanced to the fire escape door behind them.

"My working assumption is that the reason we are not hearing any firing, or any commotion of any kind outside is that the compound is now, somewhat belatedly, surrounded by an overwhelming police and military presence. While opening that door and waving white flags is an option, I tend towards the view that given the kind of people the authorities are dealing with, they are likely to shoot first and ask questions later. If I was a soldier, state trooper or cop out there I wouldn't trust any of the lunatics who broke in here to honour a flag of truce, would you?"

Dwight Christie shook his head.

"So that's the plan, we get to the telephone?"

"No," Rachel said definitely. Then moderated her stance: "Later, maybe. I need to go downstairs to see what we're up against. Assuming it is 'safe', you, Mary, Cynthia," she indicated the whimpering woman, "and Kitty are going downstairs. You'll have to decide whether to lock yourself in the basement or try to contact the authorities – if the line is still up – I'll be going 'up' there," she explained matter-of-factly, her eyes flicking to the ceiling where a small panel, painted over and barely a foot square was set into the ceiling.

"What's the point of that?" The man demanded.

"I lied," Rachel admitted, almost coyly. "The north and central wings share a common roof space, or rather, access between the respective lofts. The prior occupant of the building, an elementary school, I believe, was in the middle of a renovation and modernisation program and the idea was to tie all the services in the complex back to a single electrical switch room, boiler room, telephone exchange and so on. Thus, there are access ways just big enough for somebody of my size to squeeze through."

"That's fine, lady," Christie objected hoarsely. "You didn't answer my question. What's the point? There may be a hundred fucking maniacs in the other wings..."

The man's voice trailed off; there was something in the way she was viewing him that sent a spear of ice down his spine. Her eyes were windows to a void he did not trust himself to explore; it was like looking into...*death.*

"You may be a good man, Dwight Christie," the woman speculated, her accent suddenly very...*Russian.* "Maybe, maybe not. You and me are a little alike. Just a little. We both have a great deal to atone for. This is your chance. Protect Mary and the others if you can. I cannot. That is not what I do."

She stood up.

"I will need your help to break through that hatch when the time comes. The bastards messed up my shoulder," she added half-apologetically, as if it was her fault, "so when I return I will need you to make a back for me and to push me high enough so that I can climb the rest of the way."

Dwight Christie had risen unsteadily to his feet.

"*Who are you, Lady?*"

Rachel opened her mouth to reply.

And the girl Kitty screamed...

Chapter 41

The navigation plot showed the Big E over two hundred miles north-west of Alexandria. A problem with one of the carrier's eight Admiralty 3-drum boilers had caused Eagle to slow to twenty-five knots for nearly an hour but now she was smashing almost due west at over twenty-nine knots, her stem carving imperiously through the rising swell on the edge of the storm front racing north towards distant Cyprus.

Her smaller escorts, even with their magazines full and their bunkers topped up were only a fraction of the Big E's *heft* – Oudenarde tipping the scales fully loaded at around three thousand four hundred tons and the Scorpion around two thousand eight hundred tons – and when the sea state worsened, as it surely would as the squadron battered into its dark heart, both destroyers were going to begin to ship white water over their bows and foredecks.

Although the motion of the rising swell could be felt on the carrier, especially on the flight deck and from the lofty vantage point of the island superstructure of the bridge; her length was such that she crested several waves, hardly pitched at all in this sort of 'squall'. In her post-refit configuration, she only really rolled in a strong cross sea and today she was steaming virtually straight into the weather. However, if Oudenarde and Scorpion were to keep up with the Eagle the going was going to get rough, pretty bloody actually, before it got any better.

Frank Maltravers returned to the bridge and stepped onto the starboard, outer wing perched the best part of seventy feet above the waterline. He gazed ahead and enjoyed the gale blowing in his face. With the ship making the best part of thirty knots (thirty-three or four 'land' miles per hour) through the water and the wind gusting twenty to twenty-five knots almost directly over the bow, he was standing in a wind that gusted from forty to sixty miles an hour; the sensation never failed to make him want to vent a raucous gout of joyful laughter. However, this afternoon he contained his exuberance. Notwithstanding that he and his great ship might be racing towards its appointment with destiny; every eye was upon him and the Navy expected its Captains to respect due *decorum*. For a brief interregnum he actually felt a tinge of guilt; things might be looking universally grim on the hemispheric, not to say global, geopolitical strategic level but he was having the time of his life and that seemed, just...well, wrong.

The two returning Sea Vixens circled over the carrier and dropped astern as Maltravers returned inside.

Back in 1959 the plan had included modifying the Big E for all likely 'ABC' – Atomic, Bacteriological and Chemical – War contingencies. This involved making it possible to seal up the ship basically, and the installation of sufficient plumbing and pumping capability to wash any nuclear fallout, or bacteriological or chemical contamination 'filth' off the outer hull and superstructure if the worst happened. The necessary work had been started and substantially completed in several areas of the ship, for example the island superstructure which had been practically rebuilt from scratch could be closed up and hermetically sealed for short periods of time if necessary, but unfortunately very little of the 'washing down' pipe work, and none of the new pumps or filtration units required in the event of an ABC attack, or accident, had actually been installed.

The Big E would have been one Hell of a ship if all the plans mooted for her back in the late 1950s had actually come to fruition. She would have been a hundred feet longer, perhaps five to six thousand tons heavier and very nearly a match for the biggest US carriers. It had not happened and nobody onboard loved her any less for it. Those plans would have turned her into a thoroughly modern, possibly less idiosyncratic beast and a part of Frank Maltravers's naval soul would have regretted that; at least now as the old girl pounded fearlessly towards her fate she was clothed in her true colours.

Moving to the rear of the bridge he stepped out onto the flying platform and watched the first of the two CAP – Combat Air Patrol – De Havilland Sea Vixens thump down onto the deck.

Second arrester wire!

First or second was good.

Once a pilot started regularly catching the third or fourth wire, or 'bolting' off the angled landing area to go around for another bite at the cherry it could become a problem.

Up until the advent of fast jet aircraft, landing on a carrier, even in a lump of a piston engine fighter like the four-and-a-half ton Vought F4U Corsairs Frank Maltravers had flown at the end of the Pacific War, was still, vaguely, like landing on terra firma, albeit an evolution requiring the hooking of one or other of a carrier's wires. Nowadays, landing a fifteen-ton beast like a Sea Vixen, even on a much bigger deck, was not so much a return to earth as a controlled crash. The moment the wheels hit the deck the pilot shoved the throttles through the gate in case he missed *all* the wires and – assuming he hooked *something* – in a furious, deafening crescendo of engine noise the aircraft decelerated from well over a hundred miles an hour to a shuddering standstill in a split second before the throttles were closed again.

Frank Maltravers never tired of watching the violent choreography of a landing. The moment the aircraft was stationary men swarmed out, and the arrester wire snaked back across the after deck to be re-tensioned...

The outer sections of the Sea Vixen's wings folded upward until they were vertical as the pilot taxied out of the way.

The landing, the resetting of the arrester gear, and the first fighter clearing the deck all happened in less than sixty seconds as the second aircraft lined up for its approach. Normally, aircraft would be being launched off the bow as all this was going on, not this afternoon. The 'summer squall' predicted before the squadron sailed that morning was turning into something altogether sharper, nastier and the Captain of the Eagle liked recovering his birds in the middle of an electrical storm as *much* as his pilots.

Where Eagle was heading he needed every aircraft and every pilot he had and risking either unnecessarily in the middle of a storm was tempting fate.

Rain dashed across the flight deck at a slashing forty-five-degree angle, a vicious gust of wind hit the ship as the second Sea Vixen crunched down. Its hook caught the fourth wire – a minor miracle in the circumstances – and momentarily its two Rolls-Royce Avon Mk. 208 engines spooled down.

The majority of 892 Squadron's pilots were pre-war veterans who had come back from the Far East on the Ark Royal and the Hermes. Some of their deck landings were minor masterpieces of sheer applied airmanship and eyes squeezed tightly shut triumphs of optimism over adversity.

The pilot of the No. 2 Sea Vixen had practically thrown his aircraft onto the deck when the sudden gust of wind hit the starboard side of his aircraft...

Chapter 42

12:12 Hours (GMT) – 07:12 Hours in Philadelphia
Hertford College, Oxford, England

The American authorities had been waiting for daylight to attempt to recover the bodies of Lord Franks, his wife Barbara, Sir Patrick Dean, the Charge d'affaires and half-a-dozen other bodies from the steps of the Wister Park Embassy in Philadelphia. There was, apparently, an uneasy stand-off between the mob which had stormed the compound and the heavily armed Marine and National Guard units which now completely encircled the Embassy.

"According to Fulbright," Tom Harding-Grayson reported down the distractingly noisy local line between the United States Embassy and Hertford College, less than a mile away, "the attack on the Embassy compound caught the Philadelphia Police Department and National Guard troopers completely unawares. Most of the Guardsmen were facing a crowd of about three to four thousand protesters on the park side of the Embassy, and only a relatively small number of policemen and soldiers were on duty, less than fifty, were actually guarding the front gates..."

Margaret Thatcher listened in stony silence.

Her friend, the Foreign Secretary's wife and – she had recognised latterly – her own motherly, personal advisor had intercepted her on her return from Woodstock a few minutes ago with a cup of tea and made very sure that she was left alone long enough to collect her wits.

Pat Harding-Grayson had tactfully withdrawn when her husband's call had come through.

"Fulbright freely admits that the Philadelphia PD and the Army were caught napping. They had eyes only for the events in the centre of the city. The so-called 'March on Philadelphia' by Doctor King's supporters. That and the big rally in the streets around the House of Representatives building, City Hall. Fulbright maintains that the local commanders at Wister Park did not know what to do. Two busses crashed into the area directly in front of the central wing of the complex, and a fierce exchange of gunfire ensued; while in a seemingly co-ordinated fashion the crowd to the rear and south of the compound rushed the National Guardsmen and scaled the fences to gain access to the grounds of the Embassy. It seems the order to fire on the mob either came too late or was ignored by the majority of individual soldiers. There is some suggestion that staff within the Embassy also failed to fire directly into the crowd. Thereafter, there was chaos and the 'intruders' ransacked the building. As many as ten bodies were seen to be thrown down the steps to the main entrance around dusk last night. The bodies had been stripped naked, or down to their under clothes – it is not clear which – and all were in a bad state..."

"Somebody will pay for this, Tom!" The Prime Minister snarled.

"Yes, quite," the man at the other end of the line agreed.

"President Johnson's terms are ridiculous," she went on.

"I agree." Except of course, Tom Harding-Grayson's appreciation of the 'American terms' was less black and white; nothing in diplomacy was ever black and white, there were always infinite variations of grey...

"You do?"

"No, actually I don't, Margaret."

The Prime Minister was about to vent her impatience when there was a knock at the door, and the war-reduced, still burly presence of the Member of Parliament for Penrith and the Border, stepped into the room. William Whitelaw was sporting a poker, albeit hangdog expression, but there was the hint of a smile in his eyes and a suggestion of jauntiness in his movements.

She waved him to take a chair.

"What *do* you think, Tom?" She demanded with less asperity than perhaps, her Foreign Secretary had anticipated.

"I expected them to have attacked us by now."

"Yes, well they jolly well haven't, yet!"

"Quite. In any event, do I have your licence to carry on talking to the blighters?"

Tom Harding-Grayson had been rushing towards the end of his brief update when the Secretary of State for Defence had made his entrance.

"Willie's just arrived," Margaret Thatcher told him. "I'll speak to you again in a few minutes, Tom." Putting the handset back on its cradle she viewed the newcomer, inadvertently chewing her bottom lip. "What's happened now?" She inquired, not really wanting to know.

"I think we may finally have a good picture of what's actually going on in the Gulf, Prime Minister," Whitelaw announced.

Margaret Thatcher suppressed the urge to scowl; the man looked like he was about to dance a jig. She spread her hands, inviting him to elucidate further.

"General Carver's forces have thrown the Red Army out of southern Iran and driven it back into Basra. Nobody has any idea how many Soviet tanks and vehicles we've captured or destroyed – hundreds certainly – and we've probably taken as many as twenty to thirty thousand prisoners, mostly around Umm Qasr and on the Faw Peninsula. Two of our ships, Tiger and Anzac sailed practically all the way up river to Khorramshahr and blew an entire Red Army armoured division to smithereens, our Iranian allies have chased the enemy into the ruins of Basra Industrial City on the right bank of the Shatt-al-Arab, and Tom Daly's Anzac-led brigade has invested the town of Zubayr – that's just south of Basra - blocking the Basra-Umm Qasr Road. As if all that wasn't extraordinary; the Yanks have agreed to a naval and air ceasefire in the Persian Gulf and HMAS Sydney is bound for Abadan with medical and other supplies as we speak..."

Margaret Thatcher was in no mood to rejoice.

"What of our casualties, Willie?"

This instantly sobered the man.

He shook his head.

"Our naval casualties are in the region of three to four thousand dead and missing, Margaret. Our losses in the Abadan-Khorramshahr sector will be heavy, possibly several thousands dead and wounded. In the west Tom Daly's casualties have, mercifully, been minimal, less than a hundred killed in action thus far. In addition to Centaur, the frigates Palliser and Hardy, and the New Zealand ship Otago lost in the First Battle of the Persian Gulf, all five vessels of Admiral Davey's Shatt-al-Arab squadron are feared lost. The wreck of the Tiger, and of the Australian destroyer Anzac lie grounded opposite the mouth of the River Karun, the New Zealand cruiser Royalist was destroyed by an internal explosion and the destroyers Dainty and Tobruk are grounded at Al Seeba. Essentially, we have no meaningful naval presence in the Persian Gulf at this time."

Much of this was simply confirmation of what had been feared or hoped for the last twenty-four hours.

"General Carver is in direct communication with the Soviet commander in Basra, none other than my opposite number in Russia, Admiral Gorshkov," Whitelaw guffawed, inadvertently drawing a narrow-eyed look from the Prime Minister. "Forgive me, it's just that I've learned that Carver's employing that lovable rogue, Frank Waters, as his chief translator!"

Margaret Thatcher brightened.

Despite herself, she brightened.

"Colonel Waters?"

"During the heat of the fighting around Abadan, Waters and one of his BBC colleagues, an old army man, attached themselves to Carver's Headquarters company and by all accounts, got well and truly 'stuck in'!"

"Colonel Waters..." The Prime Minister mused out aloud. "Well, fancy that. Is he injured?"

Why did I ask that?

"Walking wounded from the reports I've received."

Of course, he would be wounded; a man like Colonel Francis St John Waters, VC, would have been where the fighting was hottest and most desperate...

"Er, Prime Minister?" Willie Whitelaw coughed.

Margaret Thatcher realised with a sharp pang of no little existential angst that she had allowed her thoughts to wander. She had been a little sad to despatch the distinctly mischievous, possibly incorrigible former SAS man off to the Middle East so soon after his heroics in Iran earlier in the war. But Airey Neave had persuaded her that a 'chap like Frank Waters was a loose cannon, wasted in Oxford' and she had bullied him into accepting the BBC foreign/war reporter role which had taken him straight back to the Gulf. At the time she would much rather have kept him at home, got to know him better and given him longer to recover from his previous ordeal at the hands of the Soviets. There was something about the man which, well, fascinated her more than somewhat...

"You were saying, Willie?"

"Michael Carver is doing his level best to bluff the Russians out of Basra but sooner or later the other side will work out we don't have any air power," Whitelaw shrugged, "then unfortunately, we'll be back to square one again."

Had she been of a more contemplative nature Margaret Thatcher might have asked herself why, nearly three days on from the events in the Persian Gulf which had transformed a fast-developing regional military and political disaster into a headlong rush towards a new, seemingly inevitable, global catastrophe on the scale of, or worse, than the October War, she could be so calm.

If she was being honest, calm was a thing she had not been at any time since the news about the attack on the Centaur had exploded in their midst. Yet now she *was* calm; not because she felt herself to be in any way in control of the situation for patently, she was not. And besides, *calm* was not in her nature. It was a condition she achieved only occasionally, otherwise her internal psychic wellspring had always been a restless, questing energy that compelled her to keep moving ahead no matter what obstacle stood in her path. For all that that she was often afflicted by an odd shyness, an inability to easily mingle in a crowd, or know what to say even to people whom she knew quite well – a disability she had assumed was to do with a reluctance to 'give' too much of herself to others – she had always compensated by, literally, charging in where others feared to tread. It was her greatest strength and her Achilles heel; never more so than in recent days and now that she was 'calm' she was beginning to realise how badly she had handled the developing crisis.

"Well," she consoled her companion, "we shall cope with that if it happens, Willie."

The man arched a shaggy eyebrow.

"We have made a lot of mistakes," she went on, the heat rising in her cheeks. "Hubris, I think. Or perhaps, because we are all still very new at this," she waved a distracted hand around them, "business of governing. I'm sorry if I was rude earlier, inexcusably rude to you and others. If we – somehow – come through this, we all in fact, must resolve to do better in future."

There had been periods during the last days when she had been beside herself, beyond reason and that was inexcusable.

Conversations with Tom and Pat Harding Grayson, the Chief of the Defence Staff, a gruffly chatty five minute telephone exchange with her friend Airey Neave - her Security Minister chaffing at being 'locked up' in the Chilmark Bunker under the Chiltern Hills in Wiltshire - and the soothing words of Willie Whitelaw, his deputy Peter Carington, and latterly busying herself working on her Information Minister Nicholas Ridley's plan to win the 'battle of the airwaves', had each contributed to bringing her down from her personal castle of righteous anger in recent hours.

"Prime Minister?" Willie Whitelaw inquired solicitously.

Margaret Thatcher blinked at the man.

She had allowed her thoughts to wander...again.

It really would not do!

She had not realised that the loss of Julian Christopher – murdered by Soviet assassins at Mdina at the height of the Battle for Malta only three short months ago – still weighed upon her so heavily. They – Julian and she - had made a pact during her short visit to the Mediterranean for the marriage of the C-in-C's son to his delightful Maltese bride, Marija, and there on the night before the wedding at the Verdala Palace Julian had proposed to her, she had accepted and they had kissed...

That evening, that night now seemed so long ago as to be the stuff of dreams. She had always thought herself to be such a proper person, the Head Girl duty-bound to be an exemplary example and yet that night she had...

She had invested her whole being in the idea of *their* future together, the great things that might be done with a husband like Julian...

In truth she had hardly known the 'fighting admiral'; just that he had captivated her on first sight and that with him by her side – notwithstanding there was twenty-five years between them in age – there was no limit to what she might achieve...

Again, her face was burning with embarrassment.

It was too soon. The man she had loved was hardly cold in the ground, and the memory of their short time together still so pin-prick sharp in her mind. Often, she sensed *he* was with her. He had told her his secrets, of the woman he had loved, and lost, half a lifetime ago.

Aysha had been a dusky-skinned Vietnamese courtesan and briefly, ever so briefly, *she* had envied the simplicity and the *freedom* – within the constraints of that oldest of professions.

"I'm sorry," she murmured. She forced herself to concentrate, snapping from the trance of remembrance. "Would it be possible for me to send a personal message to General Carver," she hesitated, "and to Colonel Waters?"

The Secretary of State for Defence's attempt to remain deadpan failed dismally.

"Er, yes, I'm sure that could be arranged..."

Chapter 43

14:48 Hours (Local) – 07:18 Hours in Philadelphia
Twenty kilometres South of Tselinograd, Kazakhstan

President Kennedy's Special Emissary to the Troika on what now seemed like a doomed peace mission stared gloomily out of the window of the Tupolev Tu-114. Other than that the aircraft had flown on a generally southern heading – the sun had been in the south west most of the time - for much of the last two hours he had no idea where it was going; less still what fate awaited him at journey's end.

The great, deafening turboprop airliner had been circling for some minutes, proscribing huge figures of eight high above the clouds which shrouded much of the ground below.

Llewellyn E. "Tommy" Thompson had joined the diplomatic service as long ago as 1928. He had served in Ceylon, Austria, Switzerland, and for many years in the Soviet Union, most recently as Ambassador for five years between July 1957 and July 1962. Earlier in his career he had remained in Russia when the US Embassy was moved from Moscow to Kuybyshev in south eastern European Russia when German tanks threatened the capital in the winter of 1941; his old friend Nikita Khrushchev had never forgotten that. Such things had always mattered to the irascible, mischievous old Bolshevik. The trouble was that Khrushchev and his generation were gone and many of the 'new' men were strangers to him. The whole country – which he had grown if not to love, then to respect and appreciate for what it was, a young power seeking what it believed to be its rightful place in the World order – was *strange* to him now. He spoke Russian fluently yet he had no idea if he was actually communicating with...*anybody*.

Movement to his right snapped him out of his brooding.

Alexander Shelepin, head of the KGB and the acknowledged number two man in the collective leadership that ruled the new USSR, sat down in the rearward facing seat opposite him and viewed the US Envoy across the narrow table between them.

The Tu-114 was so noisy that unless interlocutors sat next to each other and shouted at each other it was virtually impossible to hear a word the other was saying.

"I am sorry to have neglected you, Ambassador," Shelepin began, his face a mask of inscrutability. He took a series of slowing breaths and the tension ebbed out of his dapper frame. He glanced to one of the green-uniformed KGB subalterns who had followed him into the rear passenger compartment of the airliner. "Bring tea."

The Head of the KGB studied Thompson.

"These are difficult days, Ambassador. Soon, things will be plainer. If we live long enough we may yet reach a more satisfactory accommodation than that which presently pertains."

"That would certainly be my hope, Comrade Chairman." Thompson was convinced that the problem President Kennedy –

actually, the whole State Department in fact – had had with the Soviets, pretty much since the 1917 Revolution, was that nobody 'Stateside' ever listened to what *they*, the Russians, said to them. Consequently, most Americans were profoundly ignorant about the Soviet Union, and even at the highest levels of the US government there was, and always had been, unconscionable misconceptions about even the basic structures of the Soviet political system.

Yes, 'political system'.

Even under Stalin there had been 'politics' in the USSR; not Western 'politics' but 'a political system' which had created and advanced the careers of several of the same men his masters back in Philadelphia were having to deal with *now*.

Shelepin, like all members of the ruling elite had accumulated titles – some honorific, others anything but – in his rise to the top. He remained Head of the KGB but his 'headline' title was First Deputy Chairman of the Council of Ministers of the Union of Soviet Socialist Republics. That was critically important because it meant that he controlled – day to day - both the Soviet State Security apparatus, *and* he was in effect, the Prime Minister, of the USSR, while Leonid Brezhnev, as Chairman of the Communist Party was theoretically, the country's President, and the Commander-in-Chief of the Armed Forces.

Jack Kennedy had got Khrushchev all wrong. The man Thompson had known had not been an ogre, or any kind of malevolent 'son of Stalinism'. True, Nikita Sergeyevich had been an old Bolshevik who had done terrible things – he had done what had to be done – to beat back the Nazis at Stalingrad, and subsequently been the *Man of Steel's* obedient servant during the purges of the post-Hitler War period. But unlike Stalin he had never been the all-powerful dictator. The Hungarian Uprising might easily have unseated him in 1956; likewise, the failure of several harvests in the late 1950s might have brought him crashing down. Khrushchev's USSR had been a repressed, miserable place for many of its inhabitants and the Gulag, the great archipelago of labour and penal camps still blotted the landscape of the Soviet empire, but there had been no Stalinistic 'terrors' under Nikita Sergeyevich's regime, just a constant roiling of the sort of 'politics' not even the dirtiest Western politician could begin to understand. To retain his partial grip on the levers of power Khrushchev had had to make numberless pacts with men like Alexander Shelepin.

Shelepin had 'cleaned the stables' at the Lubyanka, transformed the out of control monster that had been Lavrenty Beria's NKVD into the KGB, Vasily Chuikov had kept the Red Army faction under control, while others had kept the lid on the plethora of long-entrenched 'empires' within the sprawling, fundamentally unmanageable Soviet 'polity'.

In the end Khrushchev had found himself juggling too many balls in the air; the Cuban Missiles Crisis had got out of control and, Thompson guessed, Jack Kennedy had sensed he was dealing with a

Kremlin likely to pull the thermonuclear trigger at any moment and done the only thing he could do; shoot first with everything he had to hand at the time...

Alexander Shelepin's proper title in his capacity as a member of the Troika was 'Chairman', and Thompson was always mindful to accord Soviet dignitaries their correct and rightful honorific because it showed that he understood, at least a little, about them and their status within the hierarchy.

Shelepin nodded out of the window.

"Down there is Tselinograd."

Thompson said nothing, content to have his guess that they were flying somewhere over Kazakhstan confirmed.

"Well," Shelepin continued. "What's left of it! A big bomb went off about ten miles from the middle of the town. It wiped out half the population."

The diplomat absorbed this.

He was in an aircraft circling high above a wrecked city that SAC had probably already ticked off its target lists.

Okay, so we are hiding.

What does that mean?

Perhaps, that the Soviets have decided to tough it out?

"Do you think there will be a new war?" Thompson asked tersely.

"Possibly, who can tell?" The Head of the KGB shrugged. His attitude was one of carefully manicured indifference. "The city down there started out as a Cossack fortress; Akmolinsky prikaz, the Tsar Akmolinsk. We changed its name to Tselinograd the year before the Cuban Missiles War. It was to be the capital of the *Tselina kampanii*," he scoffed sourly.

"Ah," Thompson re-joined soberly. "*The Virgin Lands Campaign*, I recollect Chairman Khrushchev speaking of it on many occasions before the, er, war..."

"Everything is before or after a war, Comrade," Shelepin observed. "People forget that the whole Cuba thing was a mistake. Khrushchev made a mistake about Kennedy, Kennedy lost his nerve, the fucking admirals didn't tell the fucking generals that they'd sent those fucking submarines to the western Atlantic. It was one fuck up after another. At the time the Cuba 'thing' started Khrushchev was more worried about the failure of the Virgin Lands Campaign than he was about your fucking missiles and bombers. If there was war he knew he'd be dead; whereas, if he didn't do something about the bad harvests he'd be out of power and he'd probably be in a fucking labour camp!"

The American was astonished by the sudden loquacity of the man who was, by any standards, the uncommunicative dark angel of the Soviet leadership.

The Virgin Lands Campaign had been a ticking time bomb underneath his old friend Nikita Khrushchev's Kremlin right from the start.

Josef Stalin was hardly cold in the ground when plans were formulated to begin the wholesale reorganisation of the collective-farming regime, and to massively expand the area of land under cultivation in the Soviet Union.

Under the Virgin Lands Campaign Khrushchev had aimed to bring over thirteen million hectares of previously uncultivated land on the right bank of the Volga, the Caucasus, and in Siberia and northern Kazakhstan into agricultural production by 1956. Opposition to the *Tselina kampanii* had been fiercest in Kazakhstan, with leading members of the Party and Politburo predicting from the outset that the whole scheme would end in disaster. The 1957 harvest had been a failure; that in 1959 almost as disastrous and with hunger threatening to stalk the USSR Khrushchev had been forced to run down its foreign currency reserves to import grain to feed its people. Between 1956 and 1960 another twenty-eight million hectares of land had been brought under cultivation but year after year harvests disappointed, and yields declined. By 1960, the year in which Khrushchev had boasted that the USSR would surpass US grain production the Soviet Union still remained dependent on imported grain from Africa, Europe and of course, the United States.

The problem was that although the Virgin Lands Campaign had been embarked upon with typical Soviet gusto, little or no thought given to the long-term fertility of the land. By the time Jack Kennedy moved into the White House Khrushchev was in the middle of belatedly initiating a great, nationwide program to build sixty new fertilizer production plants. However, even that was far too little too late; for even had the plan come to fruition Soviet farms would have still only been able to 'feed the soil' of their fields at approximately half the input rate of the average American Midwestern farmer.

What with one thing and another by the time of the Cuban Missiles War Khrushchev was a man living on borrowed time. History, Thompson reflected, is more often about the ploughshare than the sword, always accepting the caveat that the one is sometimes indistinguishable from the other in the long run.

"Back in October 1962 President Kennedy was preoccupied with the Sino-Chinese war in the Himalayas, and with the growing disorder in the cities of our Deep South," he offered as thoughtfully as one could when one had to virtually shout to be heard about the thunder of the Tu-114's four massive Kuznetsov NK-12MV fifteen thousand horse power turboprop engines driving gigantic twenty feet diameter contra-rotating propellers. Even throttled back to minimal cruising power as the airliner gently circled, Thompson suspected he would be a little deaf for several hours after disembarkation.

Alexander Shelepin was suddenly sitting forward, elbows on the table between them, pinning Thompson back in his seat with unforgiving, remorseless eyes.

"These are bad times, Comrade Ambassador," he said. "But with bad times comes opportunity. Opportunity for people like us, for our countries and for the future of the World," he added, his lips twitching into a horrible parody of a smile. "If there is war over two hundred Red Air Force bombers will fly one-way nuclear missions to America,

Great Britain, and to targets in the Mediterranean and the Persian Gulf."

Thompson's jaw was agape; a thing he only realised much later.

"Two hundred?" He checked, wondering if he had misheard. "Two hundred bombers?"

"Two hundred, maybe three hundred; precise numbers don't really matter at a time like this. The Red Air Force is always very imprecise about such matters, anyway." Shelepin's eyes narrowed. "Surely you did not think we would be so *stupid* as to flatten Bucharest, attack Malta and invade Iran and Iraq – historic British-American spheres of influence – without *some* kind of insurance?"

"Two or three hundred bombers capable of reaching America? That's impossible!"

"Why? Because your General LeMay boasts he bombed us '*back to the Stone Age*'?"

Thompson was momentarily speechless.

"I have made – or rather, my friends in the Red Air Force, have made arrangements for you to speak to your State Department," Shelepin informed the American diplomat.

"What am I supposed to tell the people in Philadelphia?"

"Tell them that this time we are ready to fight a war. Last time, although some of our missiles were being fuelled and several squadrons of bombers were at a high state of alert, nobody in the Kremlin actually believed what was happening until the first of your Minutemen and Polaris missiles began to strike the Motherland. The last decision Khrushchev made was to hold back all our bombers that hadn't been hit. Had you mounted a second attack on us that night we would have sent all our surviving bombers to North America and killed a hundred million of your people. We are stronger now; you are weaker. This is what you will tell your President Johnson."

Chapter 44

07:19 Hours (EST)
Command Post, 3rd Marine Regiment, Wister Park Command Post, Philadelphia

Much to fifty year old General William 'Westy' Westmoreland's surprise the rebels inside the British Embassy, presumably sane enough to be mindful of the 90-millimetre rifles of the M-48 tanks lined up on the West Wing – from both the front and back - of the Embassy, had not fired on the stretcher parties which had entered the compound under a flag of truce at dawn to recover the bodies strewn across the steps in front of the West Wing of the partially wrecked Embassy.

A dozen Marines had volunteered to go in stripped to their skivvies; and the whole operation to retrieve the eight bodies had taken less than ten minutes. The man with the preacher's righteous voice at the other end of the line had said 'even the ungodly deserve to be laid to rest with dignity'.

From the state of the bodies the Marines had carried out of the compound it was obvious that the 'ungodly' had been granted precious little 'grace' in life. Some of the things the rebels had done to the Ambassador, his wife and the other senior members of the British diplomatic mission turned Westmoreland's stomach. It was only the fading hope that against the odds, other embassy staff might still be still alive in the hellhole compound that stopped him ordering the whole place razed to the ground.

Those faint hopes were dying fast.

A few minutes ago, there had been explosions and bursts of automatic gunfire in the North Wing of the Embassy compound; most likely more prisoners being executed...

Westmoreland had had some dirty jobs landed on his plate in the last couple of years but this one trumped everything. There was something sickening about the cold-blooded torture and killing of civilians that *always* got the bile rising in his throat. Once upon a time he had honestly believed that there was such a thing as 'honest soldiering'; in which decency and moral purpose were the guiding lights.

Back in the beginning he had been an artillery officer; a trade he had plied through Tunisia, Sicily, France and Germany in the Second War, ending up Chief of Staff of the 9th Infantry Division. That had been a 'good war' fought against profound evil. He had commanded the 187th Airborne Regimental Combat Team in the Korean conflict, a less morally unambiguous but still relatively 'good war'. Thereafter, he had attended a management program at Harvard Business School and become an instructor at the US Army Staff College. More recently he had commanded the 101st Airborne Division, and at the time of the October War had been Superintendent of the United States Military Academy at West Point. Within weeks of the war, he had returned to

Washington as the Personal Military Assistant to Secretary of Defense, Robert McNamara and become, to all intents, a 'corporation executive in uniform'.

In one way it was a relief to be in the field again; in another, a nightmare. The World was sliding towards a new thermonuclear abyss and Curtis LeMay had ordered him to sort out the Philadelphia PD's shit for them! His place was beside McNamara at a time like this; not out here in the boondocks dealing with a bunch of crazies...

"Sir," a Marine corpsman murmured at his shoulder.

"Yeah, what is it, son?" Westmoreland's tone was sternly paternal. He tried very hard never to take out his existential angst on his subordinates.

"There's another call from within the Embassy compound, sir."

Westmoreland frowned.

The man he had been talking to overnight – a religious fanatic well-known to the FBI called Galen Cheney whose pre- and post-October War charge sheet read like a short, and very gruesome history of Murder Incorporated – had not picked up the phone when Westmoreland had attempted to put a call through to 'thank him' for allowing the recovery of the bodies on the steps.

He had not really believed there was any real possibility of a dialogue with the madman; but by then he had already missed the best – pre-dawn – opportunity to mount a full-frontal assault on the Embassy complex. That was another thing he was going to have to hash out with the Commissioner of the Philadelphia PD; whose officers had, by refusing to surrender their positions until first light effectively hamstrung the 3rd Marines' attempts to move into optimal forward positions.

Not that the delay was wholly a bad thing.

The stretcher parties who had recovered the bodies of the dead diplomats had had a good long close up look at the approaches to the North, West and Southern Wings which adjoined each other obliquely overlooking the south-western grounds of the compound. Able to observe from close quarters, Westmoreland's men had confirmed the accuracy of the plans he held for the layout of the buildings, counted gun barrels sticking out of windows and the faces lurking behind the cracked and shattered glass of windows.

He now knew he could trust the external plans of the compound and had a rough head count for the number of 'rebels' still inside it. The Philadelphia PD had detained over a hundred 'runaways', his boys another two dozen. To a man – and woman, which disgusted Westmoreland – the prisoners claimed to have been 'just swept up in the demonstration', and later to have been held as hostages by the 'men inside'.

He hoped they all rotted in Hell; preferably after they had been hung by the neck until dead or lined up and shot for the traitorous animals they were!

"It's a woman, sir," Westmoreland was informed.

He raised the handset to his head.

"This is General Westmoreland," he said tersely.

"My name is Rachel Piotrowska," the woman informed him without preamble. She sounded...*Russian*.

"Are you..."

She cut him off.

"I don't have much time. I talk, you listen, General."

Okay, he could do that.

"Go," he invited brusquely, "I'm listening."

"There are five of us still alive on the second floor of the North Wing. Everybody else is dead. I estimate that Cheney has approximately ten to fifteen of his original disciples with him. They have access to half-a-dozen SLRs, the British Army version of the Belgian FAL assault rifle, and perhaps seven or eight Sten guns stolen from the Embassy armoury, and no more than two or three magazines per weapon. They may have grenades, I don't know. In addition, there may be up to sixty other insurgents, including as many as half-a-dozen women. The survivors in the North Wing are Mary Drinkwater, Cynthia Nansen, a teenage girl called Kitty who was brought into the Embassy by her father, a rebel, and a former FBI Agent called Dwight Christie who claims to have been a captive of the insurgents. They are lightly armed..."

"What about the rest of the Embassy staff?"

"They are all dead, General Westmoreland."

The woman's voice was dull, mechanical.

"Are there any rebels in the North Wing?"

"No, General."

"What was that shooting a little way back?"

The woman ignored the question.

"The four survivors on the second floor will exit the fire escape the next time they hear gunfire and explosions in the central, West Wing of the building. I suggest you warn your troops covering the North Wing not to shoot at *my* people when they emerge into plain sight."

Westmoreland's mind raced.

"How will they know when my people plan to attack?"

"They won't. I'll be the one causing the explosions and doing the shooting. All *you* need to do is make sure *your* people commence their assault the moment you hear the," she hesitated, "excitement begin."

"How will they recognise you?" The man asked.

Westmoreland could have sworn he heard her stifle a laugh.

"Let me worry about that, General. All you have to do is kill everybody in the West Wing and the South Wing of the building."

Chapter 45

15:20 Hours (Local) – 07:20 Hours in Philadelphia
USS Dewey (DLG-14), South of Kharg Island, Persian Gulf

Lieutenant-Commander Walter Brenckmann was not really sure why he had been taken to the stern of the guided missile frigate and escorted down into the crew quarters to be shown the chopped up remains of a flying suit.

Having found a spot amidships on the weather deck where he could stare at the oil-streaked water, occasionally catching a glimpse of the bow of the Kitty Hawk still lurching out of the sea like a broaching whale trapped in time and space; he had been trying to put off the moment when he asked for another shot to deaden the pain in his arm, and hopefully, to quieten his roiling thoughts.

The bow of the sunken carrier was like an accusation.

It was a racing certainty that there were still men trapped in that great steel sarcophagus, and equally likely that they would die in it although the small British Minesweeper HMS Tariton, approaching the battleground from the mouth of the Shatt-al-Arab with a request to offload injured men onto 'any ship with a doctor and a proper sick bay', had now offered to attempt to stand alongside the sunken leviathan.

The British ship had first gone alongside the Forest Sherman class destroyer USS Hull (DD-945) to unload her cargo of wounded men. In the east the British oiler Wave Master still stood alongside the USS Albany (CG-10). The USS Paul Revere (APA-248), loaded down with ordnance of all varieties the fleet was in no fit state to employ, had stood off three miles to the south of the wreck site. In the absence of helicopters – those onboard the surviving ships had all been peppered with splinter fragments from near misses or chewed up by the cannons of the RAF fighters which had strafed the fleet – there was no way of transferring severely wounded men to the high-sided fast attack transport; even though the Paul Revere was the only ship in what was left of Carrier Division Seven with a fully-equipped operational hospital. Other vessels were out of sight, searching the waters many miles downwind from the scene of the two-day old...*disaster.*

There was no other word to describe what had happened...

"You say these were cut off a guy in the sick bay?" Walter queried. The shredded and cut up flight suit was spread across the end of a mess table. There were injured men lying in makeshift cots on the floor around him.

There were no badges of rank or unit, it was as if they had been torn off.

Why would anybody do a thing like that?

"The guys who pulled him out of the water junked most of his kit back over the side. Things were kind of hairy..."

"I'm sure they were," Walter agreed, trying to think. "This isn't anything anybody off the Kitty Hawk would have been issued. No, I think this is British. RAF..."

Nobody around Walter was overjoyed they had gone to the trouble of pulling a Brit out of the water. However, having nowhere else he needed to be he picked his way forward towards the sick bay.

"Sit down, Commander," a nurse ordered, spying him swaying unsteadily in the hatchway.

She planted him on a stool and kept a hand on his shoulder to stop him falling off it. Walter recollected that a detachment of nurses had sailed with Carrier Division Seven on the Paul Revere; he guessed they had been transferred onto the surviving big ships after the first or second battle...

"I think you've got a British flyer in here somewhere," he explained, feeling faint. "I checked out the bits of his suit they didn't throw over the side. All the badges are torn off..."

He was surprised when this came as no surprise to the nurse.

"Oh, right. We reckoned whoever he was he must have ejected at really high speed. The human body doesn't like that sort of thing and it probably isn't very good for whatever you're wearing at the time either!"

The woman was in her early twenties, Walter guessed. She was tired but more awake than him, obviously.

"You ought to be horizontal, Commander."

He tried to focus on the name badge on her tunic.

Lieutenant junior grade H. Katawa.

Her accent was pure Midwestern Americana, her features Japanese.

The woman must have seen his brief confusion. The guy was beaten up far too badly to be wandering around the ship on his own; so, she decided to give him a break.

"Third generation Japanese-American," she smiled. "The Government put the whole family in an internment camp in California after Pearl Harbour. That's where I was born. After we got out my Pa, he was a high school maths teacher, went up to Hanford to help make the bombs that won the war." She thought about this. "Both of them, I guess."

"My folks came from Germany," Walter chuckled, regretting it a moment later as his ribs tried to implode.

Chapter 46

07:30 Hours (EST)
The Oval Office, White House, Philadelphia

"I believe it is customary for a newly appointed Ambassador to present a *lettres de créance* – a letter of credence – to the head of state of the country to which he has been posted, Mister President," Peter Christopher said, coming to attention and nodding his head in a passing imitation of a bow to the tall Texan standing before him. "In this instance I believe a hastily drafted telegram has been despatched, and received by your office, sir?"

"It sure has, Mister Ambassador," Lyndon Johnson confirmed, grinning and sticking out his right hand. "We got off to a bad start. I'm amenable to start over if you are?"

Peter half-expected his wife to give him a jab in the ribs at this juncture, if only to remind him to stop sulking.

The aforementioned 'telegram' also included the clause that 'in the extraordinary circumstances pertaining to international relations between the United Kingdom of Great Britain and Northern Ireland, and the United States of America, Sir Peter Christopher, VC, is granted *pleins pouvoirs* in letters patent'.

He was an ambassador abroad with 'full powers' to speak and to act for his country. It was all a little...*daunting*.

He was twenty-seven years old; he had gone straight from The Britannia Royal Naval College at Dartmouth to University, back to Dartmouth again and thence – via a fascinating six-month long detour to the Ferranti Research and Development Bureau in Scotland, directly into the seagoing Royal Navy wherein, until the October War he had had a whale of a time travelling the Commonwealth, dallying with a succession of charming girls and mucking about to his heart's content with all manner of state of the art electronic gizmos. He had lived the life of Riley, been frankly, as happy as a pig in... Well, he had had a marvellous time and apart from the hard work he had had to put in earning his watch keeper's certificate which had involved a lot of boring navigational 'guff', it had been an absolute breeze...

Notwithstanding that practically everybody in Christendom seemed to be abreast of his adventures in the last few months or so, he was painfully aware that there was absolutely nothing in his life experience to date that gave him – or should have given anybody else - the remotest confidence in his ability to represent his whole country in its hour of most abject peril.

He had been the EWO – Electronic Warfare Officer - of a flotilla of destroyers off northern Spain for a few hours, the second in command of HMS Talavera for a few weeks, her captain a couple of months – until she sank under his feet – and latterly he had been a public relations flimflam man on behalf of the Ministry of Information and the 'real' Ambassador, had been that inestimably charming gentleman,

Lord Franks...

As for the West Coast Consulate nonsense; that was just another kettle of fish he had been inadvertently dropped in. But for Lord Franks promising to be on the other end of the telephone – or, 'just a telegram away' because he was an old-fashioned, salt of the earth paternal kind of man – and undertaking to call him back to Philadelphia at regular intervals to 'gee' and 'gen' him up on all things diplomatic, he might even have put his foot down and refused the posting...

No, that was a lie; one went where one was sent. That was the contract he had made with the Queen and the Admiralty and while he had breath in his body he would guard that contract with every fibre of his being!

"Yes, sir," Peter blurted. Right then if Lyndon Johnson had asked him to scuttle the entire fleet he would probably have said 'yes, sir!'

Peter and Marija had passed a somewhat iron-faced Curtis LeMay on their way into the Oval Office. For all they knew the legendary bomber commander was on his way to give the order to incinerate that part of the Northern Hemisphere his B-52s had inadvertently missed the first time around in October 1962.

Even at this early hour in Philadelphia the chants of the demonstrators nearly a hundred yards away blocking Broad Street, and presumably, most of the other local thoroughfares, trickled into the inappropriately named Oval Office. Next the whiff of tear gas would foul the atmosphere. Meanwhile, downstairs in the imposing lobby of the old bank building a very large seething, churning gang of journalists, newspaper, radio and television people had been re-admitted overnight and were corralled behind a cordon of Marines, presumably sharpening their knives for their first sight of the new British Ambassador.

Which was a problem because he planned to go downstairs and speak to the newshounds at the earliest possible moment; but hopefully, only after he had locked Marija away somewhere safe.

The President smiled wanly as if he too recognised how bizarre this encounter was, given that Peter Christopher was the putative representative of a country which – at Malta and in the Persian Gulf – was at war with his.

"What advice do you intend to give your government back home, Ambassador?"

Peter resisted the temptation to say something polite, meaningless. Instead, he risked a glance to Marija, who mirrored his tight-lipped grimace of a smile. The initial part of their induction into the 'diplomatic service' had been a series of briefings about the American 'system' and its leading lights; Cabinet members, and senior Senators and Congressmen in the main, and Lyndon Baines Johnson.

It was now that Peter dredged up pieces of what he had been told about the then Vice President. His memory affixed to one particular period of Johnson's career.

Congressman Johnson had been commissioned a Lieutenant

Commander in the US Naval Reserve in 1940 and been called up for active duty shortly after Pearl Harbour. For whatever reason – a US Senator could honourably claim all sorts of sound excuses for dodging combat, and most probably had at the time – Johnson had gone straight to the Secretary of the Navy, James Forrestal and asked for a combat assignment. Although he had not really got it, President Roosevelt had attached his young political ally to a three-man inspection committee to report back to him on the conduct of the war in the Southwest Pacific theatre.

To cut a longish story short Johnson had gone on a - single - bombing raid carried out by eleven B-26 'Mitchell' medium bombers on a Japanese air base at Lae in New Guinea. His aircraft had been hit – some said it just had an engine problem before it got to the target – and Johnson got back safely; with General Douglas MacArthur, no doubt beside himself with delight and relief that a Congressman had *not* died on his watch promptly pinning a Silver Star on a potentially influential politician's chest. Shortly thereafter, Johnson had returned to political life in Washington and reported to Roosevelt that the Army was making a mess of things because; firstly, soldiers were fighting in dreadful conditions; secondly, they were fighting with insufficient supplies and weapons, and; thirdly, they were equipped with poorer quality aircraft than the Japanese. Thus, in a few short months away from Washington DC Johnson had managed to become a decorated war hero, the scourge of complacent senior officers and administrators, and the guy who could be relied upon to stand up for the average GI!

Johnson's 'war service' had attracted raised eyebrows and no little cynicism then as now but personally, Peter Christopher thought the man deserved credit. Even his detractors admitted that back in Washington DC he had spent most of the rest of the war chivvying powerful men to 'do better'. Moreover, having presented Roosevelt with a cogent twelve-point plan to put things right in New Guinea he had been appointed chairman of an influential committee on Naval Affairs, and had commenced a one-man mission against the continuance of peacetime 'business as usual' attitudes, openly attacking the inadequacies of various famous admirals. Johnson currently held the rank of Commander in the US Navy Reserve.

"Well, Mister President," Peter observed, wondering if he was about to commit yet another heinous faux pas, "if I may speak as one Navy man to another," he stumbled on regardless, "I think there's been rather too much of the full speed ahead, and far too much damning of the torpedoes going on lately."

Lyndon Johnson nodded, sighed resignedly.

"Sit down, both of you. You need to hear something."

Peter and Maria sank a sofa while an aide scurried to a phone and spoke lowly for about five seconds. Husband and wife looked to each other, shrugged.

Chapter 47

15:41 Hours (Local) – 07:41 Hours in Philadelphia
Field Headquarters, 4th Armoured Regiment, Abadan Island

"Admiral Gorshkov seems to be fielding his second team, sir," Frank Waters reported after asking the bad-tempered Russian at the other end of the decidedly scratchy VHF link to *'zatknut'sya, tovarishch'*.

Predictably, Lieutenant General Viktor Georgiyevich Kulikov, the Commander-in-Chief of all Soviet ground forces in Southern Iraq and Iran had reacted angrily to his injunction to: *'put a sock in it, comrade'*.

Russians were an infernally touchy lot!

"The Admiral has probably skedaddled by now," the former SAS man suggested. "This Kulikov fellow doesn't sound very 'political' to me. The blighter started issuing threats. Apparently, if we want war, we can have it. I tried to tell him that we'd both given that a jolly good try the last few days and it hadn't done him an awful lot of good, but…"

The battered holder of a Victoria Cross won in another war grinned toothily at Lieutenant General Michael Carver, the man responsible for the successful execution of the greatest feat of British, Commonwealth, and Saudi Arabian arms since El Alamein, and shrugged as if to say: "What can one do with these beggars?"

Carver had been jotting in a notebook while Frank Waters 'chatted' to the Soviet commander in Basra. He sighed, put down his pen and handed the open notebook to the other man.

"Run General Kulikov through these thoughts, please."

Frank Waters read fast, his brow furrowing.

He looked up.

"You're sure about this, sir?"

Carver nodded, very much in the fashion of a world-weary university don despairing of the ways of the World.

"Comrade Victor Georgiyevich," Frank Waters re-commenced, slipping back into his Moskva accent as if it was an old, very comfortable boot. "I have conveyed the general tenor of your remarks to General Carver. I apologise for the delay but well, we were laughing so hard we started crying. Let it never be said that you Russians don't have a sense of humour!"

The man in Basra resisted the urge to snap Frank Waters's head off, recognising the change of tone of the exchange. He had blustered, the Englishman had parried. That was fair enough; one had a right to know what one was up against.

"Admiral Gorshkov has flown to Baghdad to consult with the Troika. As you will have discovered our communications are as compromised as your own in this sector, Colonel Waters."

Frank Waters glanced to Michael Carver's notes.

Okay, in for a penny, in for a pound!

"May I speak to you man to man, soldier to soldier, Comrade

General?" He inquired solemnly.

Kulikov contemplated this.

"If you wish, Comrade Colonel."

Frank Waters did not pause to translate he simply stuck his left thumb in the air.

"Everybody you deployed south of Basra on the Faw Peninsula or out into the Western Desert opposite the Kuwaiti border is now dead, wounded or in the bag, captured. I haven't got a clue how many of your boys we captured. Ten, twenty thousand and all their equipment, maybe more; honestly, we haven't had the time to start counting yet... Sorry, I'm not telling you this to make a point, or to gloat. You and I are old soldiers and old soldiers don't do that sort of thing to each other. Not after the sort of fight we've just had."

"What you say may be correct," Kulikov conceded grudgingly.

"As for what happened on the Iranian side of the river, well, until 2nd Siberian Mechanised Army can bring up its reserves – if it has any left – all you can do is to carry on falling back until our Iranian allies get bored, or your chaps stumble onto a defensible line. I'd guess that's not going to happen until General Al-Mamaleki's armour and artillery is on the right-hand bank of the Shatt-al-Arab opposite Basra. What with our forces coming up from the south around Zubayr, the bloodthirsty locals in the city and our Iranian chums on the other side of the river you and I both know that Basra is going to be a very unhealthy place for your chaps in the coming days."

"I can hold the city forever, Colonel," Kulikov grunted.

"The last thing I heard was that the Americans were threatening to bomb you if you didn't retreat north of the thirty-first or second parallel?"

Kulikov laughed contemptuously.

"The last thing I heard they were going to bomb you back into the Persian Gulf!"

"Nablyudat' za vragov svoikh blizkikh, druzey smotret' odin yeshche boleye tesno," the former SAS man observed, pithily he fancied.

Watch one's enemies close, watch one friends even more closely...

"Just so," Kulikov concurred. "Marshal Babadzhanian ought to have had you shot when he had the chance, Comrade Colonel," he added, without malice.

Again, Frank Waters elevated an affirmative thumb to Michael Carver. The latter half-arched an eyebrow, otherwise he remained impassive.

"That's awfully decent of you to say so, General!"

"You know I can't give you Basra," Kulikov continued. "What do you actually want?"

Frank Waters hesitated as if he was actually giving the matter his deepest consideration. What he, or rather, what his principal, Michael Carver wanted was a breathing space in which to form a new defensive position on the Karun River line above Abadan, and time to shorten and consolidate Tom Daly's lines above Umm Qasr. Not least among his preoccupations was urgently getting a working airstrip back into play on Abadan Island. None of these things was going to happen if he and Viktor Georgiyevich Kulikov kept harrying each other.

Problematically, their Iranian allies had their own agenda but there was nothing he could do about that; and if Kulikov was as shrewd an operator as he seemed – he was still alive and Gorshkov had left him in charge, two things which greatly recommended his staying power, if nothing else – he might just see the logic of halting the madness.

"What I want is a ceasefire line on Iraqi territory south of Zubayr," the former SAS man declared.

"What about on the eastern bank of the Shatt-al-Arab?" Kulikov queried, raising the stakes.

"North of the Karun River is an Iranian national issue."

Major General Hasan Al-Mamaleki's Imperial 3rd Armoured Division was critically short of fuel and practically out of ammunition, not so much halting to re-supply as running out of gas and bullets where it fought. For the time being Al-Mamaleki's objective was to reclaim all Iranian ground up to the pre-war border with Iraq; once, that was, he had wrecked a substantial part of the industrial area which had spread along the eastern bank of the river opposite Basra.

Like most Iranians Hasan Al-Mamaleki might not have a lot of time for the Russians, but he positively loathed and despised his Iraqi neighbours.

The Iranians were unburdened with prisoners; they were not fighting the sort of war in which prisoners asked or expected mercy and precious little had been forthcoming in the fighting of the last three days.

Nevertheless, the fighting north of Khorramshahr was dying down of its own accord.

"General Carver is prepared to undertake not to support Iranian operations north of the pre-war Iran-Iraq border on the right bank of the Shatt-al-Arab for the duration of any ceasefire agreed with Soviet forces in Southern Iraq."

Frank Waters did not add that the 'forces' under Michael Carver's command were incapable of *any* operations north of the Karun River.

"Da," Kulikov muttered, musing aloud. "Give me my prisoners of war back and I will suspend offensive operations for seventy-two hours north of Zubayr."

"What about the wounded?"

Kulikov did not need to think overlong about this.

"You can shoot them if you want."

Chapter 48

Walter Jenkins placed the tape recorder on the coffee table in front of Peter and Marija Christopher, walked the long cable across the room to the nearest wall socket and plugged it in. Returning to the machine he turned it on and looked to the President.

Forty-six-year-old Walter Jenkins had started working for Lyndon Johnson in 1939. Texan-born he had grown up in Wichita Falls and attended the University of Texas before joining LBJ's staff; after four years of wartime service in the Army he had converted to Catholicism and married in 1945. He had been with Johnson practically ever since; as a Congressional, Senatorial, Vice-Presidential and now – for the last few hours – as a Presidential aide. Back in 1951 he had stood for Congress but lost the race, probably on account of his Catholicism. In Washington circles – now transplanted to Philadelphia – he was liked and respected, his decency and integrity acknowledged by friends and foes alike. He had long ago become more of a Johnson family friend than an employee, closer than perhaps any of her husband's staffers to Lady Bird Johnson and deeply involved in the Johnsons' numerous business and financial interests.

It was hardly surprising, therefore, that the President had had Walter Jenkins 'babysitting' his 'British guests' while the rest of his fledgling administration ran around the White House doing a passable imitation of turkeys who had just learned that Thanksgiving had been moved forward three-and-a-half months.

Senator Richard Russell was beginning to fret. The weariness and strain of the last few hours were telling on Johnson also, but his old friend was finding it almost impossible to sit still.

"This," Walter Jenkins explained, a little apologetically, "is an unedited recording of the substantial part of a conversation Prime Minister Thatcher had with President Kennedy shortly before he was, er," he shook his head sadly, "was taken ill on 3rd July in the Situation Room."

Marija saw an opportunity and took it. "Is there any news of President Kennedy?" She asked, hardly daring to guess what Jackie and the poor man's children must be going through.

Walter Jenkins carried on fiddling with the tape recorder; one of the spools had come loose and he was re-splicing the thin magnetic tape to the empty, left hand reel.

"President Kennedy has not yet recovered consciousness," Lyndon Johnson growled. More paternally he added: "Jackie is at his bedside at Thomas Jefferson Memorial. The children are with Ethel, sorry, Bobbie's wife. Most of the Kennedy family are staying out at Cherry Hill, security being what it is."

"Cherry Hill is a few miles away on the New Jersey side of the

Delaware," Walter Jenkins explained. "A Kennedy family friend, Claude Betancourt, owns a big house out that way. The press and the TV folk won't bother the family so much out there." He glanced to the President. "We're ready to go, sir."

Lyndon Johnson nodded.

Peter Christopher stiffened at the boxy, electronically 'thinned' voice of the now stricken President. When he had gone sailing in Nantucket Sound with Jack Kennedy – and half the Secret Service on the yacht Gretchen Louisa – the man had been at ease, the master of all he surveyed and his level, confident drawl had reflected as much. JFK had one of those voices that sounded poetic even when he was reading diary listings; but the voice on the tape was that of a half-broken shell of the man, not the man who had stood at the wheel of the Gretchen Louisa just a month ago.

There was anger, fear in his voice.

'Thank you for taking my call, Prime Minister.'

The tape crackled and hissed with background clutter.

Peter assumed it was a copy – perhaps one of many - of the original because periodic attenuations suggested it had been hurried replicated, the original tape probably stretched here and there in the haste of the copiers to produce multiple reels.

'I am always happy to *take* the President's call.'

Margaret Thatcher's icy acknowledgement froze Peter Christopher's soul. She was a woman betrayed, scorned and calculating her revenge. Several months of angst and rage had been bottled against this very day, fomenting explosively just beneath the slick, chilly veneer of civility...

Jack Kennedy must have heard it all.

'My people,' he went on, gathering his courage, 'are telling me that the electro-magnetic pulses of two medium sized nuclear devices have been detected over Iraq in the last ninety minutes?'

Margaret Thatcher's response was delayed a fraction of a second on the line.

'They are correct in that assumption. RAF V-Bombers conducted strikes some sixty miles to the west of Baghdad over sparsely populated areas,' she snapped back. 'What of it, Mister President?'

Peter opened his mouth; and somehow, stopped himself muttering: "Oh, my God!" In the silence the Prime Minister purred dangerously into the ether.

'What of it? I trust and pray that you are not going to ask me why I did not give you forewarning of the activation of *Arc Light* protocols, Jack?'

JFK and Margaret Thatcher were trying to have different conversations; mutually bemused by their common tongue. One might have been speaking Hindi, the other demotic Greek.

'Margaret,' the President pleaded, in attempting to pour oil onto troubled waters he might as well have been pouring petrol onto a fire, 'we moved the Kitty Hawk into the Persian Gulf specifically to deter the Soviets reaching for the nuclear trigger.'

His was the panicking, baffled tone of a man who clearly did not believe *he* was having *this* conversation with *this* woman.

'Now if the Soviets 'go nuclear' we'll all be dragged into this thing.'

'Mister President,' the British Prime Minister objected, 'the reason RAF V-Bombers attacked Chelyabinsk eight days ago was to ensure that the Soviet High Command could have no doubt, no doubt whatsoever, that *we* are fully prepared to complete the work General LeMay's boys left unfinished in October 1962. If the Soviets retaliate with nuclear weapons we will do likewise.'

'Margaret, you can't...'

'Further,' Margaret Thatcher retorted, a hectoring note rising stridently in her voice, 'if the worst comes to the worst I will not hesitate to bomb the Red Army all the way back to Baghdad!'

Only a master of understatement would have described the horrible quietness which ensued as simply *a shocked silence.*

'Are you still there, Jack,' the woman asked peremptorily after a gap of about ten seconds.

'Er, yes...' Miraculously, at this juncture the President seemed to regain his composure. Suddenly, he was as hard as nails. 'I will be no part of that,' he declared. 'In fact, I must tell you now that I have already broadcast a message to the Soviet leadership disassociating myself from British actions. Via the good offices of former Ambassador Dobrynin, whom you may know elected to remain in the United States after the Cuban Missiles War, we have been in communication with the *Troika*, the collective leadership of the Soviet Union in recent days energetically endeavouring to defuse tensions arising from the sinking of the USS Providence in the Arabian Sea...'

"What?" Peter Christopher ejaculated in astonishment.

The Americans in the room said nothing.

The tape recording hissed and spat.

"There's a long gap here," Walter Jenkins explained, grimacing as if it was his fault.

Presently, the sound of voices, indistinct in the background could be heard. Jack Kennedy had tried to carry on.

'Margaret, I...'

He might have been talking to a brick wall for all it achieved.

Right then Margaret Thatcher would not have given St Francis of Assisi the time of day if he was peddling what she now knew the President of the United States wanted to sell her.

'President Kennedy,' the woman began with frigid implacability. 'I took you for many things. Some of those things were uncharitable, others it now seems, unjustly creditworthy. As we speak the United States Navy is murdering British and Commonwealth sailors, airmen and in all likelihood soldiers in the Persian Gulf. Once again you have attacked *my people* without warning, their blood and the blood of all those who will die in the next few days, weeks and perhaps, years will be on your hands for all time.'

The lady was glacially calm.

'Mr President,' she enunciated clearly, her tone was so scathing that it made the hairs on the nape of Peter Christopher's neck stand up in sympathy. 'Once again it seems as if the United States has stabbed *Great Britain* in the back...'

'Margaret, I...'

'As we speak American airmen and sailors are murdering British and Commonwealth personnel in the Persian Gulf.'

There was a new hissing silence on the line for several seconds.

Jack Kennedy must have been passed more information, reports from the Persian Gulf at that point.

'Margaret, I'm receiving news as we speak...'

'Mr President, I will not let this stand!'

Margaret Thatcher said it quietly but Peter felt as if she was shouting, spittle spraying, right into his face.

'Do you hear me?'

Those around her could have been in no doubt that in that moment she was channelling the terrible righteous anger of the whole British nation.

'Do you hear me, Mr President?'

'Yes, I hear you, Prime Minister...'

'This will not stand,' the woman said, her voice trembling with deadly intent. 'Be assured that I will use every gun, every bomb, every bullet, every weapon that I have at my disposal...'

Peter felt sick; physically sick.

'Every weapon that I have,' Margaret Thatcher continued. 'I swear I will avenge this betrayal one day. Do your worst. I will fight you with my own eye teeth if I have to!'

It was hardly surprising that the man at the Philadelphia end of the transatlantic connection was briefly lost for words.

Just in case Jack Kennedy had not got the message Margaret Thatcher had spelled it out, again.

'*My own eye teeth*,' the Angry Widow had ground out between clenched jaws.

The static roared.

'*May you rot in Hell!*'

Walter Jenkins stopped the playback.

"We believe that Prime Minister Thatcher hung up at that point," he said drily.

Peter and Marija were in a state of disbelieving...horror.

They looked at each other. And then they looked to Lyndon Johnson. The craggy Texan lurched forward in his chair, planting his elbows on his knees and fixing the new British Ambassador with a granite-hard stare.

"You see my problem, son," he growled, ignoring their earlier contretemps about titles and 'respect'. "I have to talk to *that* woman before the American people get to hear about *that* tape. If *that* gets out there won't be anything to talk about. We'll just be shooting at each other."

Chapter 49

04:59 Hours (PST) – 07:59 in Philadelphia
Hearst Avenue, Berkeley, California

The heat had been so oppressive and Caroline – well, both of them – had been so hot and bothered after their last coupling, that she and Nathan had ended up standing under a cold shower. She had felt as if her blood was boiling, light-headed and a little ill until the chill of the water, an apologetic trickle rather than a reviving waterfall, had eventually cooled her down. They had stayed under the alternatively gushing, spurting and dribbling water an eternity, and then she had started to shiver, Nathan had gently towelled her hair and very slowly she had begun to feel normal again.

Whatever 'normal' was...

The sheets they had been lying in, wrapped in, prostrate upon were soaked in sweat. She had found clean linen – Nathan was the most house-proud man she had ever encountered; the Air Force had nurtured his crying need for order, for everything to have its place and to be in it – and spread it over the mattress. Now they lay down, each on their back in their nakedness and stared into the darkness.

They had been waiting, longing for the first thunder to break through the unnatural heat, to banish the worst of the killing humidity and to bring with it a life-giving breeze. Often on hot summer nights like this electrical storms raged across the Bay Area around midnight. Tonight, the heat had just built, and built until it felt as if the atmosphere was almost too dense to breathe. It was like sucking in the air from an oven vent...

The woman gasped with alarm as the room suddenly lit up as if the drapes had been suddenly pulled back to let in the sunshine of the new day.

The flash was so bright they both blinked, blindly into the night for several seconds.

Caroline had jerked upright in bed.

She tried to catch her breath but her chest had constricted with...panic.

"Lightning," Nathan muttered, dry-mouthed. "Just lightning..."

If it had been a bomb everything around them would be smouldering or on fire, they would have permanent retinal spots in front of their eyes. Besides, if it was *not* lightning then they were about to be hit by a blast over-pressure wave...

There was a second flash, not so close as the first.

The house reverberated, windows rattled and the crash of thunder rolled across Berkeley. One, two huge claps of electrical pyrotechnics rumbling around the hills enclosing San Francisco Bay. More flashing, the heavens rent asunder in a deafening cacophony of Mother Nature's primal rage.

Rain began to patter on the roof; and then the deluge hit.

"See," Nathan said, "just a storm."

Together they rose and walked through the kitchen to stand, nakedly, in the open back door as the downpour began to flood the single-floor wartime-built house's small fenced back yard.

The street lights had gone out, and in between the lightning strikes – great jagged spears hammering into the nearby canyons and daggering into the waters of the Bay – it was pitch black. The first strikes must have shorted out the local electricity grid.

Caroline took her lover's hand.

"Come on!"

She led him out into the yard, ecstatic in the pummelling rain and euphoric to be still alive. In the bedroom she had imagined for a split second that this was how the World ended. It might still end in a blinding flash but right now she was more alive than she had ever been in her whole life.

She threw her arms around Nathan's neck.

The momentary spikes of dazzling illumination threw their faces into cruel reliefs, as if they were two lunatics dancing their way to perdition.

Two years ago, she had honestly believed that the sole purpose of her life – what remained of it – was to, by hook or by crook, become the first female Dean of Psychiatry at the Chicago School of Medicine. That had been *IT*. Getting out of the Air Force Reserve, avoiding distracting emotional attachments, and side-stepping *anything* that stood between her and her goal was to be scorned, abandoned without a second look back. Initially, in a funny sort of way the October War had not really changed much – not inside her head – even though the Chicago School of Medicine, in fact most of the University of Chicago no longer existed. Chicago was wrecked, so too ought to have been her over-weaning ambition and...*hubris*. But no, she had simply thrown herself into the 'little project' Curtis LeMay had given her; made the best of a bad deal and worked to become *the* leading authority on the 'altered psychology of the men who won World War III' in a night. It had been a fascinating 'field study', professionally and physically exhausting because of all the travelling, and possibly the most intellectually and emotionally satisfying period of her entire career in medicine.

Encountering Nathan, well, that had been a blip which had subsequently resolved itself into whatever it was now – she still did not understand that, it was too weird – but that apart, she had kept her eye on the ball and begun to plan a number of, she hoped, ground-breaking papers. It scarcely mattered that nobody was going to publish any of her output any time soon, the thing was 'the work', understanding how the human mind adapted to the unthinkable and the unknowable...

"What's so funny?" Nathan asked her.

The rain was falling in large, explosive droplets which had instantly slicked her hair and now detonated or bounced, deflecting off their naked bodies.

She went up on tiptoes and kissed him full on the mouth.

"If we're still alive in the morning the sun will come up on a new world for us all, sweetheart!"

Her voice was hoarse, cracking and she had to shout to be heard above the background noise of the storm smashing down all around them. The water in the yard was already two inches deep, tumbling off roofs and overflowing gutters like hundreds of small mountain spring waterfalls that came to life for a day or so and went dry for a year.

"Imagine what this is like for everybody else," she went on, the words threatening to stumble, one over the next. "If you've got kids, just imagine it! The October War was bad enough but most people didn't know it had happened until it was all over. This is different; anybody with eyes and ears has known something was badly wrong for days, weeks. The March on Philadelphia was going to be like a giant pressure relief valve, a sort of watershed. But everything went wrong. All that stuff in the Middle East, and the President being taken ill, and the way the bad news started trickling out yesterday. The rumours of faraway wars going horribly wrong, hardly any real facts and suddenly JFK isn't there anymore and Philadelphia is in chaos, and then Lyndon Johnson does an emergency State of the Union address and talks about nuclear weapons, American values and peace all at once. If the country was 'damaged' after the October War, this time whether there is another war or not, the country is going to be exponentially *more* badly 'damaged'. We thought the worst was over, now it turns out things could get really bad..."

Caroline realised her excitement was getting the better of her and she was starting to rant.

The man kissed her.

That was so good...

She broke contact.

"The thing is this," she continued, needing to speak while the insight was pin-sharp in her mind. "Not everybody, but most people picked themselves up after the October War and, basically, got on with their lives as best they could; they did that because they still had, at some level, an abiding faith in things. The American Dream, that sort of stuff. You can forget about that now. For example, here in California we're living in the most populous state in the Union; and one the richest. Yet if a states' rights candidate stands against Governor Brown in the next gubernatorial election in two years' time how does he - or any incumbent for that matter - defend staying in the Union? What's in it for Californians? To remain in a Union run by idiots on the East Coast who have just got us into a second global nuclear war? Or, look at it more personally. What's in it for people like us to carry on supporting the 'status quo'? Why should we pay our taxes to prop up bigots and red necks in the Deep South, or to finance what sounds awfully like a re-run of the Civil War in the Midwest? If you've got kids, why would you ever trust the government again?"

He said nothing.

God, she was something when she was het up!

Caroline had paused to regain her wind.

When next she spoke, it was with a modicum of deliberation and an odd sadness.

"Oh, God... How much damage does it do to a human psyche if you've got kids on a night like this?" She posed rhetorically. "It's bad enough being terrified by a bolt of lightning because you think it's the explosion of a nuclear bomb nearby..."

Nathan bent his face and nuzzled her brow with his.

"I think you live your whole life remembering the way you felt on a night like this and you *never, ever really get over it*," Caroline decided grimly. "The worst thing is I doubt if any of the arseholes in Philadelphia or England or in wherever the new Kremlin is in Russia, *get it*. I doubt if many of them even care. Don't get me wrong, this is as scary, scarier maybe, for the people in the White House than it is for most of *us*, but they think they are in control and that makes it bearable. Even if it all goes wrong again like it did on the night of the October War, right up to the end Johnson and the military will honestly believe that they can still 'game the system', that they can 'win'."

The man had been waiting for the rain to ease.

Instead, if came down harder. Standing out in the yard in several inches of muddy water it was like being assailed by a thousand tiny wet hammers.

The woman kissed him hard, hungrily.

He staggered as she tried to lift herself onto him.

They mauled each other as a giant trident of lightning came down to earth half a block away and the sky seemed to fall upon Berkeley like some pre-historic giant volcanic eruption, filling the world with a sound and a fury matched only by the biggest, of the big hydrogen bombs in the arsenals of the warring nations of the Earth.

Chapter 50

08:02 Hours (EST)
British Embassy, Wister Park, Philadelphia

The girl Kitty was still screaming when the woman the others called Rachel reached into the khaki satchel and walked – apparently without any marked sense of urgency - to the balustrade at the top of the circular staircase at the end of the second-floor landing. With the casualness of a woman who was scattering kitchen scraps for farmyard animals she had brandished two pineapple-style hand grenades, pulled the pins and rolled the bombs down the stairs. Without appearing to hurry, or to show the least urgency, she had stepped back and unslung the Sten gun from her left shoulder.

Dwight Christie had not actually believed his eyes.

Not at the time.

But then he still had not got used to the idea that in the last hour he had also seen the same *woman* execute three men in the coldest, of cold blood. She had not killed Dan, Galen Cheney's right-hand man, or either of the other two younger men, each armed with loaded guns in any sort of a fight. She had killed Dan with his own hunting blade – a wicked, curving weapon with a serrated edge on one side and a razor sharp one on the other. Christie had no idea how she had taken the knife off him, just that she had hit him on the back of his head, or neck with some sort of martial arts manoeuvre that – judging by the click he had heard – had probably broken or crushed a vertebra, before she cut his throat and left him writhing, gargling helplessly in a rapidly spreading pool of his own, pumping, spurting arterial life blood. She had butchered the others in the same fashion; without hesitation, with merciless efficiency.

The satchel with the hand grenades, and several fresh magazines for the Sten gun had been Dan's. The bastard had left it outside in the corridor when he came into the room to have his 'fun' with Christie, and presumably, after he felt he had cut enough pieces off him, with Rachel. The maniac had been too preoccupied contemplating taking out the former FBI man's left eye with the point of that hunting knife to notice the woman had risen from the bed behind him. Their captors had assumed she was out cold; a not unreasonable assumption given how many men had raped her...

She had moved soundlessly, the blade of Dan's knife had glistened dully as she 'danced' – *danced* in front of and around her victims, it was almost balletic, the movement of her knife hand very nearly too fast to follow, the blood arcing through space, pattering and splashing on the bare boards, bodies crumpling to their knees, toppling face first onto the floor, the air painted with crimson-speckled spittle as they expelled their last breaths across the walls – her pirouette of death.

Dwight Christie had not expected the noise of the two grenade detonations to be so stingingly, deafeningly loud. Smoke and dust billowed upward, a man screamed in animal agony.

'Everybody stay where you are!' *She* had commanded.

Mary Drinkwater, secretary and personal aide to the Ambassador and his wife, Lady Barbara, now cradled Dan's antique Colt forty-five, Christie had a dirty pattern Colt 1911 Navy semi-automatic pistol in his hand. Rachel had taken the Sten gun and left the old – breach-breaking – shotgun propped against the wall by the makeshift barricade of beds, mattresses and furniture from the bed rooms.

'I'll call you when or if it is safe to come down,' Rachel had added.

Dwight Christie wondered if he had imagined the woman saying *that*. Her tone was that of a woman who had absolutely no doubt that soon it would be 'safe' to follow her.

"Until then stay exactly where you are!"

The other woman, Cynthia, who had worked in the protocol section of the Embassy and was engaged to be married to one of the Royal Marines in of the 'Protection Detail', had not stopped whimpering since she was unchained from the bed in the room next to the one in which Christie and Rachel had been imprisoned.

Within seconds of Rachel's head disappearing from view there had been two short bursts of automatic gunfire.

Then silence.

Five minutes later there was more shooting.

Screams and shouts.

The sound of doors slamming or being broken down.

Another explosion.

And more, interminable silence broken by a single long, magazine emptying burst of automatic gunfire.

Then, just the silence...

Behind the second-floor barricade Christie had gripped the butt of the Colt 1911 so hard his hand kept cramping. He had exchanged anxious looks with Mary.

"Who is *she*?" He asked eventually.

What did it matter, they were all going to be dead soon? That was the way this ended, they were trapped and the crazy woman who had bust them out of their torture rooms was probably dead, her body lying somewhere in the wreckage of the lower floors.

"Rachel?" Mary Drinkwater asked before she realised it was a very stupid thing to be checking at a time like this.

"Yes," the man hissed in exasperation. He relented. "Sorry, this is a goddammed nightmare..."

"I don't *know* who she is or even if Rachel is her real name," the woman confessed. "I've just heard what other people have said. I don't know if any of the stories about her are true. She's just well, 'normal', with the other women at the Embassy. She's one of us, really, no airs or graces, even though she's officially the senior spy at the Embassy."

Dwight Christie's eyes – even the one half-closed and rimmed with dried blood, the one Dan had been about to excise with the point of his hunting knife when he had died – must have been on stalks.

"You're kidding me…"

Mary shook her head. Her face was bruised, puffy and her nose still wept occasional drops of blood. Despite her recent ordeal she was actually more in control of herself than the former FBI Special Agent.

"No," she grimaced. "She was in Malta before she came over here. She was very close to the Maltese Navy wives…"

This baffled Dwight Christie.

"Lady Marija Christopher and Rosa Hannay," the woman explained." Realising that the man needed further prompting she added: "The wives of two of the heroes of the Battle for Malta? I believe it was Lady Marija's brother who actually fired the torpedoes that sank those Russian battleships…"

Dwight Christie had read about the 'Navy Couples'; they had gone down a storm on the East Coast. The way he heard it they would have been given a ticker tape welcome in New York when they got off the ship…the Queen Mary or the Queen Elizabeth, he forgot which if the Brits had asked for it…

"Oh, right," he mumbled.

"Nobody knows for sure what exactly went on in Malta but I overhead some of the Royal Marines talking one day," Mary continued, speaking in a confidential whisper, "that Rachel killed thirty or forty Red Army parachutists during the defence of Admiral Christopher's headquarters on Malta."

Christie's scepticism must have been palpable.

"No, honestly," Mary re-joined. "The story is she picked up a Kalashnikov from a dead parachutist and fought her way into the headquarters building. She was the person who discovered Admiral Christopher in the hands of several – anywhere from two to six Russian thugs depending on which story you hear – and killed them all. They say Admiral Christopher died in her arms…"

Mary Drinkwater's voice trailed off into thin air.

Rachel Piotrowska was standing the other side of the barricade giving her a mildly vexed look. Neither Christie nor the embassy secretary had heard her come up the stairs or her approach.

Rachel was wearing a Royal Marine camouflage smock and had discarded her ruined skirt for a slightly oversized pair of soldier's uniform 'work' trousers. These latter were held up by a red, black and off green canvass belt. She was wearing dark plimsolls.

"You shouldn't believe everything you hear, Mister Christie," she observed distractedly.

"You were a long time," he complained.

"Yes, well," she sniffed, "it took me a while to find *something* more suitable to 'slip into'," she retorted in conclusion.

Surreally, they might have been discussing where to eat out that evening.

By now Dwight Christie was staring at the woman.

Not only had she ghosted up the stairs, stepping over the bodies of the men she had killed, and somehow managed to float silently right up to the barricade without him or Mary Drinkwater knowing she was there; but she had done it carrying a cache of weaponry sufficient to fight and win a small war!

She passed the Sten gun she had gone downstairs with across the heap of furniture half-blocking the corridor. Her canvass rucksack clunked heavily, metallically on the boards at her feet.

"Take the mags for the Sten gun out of the bag," she instructed as she unslung a Thompson submachine gun from her right shoulder and hefted it as if checking its balance and its feel in her hands.

The man stared at the gun.

She glanced down.

"A Sten gun is a heap of junk," Rachel snorted. "It usually jams if you have to load a second mag in a hurry. That's if it doesn't jam the moment you pull the trigger." She hefted the Thompson like an old friend. "This thing is like an AK-47; even gangsters can get the hang of it."

"What happened down there?" The man asked.

Rachel eyed him thoughtfully.

Dwight Christie realised he had just asked a very stupid question to which he already knew the answer.

"I killed everybody," the woman said, dully.

Chapter 51

13:10 Hours (GMT) – 08:10 in Philadelphia
Hertford College, Oxford, England

"There's nothing new from Michael Carver as yet, Prime Minister," Sir Richard Hull, the Chief of the Defence Staff reported. If he was secretly mightily relieved to find Margaret Thatcher in a self-evidently more emollient frame of mind than earlier in the day, his tone and demeanour was as always, affably business like. As every old soldier knew a politician's mood was a thing liable to wild fluctuations and it was his job to keep things on an even keel. "But HMS Eagle and her consorts are making good time."

Sometime earlier – keeping track of time was impossible when everything was going to pot around one - the Chief of the Defence Staff had passed the Thatcher twins, Mark and Carol, on his way into the Prime Minister's rooms. The children had just been presented to their mother for inspection ahead of being sent off the Sunday School at St Aldates, where later that evening the Prime Minister and several of her senior colleagues were scheduled – provisionally - to attend Sunday Service.

The old soldier in Sir Richard Hull welcomed any opportunity for prayers at a time like this. The strangest thing was that being in a situation in which there was really very little one could do about one's fate, was hugely less worrisome than being, in some limited sense, in the driving seat. One's options were so few it was pointless troubling overmuch to identify what to do next.

"Captain Maltravers broke radio silence, Prime Minister. It seems his squadron was tracked by a 'spy plane' soon after it departed Port Said. In any event, Eagle is in fine fettle and the plan remains to fly off her aircraft as soon as she is in range of the Maltese Archipelago in a general show of strength."

"Excellent. No further incidents at Valletta?"

"No, Prime Minister."

Members of the crew of the USS Bainbridge (DLGN-25), a nine-thousand-ton nuclear-powered guided missile cruiser had repulsed an unarmed boarding party overnight. At the time the Bainbridge was the only major US Navy surface vessel 'unmarked' by a Royal Navy warship, an oversight partially remedied by bringing the ship under the barrels of half-a-dozen 3.7-inch anti-aircraft guns arrayed at point blank range on the heights above her.

A second incident concerning the recalcitrance of the commanding officer of the USS Leahy (CLG-16) another modern – but conventionally powered – guided missile cruiser, had been defused peacefully by the spontaneous intervention of the captain of the submarine HMS Alliance, Lieutenant-Commander Nicholas Barrington. Barrington had taken it upon himself to go over to the Leahy, moored alongside the oiling quay in Marsamxett Anchorage to have a frank a 'heart to heart' *chat* with his opposite number. Thereafter, civil, albeit strained and appropriate professional 'Navy relations' had ensued.

Onboard the Bainbridge things had been less easily resolved. Mercifully, no shots had been fired but a general brawl had developed on the stern of the American ship when a second, stronger party of sailors, backed up with a platoon of infantrymen from the Warwickshire Regiment had attempted to board.

It seemed that the C-in-C, Air Marshal French had had to appeal to the good offices of the Commander of the Sixth Fleet, Admiral Clarey to persuade the Captain of the Bainbridge to 'see reason'.

"Things are, of course," Sir Richard went on, "tense and I suspect that they will get no less tense with the passage of time. Ideally, we would like to do something to temporarily disable the US ships in the Grand Harbour but the C-in-C Mediterranean advises against attempting such action. It would be, he feels, the straw that broke the camel's back for many, if not all our American *friends* at Malta."

Margaret Thatcher did not bat an eyelid.

"I plan to keep those ships, Sir Richard," she said pleasantly.

"Very shrewd, Prime Minister. Invaluable bargaining chips..."

"No," the woman interjected. Instantly, the angry widow was back in the room. "No! No! No! If we survive this present crisis we will need *those* ships to defend *our* legitimate national interests at home and abroad in the world."

An arched eyebrow aside the Chief of the Defence Staff let this pass unremarked. He knew the lady well enough to know that there was a time to voice the other side of the argument; and a time when it was a complete waste of breath. Moreover, the last thing he wanted to do was say anything likely to draw his political mistress out of her recently constructed cocoon of calm.

"This spy plane following HMS Eagle?" Margaret Thatcher inquired, her mood turning icy. "Presumably, it is based at *that* blasted clandestine US airfield in the Negev Desert of southern Israel?"

"That is our assumption, Prime Minister. Our sources on the ground in Israel indicate it may have a runway sufficient for it to accommodate aircraft as large as the B-52. It is unclear whether the US Air Force is still operating a squadron of KC-135 Tankers at Torrejón Air Base near Madrid, or if it has transferred it in part, or wholly, to the facility in the Negev Desert."

There was a knock on the door and Tom Harding-Grayson entered the room. He nodded to the Chief of the Defence Staff.

"We were talking about the Israeli-American base in the Negev Desert, Tom," Margaret Thatcher told him.

"Ah, yes, yet another dirty little secret that's come out in the last week or so," the Foreign Secretary remarked dryly.

Sir Richard Hull made an openly dissenting grunt of irritation.

"I know, I know," the newcomer conceded. "Our own nefarious underhand dealings with Colonel Nasser were always bound to chase the Israelis back into Uncle Sam's hands. Trust me, old man, I'm the last man in Oxford with any right to throw the first stone. People who live in glass houses, and so forth!"

The old soldier harrumphed at this, before relenting.

"Tricky thing, hindsight," he averred, ruminatively. "The Egyptian imbroglio might have served us well but for the *brave* intervention of the United States Navy the other day."

None of them had seen the betrayal in the Gulf coming; even though in retrospect the question ought to have been asked louder: *How will the Americans betray us this time?*

"We shall leave the inquests to another time, gentlemen," the Prime Minister said curtly, before leavening her acerbity with a tired, nevertheless still winning smile. She turned to her Foreign Secretary. "Where have we got re-establishing direct communications with the White House, Tom?"

"*Unfortunately*," said the dapper, grey fox of a man who had had the most brilliant mind – everybody said so, even his enemies – in the Foreign Office in the second half of the 1950s before his fall from grace; partly due to his drinking, mostly due to his intemperance when it came to expressing his views on the then 'mythical special relationship' that supposedly existed between the United States and the United Kingdom, "we are now in direct communication, courtesy of the US Embassy 'communications team', and relays at Dublin and onboard a ship in the middle of the North Atlantic with the White House in Philadelphia."

"*Unfortunately?*" The Prime Minister inquired querulously. While she had the greatest respect for her Foreign Secretary, whom she also regarded as a close personal friend; sometimes he could be infuriating 'slow' in his loquacious circumnavigation of what were seemingly perfectly straightforward matters.

"Yes, quite, Prime Minister," Tom Harding-Grayson confirmed, rather lost in the circle of his thoughts for a moment.

His meteoric pre-October War career had faltered and spectacularly imploded in the middle of 1960. At the time his wife had just divorced him and he had been drinking himself into an early grave; and even his oldest and closest friend, Sir Henry Tomlinson, the present Cabinet Secretary and Head of the Home Civil Service, had despaired. What was the use of having a first-class mind if it was perennially soaked in alcohol?

In the old days he would pithily riposte: *What was the point of having a Double First brain in an environment populated with inbred, incompetent nincompoops of the kind he had to work with in Government?*

Yes, he had gone to the same school as most of Harold 'Supermac' Macmillan's cronies – Eton – and to Cambridge with some of the dunces, too. He had played cricket and rugby with several of the idiots in his younger, salad days. Actually, what with one thing and another they had not seemed such a bad lot during the Second World War; and several of the ones who were not bright enough to park themselves behind a desk in MI5 or in some home ministry hundreds of miles from the front, had had the decency to get themselves shot or blown up. That was social Darwinism at its most piquant, the dullards obligingly putting their heads above the parapet at exactly the wrong moment. The problem was that an awful lot of that gang had survived and because of their unimaginative politics, the immobility of their shared world view, their entrenched prejudices, and the fact most of them seemed to be related by birth or marriage to the then Prime Minister, Harold Macmillan, they had ended up running the country in October 1962.

He had told the useless beggars – miscellaneous members of *Supermac's* inner circle - that if they kept on down the road they were with the Americans it was likely to end badly. And that, as they say, had been that; he had promptly been banished to an office in the Foreign Office building so far from the Secretary of State's rooms that he had needed to book a taxi to get to it.

In the Macmillan era it was simply not done to remind the men running the country – and they were practically all men – that the Americans had turned up three years late for the First World War, and that they would not have turned up for the Second at all unless the Japanese had attacked Pearl Harbour, and Hitler had – presumably because he was insane – declared war on them. Moreover, it remained his view that Roosevelt had only prioritised the European war because he believed that defeating Hitler was the most efficacious way to extract treasure from and in due course, heap ignominy on the, by then, bankrupt British Empire. This had been a thesis which went down like a lead balloon in Whitehall. Post Second World War British governments were too much in hock to Wall Street banks and the US Treasury, and so seduced by the notion of the 'special relationship' that they failed to notice that they had become meek, well-schooled tame clients feeding off scraps from the tables of the new Romans.

His had not been a soft landing. Losing Patricia had been the low point and it was a crying shame it had taken a nuclear war to reunite them.

"Surely the restoration of channels of communication with Philadelphia is much to be desired, Tom?" Margaret Thatcher asserted irritably.

"Well, yes and no," her friend parried. "The problem is that now the line is up again the blighters are doing what they always do, they are throwing, diplomatically albeit in excruciatingly polite terms, their not inconsiderable weight around and making quite extraordinary demands upon us." Tom Harding-Grayson sighed. "Which was to be expected, obviously, but..."

"I need to speak to President Johnson!"

"No!" The Foreign Secretary snapped before he engaged his brain. He hurriedly modified his tone. "Forgive me, Prime Minister. There may well come a time when that is..."

Margaret Thatcher's posture had become stiff, wary.

"What you mean is you don't trust me to speak to the Americans?"

Tom Harding-Grayson met her stare, unblinking.

There were all manner of eloquent ways to sugar coat, blur, and to obfuscate his way around the heart of the matter. But actually, he honestly did not think any of them would cut as much as a fraction of an inch of ice with his Prime Minister.

Times were desperate indeed when a Foreign Office man had no option but to resort to honest dealing.

He smiled wanly.

"No, Margaret. I don't."

Chapter 52

Llewellyn E. 'Tommy' Thompson, President Kennedy's envoy to the Troika had been staring out of the window at the awe-inspiring trackless wilderness of the mountains and deserts of Central Asia as he brooded. He had belatedly realised that the aircraft he was on, a great sleek, silvery Tu-114 transport, was no ordinary airliner. Everybody onboard – at least those men and women he had seen - wore green KGB uniforms or distinctive Red Air Force Security Corps lapel badges and there was a distinctly 'military' feel to everything around him.

"What is this aircraft?" He asked Alexander Shelepin.

The head of the KGB and the second most powerful man in the new Soviet Union had been called away about thirty minutes ago. Previously, he had been napping – in the way of all powerful men he had learned, over the years, to virtually sleep on his feet – in a seat opposite Thompson, as relaxed and supine as if he had not a care in the world.

Shelepin had remarked earlier that the aircraft would be 'landing soon'; a lie; just a way to keep Thompson off balance. On the ground the aircraft would be horribly vulnerable; assuming that its tanks had been topped off back in Chelyabinsk it could probably stay in the air the best part of twenty-four hours.

On his return the Russian had fixed the American with a thoughtful, strangely benign scrutiny. If he had been any other man Thompson might have been tricked into believing his interlocutor was amused by something.

"It is one of two such aircraft. Twin prototypes that were under development at the time of the Cuban Missiles War," Shelepin explained. "Your Air Force has," he shrugged, "or had at the time of the war a fleet of Lockheed EC-121 so-called *Warning Star* aircraft. A machine developed from the military variant of your *Super Constellation* civilian airliner. Your *Warning Stars* carry large radars, we dispensed with that. We were more apprised of the need to acquire the most sophisticated possible airborne command and control 'posts'."

Thompson listened, his curiosity not so much piqued as 'spiking'. His countrymen too easily derided the apparent inelegance and outright 'clunkiness' of many Soviet technological solutions; without appreciating that what they were actually looking at was not in any way 'inferior', simply the product of a different way of approaching common, well understood engineering and production restraints. To the Soviet 'mind' *function* was everything and *form* secondary.

"So, this is an airborne command post?" He asked.

Shelepin nodded.

"Yes, I can communicate with Soviet forces in any part of the northern hemisphere from this aircraft," he confirmed, "and if necessary, fight a war from," he glanced out of the window at the mountains several kilometres below, "from the comfort of this seat."

The KGB man's pitiless gaze was boring into Thompson's face.

"Is that your intention?" The US emissary asked, dry-mouthed.

"That," Shelepin returned, "is a very complicated question, my friend."

Thompson shivered inwardly; said nothing. Instincts born of spending half a lifetime playing high stakes poker – that was what top-level diplomacy was – with the hardest-headed men, and women, in the World warned him that the other man was tempted to unburden himself to him. It made a kind of sense; who else could the most secretive and dangerous man in the new Soviet Union confide in without, that was, having to have them shot afterwards?

"I think you are a very wise man, Comrade Ambassador," Shelepin remarked, reading his companion's thoughts. "Wiser, I think, than the fools who sent you to us. There are people in *this* country who believe that there can be peace but what peace can there be 'at any cost'? You can destroy us, bomb us 'back to the Stone Age' but you cannot defeat us. To defeat us you must conquer us and that will never happen."

"President Kennedy did not send me to Chelyabinsk to offer *nothing*, Comrade Alexander Nikolayevich," Thompson objected. "He offered a pact which would enable both our great countries to begin the process of rebuilding..."

Shelepin's face contorted with contempt.

"*You* murdered a hundred million of my countrymen; we killed a few hundred thousand 'Americans'! What is there to rebuild in America?"

In a moment the Russian's expression was blankly inscrutable, his flash of temper a heart-stopping memory.

Thompson was relieved when a youthful KGB officer entered the compartment.

"The rendezvous has been achieved, Comrade Chairman," the young man barked as he came to attention, he stood so straight and tall that he almost banged his cropped head on ceiling.

"Look out of the window, my friend," Shelepin gestured to the American diplomat.

Thompson did as he was bade.

He blinked, uncomprehending for a second of so.

While Shelepin had been talking the deafening thunder of the Tu-114's four great Kuznetsov NK-12MV fifteen thousand horsepower turboprop motors had subsided, the aircraft had slowed and judging by the mild turbulence lost several thousand feet in altitude.

The nearest of the bombers was less than half-a-mile away.

There were at least a dozen of the huge aircraft, the sun glinting of their quicksilver unpainted surfaces. It was like looking at old World War II Pathé footage of the 1944 and 1945 raids on Japan, except those were not Curtis LeMay's B-25s en route from the Marianas to Nagoya or Tokyo or Kyoto, the aircraft he was looking at wore big identification numbers stencilled in Russian Cyrillic script on their wings and fuselages.

And had huge red stars on their flanks.

In the distance there were more such leviathans.

The sun glinted and flashed off their silvery hulls.

He guessed he was looking at least thirty Tupolev B-4 bombers, circling over the mountains of Kazakhstan...

Chapter 53

15:15 Hours (Local) – 08:15 in Philadelphia
USS Sam Houston (SSBN-609), Levantine Sea, Eastern Mediterranean

Commander Troy Simms had understood the logic of positioning a Polaris boat in the Eastern Mediterranean long before the revised targeting co-ordinates were run through the decoding protocols. He had figured out that 'logic' the moment he had read his patrol orders twenty-four hours out of Charleston. The Minutemen and the B-52s would cover anything beyond the reach of his AGM-27 Polaris A-2 and A-3 birds; while everything in southern Russia, Kazakhstan, Turkmenistan or anywhere in the Middle East was *his.*

Right now, even Sverdlovsk or Chelyabinsk were within the operational 'envelope' of his A-3s, around two thousand miles away. Baghdad was around seven hundred and Basra less than a thousand miles distant. The Soviet oilfields of the Caucasus were in his sights, as was Tbilisi in Georgia. The British enclave on Cyprus was a short hop away for his A-2s.

He hated the idea of having to come up to periscope depth to fix his position – assuming Sixth Fleet, the 'Advanced Emergency Facility' in the Negev Desert and the CIA's station on Crete were on line – by radio triangulation, but then there were a lot of things he did not like about what the USS Sam Houston was doing sneaking about this particular part of the Eastern Mediterranean.

Thousands of miles away in faraway oceans other boats like his would be prepping to launch their birds. He was the skipper of a Polaris missile boat; the downside was that one lived with the knowledge that this day might come.

One of the new A-3s had gone 'down' again fifteen minutes ago.

The techs had thought they were winning; they had had the bird on line for twenty minutes and then it had started flashing inertial guidance 'parity errors'. That usually meant a hardware fault, that or one or other of the sensitive 'chips' that stored the co-ordinates of where the damned thing was supposed to go was not taking orders!

Two of the A-3s loaded to replace the more reliable A-2s at Charleston were in effect, useless dead weight and that offended Troy Simms's innate sense of rightness.

Of necessity all submariners were perfectionists; if you lived and worked in an unforgiving, hostile environment in which a single mistake, a moment's inattention could very easily get you and all your crewmates killed, it tended to inculcate a meticulous attention to detail in a man. Therefore, when something onboard did not work that was *always* a big problem. Which was why, presently, the fact that two of the boat's birds were 'down' bothered him a lot more than the possibility that sometime in the coming hours he might be ordered to flush the other fourteen...

The fingertips of Troy Simms's right hand drummed the rest of his chair. Around him in the control room the tension was thick enough to cut.

"ONE-FOUR-ZERO FEET."

The four hundred feet long submarine was rising slowly, climbing up from the depths like a giant whale.

"Hold at one-two-zero feet!" Troy Simms ordered.

The command was repeated back to him.

He was bringing the boat up in small steps, pausing to listen at each shallower depth for several minutes. The whole boat was running as silently as a wraith, each command issued sotto voce, with no man moving unless he absolutely had to. Just because he did not think the British, or less likely, the Soviets, were looking for the USS Sam Houston, or had the remotest notion she was anywhere within three or four thousand miles of the Levantine Sea, Troy Simms was taking no chances.

"LEVEL AT ONE-TWO-ZERO FEET, SIR."

The big problem with targeting was in knowing where exactly the boat was at the moment it flushed a given bird. The submarine's SINS – Ship's Inertial Navigation System – was good, damned good but it was not infallible. Like any dead-reckoning system it was dependent upon its automatic inputs, course, speed, engine revolutions, drift, currents and so forth. Most of those inputs were unambiguous but every now and again tiny errors, for example calculations rounded to five or six decimal places and therefore not 'exact' accumulated and SINS began to operate with a miniscule built in 'error factor'. Axiomatically, SINS needed to be checked at regular intervals and if necessary, reset or re-centred. Before the October War this was supposedly going to be achieved by Project TRANSIT, a string of satellites placed in orbit around the Earth. However, in the absence of a 'space age' solution the US Navy and Air Force (who had the same *accuracy* constraints as the Polaris fleet) had fallen back on tried and tested radio triangulation.

Hence, the hasty creation of a network of stations in the Eastern Mediterranean that spring. The facility on the island of Crete – or rather, on Koufonisi, an island off its south eastern tip – had only come on stream ten days ago; coincidentally, around the time a similar station on the Libyan coast near Benghazi had gone off air. Two stations just about did the job but if the USS Sam Houston was to 'accurately' – that is nail her position down to within a handful of feet - re-centre its SINS ahead of flushing her birds Troy Simms wanted a three-station triangulation.

If the British knew about the stations on Crete and in Israel – which they would *if* they were responsible for putting the Benghazi node off air – then sooner or later they would also shut down the Sixth Fleet 'command and control' ship currently anchored in the Grand Harbour at Malta.

It was not as if the USS Northampton (CLC-1) was inconspicuous. Laid down as a fourteen thousand-ton Oregon class light cruiser in 1944 the Northampton had been completed in a command and control configuration – lightly gunned but with radar and communications masts practically from bow to stern – in 1951. Notwithstanding the peace dividend cutbacks, she had remained in commission since the October War and joined Sixth Fleet at Malta at the end of May, the one essential element which made Admiral Clarey's command, in battle at least, the most powerful naval fleet in history.

If the Northampton had been with the Kitty Hawk in the Persian Gulf the British would not have got anywhere near Carrier Division Seven...

"NO CONTACTS. REPEAT. NO CONTACTS."

Troy Simms sighed.

"Make our depth six-five feet, if you please."

It was time to rise to periscope depth and find out which stations were still on the air.

Chapter 54

"They had to have heard the grenades going off and all the shooting?" Dwight Christie reasoned, fingering the trigger guard of the Sten gun as he peered at the head of the stairs, expecting at any moment a dozen maniacs to rush the barricaded corridor.

Rachel took a sip of water from the canteen she had filled while she was on the ground floor.

She was sitting with her back to the corridor wall, the Thompson in her lap, visibly gathering her strength and she clearly resented the interruption.

"Nobody will be coming," she said quietly, impatiently.

"How the heck can you know that?" The former FBI Special Agent demanded.

"We're all very scared, Rachel," Mary Drinkwater intervened. She sat between the other woman and the man clasping Dan's old-fashioned Colt revolver as if it was a life preserver in an angry ocean. The girl Kitty was at the staircase, lying on her belly peering over the edge, keeping a watch. Cynthia, the only other survivor had stopped whimpering, now she lay beyond Mary curled in a foetal ball on the floor, her eyes unseeing as she stared into space.

"You're also all very squeamish," the woman who had returned from her latest killing spree dressed in military battledress fatigues groaned. "Okay," she relented, "if you really want to know, after I put the injured men at the foot of the stairs out of their misery and I killed the two guys who were still on their feet, and I forced the boy I took this from," she hefted the Thompson, "to call through to the main building. He was so scared he soiled himself but..."

Her face creased with disgust.

"The people the other side of that wall," she went on, pointing to the wall beyond where the girl Kitty was lying on the floor, "were pretty jumpy about the shooting and the grenades going off. I got the kid to tell them Dan had ordered them to kill the hostages. Us."

Rachel ignored Dwight Christie and Mary Drinkwater's goggle-eyed looks.

"The kid reckoned there are about fifty or sixty 'rebels'," she scoffed. "Most of these idiots think they are 'rebels', by the way. Apparently, the second Civil War has started and they all think they are secessionists. Well, the ones who aren't out and out religious zealots, anyway. Most of the mob that over ran the compound headed for the hills once they had had their fun. The Army took a couple of hours cordoning off the Embassy."

Christie was incredulous.

"He told you all that?"

Rachel nodded.

She had decided that the others did not need to know about her little heart to heart with General Westmoreland. They just needed to do what she told them to do; or they would die in this place.

"It's amazing what a man will say when he had a gun jammed into his crotch, Special Agent."

Dwight Christie did not have an answer to that.

"Or that's what I've always found in the past," she added, cattily. "So, no, nobody else is going to be coming up those stairs any time soon. Part of the ground floor corridor between the central wing and this one collapsed during the initial fighting; the only way the 'rebels' can reinforce this wing is by going outside and I don't think that's likely to be very healthy until it gets dark again. Which is academic because this 'situation' will be resolved, one way or another, a long time before then."

Mary Drinkwater swallowed hard.

"What did you do to the man you interrogated, Rachel?"

Rachel's expression was suddenly blank, a mask.

"After he'd told the *animals* next door that we were all dead the guy on the other end of the line asked him if he'd '*had his*' before he '*ended*' us."

"Oh," Mary Drinkwater gasped.

"He was one of the ones who raped me," Rachel went on dispassionately. "I made him tie his own gag before I emptied the rest of the clip into his groin. He bled to death – I hope in agony – while I was looking for 'something to wear'."

Dwight Christie flinched.

"Jesus...."

Rachel had already moved on. For the third time since she had returned to the second floor she checked the Thompson; clearing the breach, removing and re-homing the magazine.

Click, click, click...

"Right," she decided, rising hurtfully to her feet. Her shoulder was stiffening up, every joint ached and she felt as if she had been punched in the stomach *all* the time. There had been blood in her urine when she passed water, pausing to squat in a corner on the ground floor before she discarded her skirt. There was nothing she could do about it.

She would worry about it later.

If there was a 'later'.

"Rachel, you're not still going to try to get into the West Wing through the attic spaces?" Mary queried, her tone pleading.

The other woman ignored this entreaty.

"When you hear explosions and shooting," Rachel told her, "and I mean a lot of shooting, you and Mister Christie are to take Cynthia and *her*," she added, flicking a glance at the girl Kitty, "out via the fire escape. I suggest you try to find some white blankets, wave them or wrap them around yourselves and whatever you do leave all your weapons here, inside. Hopefully, the US Army won't shoot you on sight."

Dwight Christie had shuffled to his feet.

He swayed unsteadily and Mary grabbed his arm.

"You can't be serious? You said it yourself; there are fifty or sixty maniacs the other side of that wall! You won't stand a chance!"

Rachel met his stare, unblinking.

"We shall see," she said, eyes hard like diamonds.

Chapter 55

08:21 Hours (EST)
The Oval Office, White House, Philadelphia

"I am either your prisoner, Mister President," Peter Christopher explained, his respectful tone every inch that of a graduate of the Britannia Royal Naval College at Dartmouth addressing a foreign dignitary. "Or I am Her Majesty's Ambassador to the United States of America. I cannot and will not be both and it is not for a member, however exalted, of a foreign government to tell me how to go about my lawful business, sir."

"Goddammit, son," Lyndon Johnson exploded, before recollecting how little 'the treatment' had impressed the younger man earlier that morning, "Sir Peter," he corrected himself, "we don't have time for this... Shit!"

"I'm sorry, sir. I must disagree. Were I in a position whereby I could receive and discuss confidential advice from my government in England, I agree, that we might indeed enter into 'negotiations' as to how best to begin to resolve our mutual grievances. However, since the Embassy of the United Kingdom is presently in the hands of murderous 'rebels' I have no 'confidential' means of communicating with my government. I have said to you, and Secretary of State Fulbright that it seems to me that the best way to proceed, until such confidential means of communication have been restored, would be for both parties to declare a unilateral ceasefire, or truce. You have told me that this is impossible. Therefore, I ask you again, what are we to talk about, sir?"

Peter was aware that his wife had risen from the couch where she had been sitting with the First Lady.

"I am not a diplomat, sir. I do not understand the so-called 'complexities' of the issues that divide us. I joined the Navy to play with the latest electronic toys, oh, and to travel around and to see the World, too, I suppose. In any sane world I'd still be a lieutenant, an EWO – that's an Electronic Warfare Officer – on a destroyer. That's what I was twenty months ago, that's what I still am inside my head. Now everybody is asking me to behave like a career diplomat at the absolutely worst of all times. Frankly, sir," he sighed, "you'll understand me when I say I feel a little bit like Alice when she fell through the Looking Glass. Except Alice was fortunate not to land on her head!"

This analogy clearly perplexed Lyndon Johnson and drew a snort of undisguised contempt from Senator Richard Russell, who had just walked back into the room.

The President turned to his old friend.

"The kid wants to talk to the Press!"

"Let him. They'll tear him to pieces."

Lyndon Johnson was sorely tempted to give the young Englishmen a fresh taste of his famous 'treatment'.

Problematically, Peter Christopher was only an inch or two shorter than him and unlike most of the men to whom he applied the 'treatment' – brow beating and looming over an opponent until his moral courage failed him – it was very unlikely that the man who had conned his ship down the barrels of a Russian dreadnought and a fifteen-thousand-ton cruiser, would blink first. Particularly, while his wife was still in the room; that young woman seemed to have tempered steel in her veins!

"You are not a prisoner, Sir Peter," he admitted grudgingly. "You are free to leave or remain in this place. But..."

The younger man's eyes narrowed.

"In the present crisis," Johnson continued, "the US government cannot guarantee your safety, or, that of your wife, in the event that you elect to leave the White House."

"Sir?" Walter Jenkins murmured at his elbow.

The President turned to his long-time aide.

"Secretary of State Fulbright wishes to speak to ahead of the telephone session with the British."

The line to Oxford was already routed through to the Oval Office, and the first 'plenary' session requested by the British Foreign Secretary was now scheduled to commence at 09:15.

Things were moving too fast.

Curtis LeMay needed answers, the Navy wanted a direct Presidential command before it re-initiated hostilities in the Mediterranean or in the Persian Gulf. Dobrynin, the Soviet Ambassador was in a room along the corridor – presumably with a new and impossible set of demands – and Senate and Congressional leaders were literally beating down the doors to the White House. Downstairs in the cathedral-like lobby of the old bank building the nation's TV and newspaper men were baying for blood; outside in the streets of Philadelphia people had spilled out into the balmy summer morning and begun to converge on Broad Street and City Hall in their tens and hundreds of thousands.

The crisis over Cuba had been nothing like this.

That disaster had been twelve or thirteen days in the making, its seeds sowed eighteen months before by the new Administration's mishandling of the Vienna summit with Khrushchev and its inaction over the building of the Berlin Wall. In fact, some historians were already positing that the real roots of the disaster of the October War went back to the Suez fiasco which had shattered the myth of British and French imperial hegemony, and the inability of the West to stop the brutal crushing of the Hungarian uprising in the wake of the Suez imbroglio.

This latest *disaster* might have been brewing for months but it had exploded in the last seventy-two hours; worse, whereas the Cuban catastrophe had been a two-handed thing blundered into by America and the Soviet Union, this new crisis was a fiendishly convoluted three-handed affair.

Was Curtis LeMay right when he said the only way out of it was to hit the Soviets with everything they had and to worry about the British later?

The trouble was that other voices in the Administration counselled that the British, not the Soviets were the real problem. Fight them now or fight them later, nip the idea of a 'militarized' white British Commonwealth in the bud, or risk a new imperial colossus arising from the ashes of the October War...

Driving everything was the fact that the full horror of what had befallen Carrier Division Seven in the Persian Gulf was at last beginning to screen on TV on the East Coast; that nightmare would soon be sweeping across America like a killer plague. Mercifully, there were no pictures from the Persian Gulf yet...

The British had sunk the Kitty Hawk and seized the Sixth Fleet; twin catastrophes that made the sinking of the USS Maine in Havana Harbour, or even Pearl Harbour pale into distant, hardly significant memory. The American people would be stunned, and sooner or later they would demand revenge.

Lyndon Johnson knew he had to get 'ahead of the story'.

But how?

"Oh, shit!" Somebody muttered from the corner where the TV was on, turned down low.

"What is it?" Walter Jenkins demanded.

"That bastard Nixon is talking to Walter Cronkite!"

Chapter 56

Henry Kissinger had arrived back at the Rockefeller campaign headquarters a little after eight o'clock. Nobody at the White House was paying a blind bit of notice to anything he said and it had become clear that Johnson – or his people – was now rigidly controlling who got access to the last British diplomat standing; Captain Sir Peter Christopher.

He genuinely felt for the young man. He was in an impossible situation, the Administration wanted to play hardball with the game rigged in its favour. It was just plain dumb and showed how little LBJ, the former master of the House, understood the *proper* conduct of international relations.

Kissinger had been half-way through recounting his conversations at the White House when an aide ran – literally sprinted into the first-floor room where Rockefeller was holding court – and breathlessly announced: *"That bastard Nixon is talking to Walter Cronkite!"*

Kissinger had been trying to focus Nelson Rockefeller's mind on the fragmentary reports emerging from Seoul and the US Embassy in Tokyo about what *might* be happening in Korea. A US warship, the USS Herbert J. Thomas (DD-833), had been repeatedly 'buzzed' by North Korean MiGs in international waters forty miles east of Wonsan, overnight there had been several reports of shelling from the North across the DMZ, and it was known that at least two tank divisions had concentrated in the country just north of the DMZ opposite Seoul, only thirty miles to the south of the border in the last month.

Coincidentally, there were reports of violence on the streets of Saigon and attacks on US legations and bases throughout South Vietnam. These seemed to be guerrilla, hit and run incidents in the main but Henry Kissinger hated the timing. The Administration had been blind to the fact its several thousand 'advisors' on the ground in South East Asia were every bit as out on a limb as the weakened 'garrison' brigade left behind in Korea.

Suddenly, too much was happening at once.

What was going on in the Middle East and the Mediterranean, in the Western Pacific, the disastrous uprising in the Midwest and the civil disorder which was rapidly becoming the norm across wide swathes of the Deep South, were not the *only* issues – perhaps not even the most important issues – confronting the new Administration. At the time of the Cuban Missiles War Kissinger had wondered how much the outbreak of the Sino-Indian war in the Himalayas on Saturday 20th October 1962 had distracted, or in some way contributed to the Cuban crisis turning into a global nuclear war seven days later. In the week after China invaded the Ladakh – the 'land of high passes' – region in the Indian states of Jammu and

Kashmir, the Kennedy Administration was emerging from a summer disfigured by race riots in the South and approaching mid-term elections that nobody believed were going to go well for the Democrats. Allegedly, when told that the Soviets had medium range intercontinental missiles based on Cuba, Bobby Kennedy had turned around and asked, hopefully: *'Can they bomb Oxford, Mississippi?'*

Kissinger understood that if there was a lesson from history it was that nothing was ever as simple as it later seemed. Life, the world, and foreign relations in particular were invariably excruciatingly complicated. Hardly any decision about anything was ever taken in isolation; and most of the time there was no such thing as a right or a wrong answer to anything.

The month before Bobby Kennedy and then Secretary of State Dean Rusk had gone into conclave with Soviet Ambassador Dobrynin, and the teleprinter lines between Washington and Moscow had burned red hot, JFK had had to send US Marshals, and then troops to Oxford, Mississippi, to enforce a court order permitting the admittance of the first African-American student, James Meredith, to the University of Mississippi. The Attorney General and the President had been afraid there would be a mini 'civil war' on the streets of Mississippi between federal soldiers and armed protestors.

The moral of the story was, and remained, that most US Presidents were always more preoccupied with domestic affairs and tended to get surprised far too easily by events overseas.

Right now, Lyndon Johnson was *scared* by what was going on in the Midwest, *perturbed* by a host of other North American 'problems', but just plain *angry and confused* about what was going on in the Mediterranean and the Middle East. At the moment what *might* be going on in Korea, or South Vietnam – and the potentiality for a catastrophic meltdown of everything US post-1945 policy in the region had striven to achieve – was not even on LBJ's event horizon.

Nor, unfortunately, was it on Nelson Rockefeller's.

Briefly, the only thing anybody in the room cared about was the grainy black and white pictures on the screen of a small television set in the corner of the room. As one everybody scampered for the door, knowing there was a much bigger set in the adjoining lounge.

The air was heavy with cigarette smoke and there were bottles of Bourbon half-empty on coffee tables jammed between the chairs drawn up around the TV. It had been that sort of night and things were going to get worse before they got better.

Always assuming that sooner or later they did get better...

Richard Nixon and his chief of staff, Bob Haldeman had disappeared about an hour ago. Everybody imagined they had gone back to their rooms to shave, brush up, and to put on fresh suits. Nobody had guessed Nixon was intent on stealing a march on the election trail on a day like this!

Walter Cronkite appeared to be standing in a diner, or maybe a bar, and the 'live' pictures were grainy. Technology was marvellous but when it was 'live' it was still very cranky and the outputs often very poor quality unless the technical folk had had days, weeks or months to set up everything in advance.

Clearly, Cronkite's CBS crew had had to set up in a screaming hurry that morning.

Nixon had shaved, put on a fresh suit and affixed a solemn, worldly, I was with Ike in the White House for eight years and we did okay, look on his less than telegenic face.

Forty-seven-year-old Walter Cronkite who had been in Illinois until a few days ago, reporting on the ongoing 'insurgency' looked his normal dignified, imperturbable self. Having returned to Philadelphia because he was unable to get anywhere near the front line, he had the look of a wise old terrier that had got its teeth into a bone who had no intention of letting go.

Cronkite was one of those 'news men' who seemed to have been around forever, even though he had only found a semi-permanent television niche in the last couple of years. Back in April 1962 when he had replaced Douglas Edwards as anchorman of the CBS Evening News, he could scarcely have imagined that within months his would be the face of, and his voice the soundtrack of the cataclysm of the October War and the travails of the following twenty months. Unsurprisingly, a recent Gallup poll indicated he was the 'most trusted man' in America; there was something about his patient, gravitas-filled delivery and his peculiarly paternal, good-natured manner that inspired confidence in practically every citizen, his charm was capable of crossing racial, sectarian and state divides with a magical loquacity most politicians would have killed for.

"...it deeply pains me to say it," Richard Nixon averred, crocodile tears forming in his eyes, "but the Kennedy Administration has betrayed every American. We have confused notions of good and bad, and pursued a criminally muddled policy abroad..."

Cronkite had no intention of allowing campaigning hyperbole to drown out reality.

"Surely, this is not the time to be casting the first stone, Mister Vice President?"

Nelson Rockefeller and his people winced in unison.

Mister Vice President...

The honorific that kept on giving!

All the man had done between 1952 and 1960 was nod like an obedient puppy every time Ike opened his mouth!

"We find ourselves in a dire situation," Cronkite pressed, "the question is what would you do if you were in President Johnson's shoes?"

"This is a time for firm leadership, Walter."

"The bastard!" Somebody groaned from behind Nelson Rockefeller's shoulder.

Rockefeller had been under the impression that he and Richard Nixon had agreed to present a combined front; partly to stop Barry Goldwater out-flanking them, but also in Rockefeller's mind, to avoid unnecessarily fanning tensions and basically, because he believed that it was their duty to behave in a patriotic, statesmanlike way. He ought to have known Nixon would double cross him.

Never give a loser a second chance...

At that moment people in the room were fit to start throwing things at the TV.

More bodies were packing in behind Rockefeller.

And then an odd thing happened.

Richard Milhous Nixon made an appeal for calm.

"I urge my fellow Americans to surrender the streets to the authorities, to remain true to themselves, to remember that we are a God-fearing nation united under *His* merciful oversight. I agree that this is not a time for recriminations; this is a time for us to stand together to mourn our fallen. President Johnson has been called to the White House in the worst of times and he deserves our full, unconditional support in confronting, and hopefully, defusing this new and terrible crisis in our nation's affairs..."

Nelson Rockefeller felt sick.

He had just lost not only the Republican nomination but what, less than a month ago, had looked like a virtual shoe-in for the Presidency.

"The only thing President Johnson cannot do," Nixon was saying as if he was a cross between Confucius and Abraham Lincoln, "is to allow the crisis to fester. I want it to be on the record that I will stand shoulder to shoulder with the President whatever," he paused, "*whatever* his decision is as to the best way to proceed. If he determines that the only way to protect American lives and the American *way* of life is to wage war on those who would threaten the United States and its legitimate interests overseas; I will be by his side. I will be at his side now, tomorrow and for all time heretofore!"

There was a clanking of glasses.

"Did the bastard really just say that?" One man slurred, reaching for the nearest bottle of liquor.

Nelson Rockefeller was too stunned to speak.

His campaign for the Presidency had not just been undermined; it had been cut off at the knees.

"Would somebody get *me* drink, please," he asked resignedly.

Chapter 57

"Your helicopter is ready to take you to Baghdad, Comrade Admiral," Admiral of the Fleet, Defence Minister and third ranking member of the Troika, Sergey Georgiyevich Gorshkov was informed deferentially by a junior aide-de-camp.

Gorshkov had demanded a helicopter be available for his 'immediate use' just in case he 'needed' to stiffen Yuri Andropov's courage. Shelepin's deputy – now only one of four as a result of a recent re-organisation – at the KGB had panicked back in Budapest in 1956, and after his experiences in the hands of the Rumanian Securitate in Bucharest that spring, Gorshkov was not alone in suspecting that Andropov was 'unreliable'. In fact, like others he assumed Shelepin only kept the Commissar General of Iraq – that was joke! – around to give dissident factions in the KGB a 'sitting target' for their intrigues.

In any event, neither Shelepin nor Gorshkov wanted to risk Comrade Yuri Vladimirovich doing anything 'off script' in the next few hours. The man had practically pissed himself when the British set off those two medium-sized airbursts west of Baghdad; if Gorshkov had not kicked him out of his bunker he would still probably be hiding under a fucking desk!

Whatever happened in the next few days somebody had to keep an iron grip on Baghdad and ensure that there was no general rout of the dispersed but still formidable Red Army forces unengaged in the north of Iraq.

Gorshkov's aircraft had landed at Al Habbaniyah some fifteen minutes ago while he was still 'in radio telephone conference' with Alexander Shelepin. For the last ten minutes he had been sitting staring out of the window across the shimmering, glassy surface of Lake Habbaniyah.

The Revolution demanded hard decisions, adherence to the one path. The dialectic demanded self-sacrifice, it took no account of old loyalties; it simply lit the way ahead.

Operation Nakazyvat had been an unmitigated disaster; as he – and others - had predicted from the outset. His carefully husbanded Black Sea Fleet and practically every unit of the Turkish Navy which had fallen into the hands of Krasnaya Zarya – Red Dawn – had been consumed in the diversionary attack on Malta. It had seemed like a price worth paying in the spring. If Malta could have been taken, even for a few days or weeks, Marshal Babadzhanian's two tank armies might, conceivably, have rolled down through Iran and Iraq to the Persian Gulf virtually unopposed. Of course, there had been no 'victory march'; and there was never, ever going to be one. True, the jewel in the British Imperial crown – Abadan and its irreplaceable refineries – was wrecked from end to end, and it was gratifying the way the British and the Americans had turned on each other like rabid dogs fighting over a bitch on heat...

The trouble was that from what he had learned in his short time in Iraq, even if the Red Army and the KGB could hold down the country – which he doubted, long-term was possible without committing men and resources that were going to be needed holding down the Balkans and re-establishing the Soviet writ in Eastern Europe, among other things – the USSR had just driven its last two tank armies into a veritable meat-grinder!

And for what?

In the name of some old-time Tsarist fantasy to secure an ice-free all year around warm water port?

Revenge?

If Brezhnev and Kosygin had held their nerve in the spring; and let Krasnaya Zarya off the leash the entire northern Mediterranean coast line all the way from Beirut to the Pyrenees might be in Soviet hands by now. In comparison all the grief and lost treasure in Iraq would have been a sideshow. There would have been no need to try to topple Nasser and risk, as now seemed likely a generation of enmity from the foremost regional power in the Middle East. When the West had failed to retaliate in the wake of the Red Dawn nuclear strikes in the Eastern Mediterranean, the Balkans and – abortively – against Malta in February *that* had been the time to let Red Dawn run riot, to halt the madness of Operation Nakazyvat, to retrench at home and to expel the British from the Middle East!

Now...

Now the Americans had been drawn back – whether they liked it or not – into both the Mediterranean and the Middle East and the Red Army's position in Iraq was untenable.

Brezhnev, Kosygin and Chuikov – the 'old' Troika – had been seduced by the *idea* of Operation Nakazyvat, and so obsessed with vengeance that they were blind to its dangers. The risks might have been worth it if there had ever been a realistic chance of Babadzhanian's tank armies rolling into Riyadh, and thereby denying the West the oil of Arabia but all that had actually been achieved was the destruction of the biggest oil refinery complex in the World on Abadan Island. The British would rebuild that, and in the meantime Saudi Arabian oil would continue to flow to the West in an ever-quickening river.

When Iran emerged from its current internal strife as factions vied to fill the vacuum left by the assassination of the Shah and the devastation of Tehran; it too would demand its revenge on its assailants...

Babadzhanian's tanks had dismantled the Iraqi state; whether the Red Army stayed or left the country – which was not really any kind of 'country' – Iraq would surely disintegrate into a civil war on the USSR's already troublesome Middle Eastern southern flank. The Motherland had no need of the oil of Kurdistan; half the wells in the

Caucasus were capped because of lack of demand; it might be ten, fifteen or twenty years before the USSR needed to go abroad again for 'black gold'.

Yet long before that, in five or ten years perhaps, the USSR might easily be confronted with two powerful, oil-rich enemies – Iran and Iraq – united in a common cause thwarting its lingering 'southern' ambitions. Operation Nakazyvat had achieved only one thing; generations of chaos on the Motherland's western Asiatic borders and in the process, for the moment bled the Red Army virtually dry.

Leonid Brezhnev had claimed the Politburo stood behind him over 'making peace' with the Americans. Gorshkov did not know if that was true. However, the fact the Party Chairman had left the negotiations with the Americans in the hands of Kosygin's man, Vasili Vasilyevich Kuznetsov, previously the First Deputy Foreign Minister responsible for dealings with Western Europe, a party time server known principally for never having put his head above the parapet, said everything about Brezhnev's increasing disconnection with reality. It was as if the Party Chairman did not understand that the Red Army was, right now and for the foreseeable future, *broken*. Its best men and equipment had been thrown into the deserts of Iraq and consumed; the scale of the defeat south of Basra and at Khorramshahr and Abadan was likely so catastrophic that initially, Gorshkov himself had refused to believe what Kulikov – the highly able man Babadzhanian and his lunatic sidekicks had relegated to the role of a helpless bystander - had been telling him!

The humiliation was complete.

He had been forced to fly out of Basra leaving Kulikov bluffing for time to get his people out of the city. On the opposite bank of the Shatt-al-Arab 2nd Siberian Mechanised Army was in headlong retreat, utterly routed, abandoning its armour. It was only a matter of time before the enemy – Iranians in the main who were routinely slaughtering Red Army wounded as they advanced – found a way to get across the river above Basra, and then the fifty thousand troops still south of the 31st parallel would be as cut off as were the remnants of the three divisions trapped south of Zubayr.

Gorshkov collected his wits.

"Signal Comrade Commissar Andropov that I will be delayed."

The aide-de-camp slithered obsequiously out of the small compartment in the nose section of the airliner.

Yuri Vladimirovich Andropov was nominally Commissar General of occupied Iraq. Actually, in Central Iraq all the KGB man controlled was the city of Baghdad, and a few isolated garrisons. His troops did not even 'command' the road between Al Habbaniyah and the capital. In between were the towns of Fallujah and Abu Ghraib, both rife with renegade Iraq soldiers who had run away when Babadzhanian's T-62s had rolled into Baghdad only a few short weeks ago.

Andropov did not know that there had been a change of plan and that, for the next few days, he was on his own. Iraq was about to become again what it ought to have been from the outset; a sideshow.

"Comrade Admiral," a voice standing over him murmured, "there is an urgent call for you in the communication compartment."

Gorshkov nodded.

"How long before the aircraft will be ready to take off?"

"Another twenty minutes, Comrade Admiral."

He had needed to be in Basra in such a hurry that when the Tu-114 had touched down at Baghdad previously there had been no time to refuel.

At the time the British had just knocked out most of the Red Army's communications in Central Iraq with two big airbursts over sparsely populated areas northwest and southwest of the capital; and things had been...confused. The next time his personal command and control station took to the air he needed its tanks topped up to the brim. If necessary the aircraft might have to stay in the air twenty, or perhaps twenty-four hours.

"Everybody out!" He ordered as he took the seat at the console and pulled on the headset.

He hesitated, took a deep breath.

"This is Black Knight," he growled.

"This is Red King," Alexander Nikolayevich Shelepin replied.

For a fraction of a second Gorshkov thought he heard a suggestion of irony in the KGB man's voice through the scrambler mush.

"I'll be in the air again in about half-an-hour," Gorshkov informed the other man.

"Good." Shelepin mulled his next words with infinite care. "Ya initsiiroval Krasnyy Voskhod Solntsa..."

I have initiated Red Sunrise.

Chapter 58

08:39 Hours (EST)
The British Embassy, Wister Park, Philadelphia

For a minute or so, or perhaps, two or three after Dwight Christie and Mary Drinkwater had made backs, and then lifted and pushed Rachel Piotrowska up into the roof void via the small access panel in the second-floor corridor ceiling, they had said nothing, exchanging anxious, vaguely comforting looks.

Rachel's damaged left shoulder had made it almost impossible for her to pull herself up and once, she had cried – a yelp of animal anguish, in fact - with pain as they tried to lift her. Eventually, she had disappeared into the darkness of the loft, and had lain very nearly exhausted on the bare rafters for several seconds before she asked for the Thompson and 'Dan's rucksack' to be passed up to her.

'Jeez, what have you got in this?' Dwight Christie had groaned, feeling the weight of the bag.

'Just grenades and spare mags; oh, and a couple of bottles of paint thinner I found in a cupboard downstairs. They might make good impromptu Molotov cocktails...'

Rachel had peered down at them.

'If that kid goes bad on you,' she said, looking at the girl Kitty. 'You know what to...'

'Yeah,' the man had interjected. 'Trust me, I know.'

'Okay. Remember, when you hear shooting, a lot of shooting, GO! Don't hesitate, just GO!'

Then the access panel fell in to place and she had been gone.

Mary had searched the rooms on the floor for white sheets or blankets.

"Put them by the fire escape," Christie suggested. "We'll grab them on the way out."

"Paint thinner?" The woman asked in a whisper. "Does that work as a Molotov cocktail?"

The former FBI Special Agent shook his head.

"Heck, I don't know. *That* broad's out of my league. I have no idea what's going through her head."

Mary Drinkwater's thoughts moved on.

"Kitty," she hissed. "Come here please."

The teenage girl approached on hands and knees, her eyes wild with fear.

"What?" Dwight Christie mouthed at the older woman.

"You're the FBI man; ask her what she's doing here?" Mary prompted.

Okay, they had to pass the time – probably *the* remaining time they had left on Earth – somehow. And besides, the nearness of the woman was beginning to remind him he was a human being. It was as if with the departure of Rachel – their personal guardian killer angel

– death, which had been on their shoulder, was stalking elsewhere.

"What the heck are you doing here, kid?"

"I came up with my Pa and brother, sir." The girl's accent had a Southern burr corrupted with a nascent Yankee drawl, she could have been brought up anywhere from Rhode Island to Baton Rouge.

"Came up from where?" Dwight Christie demanded tersely.

"We lost our farm in Mississippi a year back. Bank shut us down and took our land. Ma died just after the war, she got the first sickness that came through Jackson. It took my baby sister, too. Pa was never the same after that."

"What happened to your Pa?"

"The crowd moved forward and I never saw him or Jeb, my brother, we're twins, after that...you going to shoot me, sir?"

Dwight Christie shook his head.

"Only if I have to, kid."

Kitty glanced at the ceiling.

"*That* woman wanted to shoot me!"

"If you'd seen what your 'friends' did to her you want to kill somebody too, kid."

The girl Kitty bowed her head, she was crying.

"That weren't right," she sniffled. "Pa said there were bad men in the brethren," she shrugged, "Pa and Jeb said they'd kill any man who laid a finger on me..."

The child, she did not look more than twelve or thirteen, was sobbing now.

"How old are you?" Mary asked gently.

"Fourteen, fifteen this fall, ma'am."

Dwight Christie sighed.

The World had gone mad!

Mary Drinkwater was quiet for some seconds. She came to a decision.

"When *we* escape *you* and *I* will take care of Cynthia," she told the girl, nodding towards the woman curled on the floor behind the makeshift furniture barricade. "Whatever happens, we are not going to leave her behind. Do you understand me?"

Kitty jerked her head.

Mary put down the Colt she had been holding – not knowing what to do with it – and took the girl Kitty in her arms as if she was the child's mother.

Dwight Christie tensed; half-expecting the kid to make a grab for the gun.

Chapter 59

13:46 Hours (GMT) – 08:46 in Philadelphia
Christchurch College, Oxford, England

The Foreign Secretary put his head around the door of the small dining room where his wife was serving lunch – soup and modest chunks of dark bread – to the Thatcher twins, recently returned from their 'abbreviated' Sunday School at St Aldates Church. He had walked upstairs from his Private Office, whose staff had mostly been removed to the Chilmark bunker in the Chilterns and therefore, even on this day of ultimate crisis, was eerily sparsely populated.

In less than half-an-hour the 'talks' with Philadelphia were due to start in earnest. It had been determined that he and Willie Whitelaw should 'hold the fort' for the time being. No matter how nicely they wrapped it up the Americans were asking for abject submission; effectively telling the United Kingdom, and by implication its Commonwealth allies how things would be now and in the future.

That would never do.

Presently, the Prime Minister was hosting an emergency round table meeting with the High Commissioners from Australia, New Zealand, Canada and South Africa, the Portuguese Ambassador and the head of the recently arrived Swedish legation, the latter representing the diplomatic interests of his own country, and those of Norway, and the newly formed Danish Confederation.

At any other time, the re-emergence of the variously damaged constituents of the 'Scandinavian polity' - each of the three countries remained traumatised after suffering directly from nuclear strikes, or fallout as bad as parts of England during the October War - would have struck Tom Harding-Grayson as an encouraging first step on the road to arriving at a new western European post-war settlement.

"I must get back downstairs in a minute," he apologised, stepping into the low-beamed room. Not normally a sentimental or tactile man, he had needed to connect with his wife, and their surrogate 'wards' before he dived again into the quagmire of the crisis.

"Did you have a chance to have a bite to eat at Hertford College, darling?" The Foreign Secretary's wife inquired.

Tom Harding-Grayson slumped into the chair across the table from her. He shook his head, looked to Mark and then Carol Thatcher, mischief quirking on his pale lips and in his grey eyes.

"I was too busy thanking my lucky stars I wasn't being keel-hauled," he chuckled ruefully. "Our American 'friends' want to hold a 'so-called' *one to one* meeting of minds between President Johnson and your mother," he explained to the twins who listened with polite interest.

Carol and Mark Thatcher's mother had actually reacted quite moderately – by her lights - to his 'advice'; and moreover, politely heard him out as he explained his reasoning. He could not be sure how much of what he had said had been taken to heart; but for the moment she was prepared to leave the 'talking' to the 'people in Philadelphia' to him. This established, they had gone on to discuss the invidious position of 'the Christophers', who had it seemed, been unwittingly 'press-ganged' by LBJ into murky diplomatic waters so deep they might easily drown.

The Foreign Secretary still had no idea what the Americans had been thinking drawing two young people with such a high, and from everything he had heard, a remarkably 'popular' public standing in America into the crisis.

Peter Christopher and his beautiful wife were indubitably 'remarkable' young people but they were in an impossible position, and in his mind Sir Peter's *pro tem* installation as Ambassador – an interim measure he hoped would stop the Johnson Administration taking further 'liberties' – was a wholly cosmetic gesture. Tom Harding-Grayson had no intention of allowing the gallant young tyro to engage in any kind of 'negotiations' with wily old hyenas like Bill Fulbright and Dick Russell!

He took it as read that his opposite numbers in Philadelphia had, by now, worked that out for themselves. If they had played their hand a little better, with a tiny bit more forethought, they might actually have engineered a situation in which Peter Christopher might have been their unsuspecting dupe.

He suspected that they had misjudged their man and missed their moment of opportunity. All things considered he was astonished that his adversaries across 'the pond' had 'mucked about' so much in the last few hours. They ought to have sorted out the 'communications problem' first, not last.

The irony was that the Soviet delegation in Philadelphia, headed by former Ambassador Anatoly Fyodorovich Dobrynin was – and had been for the last few months, and remained – in 'secure' and very 'secret' communication with his government back in the USSR, while Her Majesty's man in America, Captain Sir Peter Christopher, VC, was virtually incommunicado!

The Americans were being unbelievably stupid over that.

Johnson's people could rig a direct – sufficiently confidential – voice link for Sir Peter in five minutes flat if they wanted to; if that was, they actually wanted to negotiate. They clearly regarded Peter Christopher as irrelevant, other than for employment as some kind of public relations stooge. It seemed that pictures of the President and 'the Christophers' would adorn every newspaper front page in the United States if the moment seemed propitious to their hosts.

It beggared belief that the US authorities had apparently sat on their hands while a mob ransacked the British Embassy and murdered its occupants; now they were holding the senior surviving accredited UAUK diplomat and his wife hostage at the White House. Presumably, Johnson's people would want to keep the young people 'sweet', just in case they needed to be wheeled out for the cameras to show that LBJ was in charge, or simply to administer some gratuitous ritual humiliation upon them and the 'British Empire'!

Tom Harding-Grayson realised he had got lost in his thoughts.

He blinked back to the here and now.

"That's a good thing, isn't it, Uncle Tom?" Carol Thatcher asked with the curiosity and innocence of a child who would be eleven in August. "That they want to talk, I mean?"

"That they want to talk, yes, my dear," the Foreign Secretary lied. The sort of 'talk' that Bill Fulbright and his new master had in mind was probably more like the conversation a cat had with a cornered mouse. "But your mother and Mister Johnson do not know each other very well and," he shrugged, grimacing whimsically, "this is a very bad time to be trying to get to know each other. She has asked Willie Whitelaw and I to, er, do the honours for the time being."

Mark Thatcher had put down his spoon and his face was twitching with quiet angst, and a rebellious mop of dark hair chose that moment to flop across his brow.

"Will the Americans attack us again, Uncle Tom?"

The Foreign Secretary could feel his wife's sudden unhappiness, her silent intake of breath.

"Not if you mother has anything to do with it." He sighed. "The thing you must always remember, young man," he went on, "is that the Americans always do the right thing in the end, but *only* after they have tried everything else first; which," he smiled, "is pretty much where things stand now."

The boy did not know what to make of this.

"Do you know who said that?" Tom Harding-Grayson asked.

Mark Thatcher shook his head.

"Winston Churchill. Things turned out all right in the end when he was charge."

The Foreign Secretary glanced at the clock on the wall above his wife's head.

"Forgive me, I must run. Have Nick Ridley's people sent over the draft of the Queen's speech yet, my dear?"

"Not yet. There was a call about that shortly before you got back," Pat Harding-Grayson nodded.

The Minister for Information, the UAUK's chief propagandist had asked for her 'insights' before the final version of the 'address to the Commonwealth' scheduled to be broadcast at six o'clock – 18:00 hours Greenwich Mean Time – was finalised.

Much to her discomfort, word that she was the Prime Minister's 'amanuensis' and mentor – she was no such thing and would not have presumed to be such a thing – was uncommon knowledge in Oxford.

Pat Harding-Grayson regarded herself as Margaret Thatcher's friend; that was honour enough. If she advised her younger 'friend' upon matters of couture, and when pressed, offered 'thoughts' on papers she was drafting, or 'talks' she planned to give, that was simply what a friend did. At times such as this it was one's patriotic, and sisterly, duty to serve a woman like Margaret Thatcher in *any way* one could. For example, she had become the twins' de facto guardian, and she and her husband – a childless old couple well beyond such things – had become 'uncle' and 'auntie' to Carol and Mark. Having never felt remotely motherly, having never brooded, not for a single day about the absence of small pattering feet in any of her abodes over a long and fulfilled professional and emotional life, Pat Harding-Grayson had surprised herself of late by how attached she had grown to the two Thatcher siblings. It was as if something had been missing all these years and she had never known it.

In any event, much though it was touching for people to consult her over the texts of public pronouncements, or this or that turn of phrase, she hated it when it was assumed that she was in any way one of the real movers and shakers in Oxford.

"Nick thinks the thing should be somehow more 'poetic'," she explained to her husband. "Personally, I think that's muddled thinking but Nick's one of the cleverest people in Oxford. I'm literally, only going to read it through while the courier waits."

Tom Harding-Grayson was mightily impressed by how quickly Nicholas Ridley, the MP for Cirencester and Tewksbury, had grown into his role as the Government's 'information Tsar'.

The Prime Minister had plucked him out of the late Iain MacLeod's 'back room circle' on the advice of the Chancellor of the Exchequer, Peter Thorneycroft, the last man standing from Harold Macmillan's pre-October War Cabinet, and her friend and confidante, Airey Neave, and as was her wont, she had subsequently backed Ridley to the hilt.

Airey Neave, the nation's 'Security' supremo was still chaffing at the leash beneath the Chilterns periodically broadcasting impassioned pleas to be allowed to return to Oxford. However, with the Secretary of Defence having already abandoned the bunker the Prime Minister had commanded that nobody else 'jump ship', and that was that!

The Foreign Secretary rose from his chair.

If the worst happened he had no intention of surviving in the Hellish aftermath; it was better by far to be here in Oxford with the woman he loved.

Besides, if he was stuck in a bunker in the middle of nowhere he would be missing all the fun.

Chapter 60

When the bow of the USS Kitty Hawk slid beneath the waters of the Persian Gulf it was not with a whimper, or with any semblance of grace. The behemoth's bow had projected like a jagged outcrop of basalt, the big letters 'CV-63' painted on her flight deck visible for miles, for nearly two days. Her stern lay two hundred yards away, skewed and broken resting upon its starboard side, parts of her hull less than fifty feet beneath the surface at a right angle to the bow section.

Oil and flotsam escaped, fouling the sea for miles downwind. Now and then a new body was hooked and dragged onboard the circling ships. Miraculously, two men trapped in the bow had leapt into the oily seas in the last hour and been picked up by the four-hundred-ton Royal Navy minesweeper HMS Tariton, the only vessel capable of standing close in to the looming wreck.

Walter Brenckmann had been standing at the lee rail of the USS Dewey when the muffled boom of the underwater explosion rumbled from deep within in the wreck.

It happened that he had just been joined by Lieutenant (jg) H. Katawa. Having ignored her entreaties to 'lie down and stay lying down', he had returned to the weather deck, unable to rest.

She had nodded acquaintance and lit a cigarette.

"I don't," he had apologised when she offered him her pack.

Lucky Stripes...

"I shouldn't," she confessed. She was so tired she was almost out on her feet. "Commander Sanchez ordered me to take a break," she added.

The Dewey's surgeon was a man in an exhausted trance the last time Walter had been in the sick bay; the guy was operating on muscle memory but it was only in the last couple of hours that the stream of injured and dying men had slackened.

The only people coming onboard now were dead.

"What does the 'H' stand for?" Walter asked.

"Heidi."

"Oh, right..."

"My folks couldn't make me or my brothers look more American so they made damned sure they gave us American-sounding names. I've got three brothers; Luke, John and Matthew!"

She snorted a distinctly tomboy snort.

"You're a 'Walter', Commander Brenckmann, what about your family?"

"There's a Daniel and a Samuel." He hesitated, pricked with the sort of remembered pain that never really went away. "My kid sister Tabatha was up at Buffalo the night of the war."

The woman nodded, stared at the bow of the Kitty Hawk.

"My grandpa worked in the Boeing plant at Renton in Washington State. The plant didn't get a scratch but his and my granny's place in Seattle was a couple of hundred yards from ground zero."

"I'm sorry."

"Naw," the woman shot back. "We all lost somebody. Well, all of us except those schmucks on Capitol Hill in DC."

Walter was silent.

Mistaking this for censure the woman shrugged.

"I'm a nurse. I tell it how I see it, Commander."

"No, I'm sorry," he said hurriedly.

Heidi Katawa took a drag on her Lucky Stripe, inhaled deep.

"This sure is a fuck up," she sighed, still staring towards the wreck of the Kitty Hawk.

Walter studied her a moment. She was slight, petite of build and yet tough in a way that wholly belied her gracile, girlish looks. She would be a very pretty woman if she wanted but he got the impression she did not much care about it. She was a product of the school of hard knocks, he guessed.

"That's no lie," he muttered.

That was the moment *it* happened: an underwater explosion that thudded against the hulls of the circling ships. On the surface there was little initial disturbance. Then the water frothed and bubbled around the rock-like projection of the Kitty Hawk's bow, the inevitable eruption of spume and spray delayed seemingly, for unbearably long seconds.

The Tariton, having offloaded the latest consignment of bodies to the USS Hull, was closing with the wreck. The shock wave of the underwater detonation made her pitch and roll as if she was dingy in a ten-second hurricane.

The spray cleared, and miraculously the bow of the carrier still reared high out of the water.

Only now it was beginning to move, topple.

The British minesweeper was broadside on to the fallen leviathan, her screws thrashing the confused waves as she rolled. Imperceptibly, the letters on the carrier's flight deck shortened, as if swaying, twisting away. The bow tottered, finely balanced and then gravity won out over buoyancy and whatever shattered steelwork and girders had briefly nailed her to the sandy bottom of the Persian Gulf.

HMS Tariton was turning.

The bow of the Kitty Hawk was falling.

Everything was in ultra-slow motion; like a giant whale broaching and falling immensely back into the waves, as the bow section descended thousands of tons of water were displaced in a huge local tsunami.

Even from over a mile away the sound of metal and machinery breaking lose, grinding, tumbling within the hull of the carrier rumbled dully, sickeningly.

There were almost certainly many, many men still alive in the great carcass as it surrendered itself to the sea.

Men who were surely dying now.

Walter did not want to watch it.

Still he watched, his eyes trapped by the horror of the spectacle.

The shadow of the carrier's bow disappeared into the spray which enveloped the Tariton; everybody who witnessed it thought the Kitty Hawk's final violent death throes must have taken the small British minesweeper to the bottom with her.

And yet, as the mist cleared the Tariton nosed into clear air, rocking and pitching like a toy in a bath; but intact.

It was at that moment the Tannoy sounded.

Three bells!

Instantly, men were running for their stations, jumping, skipping, stepping around the stretchers partly-blocking most of the amidships passageways.

Beneath his feet Walter felt the deck begin to vibrate as the Dewey's screws bit hard and fast into the water under her transom and the ship started to pick up speed through the water.

"What the fuck!" Heidi Takawa muttered, throwing the butt of her cigarette over the rail.

"NOW HEAR THIS! NOW HEAR THIS! THE SHIP WILL CLOSE UP TO AIR DEFENCE STATIONS. THE SHIP WILL CLOSE UP TO AIR DEFENCE STATIONS!"

Chapter 61

"...the British constitutional system of government has developed over our long history from the days of the Normans, via Magna Carta and vicissitudes too numerous to catalogue into the modern age. Prior to the cataclysm of late October 1962, I would not have allowed *my* person as your monarch to be drawn into politics; the very idea would have been anathema to me. Until that terrible day in late October a little over twenty months ago the very idea of making what some may deem to be a 'political intervention' in the democratic affairs of the kingdom would have been unthinkable, unconstitutional, and wrong."

Elizabeth the Second, by the Grace of God, of Great Britain, Ireland and the British Dominions beyond the Seas Queen, Defender of the Faith, paused and gave her husband, Prince Philip, Duke of Edinburgh, a thoughtful look.

"However, the events of the last twenty months have turned the World upside down..."

Now the thirty-eight-year-old mother of two upon whom the weight of the World – or at least a substantial part of that globe – seemed now to be weighing heavier by the minute turned her attention to *Her* Secretary of State for Information.

"I know that our intention is to be, as always, *regal*, above the fray and ostensibly to attempt to occupy the high moral ground, Mr Ridley, but," she pursed her lips, "ought one to be so, well, *wooden* at a time like this?"

"I have sent mimeographed drafts of the transcript of the speech to Lady Patricia Harding-Grayson and to a couple of fellows at the BBC office in Oxford, Ma'am..."

"The BBC?" The Queen queried with a sudden frown.

"Professional 'script writers', Ma'am..."

The Queen's frown lingered.

"Very well." As always, her mind turned to practical matters. "Do you know how long it will be before we can remove to the Library? Rehearsing in here," she gestured with the papers in her hand around the glittering, chandeliered magnificence of the dining hall, "lacks the intimacy and the innate gravitas of the Library setting."

"Quite so, Ma'am. It will be a while yet, I fear. There is a great deal to be done and the equipment is very cumbersome."

"Oh, very well." The Queen knew from experience that if she practised too long and too hard her voice would be hoarse by the time she came to make the final recording. "I have decided that Prince Charles and Princess Anne will be by the Duke of Edinburgh's and my side when I speak to the Commonwealth."

Nicolas Ridley opened his mouth to speak.

His monarch beat him to the punch.

"We shall all be attired in normal 'working' clothes," she hesitated, and took a mental backward step, "Prince Philip will of course be in uniform; but *not* one of those dreadful ceremonial ones which are covered in gold braid."

The Queen's Secretary, Sir Michael Adeane was taking notes at Nicholas Ridley's shoulder. His sovereign's word was his law; she had spoken and that was that.

Both men half-turned as one of the Queen's ladies in waiting glided demurely into the room.

"Captain Brenckmann, the United States Ambassador, urgently requests and audience with you, Ma'am."

Nicholas Ridley's eyes rolled heavenward.

Sir Michael Adeane stepped forward.

"This is very irregular," he observed. Ambassadors did not just turn up at the doors to a royal residence demanding audience.

It simply was not done!

"For goodness sake! The nerve of the man!" Prince Philip remarked drily.

The Queen handed her husband the script.

"I need to rest my voice and to powder my nose, Sir Michael," she said, rising to her feet. To Ridley she said: "We shall reconvene in the Library when the speech has crystallized into a more final, definitive form."

She took one, then another step.

"Please ask Ambassador Brenckmann to await my pleasure in the morning room. I shall join him shortly."

And as an afterthought, she turned to her husband.

"Philip, if you would entertain Captain Brenckmann in the meantime please. I know how you old sea salts love to swap naval tall tales. Poor Mr Brenckmann must be feeling awful about this, the least we can do is try to cheer him up a bit."

The Duke of Edinburgh was already struggling hurtfully to his feet; half in anticipation of his wife's suggestion, but mostly because he too felt that such a profoundly decent man as Walter Brenckmann deserved all the moral support his friends in England could muster at a time like this.

"I'm on my way," he grimaced.

Chapter 62

Forty-four-year-old Anatoly Fyodorovich Dobrynin very nearly bounced to his feet as Lyndon Johnson shouldered into the first-floor room opposite the Philadelphia Oval Office across the chasm of the atrium of the White House.

To the Soviet Ambassador it had seemed to him entirely consistent for the President of the richest country on the planet to move into a former bank while his 'home' in Washington DC was being repaired and refurbished. Government for the bankers by the bankers; was that not what capitalism was when all was said and done?

Normally the calmest and most unflappable of men, the strain was telling on Dobrynin. In the last few hours, he had been reliving minute by awful minute, that dreadful day in October 1962. What was almost as terrifying was that every time he set eyes on Lyndon Johnson he saw the toll the new, unspeakable disaster was taking on the tall, craggy Texan.

'There's another telegram coming through from home,' one of Dobrynin's aides had warned him less than five minutes ago. He had no idea if that was good or bad news; the Troika had ignored the three previous communications he had despatched since midnight, and he was in effect, still dealing with the Americans on the basis of seven-day old instructions.

Back in October 1962 Dobrynin's then master – Nikita Khrushchev - had lied to him about the missiles in Cuba. In fact, all the men in the Kremlin had lied to him, their premier emissary in Washington, about practically everything and that was why, unlike his colleague Valerian Alexandrovich Zorin, at the time the USSR's Representative on the Security Council of the now defunct United Nations, he had declined the 'opportunity' to return to the Motherland. In the Soviet Union there were far too many men who would not bat an eyelid to have him 'disappeared' in order to conceal *their* culpability for what had happened in October 1962. That was the way of things 'back home'. And, he suspected, in most countries these days.

Strictly speaking, Dobrynin had never stopped being the Soviet Union's Ambassador to the United States. The Cuban Missiles War had occurred six months into his tenure and although he had been under virtual house arrest for most of 1963, the Kennedy Administration had always kept channels of communication open. Moreover, shortly before the Battle of Washington, the State Department had allowed his staff to re-commission cipher and other communications equipment mothballed at the Washington Embassy.

He had been 'in communication' with home ever since; although the quality and the coherence of that 'communication' had been, to say the least, 'variable' since the turn of the year. Several times that spring, and at the time of the invasion of Iran and Iraq, the Americans had threatened to break off 'diplomatic relations', and attempted to quiz him – well, interrogate actually – about matters of which he had no knowledge, and would not, obviously, under any circumstances have discussed with his hosts anyway. But then the American attitude to 'diplomacy' had always been a thing dependent more on mood than reason; and would probably remain so until it finally dawned on the United States that the cataclysm had changed *everything*.

That spring President Kennedy's brother and Dean Rusk's successor as Secretary of State, William Fulbright, had formally re-acknowledged his status as Ambassador, and thereafter 'the US-Soviet dialogue' had begun again in earnest.

When Fulbright had despatched Llewelyn Thompson to Chelyabinsk, Dobrynin had honestly believed – insanely it turned out – that history might remember him for being responsible for facilitating the greatest diplomatic coup in his country's history.

His hubris had been short-lived.

Now, in the same way the Red Navy had triggered the Cuban Missiles War at the very moment he had begun to hope that common sense – sanity really – was about to prevail; it seemed as if the US Navy might have triggered a new war with not just his country, but with the British and their world-wide allies too!

None of which was President Lyndon Johnson's doing.

Johnson had inherited the unfolding catastrophe and from the expression on his face and anger in his eyes he was very afraid he had lost control.

Dobrynin forced himself to stand still.

The Soviet Ambassador's father had been a locksmith; and he had never planned for a career in the diplomatic corps. Dobrynin's first job after graduating from the Moscow Aviation Institute was at the Yakovlev Design Bureau, and he had only entered the Ministry of Foreign Affairs in 1946, aged twenty-seven. That he had advanced so swiftly in the Foreign Ministry was because he had had the great good fortune to work for that great old Bolshevik Vyacheslav Mikhailovich Molotov; with – fortunately not very closely - Dmitri Trofimovich Shepilov whose involvement in a plot to oust Khrushchev in 1957 had almost ended his, and countless other ambitious men's careers; and latterly, for Andrei Andreyevich Gromyko, a man whose death in the war of October 1962 he still deeply felt.

What, he asked himself, would those great men have said and done to slow the headlong rush to a new global war?

Unfortunately, he had no idea...

Lyndon Johnson stood over Dobrynin, glaring down at him.

The Russian was a much shorter man. Unused to being so ostentatiously bullied he instinctively shrank away before he stiffened and stood his ground.

"My people tell me," Johnson almost shouted, "that the whole god-dammed Red Air Force is heading *this* way over the Arctic?"

Dobrynin had spent his entire career in the Soviet Ministry of Foreign Affairs working on and perfecting his poker-face. However, for a split second his mask of inscrutability fractured. His eyes widened and he heard himself saying: "No, that cannot be, Mister President..."

Chapter 63

Walter Jenkins had explained that the 'scheduled talks with England had been put back until ten o'clock', informing the United Kingdom's Ambassador that he would be called when the new 'link' had been 'set up'. The visibly wilting Presidential Aide had then escorted Peter Christopher and his wife back to their pleasantly appointed 'holding cell'.

Petty Officer Jack Griffin had followed his charges back into the ante-room along the circular first floor corridor above the marbled atrium twenty feet below. Jake Karlsen – the stern-faced Secret Service Man who had shadowed him ever since he and 'the Christophers' had boarded the United Airlines Boeing 707 at San Francisco – had tried to follow him inside.

"We'll call you if we need you, pal," Jack Griffin growled. The other man seemed a decent type but even though the battered warrant officer had not been party to any of the 'discussions' going on around him, a man did not need to be a rocket scientist to know better than to confuse any of President Johnson's men for 'friends'.

This said he shut the door and stood with his back to it.

The 'diplomacy game' he decided, was not everything it was cracked up to be. Like his former Captain and Lady Marija, the rugged seaman had no illusions that they were anything other than under a subtle, polite form of house arrest at the White House.

Peter Christopher swapped a tight-lipped grimace with Jack Griffin, determining not to waste this brief interlude of privacy; their hosts having neglected to post a minder in the room ahead of their arrival.

The First Lady and her daughters were charming; and most of the Presidential flunkies were courteous, personable people but being constantly 'watched' was getting tiresome in the extreme.

Their half-drunk cups of tea were still on the coffee table where they had been when Lyndon Johnson had called the new British Ambassador and his wife into the Oval Office. Marija discovered the overlarge silvery tea pot was still warm.

"There is still tea in the pot, Jack," she announced, beckoning their scarred bodyguard as she moved to the side cupboard inside the door where she had previously seen the Johnson daughters retrieving chinaware.

Peter Christopher had been lost in rumination.

His wife's dulcet words broke him out of his spell.

"There's no need to stand by the door all the time, Jack. If the beggars want to come in they will. Come and have a cup of tea, you must be parched. You've been standing out there for hours!"

A thing Peter Christopher had acknowledged very early in his naval career was that he was *responsible*, personally and *always*, every second of every minute of every day for the welfare of the men under *his* command. Effectively, he was in *loco parentis*, and the mark of a good officer was that he put his people *first*. Right now, he was assailed by a nagging pang of guilt, realising that he had not given a single thought as to how their hosts were treating *his* man.

Unforgivably, *Her* Majesty's Ambassador to the US Government had completely lost track of time. The last few hours were a blur; a humiliating, maddening blur and his sense of personal failure was excruciatingly acute.

He had to do...*something*.

Marija, sensing Jack Griffin's unease went up to him and took his arm, leading him back to the chairs in the middle of the large – but by American standards – tiny ante-room.

"Sit down, Jack," Peter ordered, distractedly as he reviewed his options. He took a deep breath. "We're safe in here. Look," he prefaced, paused, forcing himself to slow down. "Mr Jenkins, or one or other of President Johnson's aides, or a member of his family will no doubt join us presently. When they come in I'm going to insist on speaking to the American press and TV people. If they don't like it they are going to have to arrest me."

Jack Griffin's eyes widened.

The man glanced to Marija, who half-smiled resignedly and shrugged as if to say: "They will have to arrest me, too!"

"Basically, our 'hosts' aren't interested in talking to me, or us," Peter Christopher continued, his resolve hardening with every spoken syllable. "I think we are just window-dressing for whatever President Johnson has in mind. He's tried to 'keep us sweet', as they say but he obviously thinks he can walk all over us and I've had enough of it. If our hosts won't let me talk to the people downstairs," he shrugged, his resolve such that he might have been back on the bridge of the Talavera off the entrance to the Grand Harbour at Malta. *What we shall do is charge at the beggars at full speed and see what happens...* "Then I propose to walk outside. For all the good *we're* doing inside this building we might as well never have left California. I should have known what was going on but I imagined that we were being helpful, diplomatic in fact, in accepting the President's invitation to fly to the East Coast."

Jack Griffin did not know why he was being told this. He would have killed for, and would die, if that was what it came to for the fair-haired young officer sitting across the coffee table from him, and his princess of a Maltese wife. Although he could not bring himself to say the word 'friend' in connection with either of his companions, they were in some indefinable way 'family'.

Marija touched his elbow.

"When we left San Francisco, we believed that Lord Franks was behind the invitation," she told Jack as a cup and saucer appeared before him and she poured dark, over-stewed tea. "We believed that the President had asked us to come to Philadelphia after 'consulting'

Lord Franks. But Lord Franks is dead." She swallowed, could not meet Jack Griffin's startled gaze for a moment. "As are all our friends at the Embassy in Wister Park."

"You're joking!" The ginger haired, bearded Petty Officer blurted before he knew he had spoken.

Peter Christopher shook his head sadly.

"No, I'm afraid not. Things are bad in the Gulf. Two," he hesitated, trying to sort out which day this was across international datelines, "no three days ago the US Navy attacked and sank the Centaur and all her escorts; twenty-four hours later the RAF and the Fleet Air Arm sank the Kitty Hawk and at least two of the big ships with her. As if that isn't bad enough, all the ships we sent up the Shatt-al-Arab were lost, including Admiral Davey's flagship Tiger."

Jack Griffin just stared at him.

"Oh, and we took the Sixth Fleet prisoner at Valletta," Marija added, trying to be helpful, albeit inadvertently much in the fashion of a Lewis Carroll character trying to explain to Alice that she is now in Wonderland.

"Are..." Jack Griffin had reached for the tea cup and saucer. It rattled unsteadily in his trembling hand. He put it down on the table with a clunk. "Are we at war, sir?"

Peter Christopher thought about it.

"That's the oddest thing, Jack. I don't know. There seems to be some kind of undeclared ceasefire at sea in the Persian Gulf. Nobody's actually shooting at each other in the Mediterranean so perhaps there's some kind of stand-off going on at the moment. Personally, I think we are living in a World turned upside down again. After the attack on the Centaur, I gather that the Prime Minister was so rude to President Kennedy that he had a seizure of some kind shortly after she hung up on him."

Marija had sat down next to her husband.

She shrugged apologetically.

As if on cue Lady Bird Johnson and Walter Jenkins not so much entered, as burst into the room. As Peter Christopher had surmised their hosts had, very briefly, forgotten all about them in the self-evident mounting chaos and confusion of the White House.

This, in itself, told him everything he needed to know about how seriously President Johnson took him, his role and anything he might care to say to him.

He ought to have been thoroughly disheartened.

However, when the going gets tough the tough get going!

In Peter Christopher's case adversity always brought out the bloody-minded side of his character; immediately unsheathing the tempered steel in his soul he had inherited from the 'fighting admiral' father from whom, almost to the end, he had been estranged most of his life.

Jack Griffin jumped to his feet, Peter less quickly. Marija stayed seated, saving her strength because she knew, she just knew, that there was going to be a scene.

Secret Serviceman Jake Karlsen and a second crew cut man wearing a suit tailored to conceal a shoulder holster had followed their principals into the arena.

Marija saw Jack Griffin's eyes narrowing as if he was deciding which American to shoot first.

Peter Christopher raised a hand to abbreviate the awkwardness of another round of civilities; the time for small talk was long gone.

"Mister Jenkins," he announced, shooting his cuffs, his voice ringing with command.

Marija watched it all with a serene smile.

Yes, she decided, glowing with pride. Her husband might well be back on the bridge of his ship again. His voice rang with such marvellous authority and she guessed that his thoughts, so tangled and troubled these last few hours, were suddenly pin-clear now that he had come to a decision.

"Please inform the reporters in the lobby that I will be coming down to speak to them in five minutes time."

Walter Jenkins objected.

"Sir Peter that's not..."

"In five minutes' time," the tall young Englishman reiterated, checking his watch.

Still on California time...

I ought to do something about that!

Walter Jenkins had not got the message.

"I'll have to speak to the President, Sir Peter."

"Speak to him at your convenience, Mr Jenkins," the British Ambassador retorted affably. Another glance at the watch. "In slightly less than five minutes from now I will be going downstairs. If you have a problem with that then I shall go outside to speak to the gentlemen of the press."

"Sir Peter, it is not safe!" The First Lady interjected.

"Madam, I don't give a damn. I am *Her* Majesty's Ambassador to the United States and I will communicate *my* country's case to the American people whether the Administration likes it or not. That is my final word on the subject."

Lady Bird Johnson and Walter Jenkins swapped horrified looks.

Peter seized the moment.

"Just so that there is no misunderstanding about this, Ma'am," he met both the First Lady's and Walker Jenkins's eye in turn, "if you want to stop me you are going to have to shoot me!"

Chapter 64

09:07 Hours (EST)
The Situation Room, The White House, Philadelphia

"There are survivors holed up in the North Wing of the British Embassy building," US Deputy Attorney General Nicholas Katzenbach said, carefully replacing the handset back onto its cradle.

Nothing spoke quite so eloquently to the dysfunctionality at the heart of the Administration as the fact that Katzenbach, in Attorney General Robert Kennedy's absence at the bedside of his stricken elder brother, the chief law officer of the Federal Government of the most power country on Earth, was currently acting as Situation Room 'point man'.

It was not that the immensely capable former 381st Bomb Squadron B-25 navigator, who had taken part in mounting the 'great escape' from Stalag Luft III in 1944, was remotely fazed by his temporary role. Nor in any way less capable than any other man in the inner circle around the new President; no, it was more that he could not help but be struck by how bizarre it was that his country, by any standards, a leviathan bestriding the World, had so lost its faith, its fundamental belief in itself and so comprehensively lost touch with its supposedly 'inalienable' values that it seemed utterly powerless to halt the inevitable rush to war.

Senator Richard Russell scowled.

There were more reports from Korea: US Air Force F-4 Phantoms had been scrambled in response to 'threats to violate South Korean air space', and the USS Herbert J. Thomas (DD-833) had been 'forced' to fire 'live' warning shots at North Korean MiGs making 'mock strafing runs' over her in international waters.

Bill Fulbright had characterised the reports as 'sabre-rattling', but Curtis LeMay had put his B-52s on Guam on one hour's readiness to 'rumble'. Meanwhile, the USS Chicago (CG-11), flagship of Task Force 7.2 was making preparations to depart Kobe for the Sea of Japan, while 'in country' US and South Korean forces had been placed on a local DEFCON 2 alert status and begun moving into pre-prepared positions around Seoul.

The State Department said this sort of 'shit' happened in Korea from time to time; the Department of Defense was getting 'twitchy', and Russell had used the word 'complacent' in his conversations with the Administration's 'point man' in the Situation Room.

Moreover, the reports coming in from Saigon were hardly reassuring; the US Embassy in the South Vietnamese capital was under attack by insurgents; the surrounding districts hosts to a series of small, vicious pitched battles as communist infiltrators attempted to encircle the Embassy compound.

'We're keeping an eye on things,' Katzenbach and Russell had been assured by McGeorge Bundy, the United States National Security

Advisor.

Russell and Bundy had almost come to blows.

Katzenbach regarded The Senator from Georgia, the man who was, apparently, Lyndon Johnson's de facto Vice President without the suspicion of many of his Administration colleagues. Unlike many of the Kennedy 'stalwarts' he was not a man who left enemies, embittered or otherwise, in his wake and Russell respected that.

The 'hotline' phone rang loudly.

Katzenbach smiled apologetically and snatched it up.

He understood that LBJ needed somebody he trusted close to him at a time like this; heck, LBJ had been handed the worst hospital pass in history. But it was not as if the acting President was short of available advisers!

It seemed the Chairman of the Joint Chiefs was on his way down to the Situation Room on what sounded like a verbal strafing run. Katzenbach put the phone down as Curtis Lemay shouldered into the bunker.

"I heard!" The Big Cigar growled. "CIA says this woman Westy talked to is the Head of Station of British Intelligence at the Embassy."

"What about the other survivors?" Russell demanded.

"Just a couple of female secretaries. We're still waiting for Hoover to get his thumb out of his arse to give us the low down on the male survivor, a guy called Christie."

Katzenbach tried not to groan out aloud.

"If it's Dwight Christie," he reported, "he's one of Hoover's guys. Well, one of his guys who went rogue..."

Curtis LeMay swore.

Nick Katzenbach did not need to be having this conversation. Whatever was going on in Wister Park was – however unpleasant – incidental. He needed the Chairman of the Joint Chiefs of Staff Committee to be focused on the big picture. The continental United States was supposedly under imminent threat of attack by hundreds of previously unsuspected Soviet bombers; except, nobody knew where that warning had come from and he badly wanted Curtis LeMay to stop worrying about what Westy Westmoreland was up to at the British Embassy siege and tell him where all those bombers were supposed to be, because nobody seemed to know!

He tried to bring a sense of perspective to the table.

"Ten minutes ago, there were hundreds of Soviet bombers in the air?" He reminded the angry veteran bomber commander.

"Somebody at NORAD got over-excited," LeMay grunted. "The threat board is clear at the moment."

"Has somebody told the President?"

"Where do you think I've just come from?"

"In that case you'll know that the President is about to go back into a meeting with the Canadian Ambassador, General," Katzenbach observed levelly.

"The first Red Air Force bomber that sticks its head up above NORAD's radar horizon gets taken out. Period!" Curtis Lemay barked.

"I don't give a fuck whose air space it's over at the time! If the Canucks want to go it alone, let them!"

Nick Katzenbach was about to attempt to inject a dose of reason into the debate. Senator Richard Russell, an old protagonist of LeMay's beat him to the punch.

"Don't you think we're not already at war with enough countries, General?"

No, Curtis LeMay did not think that.

The Georgian Chairman of the Senate Committee on Armed Services viewed the man who had dropped into the Battle of Washington in December last year and, most likely, saved the day by dint of sheer personal will-power, with the weary irritation of a judge who has seen the man in the dock before him once too often.

"Presently, we're at war with the British, and like them or not you and I both know that they're the wrong people to pick a fight with. We may already be at war with the Soviets; the bastards have just sent Dobrynin new instructions. Maybe, we'll know for sure if we're under attack soon." He shrugged, grey-faced. "If we aren't already at war with the white British Commonwealth, Australia, New Zealand, South Africa, I'd be very surprised. As for the Middle East," he sighed long and hard, shook his head in frank disbelief. "We left Iraq and Iran to their fates, sat on our hands when the British got into bed with Nasser in Egypt and once the news about Bill Fulbright's dammed fool mutual defence treaty with Israel gets out the entire Arab World will be on our backs forever. Right now, we don't have a Navy worth the name..."

Katzenbach was tempted to intervene to defuse the clash.

The moment came and went even though he knew exactly what Russell was going to say next and that afterwards, there would inevitably be an outburst of even angrier existential pyrotechnics.

The Chairman of the Senate Committee on Armed Services slowly rose to his feet.

"You don't get it, do you, General?" He complained sadly. "LBJ won't order a first strike. That's not who he is. You, me, all of us ought to be trying to find a way out of this that doesn't make *this* country even more ungovernable than it already is. Your B-52s can't even snuff out the rebellion in Wisconsin; so, don't even think about telling me you can bomb the fucking Russians back to the Stone Age!"

Curtis LeMay lurched towards the older, shorter man.

The explosion never came.

The two men stared angrily into each other's eyes.

Then the Chairman of the Joint Chiefs turned on his heel and stalked out of the Situation Room looking for money lenders' tables to kick over on his way out.

Russell shook his head.

"What exactly does General Westmoreland plan to do?" He inquired, picking up on the conversation he and the US Deputy Attorney General would have had, had not Curtis LeMay shown his face in the Situation Room.

"As soon as he hears gunfire and explosions in the Embassy compound the Marines will fire smoke and tear gas rounds into the building and move in, Senator."

"He seriously thinks he can take prisoners?"

Katzenbach nodded, thinking about the 'rebels' captured after the Battle of Washington. Before everything had gone to Hell in the last week the ring leaders were scheduled to go before a specially convened military tribunal in Maryland in August. Nobody doubted that the twelve men on trial represented only the first small tranche of men – and at least a score of women – with imminent appointments with the hangman. Execution by firing squad or electrocution had been ruled out; the former inferred some small element of military dignity upon the subjects, while the latter was a thing reserved for 'civilians'.

The 'rebels' were traitors, murderers, rapists and worse; for them the normal rules did not apply. The guilty would be hung by the neck until dead...

Any prisoners captured at Wister Park would suffer the same fate as their brethren in Washington, or any 'insurgent' captured in the Midwest. The crazies inside the British Embassy had to know that. Sure, they would get a trial, the nicety of having a public defender assigned – like it or not – to their cases; in the end they would hang, and afterwards their bodies would be incinerated.

Just about the only thing Congress and the Senate had agreed upon in the last six months was the 'trial and disposal' of 'enemies of the state'.

Now that the dreadful news from Wisconsin and Illinois was finally escaping into the public domain, few Americans were going to have pity to spare for any 'prisoners' taken at Wister Park.

Katzenbach forced a smile.

"You know what Westy is like," he observed wanly. "The guy's a natural born optimist."

Chapter 65

09:08 Hours (EST)
British Embassy, Wister Park, Philadelphia

Once she was shut away in the roof space Rachel lay across the rough-sawn rafters for several minutes waiting for the pain to subside, and her breathing and heart rate to return to normal. Her shoulder hurt most; but everywhere else was close behind and she was suddenly desperately tired. That was the shock kicking in; if she did not keep moving she would start sobbing, curl up, give in...

Except that was not going to happen.

Not now, not today, not ever...

It had been easier to keep her mask in place when the others were watching her. Up here in the gloom where only the faint slivers of light creeping under the eaves lit the lofts where there was nobody else to fool, where there was no need to pretend, where there was nobody to directly defend it was harder to convince herself to carry on fighting...

Not that there was any other choice...

Mary Drinkwater would have told Agent Christie about her by now. What little she knew. Only the Ambassador and the Charge d'affaires really knew *anything* about her other than the wild rumours that swirled. She had no idea, and cared less, if the American spooks who watched over the Embassy had connected her with the events in Mdina in April or knew anything of her eighteen-year career working for the British or guessed any part of what her long-time handler dryly referred to as her 'back story' in occupied Poland during Hitler's War. She could not deny that she had been with Admiral Sir Julian Christopher when he died; but around that one 'fact' she, and others had worked to subtly construct web of misinformation.

In some legends she was the great man's lover, in others his secretary, or a hostage of the Russians, and inevitably, in others she was a Kalashnikov-wielding angel of death roaming the citadel of the ancient hilltop capital of Malta.

Here in the United States, she had, of course, another history. Most of the Americans she had had dealings with still recollected her from 1961, turning up at the best parties on the arm of this, or that Senator or Congressman, wafting around the fringes of Camelot as the Kennedy boys *really* got down to partying...

None of that mattered now.

Her 'back story' was like a walk in the ruins.

The Soviets had arrested her father – a journalist and scholar, a gentle man with delicate, expressive hands – when she was eleven years old. She had never seen him again; his was probably one of the twenty thousand bodies discovered in the mass graves in the Katyn Forest by the Nazis.

Her mother had died in the Lodz ghetto when she was fourteen; or at least she assumed she probably died around then. She was among the handful of 'ghetto rats' who got out in time. She had already killed her first Fascist by then, a boy in a Wehrmacht uniform in an alley. His rifle had bought her a place with the partisans.

She had killed a lot of Fascists before the Red Army 'liberated' Eastern Europe. Skinny and filthy she had been caught by the Germans; they had thought she was a boy, no danger to them. She still heard the screams of the pigs as they burned to death in their barracks that night...

She had killed her first Russian in Ravensbrück Concentration Camp. That's where the Fascists had taken her the second time they caught her. By rights she ought to have died of typhus or starvation that last winter of the Second War. The 'liberators' had raped her, a starving seventeen-year-old kid, hardly more than a bag of bones.

So much for the great and glorious Soviet Red Army!

The British had recruited her in Berlin in the summer of 1945; they had arrested her for allegedly 'plying her trade' on the streets; but she had never been a prostitute. She had decided to survive and if she was going to survive she had needed food in her belly and friends who could help her, if sex was the price she paid that was a fair trade. Back in Berlin in those days none of the normal rules applied.

In London in 1946 she had begun to train as a nurse. Already fluent in Russian, German – not so fluent in French at the time – and English, one day she had had a visitor at the Royal Brompton Hospital.

'There is a gentleman to see you, Rachel,' she had been told.

A tall, very handsome 'gentleman' in fact.

She had not known at the time that the man she met that day in August 1946, who had taken her out to lunch at a Lyons Corner House, and quietly, smoothly persuaded her to talk about her life – practically everything – was one of the men who had tricked the Germans into defending the 'wrong part' of France before D-Day, or that he had been responsible for running the biggest 'double agent' scam in the history of spying for the last four years of the European War. He had walked with her along the Embankment, quietly, methodically interrogating – or debriefing her, he was so 'professional' a third party would not have been able to tell the difference – as they looked down into the muddy, swirling waters of the River Thames.

It had never been her destiny to be a nurse.

The tall, blond man with the perfect English manners who had always, even when he was incandescently angry with her, treated her with achingly 'proper' decorum and courtesy, had been her controller ever since.

Sir Richard Goldsmith 'Dick' White, the poster boy of wartime MI5, had been head of both MI5 and MI6 in the 1950s, and rather out of favour with Harold Macmillan's pre-October War Government; now he was the Head of all British Intelligence, Security Minister Airey Neave's partner in crime and she, Rachel Angelika Piotrowska, was the only person alive who knew all his dirty little secrets...

Presently, she caught her breath and painfully slung the Thompson over her back. Finding the submachine gun had been a lucky break. The kid hiding in the first-floor toilets had left it propped against the wall when she killed his buddies.

The grenades she rolled down the stairs had turned one man into a red mush along one wall and gutted another. He was still alive, pathetically attempting to claw his intestines back inside his abdomen when she stepped over him.

She had let him suffer.

She ought to have felt something, anything but had felt precisely nothing.

A shadow had emerged from a room waving a hand gun. She had killed the man with a three-round burst from her Sten gun. There had been two men – boys really – hiding on the ground floor. One of them had wanted to surrender, the other had been hiding...in the toilet.

It was funny the way such brave warriors suddenly want to become prisoners of war protected by the Geneva Convention and the Swiss Red Cross the moment the going got a little rocky...

The kid had soiled himself, obviously.

That was unpleasant but it also seemed to have loosened his tongue and he had answered all her questions. Well, eventually. All that sobbing and pleading, cringing and begging had been irritatingly distracting.

The little *shit* had not been snivelling and crapping himself while he was raping her; what did he think was going to happen to him when she finished interrogating him?

Focus...

The rebels had ransacked the first-floor dormitory of the Embassy Guard Detail; the armoury had been cleaned out.

The men she killed had had half-a-dozen grenades; one had had a new-looking Birmingham-made L1A1 Self-Loading Rifle, the British Army version of the Belgian FN FAL. It was a good infantry weapon; although not so good for the sort of killing that she had in mind. It was too long in the barrel, unwieldy at close quarters or in confined spaces and besides, she had the Thompson.

If she could not get her hands on an AK-47, the Thompson was the next best thing; in fact, probably even better for really close quarter 'work'.

The model she had 'inherited' was an M1928A1, one of the two variants adopted by the US Army in 1938. The gun had a Cutts compensator – or muzzle 'brake' to redirect propellant gases to counter excessive recoil and to reduce the barrel's tendency to rise during extended rapid fire – and a delayed 'blow back' action. This latter innovation stopped it juddering about too much in one's hands during 'bursts'.

The Thompson, variously styled as "Tommy Gun", "Annihilator", "Chicago Typewriter", "Chicago Piano", "Chicago Organ Grinder", "Trench Broom", "Trench Sweeper", or "The Chopper" by its proponents and devotees, fired a large .45 ACP (Automatic Colt Pistol) round at a rapid-fire rate of over six hundred rounds per minute. In other words, it spat out bullets as fast – and as reliably – as a Kalashnikov, except that its 11.43-millimetre calibre slugs were approximately twice the weight of an AK-47's 7.62-millimetre rounds.

Technically, an Ak-47 was a modern, superior weapon for aimed shooting at ranges over twenty or thirty yards but for work inside a building, a Thompson won hands down.

Its designer, Brigadier John T. Thompson – who had previously supervised the development of the M1903 Springfield rifle and chaired the board that selected the M1911 pistol for employment by the US Military - had originally called the weapon 'the Annihilator'.

Rachel picked up the gun fitted with a twenty-round stick magazine. Discovering two thirty-round 'sticks' nearby had been a very pleasant surprise.

The only thing she did not understand was how she had been able to creep up on Christie and Mary Drinkwater without either of them noticing her while she was carrying a canvas bag clanking and clunking with ordnance as loudly as a cupboard full of pots and pans in the middle of an earthquake!

Finding practical clothes that more or less fitted her, and plimsolls that reduced the sound of her footfall had been a positive boon but it was not as if she had actually been trying to be quiet when she came back up to the second floor. It was not as if there was anybody else left alive she needed to worry about in the North Wing of the Embassy compound.

She was about to start dragging herself towards the 'hatches' she knew to exist built into the asbestos firewalls in the roofs separating the three 'blocks' when she heard it.

Like a distant, very boozy party.

She held her breath.

Singing, shouting, occasionally punctuated by what she assumed was a drunken 'rebel yell'. Okay, the animals had broken into the wine cellar...

So....maybe I don't have to worry about being quiet after all...

Chapter 66

19:11 Hours (EST)
The White House, Philadelphia

Movement stopped, silence momentarily fell threateningly as Peter and Marija appeared at the top of the staircase leading down to the wide, echoing ground floor of the former bank. Jack Griffin and the pair of very worried-looking Secret Servicemen flanking Jake Karlsen went ahead of the couple, ready to clear a path through the milling crowd.

Marija squeezed her husband's hand.

She had insisted on standing at his side and bless him he had not had the heart to say 'no'.

'This is likely to be bloody,' he had protested.

'That is all the more reason for us to stand together, husband.'

Peter Christopher stared down into the throng.

What on Earth are President Johnson's staffers doing allowing all these people inside the White House on a day like this?

He steeled his resolve, glanced down at Marija and smiled a tight-lipped smile.

"For better or worse, wife of mine," he murmured.

"Until death us do part, husband," she re-joined, putting her shoulders back as if bracing to step out into a storm.

Peter Christopher took one hesitant step, and then another, more assured one. His mind was clear, his priorities simple. In that moment he was more worried about Marija – who as a result of her childhood injuries had troubles negotiating cobbled streets, and descending stairs, which regardless of her protestations were likely to be ever more exacerbated by her pregnancy – safely getting down to ground level without tripping, than he was about anything which awaited them at the bottom of the stairs.

He might not be a diplomat but he was a Royal Navy officer and that was just as good. The rules were the same in both trades. The thing was to keep the ship afloat for as long as possible, and everything else was peripheral, irrelevant flimflam.

A cordon of Marines armed with M-16s blocked the foot of the staircase. Over to the right of the stairs another detachment controlled access to the underground Situation Room situated in the bank's old vault. Peter guessed every fourth or fifth man in the crowd which had temporarily stilled as all eyes turned to the staircase, was a plain clothe Philadelphia PD or a Secret Service man. He also registered that while there were TV cameras, big bulky, clumsy things on substantial tripods set up, and cables snaking across the floor in practically every direction, that none of the equipment was actually attended.

Lady Bird Johnson and her daughters had halted at the top of the stairs, now they shrank back into the shadows as Walter Jenkins and several other Presidential aides chased after 'the English couple'.

"Sir Peter," Walter Jenkins pleaded breathlessly out of the side of his mouth. "Lady Marija, please, you have to make the Ambassador see sense..."

Peter felt Marija's grip on his hand tighten.

Terrified that she might stumble he halted, half-turned and steadied her with his free arm. She looked up at him a little sheepishly, she had indeed been about to lose her balance and but for his support she would surely have tripped...

Husband and wife gazed one to the other, oblivious of the commotion all around, and the rising crescendo of clicking camera shutters and the breathless entreaties of Walter Jenkins.

The man was only aware that he was married to the most beautiful woman in the world; and she that she need fear nothing in the arms of her very own, lifetime Prince Charming...

Fairy tales did come true.

Cinderella, you shall go to the ball...

"Wait," she whispered.

Peter frowned, then realised his wife was kicking off her shoes. She was always steadier barefoot. He could not stop himself, he bent his face to hers and kissed her mouth. She kissed him back, reluctantly broke free, her eyes bright.

"People are watching, husband," she reminded him in a tone which demurely proclaimed that 'we shall continue *this* later'.

The World, a noisy, bewildering, chaotic place intruded again into their lives. Walter Jenkins had stepped back, realising how bad it was going to look if he pursued the couple all the way down to the ground floor where his every word – perhaps, his every thought - would be transparent to the wolves.

"We will stop about five steps from the bottom," Peter warned his wife. "So that everybody can get a good photograph of us and I can say a few words. After that we shall go outside onto the steps of the White House on Broad Street. There are bound to be television cameras, lots of microphones and suchlike out there in case the President wants to say something."

Now, as the couple proceeded, very slowly down to earth, it was with a regal, oddly serene confidence like gladiators of yore resigned to their shared fate.

Presently, they halted on the fifth step. Marija shifted on her feet until she leaned her right shoulder against her husband's left side, knowing that he would extend his arm about her.

She smiled seraphically at the flashing camera bulbs as the barrage of shouted questions washed deafeningly around the couple. She knew her Prince Charming would plant a kiss in her hair before he spoke. Outside in the cold distance the World was lurching headlong towards catastrophe; right now, she was in the eye of the hurricane, watching the mayhem rushing towards her and yet inwardly she was...totally at peace.

Chapter 67

16:45 Hours (Local) – 09:15 in Philadelphia
Sevastopol Bunker Complex, Krasnoufimsk, Soviet Union

Occasional single gun shots echoed down the corridors of the warren of deep tunnels and catacomb-like caves bored into the foothills of the Urals. The bulk of the killing was over now. All that was left was to execute the last few survivors; and to clean up the mess.

Colonel Viktor Vasilyevich Konayev holstered his Makarov pistol and saluted Chief Marshal of Aviation Konstantin Andreevich Vershinin, who had sat out the 'Action' in the safety of his command post surrounded by a detachment of fifty hard-faced and heavily armed Red Air Force airborne troopers commanded by one of his nephews.

In times such as these it paid to take precautions.

"They're all dead," Konayev reported perfunctorily.

Both men understood that their part in the ongoing purge was only one of several equally brutal 'Actions' orchestrated by the dark prince of the Motherland, Alexander Shelepin. There was talk that only the Red Navy was exempt from the worst of the blood-letting, that had been the price of Admiral Gorshkov's 'neutrality' – or complicity, depending upon one's perspective – in the coup that was methodically liquidating the surviving members of the 'old guard' who had led the USSR into the cataclysm of the Cuban Missiles War, and subsequently, into the abomination of Operation Nakazyvat.

Most likely it was Gorshkov's persistently violent denunciation of the 'Persian Adventure' which had saved him from the fate which had just befallen Leonid Brezhnev, his wife and his son and daughter, and the entire Brezhnev extended family. As one would expect of the man whom Nikita Khrushchev had entrusted to 'clean up' Stalin's dirty little secret in the Katyn Forest, Alexander Shelepin was nothing if not meticulous in his work.

Death was too good a fate for the old Bolsheviks whose stupidity had resulted in the death of a hundred million Soviet citizens and the overnight destruction of everything the USSR had achieved since the Revolution, and who had then recklessly had embroiled the Motherland in a war in the Middle East it could not possibly win.

Notwithstanding much of the Motherland had been bombed back to the Stone Age, Brezhnev, Kosygin and their failed clique, witnessing the chaos Red Dawn had spread, and might yet spread more widely in the bombed lands of Western Europe and farther afield, had like men addicted to gambling, knowingly upped the ante and begun again to play 'Russian Roulette' with the fate of the Motherland.

In the distance another gunshot rang out, the discharged reverberating through the complex.

The orders were to strip the bodies naked; pull out the teeth of the dead so they could not be identified from, if they existed, dental records, and to incinerate their personal belongings. The corpses would be laid out above ground, tanks directed to roll over them several times; and then the mush would be doused in kerosene and set on fire. There was no honour in death for the losers in a Soviet coup d'état.

Konayev was not proud about putting a gun to the heads of women and children. As to the men well, that was different. They were the lackeys of the traitors who had led the Motherland to ruin, so far as he was concerned they were swimming up to their necks in treason. They had believed they were safe in their bunkers and country dachas, that the nightmare they had inflicted on the proletariat was nothing to do with *them*.

He was under no illusion that Alexander Shelepin was some kind of saviour saint; as angels went he was the darkest of dark messengers from the gods, Josef Stalin's true successor.

But the USSR had once been great under the tyranny of the 'man of steel'; and under a man like Alexander Shelepin, it might yet be great again one day.

Chapter 68

Lieutenant General Viktor Georgiyevich Kulikov jumped down from the radio truck and stared out across the muddy brown swirl of the Shatt-al-Arab.

During equinoctial phases of the Lunar cycle the river was tidal all the way north to al-Qurnah, the town at the confluence of the Tigris and the Euphrates Rivers over forty miles north of Basra. A couple of months ago it had been in spate, inundating the low-lying ground above and below Basra, turning the desert into reedy marshland overnight. Great shallow lakes still remained, their surfaces a shimmering haze, across which dusty mirages still danced even though the summer sun was slowly scorching the transient water lands back into desert.

As the afternoon drew on towards dusk – which fell fast in these latitudes – the heat was stifling as Kulikov stepped beneath a camouflage awning.

Careful to present his customarily bullish outward appearance inwardly, he was still reeling from what Admiral Gorshkov had told him before he flew back to Baghdad.

'There will be no cull of the officers and men on the ground in the combat zones,' the man designated to be the First Deputy Prime Minister, Defence Minister and second-ranking member of the Politburo of the Communist Party of the USSR, in the new post-Brezhnev era, had assured him. 'It is well known that you were opposed to the madness of Operation Nakazyvat. Until things have settled down you must bluff the British into inaction. Steps will be taken to put in place a suitable buffer region north of the marshes behind which we are withdrawing our surviving forces.'

Given that Kulikov considered himself to be a relatively well 'connected' man within the Party the news of the coup had hit him like a surprise blow to the solar plexus. The notion that the dividing line between who lived and who died was a man's stand on the mounting of Operation Nakazyvat was gut-wrenchingly sobering.

'You were appointed to command of 2nd Siberian Mechanised Army in the hope that you would be able to curtail Chuikov and Babadzhanian's worst excesses. The fact that you were side-lined by those idiots in the lead up to the final offensive proves your loyalty to your convictions,' Gorshkov had concluded.

But Kulikov was not an insider; that much had been made very, very clear to him. If he wanted to go on living he had to obey orders.

'Move your staff out of Basra but do not abandon the city to the enemy. Do what you can to draw the Iranians into the industrial area on the western bank of the Shatt-al-Arab and try to keep the British and the Australians *in contact* around Zubayr, attempt to draw them north if you can.'

'And this *buffer zone*, Comrade Admiral?'

'You will be given the resources necessary to hold Al-Qurnah.'

Forget Basra, the Faw Peninsula, Umm Qasr, Khorramshahr and Abadan Island and any Red Army troops still trapped in any of those places; they were already lost.

Right now, Viktor Kulikov was aching for the good old days twenty years ago when he had been a humble tank commander and all he had had to do was kill fascists. By the time the Great Patriotic War was over the Red Army had pinned so many medals on his chest he was beginning to worry about running out of room.

Nothing had ever been so simple since.

Nor it seemed, was it likely to ever be so again.

Chapter 69

09:21 Hours (EST)
The White House, Philadelphia

"Good morning," Peter Christopher declared in a fleeting interregnum when the clicking of camera shutters and the barrage of exploding flashlights slackened for a moment.

This was one of those occasions when having had several years of practice addressing members of one's Division on the rolling deck, or on the windswept stern of a frigate or destroyer, or of having to make oneself heard above the noise of a storm in a rolling mess deck, or on a parade ground, was invaluable.

"In the last hour or so I discovered that I have been appointed The United Kingdom's Ambassador to America. This came as a quite shock to me, to *us*," he added, glancing to Marija, "and I confess that *we* are still somewhat feeling our way with things. I am sorry we have kept you all waiting. We were disappointed to arrive in Philadelphia too late to attend President Johnson's inauguration, and since then we have been unavoidably detained behind closed doors."

Stopping to take a breath was a mistake. This he recognised too late to undo his error. A wall of indecipherable shouted questions and a couple of distinctly hostile catcalls echoed around the marvellous natural auditorium. He glanced up to the balcony twenty feet above the floor, and saw that people were spilling out of offices and side rooms, packing the rails all around the building.

"It goes without saying that Her Majesty's Government, and my wife and I, personally extend our most sincere congratulations and, in the circumstances, commiserations to President Johnson in this troubled time. Also, that our thoughts are with President Kennedy and his family at this time. Only a month ago I was honoured to join President Kennedy on the yacht Gretchen Louisa in Nantucket Sound during the Hyannis Port Summit. That all seems a very long time ago now."

The big problem was that he had to stop to breathe now and then. Mastering 'circular breathing' had not been on the syllabus at the Britannia Royal Naval College at Dartmouth. Perhaps, he ought to suggest its inclusion in future...

"What do you have to say to the families of the men you killed on the Kitty Hawk?"

Peter Christopher felt his wife's nails sink into the palm of his left hand. *Again.* That was happening a lot today!

As simple, bluff naval officers went the man standing on the fifth step of the stairs to the first floor of the Philadelphia White House was, he was discovering, much to his chagrin rather better at this 'political game' than he cared to admit.

He steadfastly refused to rise to the verbal bait.

"I grieve for the dead of Carrier Division Seven as I grieve for the loved ones of the men who died under my command in the Mediterranean in April, sir!"

"*Yeah sure!*"

However, the catcallers were lonely in the throng; and very nearly drowned out by men – and women – more preoccupied with mundane matters; such as if he thought the World was about to blow up again in the next few minutes.

"Despite everything," Peter Christopher continued doggedly, "I still cling to the conviction that our two countries have so much in common that it would be madness for us to carry on down the road we seem to be on. My father's generation fought shoulder to shoulder with Americans on a hundred battlefields less than twenty years ago. Less than a hundred days ago my ship was destroyed in battle fighting *alongside* ships of the Sixth Fleet against our then common enemy."

He was starting to get spots in front of his eyes as the camera flashes blitzed all around.

"Look!" He appealed in his best parade ground voice, hoping he did not sound overly plaintive. "My wife and I will be happy to talk to anybody who wants to talk to us," he promised. "We will talk until the cows come home or we lose out voices, but first we must go outside where we know a lot of people are waiting..."

"*Do you have any comment about the siege at Wister Park?*"

"Not at this time."

"*Is it true Margaret Thatcher was talking to President Kennedy when he fell ill?*"

"No," Peter replied, "I am given to believe that the President fell ill sometime after that conversation."

A fresh barrage of urgent interrogatives buffeted the couple on the staircase.

Marija pulled down on her husband's hand and he bent his face to hers.

"Nobody in the White House is talking to these people, husband," she hissed. "They know nothing, or very little of what has been going on. They know nothing of what their leaders have done in their name!"

That was the moment in which Her Majesty's freshly installed Ambassador to the United States glimpsed the narrowest imaginable window of opportunity.

The moment when for the first time he began to hope that in some small way, he and Marija might after all, be able to make a difference.

Chapter 70

09:30 Hours (EST)
Morris House Hotel, 8th Street, Philadelphia

"My interview with Walter Cronkite would have gone on longer but there was a rumour Johnson was going to speak on the steps of the White House, so Cronkite and his crew had to get across to South Broad Street," Richard Nixon explained to Nelson Rockefeller, sternly gloating while doing that infuriatingly intent, inclining of his head thing of his – which made it look like he was a supplicant rather than a ruthlessly mendacious turncoat – whenever he was pretending to listen to what was being said to him.

Nixon and Rockefeller's aides had stepped back; giving their contenders room to swing at each other in the hotel's downstairs lounge.

Rockefeller, the taller man was visibly seething. If he had just done what Nixon had done – basically used a monumentally dangerous World crisis to steal a march on his main political rival, with whom he had previously concluded a solemn pact to suspend campaigning until *after* that crisis was past – Nelson Rockefeller would have had trouble looking himself, let alone anybody else in the eye.

Nixon was brazen, unapologetic.

That's politics.

Nothing personal

Get over it.

What's next?

Nixon could not understand why Rockefeller had not got his retaliation in first.

If Nelson Rockefeller was angry – which he was – he was not angry enough to want to punch out the former Vice President's lights and that marvellously encapsulated the difference between the two men as politicians, and as human beings.

Very little was life and death to the billionaire Governor of New York; everything was life and death to the son of Quaker parents who had risen to be Dwight Eisenhower's loyal Vice President, and who had by a whisker, a mere hair's breadth, lost the Presidency to the seductive charm and immense wealth of the Kennedy's in November 1960.

"Presumably, you're damned pleased with yourself?" The patrician figurehead of the left wing of the GOP, the one Republican Presidential candidate whom conservative Democrats might conceivably vote for in a general election, inquired tersely of his rival.

Nixon shrugged, avoided his eye.

"I positioned the party on the side of patriotism," he offered. "On the side of national unity. The people deserve to know that the GOP is with them in this hour of peril..."

Nelson Rockefeller stared at the shorter man.

Nixon's expression was one of mild confusion; he honestly did not see what the other man's problem was.

Stalemate...

"Something's happening at the White House!"

Both Rockefeller and Nixon swung around and marched closer to the television in the corner of the room.

There was Walter Cronkite again, this time caught a little unawares. The candidates recognised Walter Jenkins fussing around in the background. The crowd had obviously been pushed back onto Broad Street and a battery of microphones was arrayed near the top of the marble steps below the grand entrance to the old Girard Corn Exchange Trust Bank.

Cronkite stepped forward and then...something utterly inexplicable happened.

The tall young man in the dark two-piece suit stepped forward, and clasping the hand of his wife, took ownership of the waiting microphones.

"That's that kid who made a name for himself in the Mediterranean," Nixon grunted, unhappy because when he saw star quality he always felt threatened.

"And his wife," Rockefeller added.

"Heck, she's cute!" One man observed in a half-inebriated locker-room leer.

"Ain't she just!" Others chorused.

"Is she *barefoot?*"

Yes, she was holding her shoes in her free hand...

"Forgive me, Mister Cronkite," the fair-haired man with the movie star good looks apologised. There was nothing tentative or explorative about his manner; he had stepped up, got straight into his stride. "I and my wife will happily speak to you and to any of your colleagues in a minute or so. But first I would like to take this opportunity to say a few words to the American people."

He took a breath, looked down and around, into the sea of faces swaying in the road to the sides and directly before him. He said nothing for several seconds; as if he understood that it would take the networks time to break into their existing programming to televise what he was about to say 'live' across the nation.

"What happened to Johnson?" Somebody asked from behind Nelson Rockefeller's shoulder.

"Quiet, please!" The Governor of New York demanded.

Somebody coughed a smoker's cough, others anxiously lit cigarettes. The room was already so cloudy it was like viewing the TV through a haze.

"My name is Peter Christopher," the man on the steps of the White House explained, eventually. His accent was positively regal; just the way most Americans liked to hear their British cousins speak. He looked to the woman by his side, his barefoot princess. "And this is Marija, my wife."

The sound of clapping came through the TV speaker.

"Yesterday, I was a naval officer and my wife and I were 'playing' at being the United Kingdom's Consuls to the West Coast Confederation. We were engaged on a public relations exercise. I am a destroyer captain; my wife is a nurse and a midwife; neither of us is a diplomat. We were sent to this great country to make friends, to tell you the stories of our country," he corrected himself, "our countries, England *and* Malta, that you, the American people, so rarely hear about. Wherever we have been in this great country we have been welcomed with open arms, we have met generous, good people everywhere; I cannot begin to list the countless kindnesses we have received just in the last few weeks from ordinary, decent, patriotic Americans." He spread his arms. "*This* is a great and marvellous country and *you* should be afraid of *nothing!*"

"Jesus, who wrote that for him?" One of Nixon's staffers whistled.

"I don't know," another grunted, "but somebody ought to be writing it down!"

"Yesterday I was a naval officer," Peter Christopher reiterated, "then everything changed. Our Embassy in Wister Park was over-run by a mob and our good friends, Lord Franks, his dear wife Barbara, and the Charge d'affaires, Lord Frank's deputy at the Embassy, Sir Patrick Dean and many, many of our other friends were murdered and their mutilated bodies thrown on the ground outside the doors to the Embassy."

Not even the newsmen beginning to close in on the microphone stand from the wings had heard that yet.

There were shouts of disbelief.

"I wish it was not true," Peter Christopher barked. "But it is and this morning I find myself the least experienced, least able man in the history of my country, ever to fill the solemn role of being Her Majesty's Ambassador to your great, wounded country."

There was a sudden hush.

It was possibly the lull before the storm.

"You will understand my feelings," the man continued, clearly falling prey to the emotions of the moment, "when I say that there are many here among us who think that life," he shrugged, "is but a joke..."

Chapter 71

09:31 Hours (EST)
British Embassy, Wister Park, Philadelphia

Rachel's left shoulder clicked and locked, agonisingly once, and then again as she crawled through the gloom, gently lifting her bag laden with hand grenades and spare magazines for the Thompson, over one rafter and another. She was moving slowly, very quietly but not *silently*, which was a problem because the rebels had stopped singing.

Perhaps, the party was over?

However, that was not the question which was preying on her mind.

If General Westmoreland did not pull the trigger when she 'got started' Mary Drinkwater, Cynthia Nansen, Dwight Christie and the girl Kitty were going to die; either at the hands of the rebels or the moment they stuck their heads outside the North Wing of the Embassy.

The authorities had put a three-star general – a man she had heard spoken of as a future Chairman of the Joint Chiefs – in command of a 'local situation', and a man like that was always mindful of the 'political' ramifications of a screw up like, for example, allowing a bunch of murderous crazies to overrun a foreign diplomatic mission. Things would be so much simpler if there were no survivors. If everybody was dead there would be a lot less finger-pointing; everybody could get on with the funerals and the remembrance ceremonies, and for the living at least, life would go on...

Or is that sort of reasoning just a symptom of how twisted I am these days?

Either way, a man with the military and political 'heft' of 'Westy' Westmoreland had the power to play the game any way he wanted; so, where exactly was he coming from?

The man had sounded like an honest broker on the phone.

A pragmatic, straight-talking, no nonsense hard arse.

Rachel shook her head.

I am over-thinking this!

Right now, she needed to do what *she* could do. That was all. There was nothing further to be done about whatever was going on outside the Embassy...

She relaxed; down below her the inmates of the asylum had started singing again.

She moved her satchel forward another rafter, desperately attempting to rebuild a mental schematic of the layout of the West Wing's second floor. The Ambassador's Office was on the middle, first floor of the central block of the complex; assistant secretaries and military attachés worked at the top of the building in smaller rooms. She could easily drop into an office which would become a prison...but risking falling into the Central Wing's corridor was equally bad...it might be full of armed men...if there were enough of them one of them might even get lucky...

No, no, you are still over-thinking this!

The object of the exercise was not to single-handedly retake the whole building; because that was not going to happen.

Make a lot of noise.

Kill as many of the bastards as I can.

Give the others a chance to get out of the North Wing...

That was it. She did not need a fancy plan. All she had to do was start throwing grenades, setting fire to things and shooting people...until...

Well, no point worrying about that because she would be dead by then...

The satchel clunked deafeningly on the next rafter.

The drunken singers carried on bawling out what might have been a hymn, or simply a psychotic chant. The maniacs seemed to be attempting to bellow out three different songs at the same time.

John Brown's body was having a bad day, apparently!

What a peculiar thing for a bunch of nihilistic end of time red necks to be singing!

They all believed they were going to heaven sometime soon, of course. Death was a thing to be embraced, preferably soaked in the fine wines and spirits they had liberated from the Embassy cellars. *They* embraced death; it was just that they did not have the moral fibre to blow their own brains out and they were therefore, waiting for somebody else to do it for them.

I can help them out with that...

At last, she crawled to a small hatch – this one a little larger than the one she had hurtfully accessed in the North Wing, some eighteen inches square. The hatch was hinged on top, on the attic side, unlocked, meant to be pushed up for easy access.

Rachel realised perspiration was dripping from her brow.

She was breathing in short, stinging gasps.

Back in the bedroom, and when she had gone down the stairs to deal with the 'infestation' on the first and ground floors of the North Wing, she had been so pumped up with adrenaline that she had hardly noticed the pain from a dozen, mostly hidden injuries, now that she had calmed, cooled down she was very nearly seizing up. Back in Mdina in April she had run into things, collected a host of bangs and bruises, nicks and grazes that she only became aware of after the killing was over; the trouble was that this time she was so beaten up already that she ought, by rights, to be in a hospital bed right now, not about to...

Rachel blinked into the gloom.

Where...what...

She suspected that she had passed out for a moment, seconds, minutes for all she knew; and there was a foul taste in her mouth as if she had been sick.

I am nowhere near where I was before...

She desperately tried to re-establish her bearings.

Where am I?

She was resting, sitting half upright with her back against the building's big iron water tank and one of the reasons her ribs hurt so much was that a heavyweight pipe was digging into her side.

Her skull felt like she had head-butted the side of the tank...

Think! Think!

The tank was approximately above the office Peter Christopher had used during his short stay at the Embassy, and the hatch was directly over where his desk had been...

What would happen if I dropped a couple of grenades into the tank?

Would that be enough to collapse the ceiling...

Rachel forced herself into a sitting posture and scrabbled in the satchel.

Stop, check, take a very deep breath; what else do I have to do?

Two grenades clunked on the boards by her feet.

She slung the satchel over her right shoulder.

It took an age to manoeuvre the strap of the Thompson off her shoulder. She re-slung it round her neck, the weight of the submachine gun pressing on her chest. If the ceiling collapsed the sling could snag something and garrotte her.

That was the least of her problems.

She might pass out again at any moment.

What had to be done had to be done NOW!

Chapter 72

09:32 Hours (EST)
Steps of the White House, South Broad Street, Philadelphia

Peter Christopher had not been aware of *any* of the alleged advantages of a so-called classical education during his years at a minor English public school in Warwick; he had not seen the point of Greek or Latin, or the rough and tumble of sport, those things just seemed to get in the way of learning about the science of the natural world.

While his fellows had been bloodying themselves on the rugby field or brushing up on their cover drive or whitening their cricket pads, he had been reading his way through the mathematics, physics and chemistry bookshelves of the Warwick School library, or thinking about girls as boys are wont in their adolescence. Oh, and corresponding with his Maltese pen friend whom, like an idiot, he had failed to recognise was his pre-destined life partner until the night the World went mad...

Concentrate man!

Anyway, all those wasted hours reciting Greek, translating into and out of the demotic; the tedium of listening to a bored master droning on about 'rhetoric', Macaulay (Thomas Babington) and John Donne suddenly did not seem quite so pointless. Like it or not those dreary dog days of his boyhood had given him a lexicon with which he might, if he applied his mind to it, now employ to communicate with his present audience.

Standing behind a battery of microphones on a raised dais overlooking the crowd – constantly in noisy, restless motion for as far as the eye could see up and down Broad Street – he was not a diplomat, a politician, anything in particular other than a performer and there was no time to be nervous. What green young officer stepping up to address his Division on the deck of his first seagoing posting could not fully appreciate the true terrors of stage fright?

He had been there many times before and this, in comparison, was a...*breeze.* On the deck of a destroyer, one looked one's men in the eye, and they you. Right now, with his voice booming into the morning airs like muffled artillery countless eyes might be upon him, but he was sightless. And of course, he had Macaulay, Donne, Shakespeare and half-a-dozen ancient Greek wordsmiths whispering in his ear...

"So," he said with a shake of the head, "*we* stand before you now as our country's only living ambassadors in the United States because somebody has to tell the American people what they have a right to know!"

Marija tugged his hand. *Too much!* Peter Christopher privately acknowledged that his voice had become too righteous, too 'whiskey priest'. He dialled down his emotions.

"Three days ago, the greater part of the Seventh Fleet, that's your

Pacific Fleet, attacked *without warning* a much weaker force of Commonwealth ships in the northern reaches of the Persian Gulf in the vicinity of a place called Kharg Island. In that battle the Royal Navy carrier HMS Centaur, the frigates Palliser and Hardy and the New Zealand ship Otago were sunk by aircraft and ships of Carrier Division Seven, whose flagship was the USS Kitty Hawk…"

No, nobody believed that.

"Two days ago, Royal Air Force and Royal Fleet Air Arm aircraft attacked and sank the Kitty Hawk, and at least two other US Navy warships, and presumably, damaged several others. This action took place as the battles on land in southern Iraq and Iran reached a crescendo."

Anger and…shock now.

"As the two battles of the Persian Gulf were taking place British, Commonwealth, Saudi Arabian and Iranian forces were in action against *two* Soviet tank armies. I don't know how that has ended; I pray and hope that *our* boys – I say *our* boys because those brave men are fighting on *all* our behalves to preserve what is left of our democratic way of life in the West – have prevailed. That fight is not a British or a Commonwealth or an Iraqi or an Iranian fight, it is *OUR* fight! What will *OUR* freedom in the Western World be worth if the oil runs out? What message does it send to the godless forces of Marxist-Leninism if *WE* just stand back and allow *them* to take what they will, whenever and wherever they wish?"

It was impossible to tell if the babble of shouts was a good or a bad thing; let alone whose side the majority in the seething mass of humanity in Broad Street were on.

It did not matter. One dealt with what was before one; and moved on. If the ship sank, it sank.

Kismet…fate…

"In the course of those land battles a force of five Commonwealth warships penetrated the Shatt-al-Arab waterway virtually to the outskirts of Basra some sixty or seventy miles from the ocean, so as to support the *Allied* ground forces. In those operations all five ships were destroyed. Throughout the land and river operations I have been describing *our* land and surviving naval units were unsupported by *Allied* air power because HMS Centaur was by then, lying on the bottom of the Persian Gulf. In the meantime, *Allied* forces were mercilessly attacked by Soviet fighters and bombers. While this city was preparing to greet Doctor Martin Luther King's March on Philadelphia, *Allied* forces were resisting tyranny in the Middle East in spite of the 'best' efforts of the American government!"

The lynch mob faction had re-found its voice.

"The American people have a right to know that all the time *Allied* forces were spilling their blood resisting Soviet aggression in Iraq and Iran and guarding the oil reserves of the Arabian Peninsula; that *THEIR* government was stabbing its friends' in the back…"

Chapter 73

Captain Troy Simms had taken the boat down to four hundred and twenty feet, hoping, searching for a protective thermocline in the water column to mask the presence of his eight-thousand-ton steel whale from...

Something or nothing; but he had gone deep and the submarine was running silently, and so slow the current was imperceptibly drawing her astern into her hardly turning prop wash.

'CAVITATION ZERO-EIGHT-ZERO DEGREES!'

'NO RANGE...'

'NO DOPLER!'

Something had 'squeaked' out there and the most dangerous fish in the Mediterranean – the USS Sam Houston - had had the fright of its life!

Yes, something or nothing.

Everybody was so tightly strung right now that a pin dropping on the control room deck would have had men jumping out of their skins.

The sound room had heard...*something.*

Something that sounded like a screw turning, or a turbine winding down for two, perhaps three seconds; one contact, on one bearing fourteen minutes ago and nothing since. Now not even a distant porpoise was sounding, the sea itself was dead as if it too was running silent.

"Trim?" Troy Simms checked softly.

"Negative bubble forward, sir. She'll hold at this depth for five minutes maybe, longer if we move bodies about."

The commanding officer of the Sam Houston did not want to get into that sort of finely balanced game of musical chairs. A submarine was like a slow-motion aeroplane; rarely in perfect fore and aft trim – level – other than by the pressure of the water flow passing over its hydroplanes like air over and under the wings of an aircraft. Once stationary, the boat would, sooner or later nose up, or down, 'stall' as would any flying machine with insufficient 'flow' over its 'wings'. That was not good but the 'quietest' boat was the one that was moving the least.

And right now, he wanted the Sam Houston to be way quieter than the grave.

"Zero revolutions," he decided.

They would sit and listen awhile.

The Sam Houston had hung around at periscope depth long enough to triangulate and reset its SINS, correcting an error of approximately one hundred feet. Navigationally, the boat was ready to flush her birds.

Final pre-launch protocols were well-advanced when the duty

sonar man had heard...*something*.

Now the 'sound picture' of the surrounding ocean was complicated by new 'noises' from a completely new bearing. The approaching, or rather, passing ships were making no attempt to conceal their presence from his hydrophones.

The boat creaked softly in the quietness.

"FAST SCREWS!"

"MULTIPLE CONTACTS!"

"BEARING TWO-TWO-SIX DEGREES!

"RANGE UNKNOWN... DISTANT. VERY DISTANT..."

But that was just a guess.

"THREE CONTACTS. ONE BEARING TWO-TWO-NINE DEGREES!

Troy Simms thought he could hear something.

Perhaps, he was imagining it.

"RANGE TO CLOSEST CONTACT ONE ZERO THOUSAND YARDS!"

Simms stepped to the plot.

Three contacts.

Heading due west like bats out of Hell.

The perverse conditions within the water column of the Levantine Sea had masked the noise of their approach; probably it was all that damned salt water leeching into the Mediterranean from the Suez Canal!

He allowed himself to relax; but just a fraction.

Three warships. One a lot bigger and noisier than the other two. He did the math, worked the angles. The British carrier Eagle and a couple of her escorts could easily have made passage this far north and west of the Nile Delta by about now.

Where were they headed?

Malta?

"The Eagle, Skipper?" The Officer of the Deck murmured.

"Could be."

"Looking for us?"

Troy Simms shook his head.

"I doubt it." Saying it did not dissolve the canker of doubt that lingered in his mind. So far as he knew the Sam Houston was on the most secret mission in the Navy; her presence in these waters – had it become known - even before the events of recent days would have caused an international incident with the British, and there was no way of guessing how other countries in the region would react. Moreover, Soviet submarines were suspected to be operating in the Black Sea, the Aegean and possibly, still operating in the Eastern Mediterranean.

"The first contact might have been some kind of crazy echo," the OOD suggested. "Some kind of thermocline quirk; it was damned nearly on a reciprocal bearing, sir?"

Troy Simms did not instantly discount this.

The first, fleeting 'target' had indeed been on a roughly reciprocal bearing to those now detected to the south-south-west.

The ships to the south and the south west were making so much noise they were obscuring the normal, background sonar clutter of the ocean.

He decided that he would take advantage of that to put a little more distance between the Sam Houston and the bearing on which the first, fleeting contact had been reported, in the process changing course randomly just in case there was something or somebody – skippers of Polaris boats were encouraged to be paranoid - attempting to hide in the boat's prop wash.

"Make revolutions for ten knots," Troy Simms decided. "Make our heading one-nine-zero. Come up to three-zero-zero feet."

Chapter 74

Rachel had heard all about the hydrodynamic pressure wave of an underwater explosion and how destructive it could be in the right circumstances. An Army Bomb Disposal officer, a lovely man who had been pleasantly energetic in bed, had once told her about how a relatively small charge set against the face of a dam, or the side of a ship was ten times more destructive than one detonating even just a few feet away.

That was how the British had 'bust' the German dams in 1943; and a couple of near misses by six-ton Tallboy bombs had wrecked the mighty Tirpitz several weeks before she was actually sunk...

Why am I remembering that now?

And what am I doing sitting on the floor of this room soaking wet?

Rachel's ears were ringing, otherwise she was deaf.

However, it was the fact of being soaking wet, sitting panting like an exhausted retriever surrounded by plasterboard, splintered wood and the wreckage of what might once have been an office that *really* confused her.

The sling of the Thompson was wrapped around her throat, the satchel with the rest of the grenades and the bottles of paint-thinner she had hoped might come in useful as improvised Molotov cocktails lay between her legs.

She blinked, shook her head.

Bad idea, she retched agonisingly.

Afterwards her head was clearer.

Without knowing it she was on her feet.

Okay...

Two hand grenades had probably been one too many, she decided, starting to piece together what had happened. What was left of the tank was hanging precariously over the hole in the ceiling under which she was now sitting.

Somehow, both pint-sized bottles of paint thinner – white methylated spirits, remained intact, banging against the remaining pineapple-style grenades, the evil unsheathed hunting knife and two spare 30-round clips for the Thompson in the satchel.

A sweep of the room.

No bodies.

No singing, either but that could be because she was still too deafened by the proximity of the two grenades going off, and the new bang on the head she must have got falling out of the attic into the second-floor office.

She thought, perhaps she only imagined the clump of bovine feet in the corridor.

The door to the office was shut; Rachel stepped up to it and without giving the matter a single thought, emptied the Thompson through it.

Her hearing was coming back.

She ignored the cries and groans, shrieks of panic and the tumbling of bodies, and the sounds of the booted feet of the men in the corridor scrabbling to get out of the hail of bullets.

Unhurriedly she threw away the empty magazine and loaded a new one. Then she picked out a grenade, pulled the pin and lobbed the evil, oval, fruit-shaped agent of death through the ragged hole in the door with sufficient force for it to bounce once and hit the opposite wall with a loud 'clunk'.

Automatically, she stepped away from the door and reached for another grenade.

The force of the blast wrenched the door off its hinges.

A blizzard of shrapnel whistled through it.

"Um, that worked well..."

Rachel already had the pin out of a second grenade as she stepped out into the corridor. There seemed to be bodies everywhere. Well, bodies and parts of bodies on the floor, some writhing, others unmoving and various weapons, including a couple of British Army SLR assault rifles, discarded in the carnage.

"Ha," she sighed.

Maybe her instructors had been right when they said that she had a 'natural talent' for 'mayhem'. She had honestly believed that what had happened in Mdina was an aberration. She had killed before, of course. She was an assassin; that was what assassins did, kill people and usually, not ask too many questions.

But Mdina had been...*different*.

The reason she had told Dick White - her long-time controller and now the Head of both MI5 and MI6 under the new, post-Battle of Malta British Intelligence regime – that she was no longer his 'hired killer' was that when she had had a chance to think about that afternoon in Malta three months ago, she had realised, with no little chagrin and horror, that she had actually enjoyed...*the killing.*

It was as if the killing had been cathartic, a cleansing quasi-religious act. Not simply revenge for all the bad things men – well, mostly men – had done to her over the years but something *spiritual...*

She ought to be afraid; instead, she was...*elated.*

A man on the ground twitched; she put three .45 ACP rounds into his chest. He stopped twitching.

There were voices, cries of alarm, the sound of movement in rooms down the corridor.

She rolled one grenade, then a second through doors slightly ajar.

Clouds of smoke and screams.

It was like a fever dream.

The Thomson juddered in her hands.

There were bodies crumbling at the head of the stairs, falling backwards; more explosions as she dropped grenades over the balustrade.

Around her splinters showered.

Now and then she felt the nearby passage of bullets.

Mechanically, she loaded the last thirty-bullet clip for the Thompson.

No more grenades!

On the floor below something was burning in the stairwell.

She flung the bottles of methylated spirits at the wall as the smoke curled up the stairs. There was a satisfying flash, several prolonged yelps and insane screeches of panic.

By then Rachel's mind was operating in a weird kind of fast-slow motion.

Things were going on slowly; there was no hurry.

Yet she understood at the same time that in reality everything was happening at breakneck speed.

She found herself at the head of the stairs, a little irritated by the screaming, asking herself how she was supposed to get past the two bodies at the foot of the stairs. The two men – she hoped they were men – were alight like human torches, wrapped in a burning embrace.

Rachel thought she smelled scorched pork...

She would have put the burning men out of their misery but she did not want to waste the rounds.

Vexed, she took the blade of her hunting – others in her past line of work would have called it a 'scalping' knife – between her teeth, threw away the satchel and adjusted her grip of on the Thompson.

A line of bullets tore into the ceiling above her head.

She stepped forward, blitzed the gunman.

How many rounds was that?

Six or seven...probably at least twenty left in the clip.

In the brief interregnum the burning men had reeled away from the foot of the steps and were rolling around on the bare boards of the first-floor central corridor.

No more bullets were coming up the staircase.

This was a thing she interpreted as an explicit invitation to join her hosts on the first floor.

Chapter 75

09:36 Hours (EST)
West Wing, British Embassy, Wister Park, Philadelphia

The building had rocked a couple of times, suddenly there was glass underfoot everywhere and choking clouds of smoke and dust.

The Thompson had piled up bodies at the head of the stairs before it ran dry. Rachel had picked up a Sten gun but it only had a couple of rounds in it.

By then she could not see more than an arm's length in front of her face. There was movement, crashing below her; and even nearby although not so much in her immediate vicinity because she had killed everybody she had come across.

A tall, scrawny kid had tried to knock her down with the butt of a long rifle; she had gutted him with the scalping knife. She had guessed he tried to hit her with one of the stolen SLRs; but when she picked up the gun she discovered it was an old-fashioned Martini Henry with a telescopic sight.

Weird...

She had heard the old gun was a favourite in the trenches back in the Great War; its trigger mechanism was still just about the quickest 'action' to be had and with modern rounds in the chamber the old rifle was a reliable killer at a range of anything up to three-quarters of a mile...

But you never expected somebody to try and brain you with one!

The kid was still whining and crying on the floor a few feet away, lost in the fog of smoke and dust. Rachel would have cut his throat but he had been one of the first animals to rape her. She would leave him dying in his own good time; she was through with him.

Somebody was shooting up the ground floor with M-2s.

Nothing sounded quite like the chain-saw ripping of a 50-caliber machine gun.

Judging by the way the rebels – supposedly eager to meet their maker – had bravely run upstairs to get away from the M-2s the Marines might actually be finally coming to the rescue.

A day late...

Still better late than never...

She stood in the corridor and waited.

She held the big knife in her right hand.

A minute or so ago her left arm had finally stopped working. She had no idea why, she was covered in blood and had no notion how much of it was hers.

The kid with the Martini Henry was the third man she'd killed with the knife and there was no clean way to kill a man with a blade.

The building shook again.

Although her hearing had returned sounds were reaching her as if from the other end of a long tunnel, dully, muted. Big engines were revving just outside the West Wing of the Embassy, there was another jarring crash as if there had just been a small earthquake.

Rachel coughed.

Tear gas or something worse...

There was shouting, a sustained burst of automatic gunfire somewhere below her feet.

General Westmoreland's boys were coming in the front door!

The shadow formed in the grey mist directly in front of her.

A big man who towered over her.

His face was a mask of blood, his right eye a gory ruin.

He was bleeding from a wound somewhere above his right hip, so badly she heard the blood squelch in his boot.

The man stood swaying.

His surviving eye viewed Rachel maniacally.

His right arm slowly came up until, from less than four feet away she was looking directly down the barrel of the biggest hand gun she had ever seen in her whole life.

She had met this man twice before in the last twenty-four hours.

The first time was when he stood over her in the wrecked lobby of the Embassy. She had had him in her sights; pulled the trigger of her gun and the hammer had come down on an empty chamber.

The second time he had ordered *his* boys to take her arms and hold her down while he raped her as hard as he could from behind...

And now the bastard was holding a long barrelled Smith and Wesson Model 29, six-shot, double-action revolver chambered for a .44 Magnum cartridge to her head. If he pulled the trigger there would be nothing left of her above the neck.

"Who are you, Lady?" The man demanded hoarsely.

"Who are you?"

"Cheney, Galen Cheney," the giant, bloodied scarecrow of a man growled, the muzzle of the gun trying to dip. He raised it again, and again, aiming between the woman's eyes.

Rachel stared down the barrel.

She was face to face with the monster responsible for the murder of her friends, and heinous crimes without number against her and the others who had survived the initial assault. He was a mad dog who needed to be put down.

"Who am I? I'm all your nightmares come at once, Galen Cheney," she purred, fearlessly.

She could have sworn the man's lips curled in a parody of amusement.

"You have no idea what's in my nightmares, lady."

He was almost certainly mistaken in that; however, she let it pass.

"If you put down the gun I'll kill you fast," she offered.

Galen Cheney thought this was funny.

He was still smiling – albeit only for a split second – when the scalping knife flashed across his peripheral vision and suddenly his still functioning eye was staring disbelievingly at the stumps of the fingers of his right hand as the Smith and Wesson clattered to the floor.

Instinctively, he reached to grab his mutilated hand with his other hand.

And that was when the scalping knife ripped into his stomach.

Galen Cheney staggered against the wall, began to slide bloodily to the ground.

Rachel watched dispassionately.

She knelt in front of him.

"It must hurt?" She asked rhetorically, smiling a tight-lipped smile. "Trust me it's going to hurt a lot more. A cut for each of my friends you've butchered, or every woman you and your maniacs have violated. That sounds fair to me. Ideally, we'd spend the rest of the day together but the Marines, or the US Army, or whoever is making all that noise downstairs will be here soon, so we'll have to...*improvise*."

Judging by the stench the great religious resistance fighter rebel leader had already voided his bladder and his bowels.

No matter, she meant to spill his guts all over the floor anyway and that was always...*messy*.

She stabbed through his jeans, carving a bloody flap beside his fly. She scowled as she worked; the blade was getting dull, nicked too many times on bone.

Soon she had the man's genitals more or less fully exposed.

Galen Cheney began to struggle but each time he moved his hands to cover his groin she stabbed or slashed at his mutilated fingers and more crimson, faeces-fouled blood pumped from the wound in his abdomen.

Rachel had not meant to twist the blade so enthusiastically before she pulled it out.

Old habits die hard...

She prodded Galen Cheney's testicles with the gory point of her knife.

"I'm a reasonable woman," she explained. "Well, as monsters go, I suppose. Which one of your testicles do you want to eat first, Mister Cheney?"

Chapter 76

09:33 Hours (EST)
The Oval Office, The White House, Philadelphia

Lyndon Johnson was speechless. Or rather, there was so much he wanted, had to say, vent, or to spew out that he did not know where to begin or who to blame first.

The Canadian Ambassador, fifty-seven-year-old Charles Richie had drifted along in the President's wake when their 'conference' – a most unpleasant affair – had been peremptorily interrupted.

Born in Nova Scotia and educated at Pembroke College, Oxford, Harvard and the École Libre des Sciences Politiques in Paris, Richie's long and distinguished career in the Canadian Department of External Affairs which had begun over thirty years before, had included stints as Ambassador to West Germany, and four years as his country's Permanent Representative to the United Nations prior to his appointment in 1962 to the Washington Embassy. A lifelong diarist and student of foreign affairs, an intellectual who often found himself surrounded by idiots, practically everything he had observed since arriving at the gaudy old bank that housed the Philadelphia White House yesterday evening, scared the living daylights out of him!

He understood that Lyndon Johnson's grasp on the reins of power was as yet tentative; but he was – in theory - surrounded by experienced men and somebody ought, by now, to have got a grip. The chaos of journalists, radio and television people in the lobby, the insanity of allowing such an enormous crowd to block all the streets for hundreds of yards in every direction around the White House spoke of a stunning degree of, well, ineptitude. The expression 'amateur hour' came to mind. The situation was so bizarre that he hardly knew how he was going to characterize it the next time he talked to his Prime Minister in Ottawa, let alone his wife or his mistress...

Although, now that he thought about it that probably was not going to be a problem because, left to their own devices, the inmates of the White House asylum were likely to blow up the World any minute.

"What is going on please?" He inquired urbanely as he shouldered past the gang of headless chickens – his mistake, White House staffers – surrounding President Johnson.

Johnson stared at him, presumably wondering what he was doing in the Oval Office but then as the President had just got up and walked out of their meeting – without so much as a by your leave - Richie felt he had a right to hear some kind of explanation. Given the 'state of play' the normal diplomatic niceties were, quite obviously, not being respected and it was readily apparent that his country needed him to at least attempt to inject a note of sanity into affairs.

An avenue through the press of bodies opened. Richie stared at the TV set, not immediately knowing what he was looking at.

And then the penny dropped. Ah," he murmured. During the last five hours he had repeatedly asked for an opportunity to speak to Peter Christopher; ever since, in fact, he had learned the putative British Ambassador was in Philadelphia. Johnson's people had politely at first, then with increasing doggedness deflected and eventually flatly refused to let him meet 'the Christophers'. From which Charles Richie had concluded that the 'Navy couple' were as much prisoners of the White House as the other ambassadors unwise enough to voluntarily pass through its Gothically ill-conceived pastiche of the greatness that was once Rome that passed for its front door.

"...stabbing its friends in the back..."

Richie sensed the sphincters of Lyndon Johnson's staffers involuntarily contracting all around the Oval Office. The American people might like straight talking but their leaders, to a man, hated it especially when it was directed at them.

"I speak to you now while the bodies of my friends at Wister Park still lie, for all I know, broken and naked on the steps of the Embassy murdered by your fellow citizens while the authorities, I can only assume, watched and let it happen. I thought this was supposed to be a civilised country?"

The Canadian Ambassador flinched.

"I am not a politician," Peter Christopher went on.

Richie had moved closer to the television.

Lady Marija, he noticed had moved so as not to be in the shadow of the barrage of microphones. She had released her husband's hand, now she stood with her hands clasped before her – holding her shoes? Surely, she was not barefoot on the steps to the White House? - nodding solemnly, looking out into the crowd with an almost beatific serenity as the wind caught and ruffled her dark hair.

A moment later she bobbed down and re-appeared without her shoes. She reached out and touched her husband's arm.

He glanced to her, nodded. "I have almost said my peace," the man announced. "I know Mr Cronkite is waiting patiently to interview my wife and I and we won't be keeping him waiting much longer."

Richie blinked.

JFK could not have done what he just did with greater aplomb.

I am in command; this is what we are going to do...

The Canadian Ambassador realised his mouth was wide open with astonishment.

"President Johnson has issued an ultimatum to the British Government. He has made six separate and specific demands and refused to consider our objections. My Government is prepared to discuss President Johnson's demands at a future time and place at the mutual convenience of both parties. However, the President must be cognisant of the fact that until US forces attacked – without warning or provocation - Allied forces in the Persian Gulf three days ago, that the United States had maintained the facade of neutrality. In the light of what has happened since it behoves President Johnson to demonstrate *his own good intentions before he can expect the Allies, including Great Britain, to take him at his word."*

Richie went cold inside.

Was that a declaration of war or a plea for sanity?

Peter Christopher raised his face, surveyed his surroundings as if noticing the great crowd for the first time.

"Representatives of the British Government will attend the United Nations in New York no later than seventy-two hours from this time with a view to restoring former good relations with the United States."

"Does the kid have the authority to do that?" The Canadian Ambassador asked himself.

"Furthermore, at the opening of that 'peace conference' the British Government will unconditionally release the ships of the US Sixth Fleet currently interned at Malta."

Richie very nearly vented a nervous laugh; the kid sure as heck does not have the authority to say a thing like that! But it doesn't matter. Everybody listening to this, watching it now or who will be watching it later when it is repeated ad infinitum across the continent will hear it and a lot of them will believe it, every word. Every single word! And then what does LBJ do?

"Pursuant to this the British Government is prepared to institute an unconditional ceasefire across the Middle East effective midnight local time. That would be in around seven hours' time."

Charles Richie fought to suppress a smile.

"President Johnson told the American people that peace remains the only policy of the American Government! I for one am prepared to take him at his word. I say to President Johnson; what is it to be? War or peace?"

The Canadian Ambassador was mouthing the words that followed. He was stunned that he was witnessing such a master class from the lips of a diplomatic virgin.

Peter Christopher ran a hand through his fair hair, composed himself for his final rhetorical flourish.

"I am a relatively junior naval officer, a husband and hopefully sometime in early December, I will be a father for the first time. My wife tells me she is carrying our daughter..."

No, I never saw that coming... Sammy Davis Junior or Frank Sinatra could not have silenced the crowd the way the dashing young Englishman had. One-minute stern bluster, the next abject humility, the common touch par excellence!

Peter Christopher spread his arms, imploring understanding.

"I ask you in all humbleness, Mr President," he said, like a supplicant in Holy orders, *"please, for the sake of my unborn daughter, for all our children,"* he continued, building up to the punch line with astonishing patience.

Now Charles Richie mouthed the words he ought to have seen coming, not the ones the old cynic in him had predicted.

"Please, Mr President. Please give peace a chance!"

Chapter 77

When the air alert had sounded the USS Dewey had led the USS Hull into the waters north of the watery graves of the USS Kitty Hawk, the USS Boston and the USS William V. Pratt - coincidentally directly towards the last resting place of HMS Centaur and the New Zealand frigate HMNZ Otago – to place themselves between the crippled hulk of the USS Albany, the USS Paul Revere, the British oiler Wave Master and the new 'threat vector'.

The deck ought to have been cleared when the ship went to battle stations but there were too many walking wounded, and too many stretchers arranged beneath awnings to achieve that fast, let alone quickly or efficiently.

The Dewey had heeled into a long, accelerating turn. Suddenly, her twin screws had gone from idling to racing and the ship's stern had dug deep into the water as she picked up momentum. Giving the wreck site of the Kitty Hawk a mile-wide berth, she had raced past the bow of the wallowing USS Albany at a distance of less than two hundred yards with the gunship destroyer USS Hull charging up from the south in her wake.

The threat was from the north; therefore, the Hull would stay south, well clear of the horizon of the Dewey's attack radars. In the old – pre-missile - days ships had formatted close together to co-ordinate their artillery, these days separation was the thing. During both Battles of Kharg Island Carrier Division Seven had been too 'bunched up', with few of its individual units able to manoeuvre freely until it was too late. Part of that was down to the brilliance and suicidal bravery of the enemy; a lot of it was down to the fleet being in peacetime steaming order at the commencement of each engagement. Possibly, that spoke as much to Rear Admiral William Bringle's state of mind, or conscience, as it did to the US Navy's current fighting doctrine.

All that Walter Brenckmann knew for sure was that the post-mortems into what had gone wrong in the Persian Gulf would go on for years, possibly the rest of his lifetime even if by some, unlikely chance, that lasted until he was a hundred and one.

Walter was still on deck when the Dewey cleared her stern mounted missile rails. With a fiery, roaring, smoking thunder one, then another twenty-seven feet long, two-stage, three thousand-pound Convair RIM-2 Terrier medium-range surface-to-air missile roared up into the still cloudless late afternoon sky like the killer angels of some lesser god.

For the first ten nautical miles the Terriers climbed at a speed of around Mach 1.8 – well over a thousand miles an hour – riding a beam from the Dewey's AN/SPG-55 tracking/illumination radar; thereafter its internal semi-active homing system took over as the missile accelerated up to a maximum terminal velocity of Mach 3.0, around two thousand miles an hour, before its two hundred and eighteen pound proximity-fused controlled-fragmentation warhead exploded somewhere within a radius of one hundred feet of its target.

Theoretically it could hit an aircraft flying at supersonic speeds up to thirty to forty miles down range; a little less if the target was at ultra-high altitude but since the Terrier could hit anything up to eighty thousand feet high that was never a major consideration. The makers – Convair, at their Pomona plant in California – claimed the RIM-2 Terrier was virtually a fire and forget sure bet at up to forty miles at any altitude within its operational envelope. But then only a fool asked a defence contractor for an honest answer to anything.

Walter suddenly realised that he probably did *not* want to be watching the rapidly disappearing missiles all the way to their targets, however distant. There had been no broadcast to the effect but any Terrier launched might potentially be tipped with a one kiloton W45 nuclear warhead.

Things were pretty messed up right now...

The Dewey's wheel had turned amidships while she cleared her missile rails. For about a minute she sprinted north, her wake dead straight.

And then she cleared her Terrier rails again.

Chapter 78

09:35 Hours (EST)
Morris House Hotel, 8th Street, Philadelphia

The men in the lounge – Rockefeller and Nixon partisans – had looked at each other in blank, shocked, very nearly traumatised disbelief when the tall, flaxen haired young Englishman with the movie star good looks and presence had laid down his challenge to Lyndon Johnson.

'*Please, Mr President. Please give peace a chance!*'

Whoever had written that line – the whole of his speech for that matter - they wanted on their side for the coming General Election campaign.

Jesus! That was as good as the stuff Ted Sorensen had fed Jack Kennedy on inauguration day back in January 1961. Heck, better!

The two candidates, Nelson Rockefeller and Richard Nixon and their senior staffers had pushed through to the front of the crowd; where seats were sheepishly, unceremoniously surrendered.

Everybody had expected Peter Christopher to carry on.

But no, he had recognised the moment and just stood there receiving the adulation – amidst a few catcalls – from the crowd in Broad Street.

"We need to talk to whoever coached this guy," Bob Haldeman, Nixon's de facto chief of staff declared.

Henry Kissinger shook his head. Sometimes he was appalled by how ignorant even very intelligent men – like Haldeman – could be about the wider World beyond the shores of the United States.

"He's a captain in the British Royal Navy, Bob," he said quietly. "I've met a few men like him. Scratch the surface of these guys and half of them can out politic anybody in this room in front of *any* crowd. Three months ago, he told his guys he was going to get them all killed and," he shrugged, "they cheered their heads off. This," he waved at the TV set, "is a breeze."

"What does LBJ do now?" Nixon asked, cutting to the chase in a way that Nelson Rockefeller would have found rude, and positively distasteful.

Kissinger opened his mouth to reply but the picture on the screen had changed. Now Walter Cronkite was talking to the 'English couple'.

"*I know nothing about politics,*" Lady Marija Christopher protested with an innocent sweetness that positively took the breath away. "*I am the daughter of a half-English, half-Maltese dockyard superintendent and a Sicilian mother, and my best friend in the World was the most remarkable woman I have ever, or will ever meet in my whole life, Doctor Margo Seiffert, who was once a Commander in your Navy.*"

Cronkite hovered like a protective uncle, knowing only a fool interrupted *this* woman.

"*I lost Margo in the Battle of Malta three months ago, as Peter lost his father and so very, very many of his brave Talaveras. Peter's best friend died of his wounds after that battle; before that I had lost my brother, Samuel, also.*"

Her tone was self-effacing – *I do not really matter, I am just a Maltese housewife but this is my story* – and yet in her eyes there was an obstinate determination not to allow herself to be swept along by events.

"*I was hurt very badly as a child. My little brother Joe and I were trapped in a bombed building for many hours. He was unhurt, I was crushed. It was many, many years before I could walk again. Occasionally,*" she prefaced with a mischievous grimace, the joke entirely at her own expense, "*I forget that I cannot run and my husband has to catch me before I fall! My friend Margo taught me to be a nurse and a midwife; and after the October War we laughed and danced with joy with every child we brought into the world whole and safe, each normal birth was a little victory for everything that was, and still is, right in our lives.*" She shrugged. "*So, Mr Cronkite, when my husband pleads with President Johnson to give peace a chance he speaks not just for us, but for everybody here in America and everywhere in the World.*"

Walter Cronkite was not a man normally lost for words.

He dragged his eyes off the young woman.

"*Sir Peter, how can President Johnson talk to Premier Thatcher when the Sixth Fleet is being held hostage in Malta?*"

"*Sir,*" the younger man sighed, "*the whole World is being held hostage by the United States and the Soviet Union. As I said just now, the Sixth Fleet will be released as an earnest of my Government's good intentions at the outset of the 'peace conference' President Johnson has directed shall be held in New York.*"

Cronkite had expected him to continue. "Less is more!" One man behind Rockefeller and Nixon whistled admiringly.

"*If there is another war,*" Marija said, and paused, waiting to be the centre of attention again. "*If there is another war,*" she repeated, "*what will become of our children and our babies? I say to our leaders; to President Johnson, to Mrs Thatcher, to the men in Russia, in the Middle East, the Far East, everywhere,*" she went on, looking directly into the lens of the nearest TV camera, "*what will become of our children and our babies if there is another war? Is the air we breathe already not poisoned enough for you? Do you wish to be remembered as the great peace makers? Or as the wicked destroyers of nations?*"

Walter Cronkite took a very visible mental backward step.

Out of the mouths of babes and sucklings...

That was when the dam burst; tears streamed down Marija's cheeks, and oblivious to the numberless witnesses she buried her face in her husband's chest. But not before everybody on the East Coast had seen her crying and understood that her tears were for them all.

Chapter 79

16:36 Hours (Local) – 09:36 in Philadelphia
HMS Eagle, 115 nautical miles north of Alexandria

Captain Frank Maltravers tried not to pace like an expectant father outside the delivery room. Not that he had or was ever likely to be in that particular situation, having eschewed marriage until middle age and not been reunited with the love of his life until he, and she, were well beyond such procreational worries. His immediate preoccupation – which was of the hair tearing out variety – was on account of the cautionary note of the most recent reports from the Eagle's Engineering Officer.

There was another problem with the main bearing on the starboard outer shaft...

It was yet another reminder that down that low in the leviathan everything was 'original', built or specified during the 1945 war or just afterwards. Eagle's long refit had started half-way up her hangar deck and kept going; practically everything below the armoured deck of that great aircraft cathedral was 'as new' as in 1944 to 1950. Some of the machinery filling those compartments deep beneath the waterline would have started life even earlier destined for other ships which were either redesigned on the stocks or cancelled. To walk into the carrier's boiler and turbine rooms was to step back into the 1940s, overheated, deafening, humid spaces filled with pipes and shin, elbow and skull endangering protrusions, a place of glass dials and wheels, levers and clanging bells and always, there was a leak in this, or that system and copious quantities of oil or condenser water sloshing about beneath the floor grills.

Actually, this was one of things that had so endeared first the Ark Royal, and now the Eagle to Frank Maltravers. The Big E was a 'real' steel fighting ship, not one of those spic and span space-age American monstrosities with their towering masts and acres of aluminium superstructure.

However, right now the Captain of the Eagle would have given his right arm to be on the bridge of a ship on which all the things that mattered 'worked', at least most of the time.

Eagle was shouldering her way to the west at twenty-eight knots on three-and-a-half shafts; if he had to shut down 'number four' completely that speed would drop to around twenty-four or five. That was still plenty to launch and recover aircraft, given the near gale still coming over the bow but it meant he was going to be two, perhaps three hours late getting to Malta and he had a horrible feeling that he did not have *any time* to spare.

The World was going to Hell in a hand basket and the way things were looking he was about to miss the party.

Two QRA Sea Vixens were being pulled onto catapults as he paced the deck, the worst of the summer storm having swiftly blown past

Eagle and her consorts, Scorpion and Oudenarde. He would let his pilots chase away the spy in the sky who had appeared again twenty minutes ago.

Both the fighters moving up to the catapult traps were armed with a single de Havilland Firestreak heat seeking air-to-air missile. These days the damned things were worth their weight in gold; like most sophisticated munitions Firestreaks had been out of production – due to 'war exigencies' until about a month ago. Eagle would have sailed for the Eastern Mediterranean ten days ago with only four of the weapons in her magazines had not the RAF flown out a consignment of sixteen 'new' birds in the bomb bay of a Valiant V-Bomber just ahead of her departure from Malta.

Without Firestreaks the Big E's Sea Vixens lacked teeth. Subsonic, without the after burners to get up to altitude anywhere near as rapidly as an F-4 Phantom or Soviet MiG-21, they were 'interceptors' from another, earlier generation. Last winter Sea Vixens flying off the Hermes had run out of Firestreaks; they had kept flying, mainly in a deterrent role but by the end of last December's battles off Cape Trafalgar they were toothless. Prototypes of the aircraft – the DH 110 – had been designed to mount four internal 30-millimetre Aden cannons but production Sea Vixens had been initially designated missile-only fighters, with the space freed up by dispensing with guns given over to advanced radar and avionics.

Eagle's Sea Vixens each now sported a single Aden cannon 'pod' on their inboard under-wing starboard hard point. Each 'pod' had a thirty-five-round magazine; that was just one or two fleeting presses of the firing button since the gun had a rate of fire of better than twelve hundred rounds per minute. The additional drag of the pods cost the host aircraft several miles an hour in airspeed and reduced the aircraft's versatility as a bomber; but then the Big E had its Buccaneers for that sort of work.

The trouble was that the moment the QRA Sea Vixens got into the air their unwanted - spy in the sky - companion was going to push his throttles through the gate and make himself scarce, and Frank Maltravers's fighters did not have the heels to catch him. Still, the enemy had got careless in the past, maybe he would again today.

The catapults hurled the two Sea Vixens into the air.

"OUDENARDE HAS MULTIPLE TARGETS BEARING ZERO-THREE-ZERO RANGE SEVEN-ZERO MILES, SIR."

The Captain of the Eagle stopped pacing, forgot about overheating bearings, the troublesome antiquity of parts of his ship and the unpalatable recognition that his primary interceptors were not quite top dog these days.

HMS Oudenarde was tracking the flagship approximately fifteen miles to the north-west. Scorpion had forged ahead eight miles to perform the same distant picket duty.

There ought not to be *any other* aircraft this far out at sea, especially not anywhere near the Eagle and her consorts.

Frank Maltravers did not hesitate.

He turned to the officer of the watch, Lieutenant Jervis Gresham, a nephew of the man who had commanded the 1st Support Group during Operation Manna.

The Royal Navy was a family; a close-knit family, and at times like this that was what made it so strong.

Pretty damned near invincible, in fact.

"Get all our fighters in the air," he ordered with a grim insouciance. "The ship will come to action stations if you please, Mr Gresham."

Chapter 80

Lieutenant-General Michael Carver read the message flimsy and passed it across to Major Julian Carver while the third man in their small circle chaffed to learn the latest developments at home in England.

Julian Calder looked up. The SAS man was thoughtful. Then both he and the Commander-in-Chief of all British and Commonwealth Forces in the Middle East turned to Frank Waters, the BBC's man on the spot.

"We are to hold where we are until further notice," Carver remarked. "Basra is somebody else's problem."

Frank Waters guessed that there was more.

"Congratulations all round on our outstanding victory, obviously," the C-in-C added, waving beyond Julian Calder's shoulder to a lurking staff officer, to whom he handed the message flimsy. "And a most solicitous inquiry, a personal inquiry, no less, passed on to me as to the whereabouts and health of a certain recently retired member of a certain Regiment."

Colonel Francis David St John Waters, VC, (retired) frowned, not really caring to be the object of some private joke between fellow officers.

"I'm sorry, I don't..."

"The Prime Minister has asked for an urgent update on *you*, Frank," Michael Carver chuckled.

"Me?"

"Yes, you!"

The other man's grin morphed into a toothy smile.

"Me?" It took a while to sink in. The World was going to pot and *the lady* was asking after *him*. He had not even realised that she had noticed his existence, not known that she gave a fig for his 'whereabouts and health'. He had only met her briefly, there had been that very odd dinner at Airey and Diana Neave's rooms in Oxford where she had ordered him back to the Gulf, and he had thought that was that.

Although she had made such an impression on him that he hardly knew how to put it into words – he had been in a state of pole axed enchantment throughout that dinner – she had seemed friendly, cool, but in no way similarly enchanted. *She* was his country's war leader, he was an old has been, a Regimental cast off. Surely, *she* would have forgotten his name the moment he walked out the door but no, not only did she know his name, she was asking after him...

The lady knows I exist!

He wanted to dance a jig on the sandy floor of the trench; and he would have had the body been half as willing as the spirit. He settled for smiling like an idiot.

"My, my," he muttered.

"Sir," a dusty subaltern called, reporting to Carver. "3rd Iranian Armoured reports a large number of aircraft approaching Basra."

Chapter 81

Alexander Shelepin, the new Chairman of the Communist Party of the USSR, had left Llewelyn Thompson alone in the company of an unspeaking minder for several minutes.

"We are ready for you, Ambassador," the dark angel said upon his return, gesturing the American to follow him.

Thompson was ushered into a chair in the main communications compartment of the Tu-114 command and control aircraft and invited to don a headset.

"To whom am I speaking?" He inquired, evenly.

"It's me, Bill Fulbright, Tommy," the familiar voice at the other end of the long-range connection replied testily. "What's going on over there?"

Thompson's hosts – or captors, it was hard to tell which descriptor applied – had helpfully place a script by his right hand; which he had studiously ignored up until now.

"That's hard to know, sir," he replied. "All I can tell you is what I know and what I've been told by Alexander Shelepin, who claims to be the new Head of the Troika."

"What the heck *is* going on over there, Tommy?"

"I'll tell you what I know," Thompson reiterated. "And what I've been told; you'll have to make up your own mind, Mr Secretary."

Fulbright waited.

"I am presently onboard a modified Tu-114 somewhere over Kazakhstan. I have had no contact with Chairman – sorry, former Chairman Brezhnev – in the last forty-eight hours. Mr Shelepin informs me that Leonid Brezhnev is dead; likewise, a number of other leading members of the hierarchy are also now deceased. He calls these men 'the traitors of the Khrushchev era'. According to him the Troika has been re-modelled into a 'collective leadership' comprising himself with Admiral Gorshkov as his deputy. He claims that a large force of Red Air Force bombers is already in the air and that in the event of an attack on the Soviet Union, the entire force will be despatched on what are, in effect, one-way suicide missions against targets in North America and Western Europe. He also claims to be aware that since the spring a Polaris submarine has been permanently on patrol in the Eastern Mediterranean Sea; and that the CIA has been spying on Red Army and Red Air Force activities in Iraq from a clandestine base in the Negev Desert of Israel..."

The Secretary of State was silent.

Thompson swallowed hard.

"The Government of the Union of Soviet Socialist Republics has requested that I read out the following text to you, Bill," he continued, his voice crackling with tension.

"Shout it out, Tommy!" The Secretary of State demanded, badly wanting, needing to hear all the bad news at once.

The US Special Emissary hesitated, his eye juddering across the close-spaced typed Cyrillic lines of the thin sheet of paper he had been handed.

"This is my first pass translation, Bill," he warned, "of a typed Russian text. Normally, I'd process such a document several times, parsing it for nuance before submitting it to its addressee..."

"Just do your best, Tommy."

Alexander Shelepin was standing with his arms crossed next to the forward bulkhead, visibly impatient.

"For and on behalf of the Politburo of the Communist Party of the USSR, I, Alexander Nikolayevich Shelepin, General Secretary of the Party and Spokesman for the Collective leadership, the Troika, hereby give notice of the following..."

Thompson took a breath, read ahead.

"The United States of America having reneged on its solemn pledge to intervene in the war in Southern Iraq and the Persian Gulf to achieve a lasting ceasefire, namely by liquidating British and other foreign invaders on the soil of Iraq and Iran, and by ensuring, by force of arms if necessary, the disengagement of British and other foreign naval forces in the Persian Gulf, the Soviet Union will respond to any aggression by the United States over its sovereign territories with a massive counter-strike against American interests globally, and against American cities..."

"Tell him!" Shelepin hissed angrily, realising at which point Thompson had paused.

The other man nodded.

"Because the United States has shown itself unable or unwilling to accept its international obligations to the USSR several 'demonstrations' have been initiated. Retaliation against the Soviet Union for these 'demonstrations' will result in an all-out counter strike by all forces at my command. Your early warning stations will by now have informed you than a large number of Red Air Force aircraft are already in the air or moving to their forward war stations. These aircraft have not been ordered to commence operations against targets in the United States or Western Europe. Not all of the aircraft currently in the air are armed with nuclear weapons; some are decoys but, in the event, that the attack command is transmitted you will have no way of knowing which of the hundreds of aircraft approaching your territory are carrying nuclear weapons. On the night of the Cuban Missiles War, you caught us with our 'pants down''. That will not happen a second time."

A deathly chill had crept down Thompson's spine.

"At this time several divisions of the Army of the People's Democratic Republic of Korea are crossing the demilitarized zone separating the two cruelly and unnaturally separated parts of the Korean Peninsula. If US forces respond to this 'action' with nuclear weapons the USSR will mount an all-out counter-strike against ONLY targets in North America."

The American swallowed hard; sensing rather than hearing the gulps of horror at the other end of the connection.

"At this time," he went on, "Soviet Air and Naval forces are hunting a Polaris missile submarine known to be illegally loitering in the Eastern Mediterranean. In future if we discover such a vessel anywhere in the Mediterranean or within five hundred kilometres of Soviet territory we will attack it immediately with nuclear depth charges and torpedoes."

"They can't do that!" Fulbright objected.

It was unclear whether his chief was protesting about the practicality or the legality of what Thompson had just read out. The envoy wasted no time attempting to clarify matters.

"At this time," whoever had drafted the text was no wordsmith but that was the least of his problems, and besides, even Dostoyevsky would have been baffled by this brave new World, "the Red Air Force is enforcing a buffer zone between foreign forces in southern Iraq and Iran and the ground held by the Red Army north of Basra. This operation also involves 'neutering' what remains of the US Naval presence in the western half of the Persian Gulf."

"What does that mean?" Fulbright demanded.

"I have no idea," Thompson apologised. "Sorry, literally, I'm just the messenger." He sucked down a deep breath of air. "There's more, Bill."

"Go on," Fulbright invited him reluctantly.

"The Soviet Union demands the reinstitution of the United Nations as a forum wherein mutual differences may be discussed; and where future misunderstandings may be resolved short of recourse to violence."

Mistakenly, the Secretary of State took this as a hopeful sign.

Thompson soon dashed his hopes.

"Ambassadorial delegations will be maintained by both countries. However, other than at the highest diplomatic level all political, economic, military and cultural contacts between our two countries are hereby severed. Violation of Soviet borders, air space or waters will result in a hostile response. The Soviet Union claims sovereignty over all regions considered – pre-Cuban Missiles War – to be within Soviet spheres of influence including territory seized during and after that war by elements sympathetic to the Revolution. In addition to the Warsaw Pact countries, under this mandate the USSR claims sovereignty over Turkey, Greece, the Balkans and all places occupied by Red Army troops in Iran and Iraq, and in Manchuria in the Far East."

Thompson was wrung out, exhausted.

"Communiqué ends," he sighed.

Chapter 82

09:58 Hours (EST)
The Oval office, The White House, Broad Street, Philadelphia

"Mister President," Walter Jenkins said to the man who had been his friend – and boss – most of his adult life, "the British Ambassador and his wife are telling the American people what they want to hear. You can't fight that. But you can seize the moment..."

Lyndon Johnson had been staring into space.

"The Russians know we've got a Polaris boat in the Eastern Mediterranean," he said, not looking up. *"Fuck it, I didn't know that until last night!"*

"General LeMay is probably right when he says the Soviets were just seeking to justify attacking the British carrier, the HMS Eagle, which coincidentally is presently traversing the same area of the Levantine Sea where the USS Sam Houston is patrolling, sir..."

Johnson gave the other man a mistrustful glare.

He had listened in on his Secretary of State's conversation with Tommy Thompson, now his incredulity was paralysing him. There were at least a dozen other people in the Oval Office but only Walter Jenkins had had the balls to actually approach him.

I should not have bawled out the others.

Those things I said to Bill Fulbright were just plain wrong...

The moment the line from Russia had gone down something had snapped. It was not just those kids – the 'Christophers' - outside on the steps of the White House making a mockery of his day-old Presidency; they were doing what they thought best and he only dreamed of being *that* brave. It was not even what was or was about to happen in Korea. Or even the realisation that unless he rained thermonuclear fire on his enemies he was utterly powerless. No, what was tearing him apart was his viscerally personal recognition that he had failed the American people. It mattered not that none of this was actually of his making; he had been excluded from all the disastrous missteps and blunders which had brought his country to this pass. But he was now the man 'in the Oval Office'.

The Administration's birds of ill omen had come home to roost on *his* watch. History was going to remember *him* as the man who betrayed the American dream...

"Lyndon!" Lady Bird Johnson whispered in his ear.

The President snapped out of his reverie.

He looked beyond his wife to where Curtis LeMay stood, a scowl like death on his face, before Johnson's desk. The veteran bomber commander looked ten feet tall and almost as wide, and unlike everybody else in the room except for Lady Bird, he was immaculately turned out. The man had put on a new uniform; one with the newest, shiniest braid. Now he was puffing out his chest, a chest covered in medal ribbons, with the confidence of a champion gladiator yearning to be released into the ring.

"We must act now, Mister President," the *Big Cigar* reminded Lyndon Johnson.

The craggy Texan rose from his chair.

He almost stumbled; from weariness, distraction and the spasm of tightness which gripped his chest. His wife touched his elbow.

"I'm okay, goddammit!" Instantly, he regretted the outburst. "Sorry, sorry." He squeezed Lady Bird's hand. "Are the girls still next door?"

His wife shook her head.

"They went to find a window overlooking Broad Street," she explained. "They wanted to watch the English couple..."

The English couple...

He moved around the desk.

"Turn that thing up so we can all hear it!" He demanded, gesturing at the TV set in the corner. Nobody was telling him anything he did not already know or fear, he might as well listen to the circus going on outside his front door.

Walter Cronkite was talking to the Canadian Ambassador.

Charles Ritchie was an interesting guy; the sort of emissary America ought to have been sending abroad before the Cuban Missiles War instead of party place men and benefactors. Before the war DC had been full of shysters and donors, good old boys lining up to claim the most prestigious overseas embassies. All except the one in Moscow, of course, that had been the one post reserved for real old pros like Tommy Thompson. Elsewhere, appointments to the top echelons of the diplomatic service had become the time-honoured cheapskate way Presidents paid off their political mortgages. International relations did not matter when you were the biggest dog on the street.

Charles Ritchie's FBI file made interesting reading; although not on account of any malfeasance, much to the Bureau's chagrin. J. Edgar Hoover always liked to have something salacious up his sleeve, but apart from an ongoing twenty-three-year affair with Irish novelist Elizabeth Bowen – a woman seven years his senior – there was nothing remotely deleterious in Richie's file. No, the man was a diarist, a man with a literary bent, an intellectual who never confused sentiment with pragmatism in his professional life and was one of his country's ablest diplomats.

The 'English couple' had moved apart, each now surrounded by a pack of newsmen and photographers; like royalty being feted, like two movie stars just off the plane at an airport...

"Is it true that Canada has threatened to pull out of NORAD?" Cronkite asked Charles Richie.

People around Johnson stopped breathing for a moment.

"No, Mr Cronkite. People should not misinterpret the fact that old friends sometimes have frank discussions with each other for the signature of any kind of rift in their good relations. However," the Canadian went on smoothly, "it goes without saying that in the event, one hopes unlikely, of direct hostilities between the United States and the old country, that we could not allow passage, for example, to B-52s bound for the United Kingdom through our air space."

Walter Cronkite was trying very hard not to be distracted by the babble all around him; and a little discomforted knowing that he and his interviewee were by no means the centre of interest on the steps to the White House.

"Surely that would be an unfriendly act, Ambassador?"

"Yes, well," Charles Ritchie smiled, suddenly grim. "Understandably, given recent events in the Persian Gulf there are some in Canada who are asking themselves when it will be our turn to be deemed 'no longer allies'," he declared dryly.

"That sounds like fighting talk, sir?"

"Prick us and do we not bleed, sir," Charles Ritchie shot back. "Now, if you'll excuse me, Mr Cronkite, I must pay my respects to Sir Peter and Lady Marija."

Walter Cronkite was not used to one of his 'guests' walking out on him and briefly, he struggled to come to terms with being jilted.

"Well, these are remarkable times," he observed, stoically. He waved at the growing scrum on the steps around him.

"You've said it, Walter!" The President groaned. Having walked over to the TV set now he stood over it, mesmerized.

ABC had got a camera in the face of Lady Marija Christopher.

The young woman had threaded her arm through the crooked elbow of a stone-faced bearded man who seemed to be twice her size. His eyes never stopped quartering his surroundings. Behind the little Maltese princess stood a man who could only be a Secret Serviceman, crew cut and cold-eyed.

"Do you think these pictures will be shown back on Malta?" Marija Christopher asked innocently. It would have been coy except she came across as completely genuine, excited and humble at once. "I had never been away from home – not more than a few miles, and never off the archipelago – until Peter and I flew to England in April."

Lyndon Johnson groaned again.

The kid was going to tell all Americans how lucky they were to live in such a great country!

"I'm going down there!" The President decided.

Chapter 83

Margaret Thatcher knew what she had heard; she just did not believe it. The chanting of demonstrators in nearby Catte Street filtered in through the open windows of her first-floor rooms overlooking the idyllic, grassy Old Quadrangle.

"He said *what?*" She demanded; her eyes wide with astonishment.

"He said '*please Mister President give peace a chance*', Margaret," Sir Thomas Harding-Grayson reported, struggling to keep a straight face. "And then Lady Marija gave voice to a most touching little homily about how President Johnson ought to think of 'our children and our babies' before he does anything rash. The Christophers are presently being paid court, rather in the fashion of visiting royalty or film stars, by the entire Philadelphia press, radio and TV corps, and the crowd outside the White House, estimated at some half-a-million strong, previously somewhat restive, is apparently, in something of a 'party mood', by all accounts."

The Prime Minister was not to be deflected.

She threw an angry look at William Whitelaw, her Secretary of State for Defence, and at Nicholas Ridley, her Information Minister.

"He, er, also," Willie Whitelaw murmured, "promised to hand back the Sixth Fleet..."

The Prime Minister was momentarily lost for words.

"I'm reliably informed," the Secretary of State for Defence added hurriedly, "that most of the American ships are useless to the Royal Navy. We only have one dry dock in the whole country, at Southampton, which could accommodate the USS Independence, we simply do not possess the facilities to safely operate a nuclear-powered vessel like the USS Bainbridge, or the manpower or technical-industrial infrastructure required to operate the advanced 'American' radar and missile systems onboard the rest of their ships..."

Nobody dared say a word.

"Captain Christopher had no right to give away *MY* ships!" The Prime Minister exploded angrily.

"Quite," Whitelaw agreed meekly.

"Absolutely," the Foreign Secretary added. "But..."

"No buts!" The lady snapped.

Margaret Thatcher belatedly realised that she was standing behind her desk, leaning towards her ministers with her balled fists resting painfully on the surface of her desk.

She was breathless.

"Those ships were all we had to bargain with!"

Tom Harding-Grayson shook his head.

"Respectfully, Prime Minister," he ventured, "the rationale behind arresting the Sixth Fleet was to stop it further 'complicating' matters in the Mediterranean, not necessarily to hold its men and ships as hostages to fortune. Sir Peter has given us a way out, an honourable way out, of the impasse that would otherwise, sooner or later, end badly at Malta. He has played exactly the same card that I would have played, had I been in his place. Moreover, he has played it with an adroitness that I fear, none of us in this room could possibly have matched. If there was any room left on his chest I'd suggest giving him another medal!"

"Um…"

Margaret Thatcher's steely blue eyes were still angry.

However, politics was the art of the possible and the last thing she wanted was a war with the United States. In fact, although she would never have confessed such a thing; had the price of peace been her flying to Philadelphia to ritually prostrate herself at Lyndon Johnson's feet – naked - she would probably have done it without a qualm…

Without a second thought, other than to her modesty, obviously…

"Um…"

Nevertheless…

"Putting aside the small matter of a Royal Navy captain making British foreign policy on the hoof without reference to the UAUK, or even the Foreign Office; what on earth am I supposed to tell Her Majesty? The Queen has just recorded a message to the Commonwealth; a message that Captain Christopher has already delivered!"

"That's true, Prime Minister," Willie Whitelaw agreed. "But that's not really the problem, is it? The Christophers have embarked on some kind of 'goodwill' adventure in Philadelphia but our military position remains perilous everywhere. Nothing has been resolved and now we are expected to fly off to New York to discuss," he spread his arms wide, "what exactly?" This last question he threw towards Tom Harding-Grayson.

The older man returned his gaze with owlish good humour.

"President Johnson's six points, Willie."

"None of which are acceptable to us!"

"Jaw jaw, not war war?" The Foreign Secretary shrugged.

"But we have no cease fire in the Gulf and the situation at Malta," the Defence Secretary shook his head despondently, "could not be more," again he paused, as if lost for words, "more pregnant with danger!"

"Yes," the other man concurred. "And we could be obliterated by either the Americans or the Russians at any time," he reminded his companions, unstintingly sardonic.

There was a knock at the door.

Major Sir Steuart – 10th baronet - Pringle, the commander of the Prime Minister's Royal Marines bodyguard detachment entered the room bearing a message sheet. He clumped respectfully to a halt before Margaret Thatcher, essaying a cursory but none the less precise and correct brief stand to attention, before bowing his head momentarily and presenting his missive.

"This has just come in, Ma'am," he reported. "Your Private Secretary indicated to me that you would wish to have sight of it without delay."

The Prime Minister had stopped trying to dissuade her faithful Marines – who styled themselves 'the Angry Widow's Protectors', or AWPs – from using the title 'Ma'am'.

The Queen was *Ma'am*. Whereas, *SHE* was 'Prime Minister' or 'Mrs Thatcher'; but some battles one simply could not win. She would explain it to Sir Steuart; he would respectfully agree with her and then the next time they met he would address her as *Ma'am...*

"Thank you, Sir Steuart," she said stiffly as she took the proffered note.

The Royal Marine marched out of the room.

Reference PM question concerning Waters, Col. Francis. C-in-C Middle East confirms status of same as walking wounded and presently attached to his staff as liaison officer and translator. Waters, Col., most respectfully expresses his humble appreciation for the PM's inquiry. He wishes to personally express gratitude for same on his return to England...

"What is it, Margaret?" Willie Whitelaw asked, interpreting the furrowing of the Prime Minister's brow as presaging new bad news.

Margaret Thatcher realised she was blushing.

Probably, beetroot red...

"Nothing, Willie. The BBC asked for information about their staff in the Gulf." She tried to wave the note sheet flimsy with airy disdain and failed dismally. "This confirms that Colonel Waters has thus far survived the battle..."

She was immensely thankful for another interruption.

This time it was her Private Secretary who delivered the news.

The Prime Minister's mood was transformed in a moment.

Her eyes were steel blue, hard and her voice rang with indefatigable resolve.

"HMS Eagle reports being under attack by Soviet aircraft," she announced.

Chapter 84

18:02 Hours (Local) – 10:02 in Philadelphia
USS Dewey (DLG-14), South of Kharg Island, Persian Gulf

"That was something!" Heidi Takawa exclaimed, re-joining Walter Brenckmann at the rail of the guided missile destroyer. "You stayed up here all the time, right?"

Walter nodded.

There had been the flash of two, and perhaps a third nuke on or below the northern horizon. The Dewey had cleared her Terrier rails seven times in succession but other than the twin trails of each rocket salvo arching heavenwards he had seen little. The terriers must have been hunting prey thirty or forty miles out, well beyond the sight of any naked eye onboard the Dewey. Five minutes ago, the ship had reduced speed to about twenty knots and the gunship destroyer USS Hull (DD-945) had ranged alongside at a distance of perhaps three hundred yards, her guns angled upwards at their maximum elevation. Neither the Dewey nor the Hull's guns had fired a shot.

"I think the Soviets just nuked the British," he confided glumly. "We were probably shooting at the bombers as they ran south to clear the engagement zone over their targets around Basra and Abadan."

Lieutenant junior grade Takawa absorbed this as she leaned her back against the side of the deckhouse behind her, eying the sleek, predatory silhouette of the Hull as she cruised with the lowering sun behind her.

"This doesn't get any better, does it?" She observed gloomily.

"No," the man agreed.

"Staying up on deck was a crazy thing to do," the woman went on. "You know that, right?"

Walter was tempted to retort that he did not need a little sister right now; but then he thought about Tabitha, dead twenty months in the inferno that had consumed Buffalo, and he said nothing.

"Crazy world," the nurse muttered. Since she was last on deck she had pulled on a new tunic, spotlessly clean and mislaid her name badge.

"The British guy woke up," she said, making conversation.

There were other men on deck now, mostly around the fire blackened Terrier launcher. One thing missile trials never really established was exactly how much damage sustained 'shots' were liable to cause the launching ship; the missile technicians prodding and poking the rails and checking out the state of the stern around the launcher were finding out the hard way.

Walter had no idea how many birds the ship had flushed in the two previous engagements against the British but she would have started out with a maximum of no more than forty reloads, and she had launched fourteen today. Maybe the only reason she had stopped shooting was that she had run dry.

"Sorry," the man's thoughts had been elsewhere. "You said something about the British guy?"

"Yeah," she confirmed, giving him time to catch up.

"Will he be okay?"

"Too early to tell. He says he's a Squadron Leader. He was the pilot of one of the," she paused, unsure if she had heard right, 'Victors?'"

Walter's mind clicked into gear.

"Handley Page Victor V-Bomber," he told his companion. "The biggest and the most advanced of the British bombers. As good as, better than a B-52, they say."

"Oh, right." Heidi Takawa was a nurse first, Navy Lieutenant junior grade second, and she had never paid much attention to the 'military stuff'.

"He did the name, rank and number deal, I suppose?" Walter queried.

"No, not exactly."

The woman was smiling, despite herself, she was smiling and suddenly she was looking at the deck plates by her feet.

"Oh..."

"He asked me where I'd been all his life."

Walter Brenckmann blinked, grinned involuntarily.

"Okay, that's different!"

"I think he asked me for a date. It was hard to tell, he's pretty high on pain meds. He said thank you for being pulled out of the sea, even though he doesn't remember any of that."

"The Brits are always very polite," Walter agreed dryly. "Does he have a name?"

Heidi Takawa half-smiled.

"French. He says his name is Guy French. Squadron Leader Guy French..."

Chapter 85

While the action had been going on there had been no time to step back to analyse what was actually happening. But now that it was over everybody on the bridge the Big E was scratching their heads, none less so than Frank Maltravers.

The Captain of HMS Eagle stared at the plot as one of the returning Sea Vixens thumped down on the deck of the carrier. While the squadron made best speed upwind and begun broadcasting fallout alerts to the authorities in the Lebanon, Israel and Egypt, the inescapable logic of the recent 'turkey shoot' slowly began to sink in.

'I'm looking at half-a-dozen bloody B-29s!' The pilot of the first Sea Vixen to make contact with the enemy had reported. The man had done his best to sound laconic but basically, there were times when some things strained a fellow's credulity.

'CORRECT THAT! I HAVE SIX REPEAT SIX TU-4 FOUR ENGINE BOMBERS AT MY ONE O'CLOCK LOW. BLOODY GREAT BIG RED STARS ALL OVER THE BEGGARS AND THEY ARE SHOOTING AT ME WITH RUDDY GREAT BIG CANNONS!'

That had been enough for Frank Maltravers.

'SHOOT THEM DOWN! SHOOT THEM ALL DOWN!'

At the time it had seemed obvious that the only reason six obsolete Soviet B-29 clones would be flying unescorted over the middle of the Eastern Mediterranean, well over a hundred miles from the nearest landfall was to attack the Eagle.

The trouble was that the enemy aircraft had never, at any stage turned onto a heading likely to intercept the Big E. When the Sea Vixens tore into them with Firestreaks and Aden cannons the Tu-4s had been circling at twenty-eight thousand feet, bomb bay doors already *open* at a range of over twenty miles from the nearest ship – Oudenarde – and over thirty-five from the Eagle. They had not even bothered to attempt to jam the carrier's command and control frequencies.

What followed was a 'turkey shoot', to employ one of those dreadful Americanisms which, normally, Frank Maltravers deplored.

The Tu-4s had blasted away with their big 23-millimetre cannons; little good had it done them. Firestreaks had accounted for four of the bombers, head on strafing runs with Aden 30-millimetre guns had chewed up the other two in short order.

And that, everybody had assumed was that!

Right up, that was, until the moment the first nuclear depth charge went off. Most likely a ten to fifteen kiloton device...

Vivid flashes had roiled like lightning strikes on the horizon and much, much later had come the rumbling thunder of the gigantic detonations rolling across the sea like the tolling of some distant doom-laden drum roll.

Presently, the fallout clouds were being driven north east towards Beirut and the eastern tip of Cyprus on the winds of the summer storm from which the Big E had so recently emerged. The squadron's meteorologist was predicting the wind would shift into the west in the coming hours, possibly causing the fallout cloud to spread across a wider front, as far south as the coast of Israel.

"Send to Fleet Headquarters," Frank Maltravers decided.

A yeoman stepped forward, pen and pad ready.

"FOLLOWING MY PREVIOUS STOP CONFIRM ALL SIX TU-4 TYPE SOVIET BOMBERS DESTROYED STOP ALL OWN AIRCRAFT ACCOUNTED FOR STOP CONFIRM SIX LOW-KILOTON RANGE UNDERWATER EXPLOSIONS FOUR-THREE TO FOUR-NINE MILES BEARING ZERO-FIVE-ZERO DEGREES FROM CURRENT POSITION STOP ENEMY INTENTION UNLIKELY TO HAVE BEEN TO ATTACK EAGLE STOP TYPE OF ATTACK INDICATES ENEMY TARGETTING SUBMARINE TARGET STOP IDENTITY OF SUBMARINE UNKNOWN STOP SQUADRON PROCEEDING SOUTH WEST AT BEST SPEED STOP FALLOUT CLOUD WARNINGS HAVE BEEN BROADCAST MESSAGE ENDS"

The rating read back the message.

"Carry on," his Captain ordered.

Things had been much simpler in the old days, he bemoaned privately. Even that time off Formosa when the Kamikazes had been walloping into the deck of the old Formidable; at least one had known where one stood with *that* enemy! Oh, yes, those where the days! The Jap planes went straight through the wooden decks of the big American carriers; whereas they bounced off the armoured hides of the British flattops. As soon as the deck crew had hammered out the dents the Formidable was back in action while, in the distance, some other poor US carrier was still fighting its fires...

"What next?" Frank Maltravers asked himself very, very privately.

Chapter 86

18:21 Hours (Local) – 10:21 in Philadelphia
Field Headquarters, 4th Armoured Regiment, Abadan Island

Colonel Francis St John Waters, VC was not often lost for words. Formerly, when taken aback by some untoward happenstance he might have murmured something along the lines of: "My, my, what a funny old World,' but today that seemed, well...*inadequate.*

Even in comparison to that time he was disturbed in *flagrante delicto* with the curvaceous, achingly sultry wife of that chap in Algiers he had not lost his tongue. And the blaggard had been pointing a whacking great big gun at him at the time!

He opened his mouth to speak.

No words came, he shut his mouth again.

Everybody was still squatting down in the deepest trench they could find; occasionally taking a peek over the parapet to check which way the wind was blowing.

The first wave of bombers had dropped tons – literally tons and tons – of high explosives, mostly although not exclusively on Abadan Island and possibly, over on the Faw Peninsula but it was a bit hard to be sure about that because everything was still shrouded in smoke and dust.

Those bombers had flown on south.

It occurred to him they might have been off to pick a fight with what remained of the American Navy; but that idea had bitten the dirt when the first nuke lit up over Basra.

A bloody great big bomb.

Anybody who had been looking in that direction – a little north of north-west – had reeled away hoping the spots in their eyes were temporary. Thirty-five miles was nothing if you were looking at a big bomb when it went off.

Frank Waters had been having a catnap at the bottom of a half caved-in communications trench. The smell of two dead Soviet Spetsnaz troopers had been less than pleasant but he was so tired he was beyond caring. The flies had kept him awake for a few minutes, and then he had drifted off into a sort of fever sleep only to be awakened by the bombing.

There had been three bombs, the first very big one, and then two somewhat smaller ones somewhere to the west. Of course, they might have only seemed smaller because they were farther away.

There had been no big bangs for a while now.

He picked himself up and shambled – he was not about to stand upright with his head poking over the parapet at a time like this – towards where the command post had been before the bombing.

Most of the recent bombing had focussed on the wrecked airfield and the still burning detritus of the smashed refinery complex south and east of the command post. Nevertheless, dust hung heavily in the atmosphere and more injured men cluttered the surrounding earthworks.

"You were right about Comrade Gorshkov and Comrade Kulikov's ambivalence about the cease fire negotiations, Frank," Lieutenant General Michael Carver remarked dryly.

"It's not as if we're dealing with officers and gentlemen, sir," the former SAS man retorted cheerfully.

Somebody pressed a mug into his hands. He looked down on what looked like muddy water sloshing in the metal container. Tea, hopefully. He was none the wiser after he had drunk it, it could have been anything. Notwithstanding, it slaked his thirst for a few minutes.

"Pretty cold, really," Michael Carver was saying. "Kulikov must have left a lot of his people in the city." He shrugged. "As for the citizens of Basra..."

Nobody had a clue how many Iraqi civilians might have still been in the city.

Half-a-million?

Three-quarters of a million?

"The wind is presently carrying the fallout to the north-east."

Frank Waters leaned his aching frame against the sandy wall of the command post. The fallout was drifting over the line of advance – and now retreat – of the routed 2nd Siberian Mechanised Army; thousands, perhaps tens of thousands of the Soviets' own men would be fouled up in a twenty or thirty-mile-long traffic jam right in the path of the fallout cloud.

If Frank Waters had not already worked out for himself that the World had gone stark raving mad; he would know it now!

Chapter 87

09:00 Hours (PST) – 12:00 in Philadelphia
Hearst Avenue, Berkeley, California

Caroline and Nathan had gone back to bed when the storm had blown over. The small hours of the morning had been cooler and they had needed a little quiet space in which to absorb what they had lived through in the preceding hours.

The man had risen first and not caring to be alone, she had followed him into the small kitchen. The power had come back on while they were in bed and the radio was on as the kettle boiled.

Nathan made coffee, placed his lover's mug before her and planted a slow kiss in her hair. She patted his hand as he sat down opposite her at the table.

"It's morning; we're still alive," she observed, not knowing whether she ought to feel glad, guilty, or foolish.

"You've got to marry me now," Nathan reminded her.

"I hadn't forgotten, sweetheart," she confessed.

They giggled, both shook their heads.

"Do you think anybody saw us out in the back yard last night in the storm?" She asked.

He shrugged.

"Do we care?"

"No," Caroline decided.

They sipped coffee, viewed each other over the rims of their mugs; and then frowned as the strains of 'Hail to the Chief' burst, crackling from the radio.

"*Ladies and gentlemen, the President of the United States of America!*"

Nathan held his breath.

"This will be good," the woman muttered, unconvinced.

"*When, twelve short hours ago I was sworn in as your President,*" Lyndon Johnson declared, "*I did not swear that oath to preside over the end of everything that we hold dear.*"

The man and woman listened with sudden suspicion.

"*There will be no false peace with the Soviet Union; but neither will there be war. In the next few days emissaries of the Soviet leadership and others will travel to New York where issues of war and peace will be hammered out by diplomats and citizen leaders, not by force of arms.*"

Caroline sighed.

"I wonder who wrote that for him?"

"*America is great. Her greatness lies not only in her military and economic might but in the fundamental values which underpin our way of life. Any other nation on Earth would have sought retribution for the hammer blows of provocation we have suffered in the last week. But I did not become your President to exact revenge on our enemies. Yes,*" *there will surely a reckoning but I chose not to make war to exact revenge. That is not the American way. My friends, we are better than that."*

"He must have one of JFK's speechwriters working for him," the woman concluded.

"How can you tell?"

"He's dropped all that good old boy, down home stuff that plays so well back in Texas."

The man grimaced.

"If you say so..."

Without consciously moving a muscle they discovered they were holding hands across the table.

"My generation, the generation that won the 1945 war and built the war machine that fought the October War; owes it to our young people to bequeath them a world in which they can trust the air that their children breathe. Earlier this morning the British Ambassador asked me to 'give peace a chance'."

Involuntarily Caroline dug her nails into the man's palm.

"Shortly before I stepped up to this microphone I decided to move on past the provocations of our enemies. For however long I am your President I will give peace a chance!"

[The End]

Author's Endnote

To the reader: firstly, thank you for reading this book; and secondly, please remember that this is a work of fiction. I made it up in my own head. None of the fictional characters in *'All Along The Watchtower'* – Book 9 of the *'Timeline 10/27/62 Series'* - is based on real people I know of or have ever met. Nor do the specific events described in *'All Along The Watchtower'* – Book 9 of the *'Timeline 10/27/62 Series'* - have, to my knowledge, any basis in real events I know to have taken place. Any resemblance to real life people or events is, therefore, unintended and entirely coincidental.

The *'Timeline 10/27/62 Series'* is an alternative history of the modern World and because of this real historical characters are referenced and in many cases their words and actions form significant parts of the narrative. I have no way of knowing if these real, historical figures would have spoken thus, or acted in the ways I depict them acting. Any word I place in the mouth of a real historical figure, and any action which I attribute to them *after* 27th October 1962 *never* actually happened. As I always state – unequivocally - in my Author's Notes to my readers, *I made it all up in my own head.*

The books of the *Timeline 10/27/62* series are written as episodes; they are instalments in a contiguous narrative arc. The individual 'episodes' each explore a number of plot branches while developing themes continuously from book to book. Inevitably, in any series some exposition and extemporization are unavoidable but I try – honestly, I do – to keep this to a minimum as it tends to slow down the flow of the stories I am telling.

In writing each successive addition to the *Timeline 10/27/62* 'verse' it is my implicit assumption that my readers will have read the previous books in the series, and that my readers do not want their reading experience to be overly impacted by excessive re-hashing of the events in those previous books.

Humbly, I suggest that if you are 'hooked' by the *Timeline 10/27/62 Series* that reading the books in sequence will – most likely - enhance your enjoyment of the experience.

'All Along The Watchtower' is Book 9 of the alternative history series *Timeline 10/27/62.* I hope you enjoyed it - or if you did not, sorry - but either way, thank you for reading and helping to keep the printed word alive. Remember, civilization depends on people like you.

––––––––––

These days I get asked a lot about my ongoing plans for *Timeline 10/27/62*; which is a bit tricky because obviously, one is always at pains to avoid putting inadvertent spoilers 'out there'.

All Along The Watchtower' is the thirteenth instalment of the series –
or rather, 'saga' as it has become - and the simple answer to the
question: what do I plan to do with the series?

Is: I shall carry on!

Other Books by James Philip

The Guy Winter Mysteries

Prologue: Winter's Pearl
Book 1: Winter's War
Book 2: Winter's Revenge
Book 3: Winter's Exile
Book 4: Winter's Return
Book 5: Winter's Spy
Book 6: Winter's Nemesis

The Bomber War Series

Book 1: Until the Night
Book 2: The Painter
Book 3: The Cloud Walkers

Until the Night Series

Part 1: Main Force Country – September 1943
Part 2: The Road to Berlin – October 1943
Part 3: The Big City – November 1943
Part 4: When Winter Comes – December 1943
Part 5: After Midnight – January 1944

The Harry Waters Series

Book 1: Islands of No Return
Book 2: Heroes
Book 3: Brothers in Arms

The Frankie Ransom Series

Book 1: A Ransom for Two Roses
Book 2: The Plains of Waterloo
Book 3: The Nantucket Sleighride

The Strangers Bureau Series

Book 1: Interlopers
Book 2: Pictures of Lily

NON-FICTION CRICKET BOOKS

FS Jackson
Lord Hawke

Audio Books of the following Titles
are available (or are in production) now

Aftermath
After Midnight
A Ransom for Two Roses
Brothers in Arms
California Dreaming
Heroes
Islands of No Return
Love is Strange
Main Force Country
Operation Anadyr
The Big City
The Cloud Walkers
The Nantucket Sleighride
The Painter
The Pillars of Hercules
The Plains of Waterloo
The Road to Berlin
Until the Night
When Winter Comes
Winter's Exile
Winter's Nemesis
Winter's Pearl
Winter's Return
Winter's Revenge
Winter's Spy
Winter's War

Cricket Books edited by James Philip

<u>**The James D. Coldham Series**</u>
<u>**[Edited by James Philip]**</u>

<u>**Books**</u>
Northamptonshire Cricket: A History [1741-1958]
Lord Harris

<u>**Anthologies**</u>
Volume 1: Notes & Articles
Volume 2: Monographs No. 1 to 8

<u>**Monographs**</u>
No. 1 - William Brockwell
No. 2 - German Cricket
No. 3 - Devon Cricket
No. 4 - R.S. Holmes
No. 5 - Collectors & Collecting
No. 6 - Early Cricket Reporters
No. 7 – Northamptonshire
No. 8 - Cricket & Authors

———

Details of all James Philip's published books and
forthcoming publications can be found on his website
at www.jamesphilip.co.uk

———

Cover artwork concepts by James Philip
Graphic Design by Beastleigh Web Design

Printed in Great Britain
by Amazon